A LEGACY OF STARS

THE LOST GOD LEGACIES

SHEILA MASTERSON

BOOKS BY SHEILA MASTERSON

The Lost God Series

The Lost God #1

The Memory Curse #2

The Storm King #3

The Godless Kingdom #4

The Lost God Legacies

A Legacy of Stars

Fable Song Series (interconnected standalones)

Song of the Dark Wood #1

Coming Soon

The Poison Daughter - October 2025

Ballad of the Heartless (Fable Song #2) - 2026

Symphony of Nightmares (Fable Song #3) - 2026

THE LOST GOD LEGACIES

SHEILA MASTERSON

Ebook ASIN: B0DPGPGMFK

Paperback: 978-1-960416-15-5

Hardcover: 9978-1-960416-16-2

Cover Design & Map Illustration: Charlotte Slegers

Family Tree & Gods List: Nicole Trimbur

Editing: Erin Larson-Burnett at EKB Books

Proofreading: Tabitha Chandler

———

To the hyper-responsible oldest children.
I promise the world won't fall apart
if you rest for a while.

May you find the one you want to tell
all your stories to.

———

A NOTE FROM THE AUTHOR

Dear Reader,

A LEGACY OF STARS deals with some difficult subjects including violence, death, mild gore, anxiety attacks, fire, drowning, misogyny, cutting of the palm for a magical exchange, and explicit sex. I've attempted to treat all sensitive topics with the utmost care, but this content might still be challenging for some readers. Please take care of yourself.

Also, please note that while A LEGACY OF STARS can be read and understood on its own, it is a second generation story and it contains character crossover and spoilers for THE LOST GOD Series.

-Sheila

THE GODS

Olney Gods

Clastor - God of All Matter

Adira - Goddess of the Sea

Aelish - Goddess of Truth

Desiree - Goddess of Love and Beauty

Sayla - Goddess of the Hunt

Devlin - God of Wisdom and Reason

Neutral Gods

Grimon - God of Death

Samson - God of Lust

Aurelia - Goddess of Fertility and Harvest

Argarian Gods

Endros - God of War and Discord

Cato - God of Manipulation and Influence

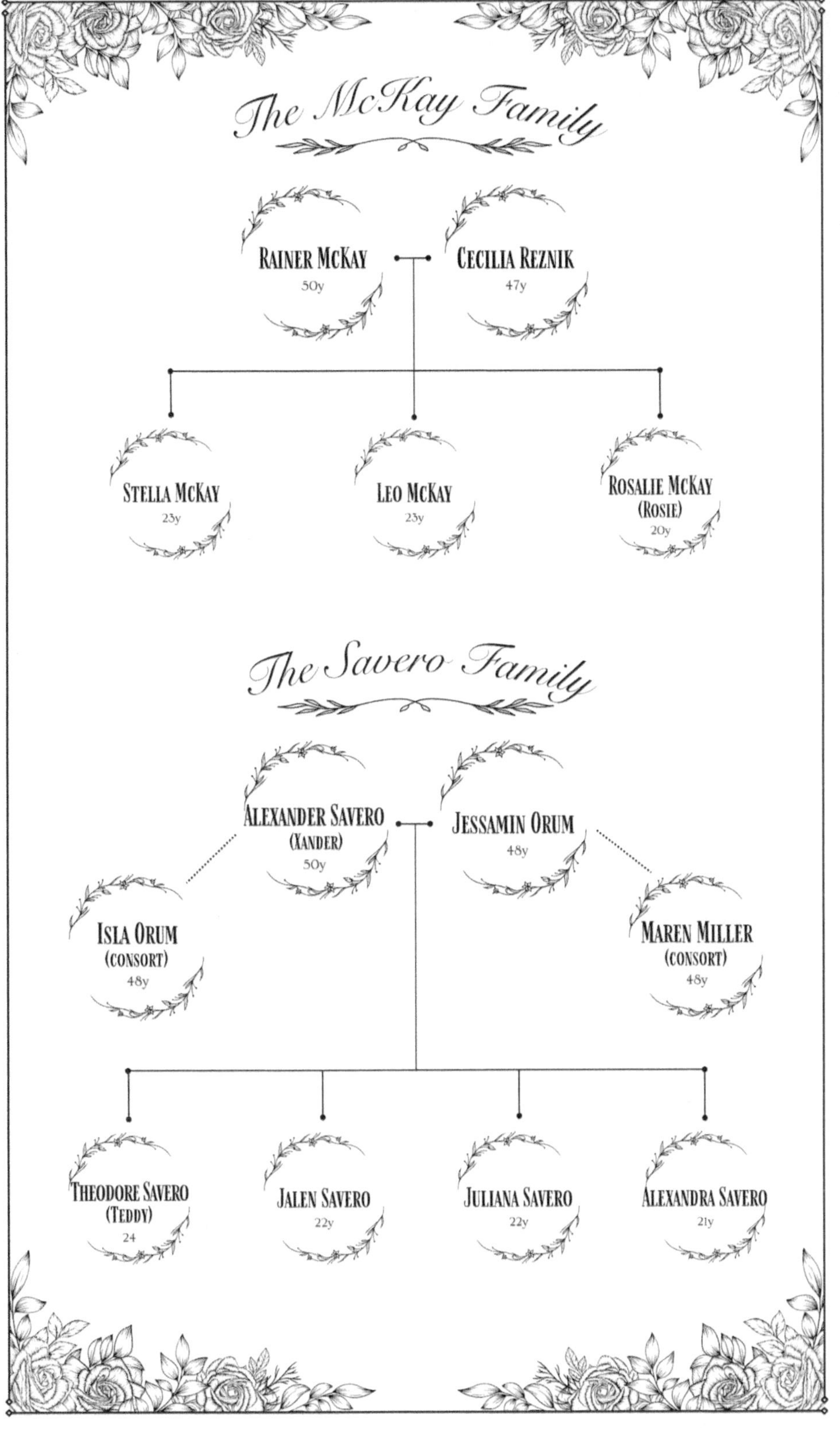
The McKay Family

Rainer McKay
50y

Cecilia Reznik
47y

Stella McKay
23y

Leo McKay
23y

Rosalie McKay
(Rosie)
20y

The Savero Family

Alexander Savero
(Xander)
50y

Jessamin Orum
48y

Isla Orum
(consort)
48y

Maren Miller
(consort)
48y

Theodore Savero
(Teddy)
24

Jalen Savero
22y

Juliana Savero
22y

Alexandra Savero
21y

Aldrena
Argaria
Ardenis
Caves
Treehouse
Cabin
Godswoods
Border Lands
Rowdane
Trickerary
Muddled Mind
INN
Alstairs
Reflection Forest
Revel Forest
Olney
Halls of Truth
May Falls
The Wilds
Wailing Woods
Shores of Adira
Heartwood Valley
Summerton
Olney City
Devlin Hills
N

1

—————

STELLA

Stella McKay was jealous, but that was nothing new.

Her earliest memory had been jealousy. At three years old she'd been outraged that her mother was giving her new brother, Leo, so much attention when Stella was used to having it all to herself.

Twenty years later, as she watched Prince Arden Teripin spin yet another lady around the Godsball dance floor, Stella's jealousy morphed into something new and more spiteful.

She fought a burning impulse to pour her wine all over the woman's pale pink dress.

Like most of the other eligible women in the Godsball tent, Arden's dance partner wore a pink dress to honor Goddess Desiree. There was a smattering of other colors around the room to honor other gods and goddesses, but almost every young woman open to courting wore pink in homage to the goddess of love.

Stella lifted the loose curls that had slipped out of her updo to stick to the back of her neck in the evening humidity and chided herself.

Her envy was irrational.

Arden looked at her every time he circled the dance floor and

I

caught a glimpse of her teal gown. She had his attention and, more importantly, his heart. This was just an act. Arden had to give equal time to every eligible lady until they announced their betrothal, but watching women believe they had truly charmed him made Stella itch.

Stella drained her glass of bubble wine in one burning gulp.

The quick-paced folk waltz was catchy, but it had been going on long enough now that it was certain to be stuck in Stella's head for a week.

Her parents spun by in a swish of silk. They were a touch too close to be appropriate at court, but no one ever gave them judgmental looks. Her parents were a fairy tale come to life, a soul-bonded witch and her guardian, a love stronger than death. Cecilia Reznik and Rainer McKay had a legendary love story and Stella wanted one too.

Stella had seen enough of her friends' parents bickering to understand that hers were deeply in love, but at times it was exhausting. Like when she came in to check on dinner in the afternoons and found them making out on the kitchen counter like teenagers, or when people told her how much she must be wishing for the same kind of love and asked about her suitors, or when their love made it feel impossible to measure up.

Everyone acted like it was a choice. Like her parents had just decided to fall in love. Really, it was pure luck that they'd been bonded as children. Few people were lucky enough to meet the love of their lives at six and eight years old.

Stella was certain that if she and Arden had that same advantage, they'd be similarly in sync.

The song came to an end and the musicians launched immediately into a slower melody that brought more couples to the dance floor. Stella stared at each duo as they spun by, trying to place their masked faces. Despite the fact that, in the past two decades, the wealth and class gap in Olney had narrowed, the Godsball Masquerade was still a night that honored anonymity as much as it honored the gods and the kingdom's history.

Unlike the Godsballs of old that her parents had told her about, Olney now distributed community funds to local dressmakers to ensure that everyone who wanted to attend could afford fine clothing that would allow them to blend into the crowd. Above all, this event was meant to kick off the Summer Solstice Festival and promote unity between the southern kingdom of Olney and their northern ally, Argaria.

Stella smoothed her hands down the star flowers stitched to her bodice. Their bright white petals stood out against the vibrant teal silk and matched her delicate flowered mask that signaled she was honoring her mother. Cecilia wore a similar teal dress, as if their resemblance didn't make it clear enough that they were family. While her mother's dress had a slimmer skirt that suited her petite stature, Stella was glad to be tall enough to pull off a full ball gown.

Leo stepped up beside her and nudged her with his elbow, handing her a fresh glass of bubble wine. "I thought you'd be out there with your prince."

"So did I," she grumbled. Telling Leo and their younger sister Rosie about Arden was a choice she made out of necessity—she'd needed them to help her sneak out to meet the prince—but Stella wished her brother was a little less smug about knowing her secret.

Leo grinned, ran a hand through his hair, and nodded at a group of ladies as they walked by. He had such an ease at social gatherings. From their first season out at eighteen, she'd felt nothing but awkward while Leo slipped into court life as if he'd always belonged there.

Even Leo could admit it was easier for him. People didn't hold him to the same standard. A woman was judged on every nuance and flaw while men were applauded for simply being respectful. The bar was set so low that Leo could hop it with little effort.

Stella had learned from the moment she entered court as an adult four years ago that there was no end to the flaws others could find in her. She was too quiet about the things people wanted to hear and too loud about those they didn't, too quick to leave a party early, too often underdressed for the occasion, quick to anger, slow to forgive, not social enough, not skilled at music or singing, and, most baffling of all, a bit too tall. As if she could will herself to shrink.

Her mother, Cecilia, had been quick to dismiss every bit of criticism, reminding Stella how far the world had come for women to still be held to such simple standards. But the gentler her mother was with her, the more frustrated Stella felt.

"How late are you staying?" Leo asked, adjusting his black silk mask so it sat more flush to his face. The silver embroidery on the mask matched that of his tunic. He was clearly trying to honor Grimon, the god of death. Their *Uncle Grim*, as they affectionately referred to him, wouldn't be caught dead in something so ostentatious. Stella had only ever seen him in black clothing with blacker detailing.

Though he wasn't related to her by blood, Stella had always felt particularly close to Grimon because he visited so frequently.

"I think I'll stay a little while longer. I didn't miss the nine bells, did I?" Stella asked.

Leo shook his head. "Have a date?"

Stella cocked her head and scowled at him. "Don't you have some ladies to lead on?"

Leo grinned. "They're being led. Don't worry. It's almost nine. I checked the hourglass on my way into the tent. Why?"

"Just wondering how much longer I have to force this smile on my face."

"I hate to break it to you, but the force is obvious," Leo said dryly. "You look like Mama when she's been at a tea too long."

"I swear I try not to but it's a terribly dull party."

"Why not talk to Kate?" Leo nodded at Stella's best friend, who stood across the tent by a table covered in rainbow-colored cakes, stacks of biscuits, and a huge mask sculpture made entirely of various fruits.

Kate chatted animatedly with a group of ladies, their colorful dresses catching the golden candlelight as they leaned toward each other to whisper. Stella normally spent most of these events at Kate's side, but she didn't want to be scolded for sneaking off.

Stella twisted her hands in her dress. "I'm just not feeling especially social. All anyone wants to talk about are suitors and it's so hard to lie."

"Then why not tell the truth?" Leo asked.

"You, Rosie, and Kate are the only ones who know and I intend to keep it that way until we're ready to tell everyone. I'm trying to be discreet."

Arden was supposed to marry a politically advantageous wife and, though Stella was a perfectly appropriate match, rising political tensions meant that Arden's choice of spouse would be under extra scrutiny. They had decided together that it was best to keep their relationship private for now.

"You're not even supposed to know anything yet," Stella said.

Leo cocked his head to the side. "Then you should have been more discreet. I'm honestly shocked no one else has noticed. Arden is better at hiding it, but it's written all over your face."

Stella smacked his arm. "Mind your business. Go chase skirts."

Leo grinned. "No chasing required. I let them come to me."

Stella didn't know why he had this sudden insistence on acting like a rake when he was so sensitive deep down, but she wasn't about to confront him about it. Leo had always needed time to come to things on his own.

Several ladies at the corner of the dance floor giggled and whispered to each other, their gazes darting to Leo. He winked at them.

"You're gross," Stella huffed. "Someday you're going to have to rely on something other than your handsome face and you're not going to have anything to say."

"That's future Leo's problem." He glanced across the room at the king and queen of Jeset and their daughter. "You think I could land a princess?"

Stella laughed. "Not on your best day."

Leo faked a wince. "Your lack of confidence wounds me." His eyebrows shot up. "Don't look now but your boyfriend is going to beat me to it."

Stella whipped her head around just in time to see Arden bow and kiss the hand of the foreign princess and gesture toward the dance floor. She gracefully followed him. The crowd parted and hushed, staring at the beautiful royal duo walking to the center of the room.

Just seeing Arden with a princess in his arms was like watching a glimmer of her worst nightmare unfolding in real life.

Of course, Princess Eleria Zim of Jeset couldn't be ugly or clumsy. She was beautiful and moved gracefully with Arden. She wore a fiery red dress woven with orange and red feathers that made her look like a phoenix.

"Who's she supposed to be anyway?" Stella grumbled.

"Some foreign goddess? Who cares? She looks beautiful," Leo said.

"You're not helping," she muttered.

Leo shrugged. "Fine, you're on your own. I have people to see anyway."

With that, he bumped Stella's shoulder and sauntered over to a group of ladies who had been eyeing him for the past five minutes.

Stella turned back to the horrors of the dance floor.

Arden gave her an uneasy glance before smoothing his face into his usual charming smile as he spun the princess around the floor.

Stella looked over the crowd, searching for just one person who wasn't completely entranced. Unfortunately, the only gaze she caught was her mother's.

Cecilia looked from Stella to Arden, her eyes narrowed.

She can't know. Stella's mother had an unnerving and supernatural way of reading people and situations and it took enormous effort for Stella to hide her feelings for the prince.

Cecilia frowned at Arden and Eleria and then looked at Stella again.

Stella schooled her face into calm indifference, but the second Arden dipped the princess and the crowd began to murmur, her control slipped. She grabbed a glass of bubble wine and a napkin from a passing waiter.

She gulped the wine, ignoring the stinging bubbles. She set the empty glass on a nearby table and tried to dry her sweaty palms on the napkin.

Arden's charm was so natural and magnetic. He glowed and his rapt attention had always made Stella feel like the sun was shining just on her. He was like that with everyone; it was a gift for a prince to be so sincere and so good at making people feel heard and understood. Stella had known him her whole life and still felt the same rush when he spoke to her. It was hard to blame other women for being so charmed.

Stella tried to reason with herself that Arden was just being a gracious host—that's why he was whispering to Eleria. The princess tipped back her perfect chin, elongating her graceful neck, and laughed. Her jet-black hair shone in the candlelight. Everyone in the tent seemed just as transfixed by the princess.

Stella twisted the linen napkin in her hands. She was certain she'd never looked so elegant while laughing. But Eleria was graceful in every movement and everyone in the room was riveted.

Anger burned in Stella's chest. Could she so easily be replaced?

"Stell-bell."

Her father's voice startled her from her fuming, and she dropped the linen napkin she'd been holding.

Rainer's gaze lingered on the hand-shaped scorch mark on the white linen. "What has you so upset, Little Star?"

She shook her head and rearranged her smile. "Nothing. I'm just too warm and I've had enough fun for one night. I think I'll head home soon."

Her father studied her. She hated lying to him. They'd always been so close, but if he knew that she was sneaking around with the prince before marriage, he'd not be a brute like most fathers. He'd do something so much worse, like sit Arden down and have a conversation with him about respect. That was a humiliation she would not survive.

Her father eyed her skeptically and nodded to the napkin. "It's been a long time since you sparked without trying."

Stella flushed. Fire magic was her primary affinity, and it was usually well-contained, but it had always followed her emotions. When she was angry, she was known to burn a dress or cause all the candles in a room to become temporary torches. She hated the lack of composure because it proved what everyone always said about how witches' temperaments matched their strongest affinities. It was embarrassing to be the stereotypical example of a hot-headed fire witch.

Stella shrugged. "It's just an off night. Where's Mama?"

Rainer nodded to the dance floor, where her mother was dancing with King Marcos. The two of them were speaking animatedly. Her mother laughed and swatted the king's arm. You could do things like that when you had saved the kingdom more than once.

"She wasn't always like this at court events," Rainer said. "She used to be so grumpy anytime she had to get dressed up, and she didn't like how I flirted with other girls."

Stella shook her head. Her father still got plenty of female attention, including from her best friend Kate, who mooned over him in the most revolting way possible.

"It's hard to imagine her being anything other than natural. Everyone loves her," Stella said.

Rainer laughed. "I promise it wasn't always like that. You'll grow into it too. Or you won't and you'll just find something you enjoy more than court events. Just don't take it so seriously." He glanced around the room. "I haven't seen you out there dancing. Is there no one you'd like to dance with? I see quite a few lonely guardians around the room."

Stella wrinkled her nose. "Papa, if you try to set me up with a *nice young man*, I swear I'll never come to a court party again to avoid the sheer embarrassment of needing my father to make an introduction. I'm fine not dancing."

Rainer chuckled. "Someday, Little Star. Someday you'll meet someone you want to tell all your stories to." He kissed the top of her head and disappeared into the crowd.

He'd been saying that to her since she was young, but Stella had begun to doubt it in recent years. She always felt she had too many edges for court. Despite her best efforts to smooth herself, she always seemed a little too sharp and cutting with her words and looks.

While she got on with most of the ladies, it never ceased to feel like work. She could never quite relax and she always felt like an extension of her parents. She wasn't Stella McKay. She was Rainer and Cecilia's daughter.

Perhaps Leo and Rosie felt the same way, but neither of them had ever said so and they both seemed so relaxed.

"I like your edges. They're what makes you you," Arden had once told her when she lamented not being softer like her mother.

She smiled at the memory. That was what she loved about Arden. They balanced each other out.

Mercifully, the song ended, and Arden bowed and kissed Eleria's hand just as the castle bells rang out.

Finally, Stella would have Arden to herself for a few precious moments. She tracked him as he politely excused himself, whispered to his guard, Falon Everett, and walked out of the tent.

The minutes dragged until finally Stella allowed herself to dash out of the tent and into the garden. She followed the familiar path through the queen's garden, rounding the corner to her favorite rose-bushes, the ones she walked to with her mother and Rosie every Saturday morning, and skirting the hedges to approach a darker, more secluded spot.

She'd barely cleared the hedge when strong arms grabbed her and tugged her against a firm chest. She bit back a yelp as she looked up at Arden's playful grin. He'd slid his mask up on his head so she could see him clearly in the moonlight.

He kissed her, slowly, his hands roaming down her bodice, pulling away to whisper in her ear.

"You are the most beautiful thing I've seen all day. All life, if I'm being honest."

Their time together was always frenzied, rushed, snuck into stolen moments in corners, closets, or the occasional castle guest room. It was thrilling, but Stella wanted what everyone else had—the time and space to go slow. She wanted to show the world their love.

They had known each other since they were children, but nine months ago, those years of friendship had shifted into something new.

She'd been standing on the beach, staring out at the waves, trying to assess if the surf was too rough for her morning swim. Arden was out for a run and stopped to talk to her. A quick conversation about storm tides had turned into a three-hour walk along the edge of the sea.

Stella had never had such an easy time talking to anyone, but Arden was such a good listener and he was one of the few people who could understand the pressure that came with being such a public figure.

She'd thought it was a one-time thing, but Arden started meeting her once a week to walk and talk, and, two months later, at the harvest festival, he'd brought her a bouquet of daisies, taken her for a walk in the gardens, and kissed her for the first time under the harvest moon.

The past seven months had been a blur of sneaking away to see each other every chance they could get, but Stella was ready for more.

"When are we going to tell everyone?"

Arden turned her so he could meet her gaze, his dark eyes bright with lust. "I have a plan for that. Something that my parents will have to honor. The last day of the festival, just before the Gauntlet Games start. I will give a speech to the people and I'm going to introduce you as my betrothed."

Stella frowned. "What if your parents are upset? I don't want to start off on the wrong foot."

Arden shook his head. "Nonsense—my parents love you already and our families are so close. They won't fight me on this. I'm certain."

"If they don't want you to marry a foreign princess, then why is Eleria here?"

Arden blew out a frustrated breath. "Stella, you know this is what I must do to ensure peace for now. Please, I have so little time with you this week. I don't want to talk about whatever foreign princess my parents are foisting upon me. I want to enjoy my time alone with you."

Stella sighed. She knew it was true. The rebel group, the Sons of Endros, had been making trouble for years, trouble that was only escalating. The mild vandalism she'd seen in her youth had turned into more violent, destructive crimes in recent years. But each time the Teripins had a foreign princess at court, the havoc died down, at least temporarily.

"You know what happened last month," Arden said.

Stella shuddered thinking about it. The Sons of Endros had murdered one of the most avid supporters of women's marriage sovereignty and left his body in the town square under their sigil as an offering to Endros, the god of war. The Sons were staunchly opposed to all of the work Arden's mother, Queen Ilani, and Queen Jessamin of Argaria had been doing to give women the right to choose their own partners, instead of being married off by their fathers.

"That's why they've scheduled this visit for the Solstice Festival and the Gauntlet Games," Arden said. "If the Jeset royals are in town, they bring their own extra security, and that means things will go smoothly over the next few weeks." He ran his thumb over her bottom lip. "Let's not waste our limited time together on worries. I don't want to talk about some other woman when you're here looking unbearably beautiful and we're finally alone."

Arden kissed her and all the doubt in her mind burned away in a flash. She slid her hands up the front of his tunic and he kissed her deeper. The routine was practiced. He was careful not to ruffle her dress as he hiked it up over her legs. She was not nearly as careful, running her hand through his dark waves and tugging him closer. There was something so intoxicating about being alone with him. There was such a reverence when the people spoke to him, but every time she looked at him she only saw her warm, sweet, romantic Arden.

His hands trailed up her inner thighs and she shivered. The anticipation was almost enough to make her groan. It had only been a few days, but *this* was right. *This* was what she'd been needing so badly.

Stella sighed into his mouth.

"I've missed you," he murmured, kissing along her jaw. "I can't wait until I can have you anytime I want. I want the world to know you're mine."

A throat cleared. Stella froze and saw her panic reflected in Arden's eyes. He practically threw her off his lap, hopped to his feet, and buttoned his pants. He tucked his shirt back into place as Stella smoothed her dress.

Arden's guard, Falon, stepped around a hedge. "Sorry, Your Grace, but someone just stumbled into the garden. It sounds like they're getting sick."

Arden nodded. He looked as disappointed as Stella felt as he pulled her into one last quick kiss. "I'm sorry."

Stella smiled weakly, shoving down her frustration. "I know."

"I love you. Soon we won't have to hide. I promise," Arden whispered.

With that, he ducked away with Falon on his heels.

Stella adjusted her dress and hair and waited a moment before walking back through the garden. Just inside the entrance, a woman was bent over, vomiting into a bush.

"Are you—" Stella's words turned to a gasp as the woman turned to look at her. "Mama?"

Cecilia's usually rosy cheeks were pale and her eyes glassy in the torchlight. "I'm fine. A bit too much bubble wine."

They stared at each other in the half-light. Her mother was a terrible liar. The joyful noise of the party grated against the seriousness of the moment.

"You're never sick," Stella said at the same time Cecilia said, "Not a word to your father."

Stella stared at her mother. Her eyes were shadowed a bit, but she was otherwise so well-preserved that people occasionally mistook her for Stella's older sister. While Rainer's hair had begun to go a bit gray around his temples, Cecilia's was still dark and wild, not a hint of dullness in its vibrant color.

Now her skin—porcelain and glowing most of the time—looked sallow.

"Will you get me some mint and water from the refreshment table?" Cecilia rasped. "I won't have your father worrying. You know how he can be. He loves something to fuss over and I'd rather not be his new project."

Stella forced her face into a tight smile and nodded. She swept into the tent as stealthily as she could, trying to slow her thoughts. Both of her grandmothers had died of the wasting disease. Stella had worked at the healer's clinic with her mother long enough to know the signs of it. It always started the same—with fatigue, lack of appetite, and vomiting.

She gathered some mint in her trembling hands, trying to recall if her mother's appetite had been normal in recent weeks. Her recollection was perfect thanks to her memory magic, but the power only perfectly preserved memory when she was paying attention. Frantically, she called on her magic and sorted through her recent memories.

She'd been so concerned about her relationship with Arden over the past few weeks that she'd scarcely noticed much else. Stella forced herself back to the present moment, the perfectly preserved memories dissolving as she opened her eyes to the party. She grabbed a glass of water and dashed back to the garden where her mother was waiting.

Cecilia swished the water and spit it into a bush before ripping off a few mint leaves and chewing them. She drank some water as she chewed more leaves and her color slowly returned to normal.

"Gods, you look like your father when you're worried," Cecilia said. "Stop frowning like that. This happens to women my age. I'm sure it's nothing, but I'll see Lyra at the clinic on Monday and all will be well."

Stella frowned. Her mother was barely old enough to be going through that particular change, and as far as she knew, vomiting wasn't a symptom.

An intuitive knowing hung between the two of them like a thread pulled too tight.

"Little Star, go back and enjoy the party, and don't give this another thought. It was probably the heat and the wine. I'm going to have your father walk me home—"

"I'll come with you," Stella insisted.

Her mother shook her head. "Nonsense. You're young. You should have your fun. What were you doing out here anyway?"

Stella looked away. "Looking at the roses."

Her mother bit back a laugh. "Oh really? I've spent an evening or two admiring the roses myself. I hope you're being careful and using your monthly preventative spell so you don't have any rosebuds of your own before you want them."

"Mama!"

Cecilia brushed Stella's cheek with her fingertips. "I'm not judging, and I don't need to know who he is. All I care about is that he's treating you well, that he respects your wishes, and that you're being responsible. And gods help us, do not let your father figure it out. He likes to pretend like I'm the protective one, but he'll be insufferable and I doubt you want him sitting your beau down for a lecture."

Stella nodded and walked back into the party without any further urging. Her cheeks still burned with humiliation. She waited for her mother to walk by. As soon as Cecilia passed, Stella rushed from the tent, tearing down the trail to home.

The house was dark, but she followed the glow of candlelight up to Rosie's room.

Her younger sister was awake in her bed, a book of their parents' fairy tales open on her chest. "What's wrong?" she asked as soon as she saw Stella's face.

Stella considered telling her. All she'd wanted was a few precious moments alone with Arden. Instead, she'd stumbled upon a terrible secret.

Rosie was old enough for the truth at twenty and she was also a talented healer, so she'd likely know more symptoms. But she looked so peaceful and Stella couldn't rob her of it. What was a big sister's job if not to protect her younger siblings? She'd been doing it for Leo and Rosie since they were all young. More than once she'd set a handsy boy straight or threatened a bully in Leo's training program.

Stella cleared her throat. "I was just sad that you decided not to join the party tonight."

Rosie frowned. "I don't feel ready for all of that attention." She set the book aside and sat up straighter. "That's not why you're upset."

"No, it's not."

They stared at each other for a long moment.

"Can I sleep in here?" Stella whispered.

Rosie nodded, her brow drawn in worry, but she said nothing. That was the best thing about her sister—the way she understood when silence was best. Stella unbuttoned her dress. It slid down her body, puddling on the floor. She smoothed her chemise and unpinned her hair, slipping into the bed beside Rosie.

Usually it was Rosie sneaking into her bed when she had a bad dream or was worried about something, but her sister didn't seem concerned by the shift in roles. She just smoothed Stella's wild hair.

"Let me tell you a story," her sister whispered.

Rosie opened the book, and, as she had so many times before, Stella let the tale carry her away from her worries for a while.

2

TEDDY

Teddy Savero was a creature of habit. He loathed being in Olney. The weather was unbearably humid, the people were too chatty, and it was impossible to find a private place to train.

Sand kicked out behind him as he ran, sticking to the backs of his calves as he sprinted down the beach.

As the future king of Argaria, Teddy needed to control his public image, and he didn't want any Olney hunters getting a glimpse of his fighting technique before he'd eyed them up first. That meant he was stuck running along the godsforsaken beach.

Being the future king was as much about cultivating the right image as it was about living up to it in every aspect of life. The last thing he needed was to look weak in an allied kingdom. He was the son of two warriors, and fierce as anyone in Argaria, but it only took one slip-up on foreign soil for tongues to wag.

The hunters were the foot soldiers of both the Argarian and Olney armies, not only trained to be expertly good at tracking stealthily, fighting, and spying but also equipped with exceptional observational skills. Their training focused heavily on finding an opponent's weakness and Teddy didn't want his to be fodder for foreign gossip.

His mother, Jessamin, was once the leader of the army in the Queendom of Novum and had brought those skills to her role as Queen of Argaria, helping to teach their hunters new fighting styles and battle techniques. His father, Xander, was a warrior who'd saved Argaria not just from the trickster god, Cato, but also from the invasion of his vicious cousin, Vincent. Teddy had a lot to live up to, and the voice in his mind never seemed to run out of ways that he could improve with just a few more hours of practice or a few more turns in the ring.

A run on the beach had seemed the next best thing to burn off the restless energy in his body. But now he was panting from the humidity, a brutal sand coating tearing up his ankles, and the idea seemed ridiculous.

Teddy paused, looking out at the Adiran Sea, sweat dripping down his back as he tried to catch his breath. He drew in deep gulps of salt air, trying to match the soft rhythm to the bright cerulean waves crashing on the shore. The longer he held still, the more he wanted to run. But no matter how far he went, he would not outrun the hard conversation he needed to have with his parents.

Teddy had planned a hundred different futures, but each year he found himself caught in the same cycle of kingdom visits and elaborate balls. Escape was an unsolvable riddle that teased him with its simplicity. He could walk away, and yet, he wouldn't. Because staying was right, and he could not bear to be weak enough to leave. What would people think of a prince who ran from his problems? They could never learn to trust a king who lacked the courage to make hard, unselfish choices.

Soft footsteps drew closer, but Teddy didn't bother turning. He knew who it was by the crackle in the air. It was the subtle warning that preceded the Storm King.

"Thought I might find you here. I spent quite a few mornings down here myself," Xander said, glancing up at a cottage that sat on the cliffs high above the sea.

"When you were married to *her*."

It was childish not to say her name. Despite the close relationship between their families, Teddy had never warmed to the woman who'd broken his father's heart. Logically he knew that his father had made mistakes, but over the years the world had run away with their fairy tale, leaving Xander as some interloper keeping fated lovers apart. The simplified version of the story was one love story instead of two.

"You can say her name. She won't appear...sadly."

Teddy rolled his eyes. "How do you still hold her in such high esteem?"

"Because I don't care about the stories or what other people think," Xander said. "I was there and I know what happened and Cece will always have my respect and affection. She is my dearest friend, second only to your mother." His father tugged up his tunic, showing the scar over his heart. "You think I'd so easily forget the person who saved my life and then helped me save my kingdom— and at great personal cost?"

Teddy shook his head and looked away. He held his tongue.

In his weaker moments, Teddy wondered if the way his father spoke so freely about Cecilia Reznik was the reason Isla had left him. There was nothing wrong with holding an old love in high esteem, but Xander spoke of her and wrote to her often.

Isla was a confident woman—a consort needed to be. But everyone had their limits.

Teddy was close with both of his parents' consorts. While the king and queen were often focused on his siblings, who were eternally getting into trouble, Maren and Isla had both made a point to pay him as much attention for behaving himself as his siblings received for not doing the same.

Teddy had taken Isla's leaving particularly hard, no matter how many times his father insisted it was temporary. Teddy had never suffered the same delusion. How the man could survive so much and remain an optimist was beyond Teddy.

"I know you hate the disruption to your routine," his father said. "I'm sure Jalen would be happy to spar with you."

Teddy crossed his arms. "Jalen's too busy chasing girls to spar this week."

"Care to throw down with your dear old dad?" Xander asked.

Teddy nodded to the guards standing a respectful distance away. "They'll let me hit the king?"

Xander chuckled. "They'll let you try. Me, on the other hand—"

Teddy shook his head. "It's all right. I was just going to go for a run and save the sparring for another day."

"I'm going to visit the fighting rings this afternoon to see the competition for the Gauntlet Games. Warriors won't start declaring until the magical binding ceremony in a few days, but I'm sure there will be enough men there bragging about their plans to join," Xander said.

It was an olive branch, but Teddy wasn't ready to make peace.

Teddy shrugged. "I have no interest in the Games."

His father laughed. "Of course. You've always been too smart for petty shows of strength. I'm all for fighting, but that tournament is no place for the heir to the throne. You and your siblings best stay as far from that competition as possible."

"You might want to remind Jalen, then," Teddy said. "He fancies himself invincible and you know how he gets when someone tells him he can't do something."

His father smiled fondly. "Yes, well, he gets that as much from your mother as me." He rubbed the back of his neck. "I'm more concerned about your sister. Alexandra was up at dawn to watch the Olney hunters and guardians train. I have four children, but it's always the same one giving me heartburn."

"She's bold, but not stupid," Teddy said. He looked out at the glittering sea, trying to settle the nervousness in his stomach.

It was now or never. His father was in good spirits and this was the chance he needed to get Xander on board with his marriage plans.

Teddy wanted Grace by his side this week and in life. She had such a different way of seeing things. He'd been so relieved that the Farlans had accompanied them to Olney for the festival. He couldn't imagine being away from her for weeks. Fortunately, Grace's extended family was in Olney and she would be close the whole time. She was the only thing that made the constant daily demands of his life manageable.

Grace could read people so well. She picked up anything Teddy missed, she directed his missteps, and when she was beside him, he felt calm. The woman was intelligent, beautiful, and born to be a queen.

Plus, she felt a natural choice for a wife since their fathers were so close. Evan and Sylvie Farlan had been loyal friends to the kingdom and some of his father's closest advisors for years. When he wasn't busy helping raise his three daughters, Evan took a special interest in Teddy's training, in particular when it came to assessing threats in a crowd and prying secrets from people who weren't eager to share. He was too clever not to have noticed Teddy's interest in Grace, but he hadn't said a word about it. If Teddy wanted to make his intentions known, he'd have to start with his own father.

"I was hoping to bring Grace to dinner tomorrow night."

His father frowned. "Grace is lovely and your affection for her is clear, but that's unwise. You don't want to give her the wrong idea."

"The idea that I value her and she's an important part of my life?" Teddy asked.

"The idea that she's a real prospect for marriage. We've indulged you thus far because we love Grace and you thrived with her support. It gives me no pleasure to remind you that you must marry for alliances. You're always so rational and you know how perilous our position has become with the Sons of Endros making so much havoc. Besides, Grace will be there with your Uncle Evan and Aunt Sylvie and her sisters anyway. No need to give her hope for something that can never be."

Teddy wanted to break things and make a scene just to prove he could. But like everything else, his anger had to be tucked away in a neat little box. People thought being king meant having power, but it really meant trading away all your personal power for the good of the kingdom. As if one man could even know what was best for everyone.

"Giving her hope for what can never be—like you with Isla?" Teddy asked.

His father flinched. It was a low blow. Xander had presented a calm front outwardly, but the wind had left his sails since Isla had left months earlier. Teddy had never seen his father so low.

He still couldn't believe Xander had asked Isla to resign as commander of the Argarian army. Things had been tense for months, with the Sons of Endros popping up and destroying property in Ardenis and Olney City alike. When they started murdering progressive public figures, it was clear something needed to be done to keep the faith of their people.

Isla wanted to continue to monitor them and not give them the attention of meeting them head-on. But Teddy's father faced intense political pressure to resolve it.

When Isla wouldn't compromise, Xander was forced to ask her to resign.

Instead of surrendering her position, she'd taken a battalion of her most loyal warriors with her and disappeared in the dark of night.

She'd left without even saying goodbye to Teddy. The woman who'd helped raise him, who had taught him everything she knew about combat and strategy, had left him without even a note.

The world felt tilted and oddly off-kilter without her. His whole family was shaken by the loss. But Teddy couldn't blame her for feeling betrayed by his father's callous decision.

"Believe me. I know the pain of not being able to give a woman what she wants," Xander said. "I'm trying to save you from the same."

The guilt was a gut punch. "I—"

"You think *I* don't know?" Xander scoffed and ran a hand through his hair. "I never wanted to rule, but I did what was required of me because being in this family means thinking about the greater good."

"Funny, it feels like that only applies to me."

Xander's eyes lit with anger. "You think your sisters will be able to love freely? That we won't have to think strategically about their marriages? Your brother and sisters might have more freedom now, but make no mistake that they will be in a similar boat later," Xander said. "This peace is such a delicate thing. I've been able to do so much good over the past twenty-five years as king. I have tried to make this role more bearable, to spread around the power so the people have more. But everyone has very quickly forgotten what it's like to truly be at war. Things are more delicate than they should be." The king shook his head, looking more world-weary than anyone his age should. "That's why we're here. To honor the alliance between Olney and Argaria and to bear witness to the contained violence of the Gauntlet Games."

"I know," Teddy snapped.

"Do you?" Xander challenged, his gaze piercing. "You know our history. You know what this peace cost me. There are stories you know and stories you don't, but just because you've been insulated from the worst of it doesn't mean that you have no sacrifices to make." The king ran a hand through his hair and sighed. "I wish things could be different for you. I wanted you to have choices I didn't. But I have fought hard and only managed to find the most tentative peace. That failure is on me. I'm sorry you must suffer for it."

Teddy hung his head. His parents both had to make sacrifices and, although they weren't a love match, they had clear affection for each other and a wonderful relationship.

"But did you not sacrifice so future generations wouldn't have to? Grace has family that are well-connected in both kingdoms. They're close family friends and she has the right temperament to be queen."

Xander pursed his lips. "But she does not have any political appeal. Aldrena has yet to renew our trade routes, and if they don't, our merchants and farmers can easily make life hell for us. At the same time, the aristocracy will relish in our failure and use it as a reason that anyone else should be on the throne and they won't be talking about you, Teddy. A good king understands how to pick his battles." His father placed a hand on his shoulder. "I'm sorry to ask it of you, but you must always be king first, and a man second."

As if Teddy didn't already hold himself to that very impossible standard. If only he could figure out how to shut down the part of him that wanted this one thing—maybe then he'd truly be the perfect king.

Ever since his parents had begun to float the idea of Aldrenian princesses, he'd made the tentative plan to go to the Temple of Desiree, goddess of love, and get irrefutable proof that he and Grace were meant to be. The type of bond that Desiree's priestesses granted was goddess-blessed. Teddy was not terribly romantic at heart, but people respected those bonds and it was one of the few things that would make his parents bend. Even a princess could not be a better option than his perfect match. They might be frustrated after the fact, but they would realize the wisdom of his choice once they saw how he and Grace ruled together.

Movement over his father's shoulder caught Teddy's eye. His father's guards, several paces away, turned too.

Teddy's sister, Alexandra, ducked out of a cave hidden along the jagged cliff face.

Xander turned, following Teddy's gaze.

Alexandra froze, a bright smile on her face. "Good morning, Papa," she said cheerfully. "Don't you just love this summer weather?"

"And where are you coming from, Alexandra?" their father asked.

Xander was too smart to ask such questions, especially given the stories about what he was like in his youth. Alexandra's hair was mussed, her tunic rumpled, and her lips swollen. She was clearly coming from the most recent in a long line of inappropriate trysts.

Teddy could never decide if his father preferred to feign ignorance or if he was entertained by her improvised excuses. Alexandra and Jalen always seemed in a tense competition to be most like their father and most at odds for his attention.

Alexandra gave him her winningest smile. "If you must know, I was making an offering to the goddess of the sea. Why else would I be on the beach so early?"

"I certainly can't fathom what else you'd be doing. Let's make sure no one else does either," Xander said.

Alexandra curtseyed. "Of course, Papa." She turned to scurry away but stopped when their father spoke again.

"You can expect a conversation with your mother and Maren about this."

Alexandra's shoulders tensed, but she didn't turn, continuing to scramble up the beach toward the trail to town.

The king shook his head, turning back to look at Teddy. "Think about what I've said. I'll see you in a bit."

Teddy wished he could scream—transform his frustration from a stoic grunt to an angry throat-shredding howl. But a good prince was a blank canvas upon which a kingdom could paint their hopes. It didn't suit to be wild or reckless when he had an obligation to be cool and solid as granite. So he forced his anger to look tidy, jammed it into the faint lines of a frown. Inside, he was a violent storm on a raging sea, but on the surface he was calm.

Be steady, the voice in his head chided. *Never let them see you sweat.* A king needed to be unmoved by aristocrats and common men alike. His father was always testing him for weak spots, making sure he wouldn't crack under pressure, and though it was out of love and experience, it still chafed that Xander didn't trust that he could take it. Teddy hadn't broken yet and he certainly wouldn't today.

His storm magic stirred beneath his skin, reaching out for the clouds above, aching to spin his frantic, unsettled emotions into a tempest. As much as he loved his magic, that power was wild. Though he always felt the rhythm of a storm and could weave it together like he was directing a symphony, there was always a strange call of the void—a reckless urge to simply let it go and see what happened.

He tore down the beach, trying to sort through the chaos in his mind. His mother had once told him that being royal meant you could only choose a few nonnegotiable things. If he wanted to rule well, he had to choose wisely what he could live with and what he couldn't live without. Grace was his nonnegotiable thing. He needed her to ground him and keep him sane, and while having consorts had worked for his parents—at least for a time—Grace was not the type of woman to abide being in second place. Nor did he want her there.

He was so lost in thought as he wandered further that he nearly jumped out of his skin when he noticed someone in the water.

She rose from the waves like a siren blooming from the sea. The dark green material of her bathing gown clung to her fair skin and her hair dripped down her back in a dark waterfall. For a moment the clouds parted, the sun shining through in a bright slash where she stood. She was lovely, ethereal and so graceful as she stretched her arms up toward the sunshine. The sopping fabric of her dress clung to her soft curves as she moved.

He must have made a sound because she turned and looked at him and then the sunlight seemed like a joke highlighting his mistake. It was Stella McKay who stared at him with a crease forming between her brows. Stella McKay, his nemesis. Stella McKay, the woman who managed to annoy him by merely existing in her perfect daydream bubble. Stella McKay, who was as reckless and emotionally volatile as Teddy was cautious and controlled.

He hadn't recognized her with her wild curls flattened by seawater. He should have known her at a glance. Not only had he seen her every summer and winter solstice for his entire life, but she bore a striking likeness to her mother, who was captured in numerous art pieces in Argaria.

Stella had the same dark, waist-length curls and fair skin that pinked with the slightest bit of exertion, but where Cecilia was short and petite, Stella was tall, only a few inches shorter than Teddy, and her eyes were bright green like her father's instead of cerulean like her mother's.

He stared at her, trying to figure out how he hadn't recognized her on sight for what she was: the bane of his existence.

"Can I help you, *Your Grace*?" Her voice was laced with contempt as she stepped out of the surf and dipped into an offensively shallow curtsey.

That was fine. The feeling was absolutely mutual. Stella was as spoiled as she was ungrateful. Her parents lavished her with praise for doing nothing. She had the freedom to wed anyone she wanted and she possessed the admiration of the people of both kingdoms for no reason other than being the only birth child of Olney's golden fairy-tale couple.

He sneered at her. "No, I don't believe there's a thing you can help me with."

"Of course not. You just do whatever you want," she grumbled, stomping by him and picking her towel up before stalking toward the cliff trail. "Royal prick."

He watched her retreating figure.

Perhaps Stella had done him a small favor. She was right. He could do whatever he wanted. His father was the one who'd taught him it was easier to beg forgiveness than ask permission. Xander couldn't fault Teddy for going after what he wanted. Tomorrow he and Grace would go to the Temple of Desiree and, once the witches there confirmed he and Grace were meant to be, they'd be bonded to each other and then he'd finally have proof enough for his parents that she was the only viable option for a wife.

3

STELLA

Stella knew something was wrong the moment she walked into the house. The scent of warm cheese and melted butter hit her as she crossed the pristine foyer. The space was normally a mess in the afternoons, her mother tossing her shawl or kicking off her shoes the moment she got in the door from work. But there were no clothes strewn about the entryway. Everything was neatly hung on the wooden hooks by the door.

It was so unlike Cecilia, who left her signature gentle mess of empty teacups, rumpled blankets, and dog-eared books in every room she entered.

A clatter sounded in the kitchen, and Stella rushed down the hall to check on it.

Leo and Rosie stood in the kitchen doorway, whispering to each other. While they weren't blood-related to each other or her, Stella often saw similarities in their mannerisms that made her smile. Their mother had always said that the fates brought them all together and Stella had always been comforted by the idea that they belonged to each other even without being bound by blood.

"What's going on?" Stella asked.

Leo nodded to the kitchen. "Mama's cooking."

Stella pushed him aside to see for herself. Sure enough, Cecilia was buttering bread and slicing cheese and humming with a determined frown on her face.

Panic sprung to life in Stella's chest. Her mother never cooked, preferring instead to be food taste-tester and designated chef-kisser, sitting on the counter while Rainer sliced vegetables or seasoned meat.

"Did she say why?" Stella asked.

Rosie shook her head. "No, she hasn't said anything, but she didn't want any help. Papa is out making a delivery and we don't know what to do."

"I'm sure it's nothing," Stella said.

Rosie whipped her head around to look at her, her shiny dark hair sliding over her shoulder. "What do you know?"

Stella shrugged. "Nothing."

Leo turned and frowned. "You're such a bad liar."

Stella held her hands up to ward them off. "I know what you know. She's just been *off* recently."

"Off how?" Leo whispered. His face turned serious.

Now that he was twenty-three, he liked to play it cool publicly, but Leo had always been a mama's boy. When he first joined their family at three, Stella couldn't stand him because he was so attached to their mother. But he'd come from such a traumatic event that he needed the comfort of Cecilia's steady presence, and he was wary of their father because of the violence in the home he'd come from.

It took a long time to pry him away from her mother and even longer for him to feel at ease in the family. And, once he'd opened up, baby Rosie joined the family as well and he took to big brother duties instantly.

Seeing them both so grown, Stella couldn't believe she'd ever felt jealous of the two people she loved most in the world.

Leo ran a hand through his hair, which had turned a light golden brown from so much time outdoors. He had grand plans of training for the Gauntlet Games, but there wasn't a chance he'd risk upsetting their mother by entering the dangerous competition.

"It's no big deal. She's just *off*," Stella said.

The front door opened behind them and they all jumped as their father walked into the house.

Rainer grinned at them. "What are you three conspiring about?"

"Mama's cooking dinner," Rosie said.

Their father frowned, peering into the kitchen. "She is? And do we have a backup plan?"

As he said it, their mother let out a string of expletives and pulled a tray of what looked like scorched lemon cakes from the fire.

"Sweetheart," their father said, pushing into the kitchen. "Do you need some help?"

Cecilia turned, her hands on her hips. "Don't manage me, Rain. I'm just trying to do something nice for all of you."

Stella walked into the kitchen. "I'm happy to help, Mama."

Cecilia pointed a wooden spatula at her children. "Oh, I know you three have been plotting. You don't think I can do it, but I'm just making fried cheese sandwiches. I think even I can handle that. Even if the lemon cakes burned. I just won't cook these as long."

Their father started to speak. "I can—"

"Rain, honestly, I can do it," Cecilia snapped.

He gave her an indulgent smile.

She put her hands on her hips again. "Don't give me that look."

"Maybe I just like you in your usual role of chef-kisser," Rainer said.

Cecilia cocked her head and angled the spatula toward him. "Why don't you be the chef-kisser?"

"Don't mind if I do," he said, scooping her into his arms and kissing her.

He ignored the chorus of groans from his children.

"Stop or you'll spoil all our appetites," Stella said.

Rainer finally set her back on her feet and grinned. "Now, what's the occasion?"

Cecilia stepped away and removed her apron, smoothing her dress and brushing damp hair back from her brow. "I had a whole plan for how I was going to tell you all," she started. "I'm not even sure how to say it, but—"

"You're sick," Stella said.

Rainer's head whipped around, his brow drawn in concern. "You are?" He looked from Cecilia to Stella, looking betrayed. "And you knew?"

Stella nodded, guilt unspooling in her stomach. "She was sick at the Godsball."

"And this morning," Rosie said.

Stella stared at her sister. "You knew?"

Rosie blushed, looking guilty. "I wanted her to bring it up."

Of course she did. Rosie was the most accommodating child, the easy-to-love, relaxed daughter in contrast to Stella's fire.

Cecilia threw her hands up. "Yes, I'm sick. I thought maybe it was wasting disease and so—"

"You didn't tell me," Rainer said. He cupped their mother's face in his hands. "Cece, I thought we had settled this. What did I say to you all those years ago?"

She smiled up at him. "There's no darkness you won't follow me into. I know. I just wanted to know which darkness it was before I pulled you along with me. But that's not what's wrong with me."

She drew away from him, grabbed her stool, and placed it in front of the windows that opened up to their back garden. She stepped up onto it with a flourish. "Now I need you all to listen and stop interrupting."

"Look out, she's on her scolding stool," Leo whispered.

Rainer had built Cecilia the stool so she could reach the upper shelves in the kitchen, but as the children grew taller than her, they had branded it her "scolding stool" where she could stand eye-to-eye to admonish them. Those occasions were rare enough that it had become more of a joke.

"I saw Lyra this afternoon and I feel rather foolish for going to the worst possible thing. I should have realized what was happening," Cecilia said.

"Out with it, Mama," Stella snapped.

Cecilia's whole face lit up and her eyes locked onto Rainer. "I'm pregnant."

The words knocked the wind out of Stella. She was hit with immense relief, followed immediately by a new world-tilting worry. The revelation rocked the steadiest ground beneath her feet.

It was no secret that her mother had always hoped to give birth to more children, but so many years had passed with them trying that Stella had assumed she'd be their only one. Pathetic as it was, it was the thing that had always made her feel special. Leo had his fighting. Rosie had her art. But Stella hadn't found her place in the world. All she had was her goddess bloodline.

It was ridiculous to be jealous of a baby, but when she looked at the joy on her mother's face, she felt the distinct prickle of envy.

Leo blew out a breath. "But you're so *old*."

Cecilia rolled her eyes. "Thank you, Leo. I'm aware. That's why I assumed it was something else."

Rosie clapped her hands, bouncing on her toes. "So we're going to have a new baby?"

"Lyra confirmed it. She assumed I knew. She and Mika had apparently noticed a couple of weeks ago." She looked at Rainer. "Say something, Rain."

Rainer crossed the room and swept her into a kiss. Leo groaned, but Rosie continued delightedly clapping. Their parents kissed for a not-at-all-appropriate-in-front-of-their-children amount of time before Rainer dropped to his knees, his mouth next to her stomach.

"Hello, baby, this is your father. We are delighted that you're here, but please stop making your mother so sick."

He stood and helped Cecilia off the stool, and she turned to the children. Leo and Rosie both hugged her, but Stella hung back.

She should have been happy, and she was. Her parents had tried for more children for a long time. She thought they were content. Though her parents made a point of treating them all with equal love and attention, Stella had always felt special being the only biological child of a legendary soul-bonded couple. What if the new baby was more magical, more talented, or simply easier to love?

Finally, her mother's gaze leveled on her. "Say something."

Stella wanted so badly to be gracious and excited like everyone else, but her mother was always looking at her like that—like she wanted understanding when everything came so easily to her.

"I guess it will be nice for you to have another reason to be the center of attention." The words were too sharp and wrong for the mood, but Stella had no softness to offer. Not when her life had been tipped on its side.

Her mother flinched, her eyes going glassy as she turned and walked out into the garden.

Stella didn't need to look to feel her father's eyes on her, to sense his disappointment. He followed Cecilia outside, shaking his head.

Rosie and Leo hovered in the doorway. Stella hated their assessment. The way it was so easy for them to say and do the right thing.

"That wasn't very kind," Rosie said.

"I don't know why you're so happy to be replaced," Stella snapped. "You're the baby. Aren't you worried about losing your privileged spot? Don't you resent the way they've pined for a biological baby? Doesn't it make you feel like an outsider?"

A look passed between Leo and Rosie, some silent language conspiring in that quick glance.

"You're the only one who ever makes us feel that way," Rosie said. "Mama and Papa never do."

The words were a gut punch. Guilt swept through her. Stella loved Rosie and Leo. She was so grateful for her siblings and loved their talents and quirks more than anything. They'd always felt like her team, and she hated that she'd been anything less than accepting of them.

It didn't matter that Rosie and Leo had both come from other families. Stella had always felt like they belonged to her.

Leo scowled at her, took Rosie under his arm, and guided her toward the foyer. The front door slammed a moment later.

Stella stood alone in the kitchen for a long time, staring out at her parents in the garden and watching a great love from afar.

4

STELLA

"Stella, I swear to the gods if you don't move your fine ass, I am leaving without you," Kate bellowed from somewhere on the first floor of the McKay Estate.

Stella had always loved the huge house where her mother grew up, but its sheer size meant that someone was always yelling between floors.

Stella rushed down the stairs, around the corner and into the kitchen, and nearly barreled into her best friend. "A face like a lady, but the boisterous voice and colorful vocabulary of a sailor," she said affectionately.

"I have to speak up if I want to get a word in edgewise in my house," Kate said with a grin. "Now tell me how good I look."

Stella laughed as Kate turned in a slow circle. Her fuchsia dress swished around her legs. The high neckline in the front fastened around her neck and left her whole back bare.

"Scandalous," Stella teased.

Kate pretended to toss her dark hair, which was meticulously pinned up on top of her head. "Thank you for noticing."

Stella smoothed her hands down the lilac silk of her own dress. "And me?"

Kate pressed her lips together for a long moment, as if debating whether to say something. She was one of the few people who knew about Arden, but the prince had not done as good of a job winning Kate over as he had Stella.

"Of course you look gorgeous. I just hope you're not getting your hopes too high," Kate said.

Stella looked around the kitchen for anything to deflect from the same conversation they'd had many times before. Kate didn't have to like Arden, but she could at least be supportive.

She glanced out the windows into the garden. Her parents sat in their fancy evening clothes, necks craned, looking up at the barely darkened sky. They whispered to each other, her mother taking the teacup from her father's hand and sipping from it.

It had been a full day since her mother dropped the news of her pregnancy and Stella still felt unsettled.

"They're so—"

"In love?" Kate finished for her.

Stella rolled her eyes. "Yes, but this whole thing is a lot. The way they sit there staring at the sky, passing the same glass back and forth and saying, *'sugared with stars'* like it actually means something?"

Kate laughed. "You *are* jealous. You want what they have. And why shouldn't you? You're their baby. They are the standard."

Stella hated that it was true. Even now, with her father surely switching to some sort of tea instead of the whiskey they normally shared, they sat there together on a blanket, whispering to each other, as in love as they'd always been.

"They are. It's easy for them, like it is with me and Arden."

Kate ignored her, watching as Rainer rose from the ground and helped Stella's mother up, kissing the scar on the outside of her hand and the one inside her wrist.

"I don't blame you for feeling like no man at court can measure up to the example your father sets," Kate said, fanning herself. "And he looks so good doing it."

"Ew, Kate," Stella said.

"It's not my fault. Ever since I caught him and your mom that one time, I swear—"

Stella covered her ears. "Stop, I beg you."

"He looks at her like he worships her," Kate said, gazing longingly out the window.

If Stella wasn't so used to seeing it herself, she might have been disturbed, but mostly it just made her roll her eyes now. "He does."

Kate waved a hand like it was obvious. "So it makes sense that you want a man who will worship you."

"Because he's like my dad?" Stella wrinkled her nose. "Gross."

Kate threw her hands in the air. "No, because you know whoever you choose to love, your relationship will be held up against *theirs*."

Stella squirmed, picking at her nails and avoiding Kate's eyes. She didn't like that it was so clear for her friend to see. That meant that everyone else would think it too. How could she compete with her parents' history, what with the bond that allowed them to understand each other so fundamentally?

Arden was magnetic, creative, and thoughtful, but it was impossible to give their relationship the privacy to grow when he was such a public figure. She didn't want Kate or anyone else's scrutiny. Not when things were going so well with Arden—when they were so close to making things more serious.

"Shall we go?" Kate asked.

Stella turned away from the windows and threaded her arm through Kate's. "Let's."

They hurried out of the house and down the trail to town. It was a quieter night for the Solstice Festival, meant for smaller household and bar parties.

"It's more deserted out here than I expected," Kate said as they walked into the main square in Olney City. Torches along the street kept the area well-lit, but there weren't many people milling about.

Boisterous music spilled out of the doors of the surrounding bars, but the streets were far less crowded than they had been in years past, thanks to the escalating rebel attacks leading up to the Solstice Festival events.

The Sons of Endros had been wreaking havoc in the kingdom since Stella's parents had helped end the war between Olney and Argaria more than two decades earlier. When Stella was young, the attacks had been few and far between—the careless tantrums of men too rooted in their ways to allow the fighting to end.

Recently, however, those attacks had become more organized and much more frequent. The Solstice Festival was normally a week long with events every night, but for the sake of security, King Marcos had reduced the larger events to every other night so that some of the kingdom's hunters and guardians could stay sharp and rested, instead of constantly guarding the royal family and visiting dignitaries.

"At least tomorrow will be exciting again," Stella said, taking one long glance down the mostly empty street. The hairs on the back of her neck prickled like she was being watched, but when she turned, there was no one.

"I know you're right, but it seems a waste to use such a breathtaking dress at a party where there won't be any real courting prospects," Kate said. "Good thing I have the perfect one saved for tomorrow night. Maybe I'll bring some excitement to the Gauntlet play."

Stella laughed. She'd always liked watching the Gauntlet play as a child. She grew up on stories and loved that her parents were so intricately woven into the tale of their two kingdoms. In recent years, though, she hadn't loved the scrutiny. People always came up to her teary-eyed afterward to reassure her that she would find the same kind of love her parents had, but their words felt more placating than sincere.

Rainer liked to say that she had inherited her mother's face for truth-telling. Stella was not good at hiding her displeasure, and over the past few years, those comments had become difficult to smile through.

Kate tugged her toward the large castle walls. The guards at the gate nodded and Stella and Kate followed a trail of rose petals that led through the castle gates and into the party. They stepped through a large floral archway into a glowing, whimsical wonderland.

The courtyard outside of Olney Castle had been transformed. Tall, white candles surrounded by colorful floral bouquets ran down the center of the long dining tables.

The more intimate gathering of the royal families and a few select families of the court, like Kate's, had become a tradition over the past few years and Stella always looked forward to it.

"I didn't know Rosie and Leo went ahead of us," Kate said.

Stella glanced at her siblings, who stood on the far side of the courtyard, looking at a large ice sculpture that held chilled bottles of bubble wine. Guilt uncoiled in Stella's stomach. She needed to apologize to them both, but not in front of everyone. She'd have to find a quiet moment when no one was paying close attention.

Kate turned an assessing gaze on Stella and arched a brow. "Oh? Are the perfect McKays fighting?"

"Of course not," Stella said.

Kate scoffed. "Must be nice. When you only have brothers, the fighting never stops. What is it this time?"

Stella wrung her hands. "You can't say anything. It's not public knowledge."

Kate's eyes lit up, and she grabbed two glasses of bubble wine from a passing servant's tray, handing one to Stella before settling in for gossip.

"My mom is pregnant," Stella said.

Kate stared at her for a full thirty seconds before the words sank in. Her face twisted from an expression of shock to a smirk.

Stella held her hands up to ward off whatever obscene thing Kate was about to say. "Do not even say it—"

"I knew your dad had it in him. I swear my life changed the day I heard him say the words 'good girl.'"

Stella groaned. "My stomach is not strong enough to hear that story a second time."

Kate fanned herself and held her glass against her neck. "I should thank you for inviting me to sleep over after our first Godsball. If I hadn't, I would never have caught them in the act. I didn't know older married people still had hot sex in their kitchens."

Stella shivered with disgust and covered her ears. "Stop ruining my life, you deviant."

Kate cackled and turned back to the party, which was beginning to fill with guests.

A squeal cut through the din of voices and Stella turned to watch her mother throw herself into the arms of the king of Argaria. Xander Savero laughed and whispered something in her ear before stepping back and making her twirl. Her mother's cheeks pinked, and she laughed again as Queen Jessamin hugged her and kissed her on the cheek.

"It's so weird how your family is so casual with King Xander," Kate whispered. "You know he's handsome for an older man. Your mother really knows how to pick them."

Stella slapped her arm. "Stop it. I can't think about him that way."

"Do you not have eyes? What about his sons? Prince Jalen is gorgeous, though you can just tell from looking at him that he knows it. Prince Theodore is very good-looking. He has that whole intensely serious, broody thing going on."

"Teddy is a jerk, Kate. Jalen is a year younger than us but at least he's charming."

"And a flirt from the looks of it," Kate said, nodding to where Jalen leaned against the table, a rose in his hand extended to Lady Amy Sharp.

At the head table, Xander pulled a pink rose from behind his back and handed it to Cecilia.

"The apple doesn't fall far," Stella grumbled.

"Stella?"

She spun and came face to face with the two Savero princesses.

Juliana was twenty-two and had always been close with Rosie. The two were constantly writing letters to each other and spent all the solstice holidays practically attached at the hip. The princess was tall like her mother with flawless golden-brown skin, dark brown eyes, and hair that was always immaculately styled in intricate braids. She was all elegant grace and stylish dresses, but looks could be deceiving. The middle daughter of the Savero family was well-trained by her warrior parents, as deadly as she was regal. Her dress probably had no less than six blades hidden within the bodice.

Juliana pulled Stella into a hug. "It's good to see you. You're looking lovely in lilac," she said.

Stella smiled. "You look beautiful as well, Jules. The beadwork on that dress is gorgeous. Is it from Novum?"

Juliana nodded, glowing with pride in her mother's homeland as she spun so the candlelight caught the silver beading on her dress. "I think it adds to my ice princess ethos."

Stella nodded. "It certainly does. You remember Lady Kate Crawley."

Juliana and Kate kissed cheeks as Stella turned to greet Alexandra.

Of all the Savero children, Alexandra was the one who bore the most striking resemblance to the king. Her skin was lighter and more olive than her siblings, and she had his bright hazel eyes that were always lit with mischief.

Kate looked at the king and then back at Alexandra. "I hope you'll forgive me for saying so, but you look just like—"

"My father. I know. Mother says it every day," Alexandra said. "Fortunate for me that the men and women of Olney think that's a good thing."

Stella laughed. "So happy court life hasn't tamed you, Alex."

Alexandra brushed her hands together like she was trying to rid herself of crumbs. "I dared them to try. They haven't risen to the occasion as of yet."

Stella had never met a more self-contained twenty-one-year-old than Alexandra Savero. Alexandra had always had a steady confidence about her and no fear of the attention being royal brought.

"You look very lovely," Stella said, eyeing the silver beading forming a scalloped pattern that looked almost like chain mail on her bodice.

Though Alexandra rarely wore anything but her leather armor, she looked just as at ease in the elegant dress that showed off her tall, slender body and a daring amount of cleavage.

Stella looked at the crowd. "Where is Aunt Isla?"

Juliana and Alexandra exchanged a look. "She's gone away for a while."

"Away?" Kate asked. "Like on a mission?"

King Xander's consort, Isla, had long been the general of the Argarian army and had shared responsibility for Argaria's network of spies with Evan Farlan.

Alexandra swiped a glass of bubble wine from a passing tray and took a long sip, refusing to meet Stella's gaze. It was no secret that Alexandra idolized Isla. She'd spoken of going to the elite Novumi warrior academy, Callemoore, every summer visit since she was old enough to hold a weapon because she wanted to be trained in the same way the consort was.

Juliana cleared her throat. "No. Not a mission. Perhaps more permanent this time. Our father was forced to make a difficult decision and relieve her of her duties."

Alexandra scoffed. "You mean to bend to the will of weaker men."

Juliana glared at her. "You know well that a king cannot rule without the allegiance of his people, Alex. We should at least *support* him even if we don't agree with his choices. Or is granting a loved one the grace to make their own mistakes a courtesy that you expect us to only extend to you?"

Stella stared at them. The two princesses were so different, but never so publicly at odds with each other.

"I don't understand," Kate said. "Isla is such an asset. She's a legend. Why would he relieve her of her duties?"

Juliana cast a wary glance around the party and sipped her wine. "Old prejudices die hard. She's been in the role a long time, but there are still men who are too proud to fight and train beneath a woman, especially a foreign woman."

"Men would rather let their kingdom be overrun with rebels than follow a woman into battle. The decades change, but the men stay the same," Alexandra said bitterly.

Stella's gaze slid to the king. Xander looked as jovial as always, smiling indulgently at Cecilia as they sat down at the table. There was an ease between Cecilia and the king that spoke of a long and intimate history. Stella had always wondered why it didn't bother her father more, but Rainer seemed entirely content watching the two of them. She supposed he was still riding the high about the baby news. Stella was the only one in the family feeling any semblance of apprehension. Even her mother, who was sick every day, seemed to be in great spirits.

Kate followed her gaze and whistled. "Gods, your father looks incredible. I love when he rolls up his tunic sleeves like that. Those forearms are so—"

"Kate!" Stella snapped. Her best friend was so good at interrupting awkward conversations with even more awkward ones. "How many times do I have to tell you not to talk about him like that? It grosses me out."

Juliana smothered a laugh, and Alexandra smirked.

Kate shrugged. "I don't know why you're grossed out. You have half those good looks."

Stella rolled her eyes. "Stop it or I'll start flirting with your brother."

Kate gasped in faux shock, her hand coming to her heart. "You wouldn't *dare*."

"Why not? He's one of the most eligible bachelors in Olney."

Kate made a gagging noise. "Don't remind me. If one more lady tries to initiate a friendship with me just to ask about him, I'm going to lose it."

Kate's brother, Gregory, was handsome, but Stella had once seen him tell a lady that her eyes were as brown as mud, so his idea of romance might need some work.

A bell rang, the signal for the guests to take their seats, and Stella was saved from any more awkwardness with the princesses.

She walked up alongside the table, searching for her name card and finding it toward the head of the table, only a few seats down from Arden. When he spotted her, he rounded the table and pulled out her chair.

He looked so handsome in his hunter-green tunic. His tan skin glowed in the candlelight.

"You look gorgeous," he whispered as he pushed her chair in for her. "Just a few more days until I can show the world you're mine."

Stella fought a smile, trying to keep her face neutral as he walked back to his place at the table and the king of Olney stood to speak.

Kate sat down beside Stella. "Ready for the corny speech?"

Stella smothered a laugh.

King Marcos stood tall at the head of the table. His dark hair was peppered with gray around the temples, but he still had the build of a warrior. Queen Ilani stood beside him. She was regal and beautiful, and though her features were more delicate, her eyes held a fierce guile that was absent in her son. Stella had always thought Arden favored the best of both of them. He had the king's kind eyes that invited trust, but Ilani's clever, strategic mind. Arden would make a great king one day, and Stella thrilled at the thought of being his queen. They could be a team the way his parents so clearly were.

"Thank you all for being here tonight for this dinner under the stars," King Marcos said. "Queen Ilani and I are honored that our dear friends, the Saveros, have joined us to celebrate our long, prosperous alliance. Please be sure you make King Xander, Queen Jessamin, and the princes and princesses feel welcome."

Stella scoffed. As if anyone could make prickly Teddy Savero feel welcome. His face was always either devoid of any emotion at all or pinched in disdain.

"Ilani and I are also happy to welcome the Zims, Princess Eleria Zim and her parents, King Limin and Queen Frella, who have traveled all the way from Jeset to celebrate with us."

The foreign king gave King Marcos a sharp nod. Stella had been trying to ignore the fact that the beautiful princess was sitting just a few seats down, but now it was impossible. The proximity made her want to down her entire glass of wine, but it would have been rude while the king was toasting.

King Marcos paused and smiled warmly at the visiting royal family. "King Limin and I are also delighted to make a very joyful announcement tonight. After many years, we have further fortified our already strong kingdom by solidifying our friendship with Jeset. Just moments ago, we confirmed the details and are happy to announce that Prince Arden and Princess Eleria are betrothed."

The crowd erupted in applause, but Stella could scarcely hear it over the pounding of her heart. She was winded by the proclamation. Arden looked just as stunned by the words. His face was drained of color and his hands flexed at his sides. Stella's gaze darted to Princess Eleria, who looked suddenly pale, her smile the tight line of a woman white-knuckling her way through a banquet she'd rather run from.

The world tilted, a sick feeling settling in Stella's stomach. She felt betrayed.

How could Arden not tell Stella this was a real possibility?

Kate grabbed her hand. "Stella?"

She'd been talking, but Stella couldn't make out the words.

"What?" Her mouth was so dry it came out like a death gasp.

King Marcos raised a glass. "A toast to my son, Arden, and daughter-to-be, Princess Eleria."

Stella grabbed her wine and knocked back the rest of what was in her almost-full cup. Her heartbeat drowned out the noise in the courtyard. She set the cup down with a clatter, her gaze locking on Arden across the table.

It was a mistake; her eyes immediately began to burn with tears. She stood with a start.

"Stella—" Kate reached for her, but she ducked away.

Stella felt like she was moving in slow motion as she slipped from the table and through the crush of servants presenting the first dinner course.

She needed air. Her chest was too tight, the evening too warm, her eyes too blurry.

Everything had fallen apart so quickly. How could she have been so incredibly naive? She'd always thought herself so above court politics. She felt better than the ladies she'd watched moon over men whose families were making alliances they chose not to see. She'd thought those ladies so silly, but now she was one of them. Swooning over a prince like she had a right to him—when she was nothing but a party trick to be trotted out. A lovely little result of a great love story she'd always fall short of living up to.

Her parents were extraordinary, and Stella was just another common lady—a dreamer with her head in the clouds. Things with Arden had always been effortless, but now she wondered if she'd read it all wrong—if she was so blinded by the shine of him that she'd thought they were more.

She barely ducked around a servant carrying a tray of bubble wine before stumbling into the queen's garden. She was practically running by the time her feet hit the familiar garden trail. The shadows of the path seemed to reach for her, the dark as eager for her as she was for its shelter.

"Stella! Slow down." Arden's voice cut through the foliage behind her and she took off at a sprint, her dress billowing out behind her.

"Leave me alone," she said in a loud whisper, running deeper into the maze of gardens.

It was no use. Arden was still on her heels.

"I have an idea. Just let me talk to you. I didn't know—"

Stella stopped and turned on him so fast he almost ran into her. "What idea could possibly fix this? You're engaged to marry some stranger!" Her words were a harsh whisper.

Arden ran a hand through his hair, making a mess of his dark waves. "I didn't ask for this. I didn't know my father was even negotiating it, let alone announcing it to the world. He's not trying to be malicious. He's just not used to someone saying no to him."

"As if you would!" Stella said. "I thought—" She was mortified by the raw emotion in her voice. "I thought you and I had something different. I thought we could have the kind of love my parents have. I know there's pressure on you to always go along with what's expected of you. But I thought this ease between us was what you wanted."

Arden winced as if wounded by the words. Anger and frustration swirled in his dark eyes. "For you, I could stand up to them. For you I will." He cupped her face in his hands. "I won't lose you, Stella."

He kissed her with a tenderness that melted the ice in her veins.

This was real. Everything at that table had been a performance, but this kiss was the real him. Arden's hands in her hair, his heart beating wildly beneath her palms. That was what mattered.

He pulled away, his forehead resting against hers, lips brushing hers. "Go with me to the Temple of Desiree. We'll leave tonight and by tomorrow afternoon we'll have proof that we're soul mates and our hearts will be bonded together. There will be nothing my parents can say to that."

"I'm sure they'll have plenty to say," Stella said. She stepped back, needing the distance between them to think.

"They won't. It's easier to beg forgiveness when we prove we're right, because I know we are. I've never felt like this about anyone. I love you. Who can argue once we have that bond? You know that's a thing our parents will respect. My father is terrified of upsetting the gods. Just trust me on this. It will be enough to convince them it's a good idea and then we can finally be together. Meet me at the royal stables at midnight and we will ride to Heartwood Valley." He took her hand in his.

The sudden impulsivity was so unlike him. He could be romantic in moments, but he was so rarely spontaneous. Spontaneity was not a luxury for princes. He always had to be aware of appearances.

He curled in on himself, looking agonized by her silence. "Please, Stella. I love you and I can stand up for what I believe in. You mean too much to me and I need you as queen. Our people do."

Seeing him so undone at the thought of losing her sent a reckless thrill through Stella.

"You think I'd be a good queen?" she asked, fighting a smile.

He lowered to his knees, brushing a kiss to her knuckles. "You would make an exceptional queen. You're kind and beautiful and have such brilliant ideas. You were made to be my better half. Just give me this chance to prove I deserve you."

Stella was torn between logic and the sweeping romance of the offer. It was unlike him to go against his parents' wishes, but this was just the grand gesture she'd been dreaming about since he first started speaking to her on the beach. She wanted the world to know that she was special to him—not in the way he made everyone who spoke to him feel special, but in the way she made him feel that back.

A warning bell blared in the back of her mind. It was the echo of her mother's voice chiding her to be careful about handsome, sweet-talking men who made big promises.

But Arden was noble and not prone to chasing whim. He had been listening all along and he wanted to give her the exact thing that she'd always wanted. She could have a grand, sweeping love story of her own, and all she had to do was take a leap of faith.

It was not the question she'd been hoping he'd ask from his knees, but her response was the same anyway.

"Yes."

5

TEDDY

Looking down the long, white marble hallway of the Temple of Desiree, Teddy felt suddenly uncertain. Impulsivity did not come naturally to him, but it was now or never.

Seeing Arden Teripin tossed into a political marriage so publicly had been the wake-up call Teddy needed. He was not about to sit back and wait for the same thing to happen to him. Not when he was certain of who he wanted by his side for life.

On the surface, his decision might have looked rash, but really it was calculated and strategic.

Any doubt in his mind was wiped away when his partner in crime grinned up at him. Grace Farlan was meant for him.

They'd been waiting to get into the main temple for nearly an hour. They'd arrived before dark and were led to guest suites to change and eat before the ceremony. Now they were finally ready to be seen by the goddess.

Moonlight poured in through the tall windows that lined the hallway, casting Grace's face ghostly white and her hair silver. She smoothed her elaborate fuchsia dress. It was a bit much for the occasion. Though she'd traveled in riding clothes, Grace insisted she wouldn't meet the goddess in anything but her finest gown.

She caught him studying her. "I know that face. You're hedging."

The tension left Teddy's shoulders. "I'm not. It's not you. You're perfect."

There was a flicker of something in her eyes. "I'm not—"

"You're perfect for me," he corrected.

For years he'd watched men of the Argarian court approach Grace like she was a rare jewel and not a person. Beauty made fools of men, but Teddy had been lucky enough to know her underneath the carefully curated facade. She was steady, kind, and mesmerizing at commanding a room. She always put Teddy at ease.

The line shifted forward.

Grace hesitated, staring out at the moon. "What if—"

Teddy could practically read the thought. *What if they weren't meant for each other?*

"Not possible," he said, brushing a kiss to her temple. "There is no one else in this world better suited to me."

She smiled, but there was still a nervous pinch of her brow. "Glad to hear you say it."

Teddy chuckled. "You were testing me?"

"Well, simply suggesting we come here is very romantic," Grace said. "But I wanted to make sure you're actually ready to commit. No use subjecting myself to this process if you have reservations."

In that moment, Grace's grin wiped away every fear that clouded his mind. Her sense of humor kept him on his toes. It came with the territory of being the daughter of the Argarian spymaster and the Olney ambassador. Years ago, her parents Evan Farlan and Lady Sylvie Brett had helped Teddy's father wrestle control of his kingdom out from under an usurper. Grace read people as well as her father and manipulated them with the same cleverness as her mother.

This had to work. The life stretched out before Teddy, as the husband to a stranger, doing every single thing that was expected of him, being perfect in a way that no one else had to be, would be miserable. An heir belonged to their kingdom. He would never get to be his own person, never get to choose his path forward, and every move he made would be scrutinized.

The people of Argaria didn't care what could be proven. They only cared what seemed true and the rumors of his father's parentage hadn't dissipated no matter how long he was king or how much good he did for the kingdom. It was an easy blade for any lord Xander offended to wield whenever he did something that chipped away at their power.

That was all compounded with the rising popularity of the Sons of Endros. The only thing that had kept the Saveros secure in their rule was their alliances with Novum and Olney and the support of the common people. But if Teddy could give them a sweeping love story, perhaps they'd buy into it with the same vigor they'd brought to other romantic stories in their history.

The line surged forward again and Teddy's stomach twisted with excited apprehension.

Grace squeezed his hand and leaned in close. "And if by some chance we aren't matched, all will still be well."

Earlier she was thinking of his reservations, but now he wondered if she had her own. It was a huge commitment to be connected to someone so intimately. If the priestesses offered them a heart bond, he would sense all of Grace's emotions and she would sense his. Gods knew that would be a lot for anyone to take.

She squeezed his hand again. "Don't look at me like that. I respect the gods, but I need you to know that I don't need their approval and neither do you. We can never be certain of their motives. I just don't want you to be blindsided if this doesn't go according to your plan."

Teddy studied her face for any hint of apprehension, but she only smiled and nodded determinedly toward the priestess waiting in front of them. It was their turn.

Just beyond the doorway where the priestess stood was the temple where the ceremony would be performed. He placed his hand on Grace's lower back and guided her forward.

The priestess wore blush-pink robes, her tight curls twisted up on top of her head and wrapped in a crown of bright florals. She had luminous dark brown skin and full lips that were painted a dark berry color. Teddy had always heard that Goddess Desiree had the most beautiful priestesses, and this woman was even more striking than he'd imagined.

Grace elbowed him, clearly noticing his gawking.

"Welcome, lovers. I'm sure you're eager to get started, but first I need to be sure you're aware of the rules," the priestess said in a low, sultry voice. "If you cut your hand here and spill your blood in the bowl, you'll be bound to the results inside. This means if you aren't a match, then you'll be sent away without a bond. You can still be together, of course. Plenty of people are happy together long-term without their hearts bound, but if you are heart-fated, then you'll receive a temporary bond that will last until the new moon in two weeks. If you still want the bond at that point, it will become permanent. If you don't solidify it, the bond will fade by the end of the month."

"How do we solidify it?" Grace asked.

The priestess gave her a smirk. "Every bond is as individual as its duo, but you will know when it happens and once it's solidified, it's permanent, and even we cannot break it."

"Not even with severing?" Teddy asked.

Grace scowled at him for even asking, but the question was a reflex of morbid curiosity. Isla had once witnessed a severing and had told Teddy how the process was excruciating physically, emotionally, and mentally.

"Not even with severing. We don't have a way of doing so with this type of bond as of now because it's borne out of more free will than the guardian and witch soul bonds of old," the priestess said.

"Are you sure you want to be tied to me, Grace?" Teddy asked. "That you want to be queen? I wouldn't blame you if you didn't."

Her face softened. "Don't doubt me now. Whether you feel like you were meant to be king or not, I think we both agree that I am made to be queen."

He studied her. It wasn't a direct answer, but she had a habit of deflecting when she was nervous.

Grace looked at him expectantly. She was waiting for him to go first.

Teddy held out his hand, and the priestess grasped it. She drew her ceremonial blade across his palm. It was so sharp he didn't feel the cut. Blood bloomed in a bright line over his skin. The priestess followed suit with Grace and then pressed their two palms together, allowing the blood to drip into the bowl. The droplets spread like smoke in the water and then dissipated completely.

When the priestess was satisfied, she released his hand and gave him a piece of linen. Teddy blotted the blood and used his magic to heal his palm.

His stomach grumbled loudly as he finished. Channeling healing burned through his energy quickly. If he was wise, he would have had more to eat earlier, but he'd been too nervous for the ceremony.

Healing was one of the first elemental magics he had learned to summon, right after his primary affinity of storms. For a young prince in a conflicted kingdom, there were few skills more practical than the ability to heal. The power to channel magic from the natural world passed through bloodlines, as did elemental affinities. Plenty of people in Olney and Argaria were born with no magic, even if they had witch ancestors. Teddy had been relieved when he took to summoning storms with the same ease his father had. It took longer to learn the other elements, and he would never wield them with the same efficiency, but that was true for every other witch in the two kingdoms.

Primary affinities were always the most efficient use of magic. Secondary affinities burned through a witch's energy stores in swift and chaotic ways, and if they didn't eat or rest enough, they could easily find themselves fainting on the battlefield.

Grace wiped the blood from her palm and healed the wound with her magic so that, when she drew the linen away, there was no sign of the cut. Though she was most adept with earth magic, she'd spent a great deal of time refining her healing, because her father had drilled into her the importance of being prepared for the worst.

Teddy met Grace's icy blue eyes. She smiled and the whole world narrowed to her. He'd known her his whole life, and now she was vowing to spend the rest of hers connected to him. She was his constant, his light that always guided him home when he felt lost.

He was suddenly overcome with relief that she'd gone along with his crazy plan. Dragging her to this temple in the middle of the night was a lot to ask, but she'd done it without hesitation. Now she stood before him, looking weary but so lovely that he had to fight the urge to kiss her out in the open. If all went well, they'd be set up in a retreat room post-bonding so they could learn to manage the new impulses and emotions that came with the connection. He'd have plenty of time to express his gratitude then.

"Please continue into the main temple and proceed around the edge of the room to line up next to the other visitors," the priestess said.

Teddy nodded and led Grace into the large space. As they crossed the threshold, he glanced at the starry sky through the circular opening in the center of the temple ceiling. There was no going back now.

A holy woodsmoke haze clouded the dim space, nearly overpowering the smell of roses and freshwater emanating from the spring that ran through the center of the temple floor. Several other couples huddled around the edges of the room, their wide eyes focused on a group of priestesses seated on cushions at the center of the room. Their eyes were closed, their faces relaxed in meditation.

Teddy ushered Grace to the edge of the room behind the rest of the lovers. He kissed the place on her palm where the mark had been. "I know I sprung this on you and that's unlike me, but I hope you'll take it as a sign of my seriousness about you and not just a brash decision with my back against the wall."

Grace brushed a lock of his hair back from his forehead. "I know your heart, Teddy. I've always known it and I have no doubt that you have thought this over—likely for a great deal longer than you should have. You need not agonize for me, too."

She knew him so well. Though he'd decided yesterday, he'd spent the following twenty-four hours talking himself through every possibility—Grace rejecting him, their parents catching them, his father's fury. No matter how he turned the problem over, though, the answer was clear. He wanted Grace more than he wanted to make anyone else in his life happy.

For once, he was choosing himself. The kingdom and all its alliances would be better for it. Grace would not only be a good partner to him, but a wise queen.

"Don't worry so much," Grace whispered. "If there's one thing even your father can't argue with, it's a magical bond."

Although the heart bonds created by the priestesses of Desiree were different from the soul bonds that were occasionally granted to witches and their guardians during the war, the people of Olney and Argaria had come to value them just the same thanks to tales of the heroics and romance of Cecilia Reznik and Rainer McKay.

A priestess in pale pink robes waved them forward. "Names, please?"

"Grace Cecilia Farlan."

Teddy cleared his throat. Most of the other couples in line around the edge of the wall seemed to be out of earshot, but he was still a little worried about what scandal he might cause. "Theodore Davide Savero."

The priestess gave him a knowing smile and wrote his name in the book.

"What is this for?" Teddy asked.

"We always keep records of who visits. A guest book of sorts. If you're bonded, you'll also be entered into the book of bonds so we can accurately trace the history of all duos."

"How many bonds do you grant in a day?" Grace asked.

"It depends on how many couples in the room have true heart bond potential," the priestess said, brushing her auburn hair behind her shoulder. "On a good night, we might have ten or fifteen percent of those who show up, but hearts can be fickle. And a heart bond is hardly necessary to have a happy relationship."

Grace nodded. "And how many of those couples solidify their bond?"

"Such a curious one," the priestess said with a smile. "It's a deeply personal choice. Perhaps half of them. For some, the connectedness is too overwhelming. It's not like when guardians and witches were bonded for the Gauntlet. Those bonds were created when the duos were just children. Children adapt so quickly. It's harder for adults to adjust to the intensity."

Teddy's curiosity got the better of him. "How does the heart bond differ from a soul bond? Will I feel everything Grace feels?"

The priestess folded her hands. "Heart bonds are very similar in the way they allow you to locate each other easily in a crowd and feel what the other does, but they don't usually run as deep as soul bonds and they cannot retrieve a soul that's lost, as in some of the more famous soul bond stories."

Teddy nodded stiffly, apprehension twisting in his stomach. Would Grace love him less if she felt his constant nervousness, or the way envy flooded him every time he watched his three siblings do little more than fight, fuck, and flirt while he carried the weight of a kingdom on his back? Would she love him if she could sense the depth of his pettiness? The rare moments when he lacked confidence?

Grace slid her hand into his and squeezed as they followed the line of fifteen other couples hoping for a bond. Finally, they came to a stop and he and Grace turned to face the center of the room. From their place along the wall, Teddy took in the starlight pouring through the open roof that shone down on the meditating priestesses at the center of the room. On the far side of the space, pink and red flowers and white taper candles in candelabras covered a large white marble altar.

Teddy glanced back at the door. There were a few couples behind them, bringing the total number to twenty couples.

A commotion at the door caught his attention. The priestesses in the room who had been in meditation looked up and began to whisper to each other. They rose to their feet and two of them split away from the group to go to the door.

Teddy's hand went to his dagger. Out of respect, he'd left most of his weapons outside the temple, but it was very foolish of him to be traveling without the protection of guards, and even more insane to be unarmed. There was always a murmur of discontent leading up to the Gauntlet Games, but it seemed at a fever pitch this year. Someone could have seen him slip away. The Sons of Endros could have tracked them.

Sweat rose on his lower back as he scanned the room again.

Several priestesses had positioned themselves around the room, their pink robes making them easy to identify, but they seemed calm and unconcerned by the commotion. Perhaps this was just how the goddess made an entrance.

The whispers swelled in the hallway. Teddy tucked Grace behind him.

But it wasn't attackers who stumbled into the room.

It was Stella McKay and Prince Arden Teripin.

"You've got to be kidding me," Teddy grumbled.

The priestesses fawned over Stella, rushing to greet her. At least she had the sense to look mortified by the attention.

"I don't need any special accommodations, but if Aunt Desiree is here—I mean, if the goddess is in, I would love to speak with her," Stella said.

Arden brought a hand to the small of her back and gave her an indulgent smile that faded the moment his gaze snagged Teddy's.

Teddy was shocked to see Arden there. They'd grown up together, and while Arden was kind and intelligent, he wasn't terribly serious about relationships—or much else, as far as Teddy had seen. He certainly didn't seem the type to be courting the daughter of the famed fairy-tale couple of Rainer McKay and Cecilia Reznik. That kind of example had clearly set Stella up for some huge expectations in relationships, and Teddy was shocked that she thought Arden was the one to fulfill them.

Arden arched a brow and smirked as he crossed the temple.

"And here I thought your betrothal to someone else was announced just last night," Teddy said.

Arden shrugged sheepishly. "I see I'm not the only prince unwilling to leave his spousal decision-making up to his parents."

Stella stepped up beside him, rolling her eyes as she noticed Teddy. "Oh, thank goodness. I thought I sensed a dark, brooding energy in the temple. I was worried there was a haunting, but your presence explains everything."

Her contempt was confounding. As if she wasn't as much a thorn in his side. She seemed to be under the impression that his life was so easy. *Clueless, impossible woman.*

Teddy gritted his teeth. "I didn't expect to see you here."

Stella cocked her head to the side. "Oh, excuse me, Your Highness, I didn't realize you had singular claim on love." She grabbed Arden's hand and tugged him back to their place at the end of the line, glaring daggers at Teddy as if *he* were an interloper.

Grace squeezed Teddy's hand again, offering a conspiratorial smile. "I don't know why you let her bother you. We're friends. She's always going to be a part of our lives. I've watched you get along with truly detestable nobles at court. Why does Stella get under your skin so easily?"

Teddy crossed his arms. There had been a time when they were children that they'd been friendly. But somewhere in their teen years Stella had turned into a boisterous, wild thing of a woman, and he'd turned into the heir to the Argarian throne. It seemed she always had as much freedom as Teddy had structure, and even though that was the way he preferred it, her sheer exhaustive whimsy irritated him.

Stella had never been crushed under a kingdom's worth of expectations. She had never been humbled by impossible shoes to fill. She should have felt the heat the way he did, having inherited such a similar history, but it all seemed to slide right off of her. She was so unaffected, when he was so shackled by it.

A hush went over the room as a priestess in a deep scarlet robe appeared from the doorway that led to the waterfall outside the temple. Immediately, all of the other priestesses fell to their knees. In a wave of movement, they touched their fingers to their foreheads, lips, and then hearts before opening their palms before the woman in scarlet.

Several of the couples in line fell to their knees as well, heads bowed in reverence.

"What's happening—" Teddy started, but then the woman in the scarlet robe stepped into the moonlight and the air rushed from his lungs as prickling magic hit him.

Grace went rigid beside him and lowered to her knees just as he shook himself from his stupor and knelt beside her.

Teddy kept his eyes down. The scent of roses filled the air, magic pressing in on him from all sides, but he held perfectly still like prey caught in the sights of a predator. All witches could sense magic, and he'd never felt something so strong all at once like this goddess fully in her element.

A soft hand came to his chin. "Rise, Your Highness. I can't imagine you're a man often on your knees."

Teddy met the bright blue eyes of the strikingly lovely goddess. Her dark, curly hair was wild around her shoulders and her brown skin glowed as if reflecting the moonlight.

Teddy rose to his feet. "Goddess."

Her red lips tugged into a grin. "You look like your father."

Teddy fought not to frown. He knew it was a good thing. Ladies of the kingdom still fawned over his father, but Xander had never mentioned meeting the goddess of love and beauty. It was just like the king to skip over something that important.

Desiree tilted Teddy's chin up into a slash of moonlight. "Less humor in the eyes, though. That must come from your mother's side. What does a young, handsome prince have to be so serious about?" Her eyes slid to Grace, who still had her face cast down toward the floor in reverence. "Lady Farlan, you may rise."

Grace rose to her feet, her eyes wide.

Desiree smiled and brushed a hand over Grace's cheek. "Long ago I blessed the Brett line with beauty. Your mother made good use of it. Seems you've done the same."

Grace nodded emphatically. "Of course, goddess."

Satisfied with their deference, Desiree turned her attention to the end of the line, where Stella stood bouncing on her toes, a wide smile on her face.

"There's my beautiful girl." Desiree held out her arms and everyone in the room held their collective breaths as Stella threw herself at the goddess.

"It's been too long," the goddess said, pulling back to look at Stella's face. "Have you seen your other aunties? Am I still your favorite?"

Stella grinned. "Of course you are."

Desiree looked over her shoulder. "And who have you brought me?"

Stella waved Arden forward. He bowed his head to the goddess.

Desiree pursed her lips. "Ah, I see."

Teddy waited for her to say more, but her smile morphed from welcoming to playful before she turned and walked back to the center of the room.

Stella and Arden returned to their place in the line of lovers. The curved shape of the temple meant that Teddy could see almost everyone who was present and he was relieved when he didn't recognize a single face in the group aside from Arden and Stella. Hopefully that meant no one would recognize him and this would stay a secret for now.

Desiree spun in a circle at the center of the room and clapped her hands. "Yes, yes. You're all humble subjects, but please rise. We have quite a crowd tonight and I want to be certain I get a good look at all of you. I appreciate you all being here this evening and offering up your blood in exchange for my vision. Because I can't hold my physical form in this realm long, I will bless my priestesses with my vision for tonight's event, but I will be watching and guiding you as your bonds are formed."

The room filled with the potent scent of crushed rose petals, and the priestesses in pink robes moved toward the center of the room. The goddess touched each one of them on their foreheads and, one by one, they returned to their section of the room.

Teddy watched as one of them spoke in quiet tones to a couple. She stared at them for a long moment, then took each of their hands. Her eyes seemed to glow momentarily. Then she dropped their hands and shook her head. The man and woman looked crestfallen, but another priestess quickly came to escort them from the room.

Teddy stared after the retreating couple. His stomach flipped. In a moment, their dreams had been dashed.

A thrilled squeal on the other side of the temple drew his gaze. A short red-haired woman and a tall, lanky hunter were hugging each other tightly, a priestess standing back and smiling serenely at them.

The joy of their union bolstered Teddy. That would be him and Grace, just as soon as it was their turn. He was certain of so few things, but that was something he knew down to his bones. The priestess nearest them was busy with another couple, so Teddy took his time assessing the space. It was an old hunter's habit drilled into him by his parents and Isla.

Always know all the exits in a room. Always have a plan for the easiest way to fight your way out. Never let your guard down.

The closest exit was behind a large flower-covered altar. He didn't know where the doorway led—likely to the private residence of the priestesses.

There was also the exit on the far side of the room that led to the swimming hole and waterfall outside, and the hallway they'd entered through, which was the most likely place an attacker would enter. Teddy kept his eyes trained there. It settled his mind to have something to do.

A man rounded the corner, striding across the temple with purpose. Teddy brought his hand to the dagger at his hip. There was no telling what kind of trouble a hunter might want to start in this temple, but Teddy was ready to spring into action.

The man came to a stop on the far side of the room in front of a petite, dark-haired woman. She stared at him, wide-eyed, and Teddy took a step in their direction. Then, the woman threw herself into the man's arms and he spun her in a circle.

Teddy relaxed and blew out a breath.

Hushed whispers broke out to his left.

"No, you don't understand. Goddess, please. You're making a mistake. He's here with me."

Teddy turned toward Stella's voice.

The goddess clicked her tongue. "Ah, my darling. He is meant to be here. Just not with you."

Teddy sucked in a breath at the brutal, casual tone of the goddess's voice. It was in such stark contrast to the devastation on Stella's face.

Desiree was leading Arden away from Stella as the prince looked over his shoulder helplessly.

Teddy shouldn't have found it satisfying, but there was something calming about being right about Arden and Stella. It was a relief to trust that he could read people well.

The same priestess who had welcomed them all into the temple stepped up beside the goddess and looked over the crowd. A soft smile appeared on her face when her gaze locked on someone.

"Do you see what I see?" she asked the goddess.

Desiree nodded. She grabbed Arden's wrist and dragged him forward. Time slowed as they came to a stop. It wasn't until the goddess placed her hand over the woman's heart that Teddy realized she was touching Grace. *His* Grace.

"*No.*" The word was a death gasp on Teddy's lips.

It took a moment for the shock to wear off and the reality of the situation to register.

Teddy stared at them. He kept waiting for Grace to argue, to turn and look to him for help, but her gaze was locked with Arden's. A silvery-pink aura glowed around them.

"Yes, these two are a perfect match," Desiree said.

"I agree," the priestess said. "You can see it all around them."

"And their heartbeats sync," said Desiree. "I just knew it was going to be an exciting night. I gathered all of my essence to stay present as long as possible."

Teddy knew that ascended gods could only stay corporeal in the mortal realm for limited periods of time. They drew strength from their worshippers, and they could wield a hint of the power they'd once possessed as gods. That was how Desiree created heart bonds. But he had not considered that the goddess might use that limited corporeal time to connect Grace to someone else.

It was a gross miscalculation. A wild bit of hubris that had led him to the conclusion he should have considered. Heart bonds were so rare that he'd assumed they would either be matched to each other or not matched at all. Teddy had never imagined she'd be bonded to someone else, let alone someone they'd both known their whole lives.

It was all wrong. Teddy could hear his father's voice in his head chiding him for making assumptions, but this had seemed a safe one.

Teddy wanted to yank Grace away from Arden. He had nothing against his Olney counterpart, but he wasn't ready to surrender his queen to the man.

Arden looked entranced by Grace. The two of them had spent plenty of time together at court parties over the years, but now they stared as if seeing each other for the first time, as if drawn together by some invisible magnetism.

Desiree placed a hand over each of their hearts and Teddy watched in mute horror as the goddess of love bound Grace's heart to Prince Arden Teripin's.

6

STELLA

Of all the impulsive choices Stella had made in her life, she hadn't regretted any as much as coming to this godsforsaken temple.

It's just temporary, she told herself. But the way Arden was looking at Grace like all of the light in the room glowed just because of her did not feel temporary.

Stella swallowed hard, trying to compose herself. She could see in her mind the web of decisions that had led to this moment—could retrace them back to Arden comforting her with the promise that they would be linked. Perhaps it was her own lack of faith to blame, because she hadn't been propelled by love in that moment. She'd been bolstered by defiance. As if she already knew it wasn't going to happen and was ready to dare the gods to try to stop her from getting what she wanted.

But this development had not changed anything. Her will was stronger than some game the gods were playing. She could weather two weeks with Arden engaged to one woman and heart-bonded to another. It didn't matter what bindings tied him to someone else. Arden was meant for her, and this was just a bump in the road. Some day they would recall this story and laugh.

Grace was a good person, at least. Not a complete stranger. Not to mention that she'd come here with Teddy, so she had good reason *not* to want to stay attached to Arden.

Still, dread crept over Stella as the reality set in. Perhaps Grace would like being attached to someone so warm after spending all her time with uptight Teddy Savero.

The priestess who had bonded Arden to Grace ushered them toward the hallway through which they had entered.

Arden looked frantically over his shoulder at Stella. *"I'm sorry,"* he mouthed.

It had been his idea to come to the temple, but it wasn't his fault that Desiree was messing with Stella.

The gods loved to meddle in human lives. Cecilia had warned her over and over—her mother had once been their pawn too. *The gods are all ancient and bored, Stella. Do not gain their interest or you'll become their new toy.*

It was easy for her mother to say now. Cecilia had lived an interesting life. She'd adventured and traveled. She'd met the love of her life.

Stella was just trying to get outside of her comfort zone, and now she was paying for it.

A hand on her shoulder startled her. She whipped her head around to meet the dark brown eyes of another priestess.

"I don't believe it," the priestess whispered. "How curious." She tugged Stella forward.

It wasn't until Teddy started moving too that Stella realized the priestess had grabbed his wrist as well.

The priestess dragged them into the silver light pouring in from the opening at the center of the room.

"What are you—" Stella stopped speaking when Desiree stepped into the moonlit circle with them.

The goddess laughed heartily. "Oh, the fates do like to play games." She nodded at the priestess. "I see what you mean."

Two priestesses stepped up on either side of the goddess. They looked at Stella and Teddy as if seeing right through them.

"What now?" Teddy whispered.

Teddy shifted under their assessing gazes, but Stella met them with a fierce defiance in her eyes.

"Look at the threads between them. They're woven in gold. How interesting," Desiree said.

"It's very curious," said the priestess who had dragged them into the circle.

"Curious indeed," Desiree said. "It's hard to believe they aren't here together. These two are meant to be."

Teddy let out a choked sound that sounded like a laugh.

Stella wrinkled her nose. "Surely you're joking."

Teddy looked offended that she thought *he* wasn't good enough for *her*.

Stella scoffed. Desiree was just trying to teach her a lesson about running off to do impulsive things. This was some sort of godly entertainment.

"You're mistaken," Teddy said. His deep voice brought the entire temple to a halt.

The humor disappeared from the goddess's face in an instant. "*Excuse me.*"

Teddy bowed his head and pinched the bridge of his nose. "What I meant is that we're not at all well-suited. I would never be with someone so—" He gestured to Stella broadly.

"So beautiful you're at a loss for words, *Your Grace*?" Stella taunted.

"So irrationally emotional," Teddy snapped.

Stella crossed her arms, jutting her chin out. "And I'd never be with someone so heartless."

Desiree's full red lips twisted into a smirk and her eyes glowed. The air filled with the scent of crushed rose petals.

"Love is an untamed thing, as strange to me as it is to all of you. If there is one thing I've learned in my many years of existence, it's that not even I can understand the mysterious ways in which it moves us," Desiree said. "I can see these threads that connect people, but I'm wise enough not to presume to understand why they connect certain loves. My job is merely to interpret what I see."

Stella shook her head violently. "But I'm here with Arden." She gestured toward the hallway, as if she had any control here.

Desiree eyed Stella. "Did you not bleed into the sacred bowl? That magic is binding. You promised to accept the outcome."

Teddy shifted beside her. He had clearly mastered his shock much better than her. Of course he had. Teddy Savero was as emotional as a stone. He had no feelings to turn off.

"If you truly think you have nothing to fear from each other, then the bond will fade in a few weeks and you'll be no worse for the wear," Desiree said.

Stella's heart thundered, pumping raw panic through her blood. She wanted to thrash around in the trap she'd been caught in, even though she knew there was no way to shake herself free. She glanced toward the exit, wishing it was as simple as leaving. She'd bled into that bowl and promised to accept the outcome.

Desiree smiled deviously as she turned Teddy and Stella to face each other.

Teddy regarded Stella with disdain, but Stella stared at him as if she'd be able to see the strange magical thread between them if she looked longer.

She couldn't remember the last time she had looked at him up close. Teddy was tall and broad, the lean muscle of his chest and arms evident beneath his finely cut tunic. His dark brown hair had a soft wave to it and fell over his forehead in an annoyingly perfect way. His face was clean-shaven, revealing a sharp jawline and high cheekbones, and his light olive-brown skin was flawless except for a faint pale scar on his bottom lip that gave his smile a roguish sort of charm.

She'd always thought his eyes were just gold, but in the silver moonlight, she could see they were light brown in the center surrounded by a ring of amber with golden flecks all throughout. Loath as she was to admit it, Teddy was striking.

He refused to meet her eyes, which left him awkwardly looking straight over her head.

Stella gave Desiree one last desperate pleading look, but her aunt was looking through them, her hands moving through the air like she was stitching an invisible tapestry.

The goddess placed one palm over Stella's pounding heart and the other over Teddy's.

The bond hit Stella like a rush of blood to the head. Goosebumps raced along her skin. The intensity of it was almost enough to make her knees buckle. She would have gone down, but Teddy caught her arm.

He was finally looking at her, studying her with a clinical sort of appraisal.

Everything tingled from the tips of her toes to her scalp, but she held his gaze as her chest warmed. Her rib cage felt all at once too full and not full enough. She wanted to draw more in, to never stop the feeling, and also she was afraid too much would make her faint.

It reminded her of the first magnificent breath after she'd stayed under the sea too long. The air felt fresher, full of the citrus and cedar scent of him, and that was all she wanted to smell.

The tingling faded, but the full feeling in her chest remained and she could not look away from Teddy. Her eyes burned, and she had the unnatural impulse to hug him and sob.

After a long moment, Teddy looked away. "Now what?"

Desiree arched a brow. "Now you thank your goddess for her blessing."

Teddy smiled tightly. "Thank you, Goddess Desiree, for this tremendous blessing."

Desiree patted his cheek. Then she clapped her hands in delight. "I knew you would see it my way. Now, go to your suite for the night."

A priestess stepped forward and took Stella's arm. Stella let the woman guide her back down the hallway to one of the guest suites. Teddy's soft footsteps followed behind them.

It wasn't until they were ushered into the suite and the door clicked closed behind them that Stella snapped out of her daze.

A large bed with pale pink linens was at the center of the room. Red rose petals were sprinkled from the doorway to the bed and across the sheets. Candlelight cast jumping shadows on the white marble walls, and large sliding glass doors on the far end of the room looked out to a private bathing pool that reflected the shimmering moonlight.

Vases of flowers covered almost every surface of the room. It was so beautiful and romantic, but Stella was meant to be here with Arden. This was the room where they were supposed to spend their first private night together ever. She'd planned out exactly how she was going to tell her parents in the morning. Of course, they would be upset. Her mother had a terrible temper, but she was also a romantic. Cecilia and Rainer would understand why Stella had been so desperate. After all, they had both done crazy things for love.

Now she was hoping that her lie about sleeping over at Kate's held up so she could wait it out until her new bond with Teddy faded and she'd never have to admit that she'd done something so stupid.

The connection felt strange. Was this how her parents felt? A heart bond differed from the fated soul bond her parents had—it didn't run as deep—but Stella felt all at once like the bond was too much and not enough. She felt too aware of Teddy's presence—over-stimulated by the sudden sharpness of this new extra sense that was entirely focused on him. She wanted to get as far from him as possible, and also she wanted to sit on his lap.

"We should strategize how we're going to handle this," Stella said, brushing her fingers to her sternum.

"I don't want to strategize. I want to go to bed and wake up and forget this nightmare ever happened," Teddy said flatly. "You can take the bed. I'll sleep in that chair." He gestured to a small red chair in the corner. He looked like a giant when he sat down in it, but he pulled off his boots with determined frustration and grabbed a throw pillow for his head.

Stella's chest was too tight, the strange pulsing of the bond too unsettling to rest. It felt like she was angry, but really Teddy was, or maybe they both were.

"Calm down. You're going to give me a stomachache," she grumbled.

Teddy turned his furious gaze on her. "I hope you're happy. You've managed to ruin the most important thing in my life."

"*Me?*" Stella shook her head in disbelief. "How could I have possibly known that you were going to be here, or that you had a relationship? It's not as if you show that poor woman any affection publicly."

"As if I could?" Teddy snapped. "I'm a prince. I lack the freedom to be as reckless as you."

Stella rolled her eyes. "Sorry. I'll leave you alone to your pity party."

"I'm not having a pity party. You have no idea how much pressure is on me on a regular basis. Grace is the one person who makes it manageable. She's so clever and—"

"Too good for you?" Stella suggested.

Teddy's face crumpled. He seemed to cave in on himself, shoulders bowing forward. "Yes, she is, but gods bless her, she still came to this stupid temple with me anyway. Now I have no way of proving to my parents that we are meant for each other. I have no case to make to them and they are so set on me marrying some politically advantageous princess."

Stella was stunned into silence, having never heard him speak so much or so openly. "I'm sorry. Arden was hoping for the same thing. I had no idea this was even a possibility or I never would have come."

Teddy kept his gaze on the floor. "I have no recourse now. Without this kind of godly blessing, I have no path forward. Forgive me for needing a moment to resign myself to this fate."

Stella slumped to sit on the bed and kicked off her silk slippers. "I wish I had a solution, but this was also my last resort."

They were quiet for a long moment.

"Why do you even want to be with Arden?" Teddy asked. "Is it just the fairy-tale idea of being queen? You know being royal isn't just wearing pretty dresses and having people write songs about you, right?"

Stella bristled. "Poor, tortured Prince Teddy. It must be so hard to have people listen when you speak. To have respect without in any way earning it. To be so handsome and frigid—"

"Frigid?"

"Frigid," she snapped. "I think I could count on one hand the number of times I've seen you smile."

"I smile plenty when I'm not in such dreadful company."

Stella scowled. *What a pompous prick.* "What have I done to you to make you hate me so much?"

Teddy winced. "I don't hate you. I just...don't...like you."

Stella blew out a breath. "Oh, that's much better."

He hesitated, looking suddenly embarrassed. "You were mean to Juliana once."

Stella frowned, racking her brain for a time when she'd been anything but perfectly nice to his little sister.

"When you were—" He cleared his throat, his skin flushing dark pink in the candlelight.

"Oh my gods, the new year celebration? When I was fourteen? Teddy, honestly, you must be joking. I was an idiot *child*."

He jutted his chin in defiance. "You made my sister cry. You told her that she was an average beauty and would never outshine Alexandra. Alex didn't stop bringing it up for months."

Stella crossed her arms. "Well, it's hardly my fault that Alex likes to gloat." She wanted to argue more, but she still hadn't forgiven Layleen Davis for making Rosie cry when she was six. She wrung her hands in her skirt and met his gaze. "You're right. Is that what started our prank war?"

Teddy nodded.

"I'm sorry I made Jules cry. She's sweet."

Teddy's lips twitched. "No, she's not." His mouth tipped into a full smile. "She's kind of full of herself. Too pretty for her own good and too proper. She could use an occasional humbling. I'd just prefer to be the one to do it."

Stella choked on a laugh. "You're awful. But she is a little too perfect."

Teddy sighed in agreement. He stared out the large windows and fell into pensive silence.

"You know, I've been so busy with traveling to Olney and trying to figure out this marriage problem that I've hardly spent any time with Grace in the past three weeks," Teddy said. "The ride here tonight was the first chance I've had. Do you think you can be homesick for a person?"

Stella stared at him, a strange lump of envy rising in her throat. "That's a shockingly romantic sentiment coming from you. Is that how you feel about Grace? What makes her feel like home?"

He rubbed the back of his neck, looking suddenly apprehensive. "She's so steady. She's much smarter than me and, honestly, it makes me feel safe because I know she's thinking of things I won't."

He wasn't looking at her as he spoke. It was almost like he forgot she was there.

Tears pressed against Stella's eyes, and she tried to blink them away. She didn't know why his words made her feel so emotional. Maybe because she'd never felt that way. Maybe because she was feeling everything he was feeling.

When she didn't say anything, Teddy turned to look at her. "Are you crying?"

She brushed the tears away with a violent swipe.

"For me?" Teddy asked. He didn't look disgusted so much as bewildered.

Stella shook her head and blinked the burning from her eyes. Truthfully, she wasn't sure if she was feeling pity for him or herself.

His face was the picture of baffled shock. "But you don't like me."

Stella huffed. "Well, yes, but it's easier not to like you when I don't know how sad your life is."

He looked suddenly outraged. "My life is great. I'm the heir." He crossed his arms and glared at her. "Are you always so—"

"Intense? Emotional?" She shook her head and met his gaze. "*Sensitive*?"

Gods, did she hate that word. Her parents had always been

careful not to label her that way, but the rest of the world hadn't been so kind.

Teddy pursed his lips but didn't say anything.

The silence stretched on awkwardly. Stella stared up at the ceiling, trying to push away the fear that she was going to lose Arden.

"You're lucky you have godly relatives. At least you have someone who can go over your parents' heads to do favors for you," Teddy said.

"You got a glimpse at the kind of favoritism I receive tonight, Your Grace," Stella said, tapping her chest. "It's not all roses having goddess aunts. Trust me. As far as I know, the only way to get real favors from the gods is to enter the Gauntlet Games."

He adjusted the pillow behind his head for the fourth time.

"You don't look very comfortable," Stella said. "I can make room in the bed. It's plenty big. You won't even know I'm here. I promise not to tarnish your honor."

Teddy leaned his head back. "I'm fine over here."

"Suit yourself, Your Grace."

Stella stilled as an idea took form in her mind. She'd said it off-hand, but it was true. The tournament was meant to channel the post-war violence into a contained event to stop the spreading rebellion, but it was also a reminder that the gods were watching. The competitors fought hard every year because the prize was from the gods, and there was nothing in the two kingdoms more valuable.

If Stella won, she could ask the gods to bless her marriage to Arden and no one in the two kingdoms would refuse her. Better yet, the entire kingdom would have seen her triumph in the Games and would want her to be queen. It would be a different path than what she expected, but she felt empowered by the idea of fighting in the tournament to win the hand of her prince. All great love stories started with a little adversity. It was the opposite of all the fairy tales she read, but she'd spent her life training for a battle that had never come. Perhaps this was the purpose of all of that work.

Besides, the Gauntlet Games were about more than just brute strength. They were about understanding the main tenets of Olney culture: Wisdom, Memory, and Magic.

Stella could admit that, after the past few days, she hadn't shown abundant wisdom, but she'd always loved solving puzzles with her father, and she had plenty of memory and magic.

She took the first deep breath in hours and closed her eyes to sleep with the comfort of a new grand plan.

7

TEDDY

Absolutely nothing was going according to plan. Teddy had woken early the morning after the bonding and fled the temple while Stella was still asleep, riding back to Olney City with Grace.

But the crowds heading into the city ahead of the Gauntlet Games tournament had slowed their progress, and they didn't get in until well after midnight.

Teddy had crashed hard from the exhaustion of the ride and had woken so late that he'd nearly missed the deadline for reporting to the competitors' tent behind Olney Castle. The priestesses had been in the middle of rolling up the scroll of competitor names when he had walked in.

It was for the best that he'd had no time to second-guess himself or consider that this wild idea had come from the least likely place.

When Stella was speaking about how the only way to guarantee a favor from kings or gods was to enter the Gauntlet Games, Teddy realized he had one last chance to get what he wanted. Of course, it was a risk, but a lifetime of happiness was worth it. Entering himself into the contest and winning meant whichever god was the gamemaker of this year's tournament could grant Teddy the ability to choose his future wife. His father would never refuse a union blessed by the gods, especially one made so publicly.

It would also be a deeply romantic story and the exact type of thing that would lend the Savero family some much-needed goodwill. It would be nice to see some rumors in Teddy's favor for once, instead of just gossip about whether his father was a bastard.

As he peeked out from the private curtained-off warm-up room he'd been granted in the bustling competitors' tent, he was grateful Grace had come with him. She peered out beside him, counting the other competitors who stretched and paced along the center walkway. Servants ran back and forth down the length of the corridor, delivering fresh water and linens and all matter of other things to those in the curtained-off rooms.

Teddy wondered who else was competing. He wished he'd gone to watch the hunters training before the event as his father had suggested. It was up to him to play catch-up now.

He knew what everyone would think when he walked into the arena in his fine ceremonial clothing. They'd think he was a spoiled prince playing warrior for a day. He needed to be ready to show them what he could do.

A particularly burly man with a fine tunic straining over his thick chest walked by, and Grace turned toward Teddy, looking pale. Her face was drawn with worry as she crossed the small space to the table and poured herself a glass of water from a crystal pitcher.

She drank slowly, not meeting his gaze until she was finished. "Are you sure this is a good idea?"

"I thought you were on board," Teddy said.

"I am on board with you doing something you want instead of what's expected for once, yes. But you'll have to forgive me for hating the idea of you entering this tournament—which is, as you'll remember from the bloodbath we saw just last year, deadly. I am uneasy with the risk you're taking for me and—" She looked away, her shoulders slumping. It was so unlike Grace to look defeated. "I don't feel worthy of that kind of risk. I wish you wouldn't enter. You've only given your name. You haven't taken the binding vow yet. You could back out."

He stared at her in disbelief. "You'd prefer I give up on you?"

Grace frowned. "No, I would prefer you be *safe*. Who knows who these competitors really are? Some of them could be Sons of Endros who will see this tournament as a way to get easy access to you. There are already enough risks to your life on a regular basis. And before you ask, no, I don't doubt you, but your attention will be divided in this competition. You will have more than defending yourself on your mind and—" She pressed a hand to her sternum. "The bond is certainly distracting at times."

Teddy took her hand. "Is he bothering you?"

Grace's face softened into a smile and she brushed his hair back from his forehead. "Always my protector. No. Arden is actually very respectful. He's trying to learn how to control it."

"Really?"

Grace nodded. "We've known Arden for years. I know this was unexpected, but he's not a bad person. I think we're all just trying to make the best of complicated circumstances, and it's actually nice to have someone share so much of himself."

Teddy felt both relieved and unnerved. Logically, he knew it wasn't Arden's fault. It was just another case of gods playing games. They had all been tangled up in the first place because the goddess had a bone to pick with Stella. But Teddy didn't like that Arden had the chance to know Grace in a way that he never had. He was not prone to jealousy, but he envied that closeness.

"This is all Stella's fault," he grumbled.

Grace laughed. The sound was soft and comforting, and Teddy could not remember the last time he'd heard it. He'd been so wrapped up in himself, he couldn't remember the last time he'd really thought about her as a person instead of just *his* person.

"Stella is hardly to blame," Grace said. "You two are so alike and you refuse to see it because you think she has it easy."

"She does," Teddy insisted, but he sounded so petulant.

Grace glanced around the room, then pressed onto her toes to kiss him. She drew back and took his face in her hands. "We don't tell each other what to do, but if you walk away from this now, we will find another way. I just want to be certain you aren't exchanging safety for instant certainty. What might a little patience buy you?"

"I've been patient. I've tried to be reasonable with my father, but he isn't having it. Look at Arden. He's betrothed to one woman, in love with another, and heart-bonded to you. I am not waiting around to make a bigger mess. I promise I'll be careful, but I have to do this." Teddy kissed Grace's forehead. "Besides, it will give me a chance once and for all to put the rumors that I'm weak and hiding behind my guards to rest. It's time to let those who doubt me see what I'm capable of—even my own parents."

Two men from somewhere deeper in the tent laughed and startled them apart. Though they were tucked into a private room that was partially closed off from the rest of the space by a curtain, for the sake of Grace's reputation, Teddy didn't want her to be caught alone with him.

She nodded and stepped away. "I wish you'd reconsider, but I trust you."

Teddy's mouth went dry. "Are you having doubts about me?"

"It's quite a lot of pressure for you to risk your life to marry me. Is it so wrong to want you to be safe? To not feel worthy of that kind of risk?"

Teddy searched her face. He sensed the specter of something she was not saying. He'd been so concerned that she was stuck with this temporary bond to Arden that he hadn't even considered how she'd feel about him risking his life. If the roles were reversed, he'd be beside himself with worry.

"I just think we should talk about it a moment before you're hurt," Grace said.

"I'm sorry. I should have considered how you'd feel about this, but I deserve to choose my partner for life and I am fighting for that choice. I love you, Gracie." He wanted to kiss her, but the rest of the competitors were beginning to mill about and he couldn't risk it. "I'll see you soon."

She waved tentatively, a tight smile on her lips as she ducked through the curtain, leaving him to stew in his nerves.

Teddy tugged on the sleeves of his tunic as he turned to the looking glass in the corner. He startled when Stella McKay's reflection appeared behind him in the glass.

She stepped up beside him, examining her own reflection. "Figures you have a full-length mirror in your royal waiting room, *Your Grace*. As if you need it."

She turned side to side, assessing the white off-the-shoulder dress. The delicate silver beading on the bodice shimmered as she moved. "Did Grace come to give you a pep talk before you introduce all the competitors?"

"I'm not introducing them this year," Teddy snapped.

She ignored the deflection, her assessing gaze sliding over him as the connection in his chest pulsed to life at her presence. "That's a very fine tunic even by royal standards."

"Competitors are supposed to wear their finest to be presented to the godly gamemaker. What else would you expect me to wear?" Teddy asked.

She stilled. "You must be joking. You're going to enter the contest, too?" Stella shook her head and barked out a disbelieving laugh. "I won't take pity on you because you're the prince of Argaria and our parents are friends. I'll put you on your ass in front of both of our kingdoms and I won't feel bad for doing it. That favor is mine."

"So you can what? Ask King Marcos to marry his son?" Teddy laughed at the thought.

But Stella crossed her arms and stared at him.

Teddy blew out a laugh. "Women don't ask for the hand of princes."

"Perhaps they should. No surprise that you're unimaginative and old-fashioned. Just when I think you can't be more boring, you say things like that." Stella shook her head. "You and I are playing for the same thing. The chance to marry the people we love. How is it so normal for you but so odd that I'd want the same thing?"

"Because you are not bound by the same responsibilities. Your plan is flawed," Teddy snapped. "You're a lady playing dress-up. This isn't another fairy tale. You're not a warrior."

She moved so quickly that he barely blocked the swing she took at his face. He caught her hand and smirked at her, just in time for her left fist to slam into his cheek. The impact drove his teeth into his lower lip.

She winced as his pain hit her through the bond. That flinch was just enough for him to catch the knee she brought up to thrust into his groin. He lifted her and slammed her onto the table beside them, only to find a dagger pressed to his throat.

Her furious eyes narrowed on him.

"Not bad." Teddy licked his lip and tasted blood. "Guess you drew first blood."

"Doubt it will be the last," she said, her gaze dropping to his lips.

The bond in Teddy's chest did a strange sort of squeezing.

"Going to let me up, *Your Grace*? Or do I have to fight my way out in this dress?" she taunted.

Teddy slowly extracted himself from Stella.

She sat up and held out a handful of dried chamomile. "Why are your pockets full of tea?"

"Why are you rifling through my pockets like a common thief?"

Stella grinned. "You can learn a lot about a man by what he keeps in his pockets."

Teddy arched a brow. "How many pockets are you groping around in?"

She glared at him. "Why? Are you jealous?"

She was so irritatingly evasive.

"You never know when you'll need an exchange for a spell," he said.

Stella cocked her head to the side, her dark brown curls bouncing with the movement. "The future king of Argaria is casually practicing spells? I never would have dreamed of such a thing."

Teddy looked away. "Sometimes Grace has trouble sleeping and the soothing spell helps her."

What he didn't want to say was that *he* had trouble sleeping and used it on himself most often.

"That's sweet."

Teddy met her eyes, expecting teasing, but she looked sincere. Two hunters stumbled by the opening to their curtained-off room. They leered at Stella, but she just rolled her eyes and waved her hand for them to move along.

She waited until they were out of earshot to face Teddy again. "Are you sure this is a good idea for you? There's a reason that my father and yours have picked their spots to compete in even the more casual tournaments over the years. They both know they would lose respect if they lost. There's wisdom in choosing battles you know you can win. You should follow their example."

As if Teddy hadn't already considered that. As if he didn't consider it in every moment ever. As if he could ever be free of it. The panic twisted his stomach, and a cold sweat rose on his back.

"I'm not saying it to be cruel. Those men competing—I've had a good look at them and at least some of them are vindictive," Stella continued.

"How would you know?" Teddy asked.

Stella huffed a sigh. "You think I'm not trained? That I haven't been doing combat drills since I was old enough to learn footwork? My parents might have preferred otherwise, but they were smart enough to know I'd always have a target on my back. Once you do the tournament binding, the only way out is through—by maiming, death, or victory. While I have confidence you'll survive the tournament, your ego might not."

Every word stoked Teddy's anxiety higher until he felt like he couldn't draw a deep breath.

Stella pressed a hand to her chest. "Hey, are you well?"

Teddy stared at her with wide eyes. There was no air in the tent. He couldn't breathe. Panic spread ice through his veins, his fingers tingling as his vision narrowed to her bright green eyes and a pinched crease in her brow.

She looked worried, but that couldn't be right. There was clearly not enough oxygen getting to his brain, and it was making him delusional.

"Teddy?" She stepped closer.

"I'm fine—" The words were hoarse.

A cold sweat rose on his back, his hands curled in, and his chest grew even tighter.

"Do you need a healer?" Stella asked, pressing a hand to his forehead, her other hand pressed to her heart. "What is this? Did you drink something? Poison?"

"Can't breathe." He leaned back against the table, trying desperately to master himself.

If Teddy failed, all of his life would have amounted to nothing. The kingdoms could descend into chaos. His family would be hurt. His people would be vulnerable. He had to be impeccable. Anything less than perfection in such a public forum would spell ruin.

He slid down the table leg and landed on his ass with his legs out in front of him. His vision darkened so much that he barely saw or felt Stella straddle his lap. She snatched his hand and placed it over her heart. He tried to pull back. Someone could see. It was inappropriate. But she held him fast.

Her other hand came to his face, her palm cool against his burning cheek.

"Breathe with me. It's going to be all right," she said softly.

She was trying to help him. He focused on the slower rise and fall of her chest, but the panic had him in its iron fist and he could not shake it. His heart beat so loud he could barely hear her.

"Gods, you're pale. Come here." She wrapped her arms around him so they were chest to chest. Her chest expanded against his and he tried to focus on following her slower, calmer pattern.

"Let me tell you a story," she murmured, her voice sounding just a little sharper, though still far away.

He felt a sudden rush of warmth in his chest. Their bond. She was sending something through their bond, or maybe it was just responding to her being so close. But the distinct feeling of calm spread through his body.

"Once upon a time, there was a village where it rained stars that granted wishes for one night every year," she said, her lips brushing the shell of his ear. "The villagers waited all year, collecting empty jars so they'd be ready."

Teddy's vision brightened, and his heart settled into a steadier rhythm. He wrapped his arm around her waist and held on tight as she continued to tell the story, her animated voice becoming clearer as he calmed.

It was pleasant, being held and told a story. He couldn't remember the last time he'd heard a fairy tale. When he was young, his father used to lie on the castle roof with him and point out fake constellations and make up stories about them, but that was so long ago. Teddy scarcely remembered any of the details.

Stella combed her fingers through his hair. He wanted to complain that she was mussing it, but it was too soothing. She smelled so good—like wildflowers after a rainstorm.

Teddy had been foolish to not even consider her competition. She no doubt had goddess-blessed bow skills like her mother, but Stella hadn't really been raised to be a warrior. She looked fit. Her dress showed off strong arms, the slit up the side offered a glimpse of a well-toned leg, and the dip in the neckline gave a glimpse of her cleavage. She was fit, but this type of fight required more than practice-ring skill.

Stella shifted in his lap. They were in a terribly compromising position. The memory of their bonding felt sharper, more vivid in the tense silence. He wanted to bend down and kiss the freckle on her collarbone.

The impulse ground against all the reasonable thoughts in his brain. He forced himself to meet her gaze. Her eyes dropped to his mouth. Heat rushed through his chest. Did she want to kiss him?

Teddy stared at her. He'd known Stella his whole life and yet she was a stranger. Her eyes were striking, almost supernaturally green with flecks of gold and framed by long, dark lashes. Her cheeks were flushed and her nose was covered in a light dusting of freckles. It was annoying how beautiful she was.

"Are you a demigoddess?" The question slipped out in some sort of half-stunned stupor. He knew she was—or it made sense that she was given her bloodline, but he had just never thought too hard about it until she was this close.

Stella laughed softly. "Yes."

"I didn't know that." *Idiot. Stop talking, Teddy.*

"You never asked."

"How does it work?"

She shrugged half-heartedly. "I heal faster without having to channel any magic. My memory affinity is stronger and more intricate than most. I have more endurance and I'm naturally stronger than other women my age would be, but I don't think it's otherwise noticeable."

Teddy disagreed. It was impossible to miss up close. The air around her held the subtle hum of magic—that, and she was so incredibly striking. It was hard to look away.

"Why are you helping me now? I'm your competition."

She cocked her head and frowned. "Sometimes we all just need a hand to hold when we're close to breaking."

"But you can't stand me," Teddy mumbled.

"And that is why I'd like to beat you when you're at your best. At least then you'll have to respect me, even if you go on hating me."

"I don't hate you. I just—" He didn't have a sufficient word for how he felt about Stella McKay. He cleared his throat. "How did you know how to calm me down?"

She shrugged like it was nothing. "My father used to do it for my mother when she had a hard day. It's been a long time, but he used to do it for us when we were little too. A hug and a story—when I was young, there was nothing that combination couldn't fix."

"And now?"

Stella smiled sadly. "And now I'm grown up and I think all the hugs and stories in the world wouldn't change the fact that the love of my life might be meant for someone else."

Teddy frowned. "You don't know that. The gods play games."

Stella's eyes lit up. "You think so?"

Teddy nodded. "Would anyone know better than us? Our families?"

Stella smoothed his tunic and combed her fingers through his hair. The movements were intimate—only Grace had done these things for him. It felt strange for Stella to be doing them now.

"Maybe you're right," she said. "Maybe this is a test from my Aunt Des. I guess I'll find out after the tournament. Now, will you let me up?"

He hadn't even realized he was holding on to her waist. He jerked his hands away like he'd been burned, and she grinned as she rose to her feet and helped him up.

Teddy tugged at the linen sleeves of his tunic and turned to fix his hair in the mirror. Then he whirled back to Stella.

"Aren't you nervous?" Teddy asked.

She flipped her hair over her shoulder. "Of course. But I'm more afraid of my parents' reaction at the moment. I'm compartmentalizing."

Teddy stared at her in disbelief. He'd seen the competition. Most of them were big and burly enough that Teddy was sweating it. Stella certainly wasn't slight, but she was probably the smallest contender, and, demigoddess strength or not, she certainly hadn't received the same kind of training he had.

Rainer McKay was the most talented swordsman he'd ever seen, but Teddy couldn't imagine that he'd made sure Stella was comfortable with killing. Surely she knew how to defend herself and would be a competent fighter, and she had a sharp tongue, but she was too empathetic for this kind of violence. That empathy would be a liability that Teddy could not afford.

Stella pointed at the tent entrance. "No one out there is half as tough as you and I. None of those warriors know what it's like to be under so much scrutiny every moment of their lives. Only you and I know what the weight of perfection feels like."

Teddy scoffed. "What do you know of it?"

She laughed bitterly. "Oh, you think it's easy to be the daughter of the perfect love story? Do you have any idea what other people expect? Gods, do you have any idea what *I* expect?" She shook her head. "Everyone in this field thinks they are resilient, but few of them are mentally tough. The only person I am worried about beating is you."

Teddy licked his lips. "Are you sure you want to do this?"

"Why? Are you scared you'll be beat by a woman? Will your royal ego survive?"

Teddy bristled. How she could go from being so soft to so biting in mere moments was disorienting. "No. I'm worried it will take something from you that you can't get back. Have you ever killed a man?"

Stella stared him down for a long moment. "No. But I'll do what I must."

"Did Arden stop to see you off?"

Stella looked away. "He can't sneak away because he has to entertain the princess and her family, but he sent me a letter this morning."

"How gallant," Teddy said.

She ignored the jab and nodded toward the binding room. "Shall we?"

Teddy nodded and fell into step beside her as they walked by several curtained-off competitor areas. Most curtains were pulled back, the competitors already having made their binding commitments and entered the arena. But the one toward the entrance was still closed.

A familiar laugh bubbled up from behind the curtain.

"What the—" Teddy shoved the curtain aside and nearly barreled into his sister. "Alex?"

"Teddy?" She stared at him with wide eyes, a beautiful priestess in Goddess Desiree's rose-colored robes standing before her. The priestess's robes were half-unbuttoned, a hint of pale cleavage peeking out from the gap.

Teddy averted his gaze immediately. "What are you doing in here, Alex? This is the competitor tent."

She was quiet for so long that Teddy finally looked up and met her eyes. Recognition tore through him.

"You're going to enter the contest."

Alexandra glanced over her shoulder at the priestess. "I'm sorry my very rude brother interrupted our talk. Could you give us a moment? I'll find you in a little while."

She winked, and the priestess flushed bright pink, then finished buttoning her robes and scurried away.

Alexandra's charm was as uncanny and mesmerizing as it was exasperating. She turned her attention back to Teddy, hands on hips. "I was trying to get insights into whether her goddess is going to be the competition judge."

Teddy arched a brow. "Was the answer inside of her robes?"

"Well, brother, I'm not certain since you barged in before I could get a good look. Should I call her back in to check?"

A soft laugh behind Teddy startled him. *Stella.* It was irritating how the bond in his chest hummed softly at her proximity. He'd momentarily forgotten she was with him, but now his body was remarkably aware of her. The soft springtime scent of her skin hit him, and his body surged with warmth, remembering her in his lap moments ago.

"This is family business," he grumbled, turning to glare at Stella.

She waved a hand. "By all means, proceed with your business."

Alexandra pulled a throwing knife from her leather vest and examined the gleaming blade with faux boredom.

"Why are you in the competitors' tent, Alex?" Teddy asked.

"I presume the same reason you are?"

"Absolutely not."

"Why?" Alexandra asked, her golden eyes lit with a challenge. "Afraid I'll exploit how you leave your left side open after a turn?"

Stella smothered a laugh.

Alexandra grinned broadly. "He also has a temper. If you smack his ass with the flat end of your blade, he will just lose it."

Stella laughed harder. Teddy ignored the way the bond buzzed at the sound.

"Alex, you can't compete, because I can't lose, and you can't either."

His sister crossed her arms. "If you can't lose, perhaps you shouldn't enter because I have no intention of surrendering so you can take the glory."

Teddy threw his hands up. "Always you with the glory. This isn't one of your Novumi legends, Alex. There are more important things than glory. This is the only way for me to have any kind of peace in my life. I'm not using this to prove a point to our parents. I'm entering because I need the right to choose my own life partner and the only way to convince our father of that is to win this stupid contest."

Stella stepped closer to him, and he tried not to flinch. The pull to her was so constant and irritating. He rubbed his sternum as if he could swipe away the magical connection.

"Are you well, brother?" Alexandra asked.

"I have myself to worry about. I cannot also contend with your recklessness. I can't protect us both in that arena and you know it, Alex."

"That's why I'll protect myself," Alexandra said.

A bell rang outside—the ten-minute warning to competitors. Teddy did not have time to argue with his sister. He needed to enter the competition officially and get out in the field to face his competitors.

"Fine. A hug for luck before I have to embarrass you in front of two kingdoms," he taunted.

Alexandra would never have gone for it if he didn't bait her. But she pulled him into a hug and clapped him on the back.

Alexandra was not as affectionate as Juliana, but she let Teddy hug her all the same. He'd always been the one to have a soft spot for her, letting her tag along to his training when she was little. Perhaps that had earned him more trust. Trust that he was going to abuse now. But that same trust would get her hurt in the tournament, and it lent him the certainty he needed. He just wanted to do what was best for her.

Ever so carefully, he slid his hand up to the nape of her neck. His other hand slipped into his pocket and he grabbed a small handful of loose herbs. Soundlessly, he mouthed the soothing spell he knew by heart. It was some of the first magic that he'd ever learned, but he'd only used it on Grace or himself to sleep. He'd never tried it with someone else.

Where summoning was inside magic, pulling an element through the channel of your body, spellwork was outside magic that compelled the physical world to bend to your will. Because it came from outside the body, it didn't use his energy supply. It required some sort of exchange from the physical world. The chamomile worked well because it was a soothing herb, and as he whispered the incantation, the herb turned to ash in his hand—a clear sign that the exchange for his spell had been accepted.

"Rare for you to show such affection. Are you going soft in your old—" Alexandra's body tensed. "Teddy, no." But her words slurred into a rush of breath and she slumped against him.

"What did you do?" Stella asked.

"I just put her to sleep with a soothing spell. All the more reason she isn't prepared for this competition," Teddy said, lowering Alexandra's limp body to the plush chair in the corner of her room. "She's too emotional and impulsive. It's just lucky that she hasn't already entered the binding tournament pact."

Stella narrowed her eyes at him. "You can't just put people to sleep when they do things you don't like."

"I know that, but—"

He'd already been far too vulnerable in front of Stella McKay for one day. He didn't know how to explain to her that his baby sister was different. While Jalen and Juliana had always had an ease about them, Alexandra had always fought the role she was expected to play. The difference was that she could act on her impulses. As jealous as her freedom made Teddy, he was almost relieved to see someone struggle under the weight of expectation and be so vocal about it.

Teddy and Alexandra had bonded over that struggle, and he always felt so much more protective of her. He'd managed to keep her from making any mistakes that would have permanent consequences so far. He could do it once more.

He gave Stella his most pleading look. "She's my baby sister. Would you let Rosie compete?"

Stella crossed her arms, and her cheeks flushed. "Rosie is a grown woman. I would respect her choices."

Teddy blew out a breath. He was destined to be surrounded by stubborn women. "I respect Alexandra's choices in many things. All other things, in fact—but if she is out in that field, I will be distracted the entire time."

"Sounds like your problem."

"Stella, I know. But my—" He ran a hand down his face and glanced at Alexandra slumped in the chair. "Alex has been through a lot lately. Her first love broke her heart right after Isla left. Surely you noticed the consort's absence. My father asked for her resignation. He didn't want to, but he was getting too much pressure with the rise of Sons of Endros attacks. I'm very close to Isla, but Alex worships her."

He let that information sink in, waiting for judgment on Stella's face, but she just looked sad.

"Jules mentioned that. I'm sorry to hear it."

"Now Alex is heartbroken and without the person she would most like to talk about it with. She is dead set on going to Callemoore because she thinks the only way to prove her worth is by completing the Final Forging test as my mother and Isla have. Alex is very talented, but she is not an elite warrior yet, and if she continues to be in such a rush, she will meet her end before she can get there. I don't want to stop her. I just want her to have the time to get there. *Please.* There's so much of my life I can't control, but I can protect my siblings. I can protect Alex from this. You know what it's like to be the oldest—to want to kill anyone who hurts them. It's not rational."

The crease in Stella's brow disappeared. "You love her."

"Of course I do. She is a pain in the ass, but she is still my sister. I won't always be able to protect her. But I can save her from this."

"What do you want me to do?" Stella asked.

"You said you were good with memory magic, right?"

Stella licked her lips and nodded.

"I'm not as precise with memory. When I've tried to practice on people before, they always know something is missing," Teddy said. "Will you remove the memory of wanting to add her name to the competition? Give her the idea to just go seek out that priestess, maybe in a more discreet location. She is such a magnet for scandal."

Stella pressed her hand to the back of Alexandra's neck. She hesitated. "I can't promise she won't remember. I'm uncomfortable doing this to someone I know without their permission. If you take this choice now, she might make a worse one later. I understand the impulse to protect, but you have to let her make her own mistakes."

"Just not this particular mistake."

Stella only hesitated briefly. She closed her eyes, and the air prickled with her magic. Her brow creased in concentration as she went to work, carefully removing the memory from Alexandra's mind.

A moment later, when Stella blinked her eyes open and nodded that it was done, relief washed over Teddy. It was bad enough to compete while bonded to Stella and her moodiness. Worrying about Alexandra would have been way too much to manage. As annoyed as Teddy was with their father at the moment, he knew that losing Isla had taken its toll. Something happening to Alexandra at the same time could break the king. Teddy didn't wish him more pain.

Outside the tent, the crowd began to cheer.

Stella stood a little straighter and smoothed her dress. "We have to go. You certain you want to leave her here defenseless?"

Teddy nodded. "I didn't use the full spell, just a temporary version. She should wake up in twenty minutes. Once the binding ceremony is over and she's barred from the tournament. Even if she remembers, she won't be able to enter herself."

He cast a nervous glance toward the opening in the tent that led to the commitment room. A priestess in golden robes stood waiting for them at the entryway.

"Having second thoughts, *Your Grace*?" Stella taunted.

Teddy glared at her. "Of course not. I was just wondering if it was worth taking one last try at convincing you not to enter."

She smiled broadly. "Sorry, you're not getting off that easily. Let's go."

Stella bumped his shoulder as she walked by, her dress swishing around her as she walked into the binding room. Teddy trailed behind her, pausing in the doorway.

The gold-clad priestess spoke to Stella in a hushed tone. Stella nodded and closed her eyes in silent concentration. Then she extended her hand over the bowl. The priestess pulled out a golden ceremonial dagger and Teddy fought the instinct to knock it out of her hands and yank Stella away.

Instead, he watched as the priestess slid the blade across Stella's palm. Stella didn't even flinch, but her pain hit Teddy in the chest. She squeezed her hand into a fist and allowed her blood to dribble into the bowl.

"I commit myself to the Gauntlet Games' challenges of wisdom, memory, and magic. I bind myself to the outcome of this tournament and promise to compete until I am eliminated by challenge failure, injury, or death," Stella said.

The conviction in her words sent a chill through Teddy's blood. Death had always been a possibility. Logically, he knew that, but was Stella really willing to die for someone who hadn't even stopped in to see her off?

A jolt went through Stella's body and Teddy felt the binding snap into place as the magic hit him like a blast of wind.

"It is done. Welcome to the competition, Stella Selene McKay," the priestess said. She flipped Stella's hand over and healed the cut on her palm.

Stella nodded and left the tent.

Teddy took her place in front of the priestess.

"The Gauntlet Games were designed to keep the peace in Olney and Argaria. So long as peace is kept, they will endure as this binding will endure until this year's tournament is over. Theodore Davide Savero, do you understand that, once made, this binding promise to the tournament cannot be broken? You may only exit by failure to complete a challenge, debilitating injury, or death. If you don't show up for an event, or if you try to leave early without attempting a challenge, you will experience intense burning in your blood that won't let up until you complete the required task. Do you understand?"

The weight of the words pressed in on Teddy from all sides, but this was the only way. He thought of Grace and hesitated only a moment before holding out his palm for the priestess and surrendering to the outcome of the Gauntlet Games.

8

STELLA

S tella squinted into the blinding daylight at the end of the tunnel as she followed the line of competitors toward the arena.

She'd felt so certain when she'd woken at first light that entering the Gauntlet Games was the right choice. Outside the Temple of Desiree, when she finally met back up with Arden, he'd been adamantly against it, but as they rode back to Olney, he slowly came to see her side. The tournament usually lasted about two weeks and that would be a blip compared to a lifetime together.

Every step so far had been fueled entirely by the determination in Stella's heart. But, standing in the shadow of much bigger competitors as she marched to face the crowd, her certainty wavered.

It wasn't just Teddy's jabs about how this would be different than training. The more present terror was how her parents would react when they realized she'd entered. She was more afraid of their disappointment than whatever challenge the godly gamemaker would throw at her.

She leaned to look around the man in front of her, squinting to try to spot her parents in their place of honor as guests in the royal booth, but the tunnel didn't have the right angle to see anything but the wall on the far side of the arena and the long stretch of dry dirt to get there.

Stella pressed her hand to the beaded bodice of her dress and took a deep breath.

The man in front of her glanced at her out of the corner of his eye and smirked. "Nice dress."

Stella stared at him for a moment, trying to assess if he was taunting her, but his eyes looked more playful than anything else. He wore fine leather armor that looked from the intricate stitching like it was Novumi, but the coin marking on his left wristguard indicated he was a mercenary. What would a warrior for hire want from a tournament like this?

The man arched a brow and looked at her expectantly.

"Thank you," she whispered, her mouth suddenly dry. "It's from Novum."

He winked. "I can tell."

Cecilia had the dress made for Stella for this very event, which she was supposed to be watching from the safety of the royal booth. Her mother had helped lace her into the corset top and sat beside her while Rosie did her hair. Stella hadn't been able to meet her mother's eye the whole time, and she had done her best not to look at Rosie at all because her baby sister was a truly terrible liar.

She prayed Leo and Rosie had done as she asked and kept her parents distracted. Hopefully, they were so busy with the Saveros that they hadn't even noticed her absence yet.

Anxiety pulsed behind her breastbone. She wanted to claw the bond right out of her chest. Behind that steely exterior, Teddy was an anxious mess, and it made it impossible to tell how much of what she was feeling was actually hers and how much was him.

Stella was vaguely aware of a priestess in gold robes giving instructions to the man at the front of the line, but horns sounded inside the arena, drowning out the sound of her voice.

The line of people started moving and Stella tried breathing in and out for even counts, the way her mother had taught her to do when she was young and still learning to control her magic.

She could hear her mother's soft, chiding voice in her head as she stepped into the glaring sunlight. *"Breathe, Stella. If you don't control your emotions, they will control you and your magic."*

She'd grown out of most of the fits and starts of fire magic, but there was something in her that never really stopped burning. Now the magic sprang to life, rushing through her veins at the first hint of nervousness. She opened and closed her hands several times, trying to soothe the subtle tingling of her power.

She repeated the words her mother had taught her when she was too young to fully understand them. *Brave with my hand. Brave with my heart.*

Her mind filled in with perfect color, sound, and scent as the vision took shape. It was one of her earliest memories.

---

*S*TELLA'S *MOTHER SAT NEXT TO HER ON THE BEACH, HER CHEEKS FLUSHED from the cool breeze that blew in off the sea. Her father stood knee-deep in the waves, beckoning her toward him.*

Cecilia had baby Rosie asleep on her shoulder, her other hand rubbing Leo's back as he slept soundly on the blanket beside her.

"I want you to come in with me, Mama," Stella whispered. "What if I go under and can't come back up?"

Cecilia smiled. "Your father won't let that happen and he is the best swimmer I know. He's out here every morning. No one knows the sea better."

Stella dragged her toe along the sand and glanced at her father again.

"I know you're nervous, but let me teach you a spell for courage," her mother said. "You just say, 'Brave with my hand. Brave with my heart.'"

"But what's the exchange for the magic, Mama?" she had asked.

Her mother had told her from the time she was young that all magic required an exchange. Her fire magic had been bound until she could control it, but once she learned to wield, it would burn through her personal energy reserves the same way running or dancing did, and if she used too much too fast, she would fall asleep. But spells, like the one her mother was describing, required herbs or blood or something else in exchange.

"In this case, you only need your will, and fortunately you have plenty to spare, Little Star."

Stella frowned at her mother. "So I just say it and it will work."

Her mother nodded. "It doesn't hurt to repeat it."

<hr>

STELLA SNAPPED OUT OF THE MEMORY AS SOMEONE TAPPED HER shoulder.

She whipped her head around to meet Teddy's gaze. She had been mindlessly following the procession into the arena. The crowd roared from the stands around them as the man two in front of her turned to the right and took his place facing the royal booth.

It was almost her turn. In a moment, they would announce the competitor in front of her and he would step away and then her parents would see her and know what she'd done.

Her heart pounded with the sheer nauseating guilt of making them worry.

The man in front of her stepped away and her gaze didn't go to her parents. Instead, she saw Arden immediately. He smiled at her. He looked so handsome in a light green tunic with gold embroidery. But, more than that, he looked proud—certain of her in a way that made her stand up straighter and finally take a deep breath.

She could do this. It was just a few more minutes and then which-ever god created the three challenges would be introduced as gamemaker. She hoped it was Aelish. The goddess of truth could be blunt and confronting, but she was less prone to violence and less reckless with human lives.

Murmurs rushed through the crowd as they noticed Stella.

"Stella Selene McKay!" the announcer shouted, and the crowd roared.

Stella walked to her place beside the other competitors with her chin held high and turned to face the royal booth.

Her mother's wide blue eyes stared back at her. Stella swallowed hard and smiled in a way that she hoped would come across as reassuring and not smug. She couldn't bear to look at her father, but she could see the way his hand had a white-knuckle grip on the arm of Cecilia's chair.

The noise of the crowd crescendoed to a deafening level as the announcer shouted, "Theodore Davide Savero."

Every head in the royal booth whipped toward Teddy as he stepped up beside Stella.

His anxiety squeezed like a fist around her heart. She imagined shoving it out of her chest. How had her mother described the bond? Like a door between two hearts? Stella tried to slam her door closed.

Out of the corner of her eye, she watched Teddy. He was the picture of handsome stoicism, his shoulders back, hands clasped behind him, and gaze staring blankly ahead like he could see straight through the crowd. But inside her chest, his fear was like a wild bird thrashing against the bars of a cage.

King Xander was looking at him with practiced apathy. Stella knew the king well enough to know that he was probably just as nervous as her parents, but had spent a lifetime learning not to show it. Queen Jessamin sat perfectly still beside him, her lips tipped in a proud smile as if she'd expected this all along.

A swarm of hunters in dark green Olney regalia marched into the arena and positioned themselves equidistant around the walls. Stella would have felt a bit more comfortable if they had stationed guardians around the arena, since they were the most talented warriors, skilled at defending a position or important person. But the majority of the guardians were probably busy protecting the royal family and visiting dignitaries.

Security was more intense than Stella had ever seen it at the Gauntlet Games, but so much rode on this year's tournament. When the war between Olney and Argaria ended more than twenty years ago, the people were restless in peace. Stella's parents and the kings had created the Gauntlet Games as a way to channel that agitated violence into something contained. It served the secondary purpose of reminding people of the main tenets of their kingdoms: Wisdom, Memory, and Magic.

While it had kept war from breaking out and strengthened the alliance between the two kingdoms, the Sons of Endros had still managed to create tiny fissures of distrust in the last few years. The Gauntlet Games would be the first proper test of the emotional temperature of their people since King Xander had dismissed Isla as huntmaster of the Argarian army.

This would be an obvious place for the Sons of Endros to probe for weakness in either kingdom or the alliance between the two. That was probably the reason for so many hunters around the periphery.

The announcer stepped into the center of the arena and trumpets blared, calling the bustling crowd to order again. The man mopped sweat from his brow with a handkerchief and lifted his hands in greeting.

"Ladies and gentlemen, at the behest of Their Majesties King Marcos and Queen Ilani Teripin of Olney and King Alexander and Queen Jessamin Savero of Argaria, I welcome you to this year's Gauntlet Games. We honor the original Gauntlet by keeping the peace it created through a three-challenge tournament. We have sixteen competitors eager to get started and prove they have the mettle to best their peers in challenges of wisdom, memory, and magic."

The crowd broke into applause.

"Without further ado. It's time for our godly gamemaker to appear."

Stella held her breath as she glanced at the throne of honor, elevated slightly higher than the royal booth. Bright florals covered the railing in front of it and framed the intricately engraved golden chair.

Stella felt the crowd's anticipation match her own. Several men patted their pockets in the hope they gambled on the right god.

Since the god in charge of making up the three tournament challenges rotated each year, many in Olney took bets on who would show. The frontrunner for this year's games was Devlin, the god of wisdom and reason. He had not participated in five years, but was known for his games and puzzles, which made the tournament more fun and exciting to watch, and less violent.

Stella had her fingers crossed that it wouldn't be Sayla, as the goddess of the hunt had an unnervingly casual attitude toward murder.

Stella was about to rank the gods in preference in her head when the air swirled and a blazing column of fire rose from the center of the arena. Teddy's panic hit her through their bond before her eyes could register who she was seeing.

The god before them was tall and strong with dark hair that was silver around the temples. He brought his hand to the golden sword on his hip and fear sliced through Stella. She had only ever laid eyes on him in artistic depictions, but she knew that supernatural fear in the air immediately.

Endros, the god of war and discord, stood in the center of the arena, clad in golden armor and a broad smile.

Gasps went through the crowd, low murmurs turning into panicked whispers.

It had been twenty-five years since anyone in the mortal realm had laid eyes on the god of war—since the battle that had ended the war between Olney and Argaria and Cecilia had sent him from the realm.

Now that he was ascended, he could only appear for short periods of time in the living world and his power to create war and fear was much weaker. But even with limited power, Endros was a god whose effect on the human world was terrifying.

Endros held up his hands to silence the crowd. "Yes, I imagine it comes as quite a shock, but as you say each year—this position is open to the god who wants to claim it. I have not done so in twenty years, while others have regularly played the gamemaker. Who better to test the contenders' understanding of the principles of this kingdom? To design a war game?"

A smattering of tentative applause broke out.

Endros held up his hands. "Yes, I can see you're unconvinced. So let me state my true intention. I thought that I was due and I wanted the chance to say once and for all that I condemn the acts of the Sons of Endros."

More murmurs cut through the crowd. It was clear that the people of the two kingdoms weren't won over.

"These men who use my name do not act at my encouraging. They are merely children—boys playing at war. I am not the god of war games. I am much greater than that and these acts are an insult to all I stand for. I condemn them and their frailty. They are no sons of mine." He placed his hand over his heart and bowed to the crowd.

Shock went through the spectators in a wave.

Even Stella might have believed it if her parents hadn't taught her never to trust any of the gods.

"I have no sons to speak of," Endros added.

Several people gasped. It was meant to be an insult to his true son —Cato, the god of manipulation and influence. Cato, with his meddling, had a hand in his father's death, and Endros wasn't the type to abandon a grudge.

Endros grinned at the royal booth and offered a mocking bow. "Thank you for having me, Your Graces. I'm so excited to see what this year's competitors are made of."

Stella should have been more afraid of what the god had in store for her, but her mind was fixated on the fact that she was in for the scolding of her life when she got out of the arena. Some survival instinct in her brain wanted to focus on the more manageable problem instead of the suddenly much more dire threat of death.

Entering the Gauntlet Games was one thing, but once their parents realized they were bonded on top of Endros being in charge of the Games, Stella and Teddy would never hear the end of it.

The only consolation was that maybe Cecilia could convince Desiree to remove the bond and end that irritating distraction. That alone might be worth whatever lecture Stella would have to sit through.

Endros raised his hands. "I know you're all eager to get to your opening parties and place your bets on your favorite contestants or maybe to bet against those you think will be eliminated early." Endros winked at Stella and raised his hands high. "Let the Gauntlet Games begin."

9

STELLA

Stella and Teddy were allies in nothing except this battle with their parents.

Now that the opening event had dissolved into afterparties, Stella and her parents and Teddy and his were gathered in the McKay Estate living room.

Cecilia paced and Stella could tell she was winding up for a tirade. For once, Rainer wasn't trying to stop her.

Teddy's parents had taken a completely different approach. King Xander and Queen Jessamin stood by calmly, whispering quietly to each other on the other side of the room. Their lack of drama unnerved Stella more than her mother's bluster.

Cecilia stopped and spun toward Stella, pinching the bridge of her nose. "So let me get this straight. First, you lie to us and say you're sleeping over at Kate's house and instead you run off to the Temple of Desiree to get heart-bonded in the middle of the night without telling any of us. Then you enter yourself into the Gauntlet Games to 'fix' this problem. This isn't storytime, Stella Selene, this is real life. Those are real warriors and you have never seen a battle."

"I'm aware of that, Mama," Stella said. "But it's the only clear path to what I want."

Her mother continued pacing the sitting room, wringing her hands. Rainer leaned against the doorframe. Stella gave him her most pleading look, but the crease in his brow remained. He was usually a pushover for her and her siblings, but safety was always his greatest concern. She wouldn't be getting off easy this time.

Stella cleared her throat. "It's not a big deal, Mama—"

"Not a big deal!" Cecilia spun on her. "Not a big deal to run off? To come back heart-bonded to a *prince*? To enter yourself into a deadly competition? Really? Tell me—does it feel like not a big deal?" Cecilia tapped her sternum.

Stella hated the constant reminder of Teddy's cresting waves of emotion in her chest.

How on earth did her parents deal with this? Was it like this for everyone? Surely Arden would be steadier.

A floorboard creaked on the stairs just outside of the living room. Leo and Rosie had been sent to their rooms to give Stella, Teddy, and their parents some privacy, but it was clear they were just listening from their perch at the top of the stairs.

"There's nothing to be done now," Stella said. "It will fade in a few weeks and all will be well."

"And what of the competition?" Xander asked.

Stella winced. "We hoped my parents could advise us on how to control our temporary bond better."

That was the entire reason she and Teddy had fessed up about what they'd done. If they were just navigating it in daily life, they probably could have gotten away with it, but in the Gauntlet Games, feeling each other's every rush of panic and pain would be very distracting.

"As if it's such a simple thing to learn," Cecilia snapped. "All for some man."

Rainer finally stepped in. He brought his hands to Cecilia's shoulders. "If anyone should understand impulsive decisions made for love, I would think it would be you."

Cecilia cast him a scathing glare. "Then wouldn't I know best?"

"I take offense to that," Xander interjected.

Cecilia shook her head and pointed at Xander. "You stay out of this, Xan. You may be king, but this is my house and my daughter." She turned and poked Rainer in the chest. "And you! Could you be any more wrapped around her finger? She lied to us, ran off with an unmarried man. Then she entered herself into the Gauntlet Games in the year it's being managed by Endros!"

Rainer blew out a breath and gave Stella a look that said he knew there was no winning. No matter who he sided with, he'd face fury. Stella had inherited her mother's temper—it burned hot and fast but fizzled out quickly, though she had the same propensity for thoughtless words.

"I'm saying that those of us in this room are the only ones who know about this, and both Stella and Teddy have reason not to share this secret," Rainer said, his voice calm.

Cecilia rubbed her temples. "I wonder what Sylvie thinks. It's so unlike Grace to go along with a plan like this. Gods, I'd pay good money to hear what Evan has to say about it." She muffled a laugh and looked to Xander.

The king smirked. "The Gauntlet Games aren't Teddy's only concern right now, I'd say. Interesting that these two ended up connected, though."

"It's not as if I was *trying* to be bound to Teddy," Stella huffed.

Rainer held his hands up to try to ease the tension. "Any other secrets we need to be made aware of?" he asked. "Like maybe *why* you were at the Temple of Desiree in the first place."

Stella looked down at her hands in her lap, ignoring her mother's burning gaze. "I went to be bonded to Arden."

"Teripin?" Her father was slow to anger, but she sensed it in the tone of his voice. "As in the prince of Olney? As in the man whose betrothal to Princess Eleria was announced at dinner the other night?"

"As in the prince she's been sleeping with for the past six months," Cecilia said.

Stella's cheeks burned furiously. "Mama, you said you wouldn't say anything."

Cecilia glared at her. "Trust is earned, Stella."

Rainer looked crestfallen. Stella watched as he realized she'd been lying to him regularly for months. He had always prided himself on having a great relationship with Stella and her siblings. She knew he'd be hurt that she had held something so important back.

She pressed her hand to her sternum. "Isn't being connected to His Broody Highness punishment enough? I know that I messed up, but it's only a temporary problem."

Cecilia twisted her hands in her skirt. "Maybe we could get them out of it. Maybe there's something written into the covenant of the Games."

"I don't want an out," Stella said. "I want to win." She looked pleadingly at Teddy.

He finally spoke up. "We thought maybe since you all created the Games all those years ago that one of you might have a loophole in how the rules were written."

Stella tipped her head back and sighed. "For the last time. I'm not quitting so you can win. If you want a loophole, let's be clear that it's so *you* can save face."

"I can't quit. I would never live it down," Teddy said. "I thought maybe another god could step up as gamemaker."

Rainer shook his head. "The gamemaker rotates every year, but once a god has taken up the mantle, they have to finish it—just like there's no way out for either of you once you're bound to the tournament."

Xander sighed and rubbed his temples. "We were very intentional. The covenant of the Games is bound by the gods and holds for as long as peace does. So unless you want to start rooting for a rebellion, the competitors are held to their binding promise the same way the gods are held to deliver a favor to the winner."

Stella fisted a hand over her heart. "Sayla's bow! What is happening? There's all this pressure. It feels like my heart is going to arrest."

Cecilia crossed the room and sat next to Stella, placing her fingers on her pulse. "Your heart rate is fine. Send me the memory of it."

Stella closed her eyes for a moment and passed the memory to her mother. When she blinked her eyes open, her mother's expression turned from concern to soft understanding and she looked at Teddy. "That's just anxiety. It seems His Grace is quite worried."

"How do you know?" Stella asked.

Cecilia nodded at Rainer. "Years of experience connected to your father."

"That is what Papa feels like? Gods, that must be exhausting."

Her mother laughed and it broke all the tension in the room. "You'll get used to it. Imagine it like a funnel. You can learn how to narrow it down, so just a little comes through. If it's that intense, he's probably feeling a lot."

Teddy cleared his throat. "Not to interrupt a family spat because it's entertaining, but can we not speak about me as if I'm not here?" He glared at Stella and rubbed his sternum. "And for the record, you're not a dream either. It's like a swirling river of emotions that shifts current every other minute."

"Apologies," Cecilia said. "I didn't mean to do that. I'm just at my wit's end with what to do with my daughter who seems to have temporarily lost her mind."

Stella cocked her head to the side. "I'm twenty-three years old. What are you going to do? Ground me? Tell me I can't compete in a magic-bound tournament?"

Her mother's face went red with fury.

King Xander covered his mouth, his eyes full of mirth. "Love, she could not be any more your daughter."

Cecilia closed her eyes and took a deep breath. "I know. It's so frustrating and so deserved."

Stella held up her hands. "I know I made a rash decision—several. But I'm capable of taking care of myself." She looked at her father. "Have you not trained me since I was a child to be able to handle myself? Am I not both of you? Your talent with a blade and Mama's magic?"

Rainer flexed his hands. "Yes. You're our daughter and that has clearly bequeathed you with your mother's recklessness and a healthy dose of overconfidence, but this is not training, Stella. This is a fight to the death and there are plenty of men who would love to make a point of besting you." He paled and shook his head like he was trying to rid himself of a bad memory. "I have every confidence in you, but these are tense times and you have a target on your back."

"Why don't you understand that I need to do this?" Stella asked.

"For that boy?" Rainer asked.

"He's not a boy, he's—"

"Engaged to someone else?" her mother interjected. It was just like Cecilia to pipe up when she could be the most cutting.

"Yes," Stella said tightly. "Which is precisely why I need to win this contest."

Her mother frowned and crossed her arms, then laughed. "Oh, you mean to ask for Arden's hand?"

The way her mother said it made Stella feel like an idiot for thinking it was possible. But it *was* possible. It was the only path forward now. The winner of the Gauntlet Games could ask for a favor from the gods and it had to be granted. There were limits to what could be requested. She couldn't ask to be made a goddess or ruler of either kingdom, but she could ask to marry someone she loved and they wouldn't be able to refuse her. Really, it would be a favor to her *and* Arden, who clearly didn't want to marry Eleria.

"You wouldn't be the first one in the family to make bad decisions because of sweet words from a prince," Cecilia said. "But a couple pillow promises should not be enough for you to risk your life. Do you have any idea—"

"About how you killed Endros and now he's back for revenge?" Stella asked. "Yes, Mother. I'm painfully aware that I walk in the shadow of greatness every moment of every day. I'm sure that the ascended god of war has a score to settle and you want to tell me how idiotic it was that I allowed myself to be baited into a trap. I know. But as you've all said, I'm bound to the competition and I can't change that now. So instead of berating me for my streak of bad decision-making, why don't we talk about how Teddy and I are going to survive?"

Xander stepped forward. "I'm going to choose not to be offended by that exchange."

"Look at you making good choices," Cecilia said.

The king smiled at her indulgently. "I'm also going to agree with your daughter. There's nothing we can do to get them out of the competition now. If I interfere, it will look like I'm giving preferential treatment and the Sons of Endros will have a field day with that. It will just add fuel to their fire about how they want equity."

Cecilia threw her hands up. "But they don't want equity. They want to set us back twenty years and erase all the progress we have made. If they have it their way, women will go back to being property of their fathers to be passed on to their husbands. We have worked too hard to go back. They don't want a seat at the table. They want to set the table on fire."

Stella slumped further into her seat. She hadn't even been thinking about the tense politics of the kingdom when she entered herself into the Games. Obviously, she had noticed the rise of revolutionary activities, but she'd thought the Gauntlet Games would be insulated from the influence of the Sons of Endros.

Her mother was right. Any of her fellow competitors could secretly be a member of their organization. And Stella had given them all the perfect opportunity to make an example of her. Not only was she a woman, but she was the daughter of the woman who had slain Endros—the harbinger of all the changes in women's rights that had come after.

In short, Stella had made herself the perfect target.

She glanced up and caught Teddy staring at her. His expression mirrored her own and his anxiety tangled around hers through the bond. He had probably realized that he also made a great target.

"They are both well-trained, but we have to assume that Endros will make it as hard on them as possible," Xander said, turning his attention to Rainer and Cecilia. "Fortunately, he has to make it just as hard on everyone else. The most important thing is that you teach Stella and Teddy how to manage this bond and that we keep the knowledge of it to just us. If any of the other competitors find out, they can use you against each other."

Rainer crossed the room and sat down next to Stella. He squeezed her knee. "All will be well." He sounded more like he was telling himself than her. "Your mom and I will teach you some basics to control the bond this afternoon, and then you'll come out and spar with me."

Stella's relief was profound, and for the first time, she realized just how exhausted she was from the anxiety of the day.

Queen Jessamin crossed the room and kissed Teddy's cheek. "You and I will speak later. For now, listen to everything Rainer and Cece tell you and then come back to Olney Castle ready to train with your brother."

Teddy nodded and watched his parents leave. He sat rigidly beside Stella as Cecilia dragged a chair in front of the couch so she could face them.

"You can't let anyone know about the bond. It will be a liability," Rainer said. "You're both so unpracticed. It will be distracting if either of you are scared or injured. You have to cultivate tremendous focus." He brought a hand to his heart. "Cece and I had years of practice before we were ever in real combat together, but the two of you don't have that luxury. I don't mean to be patronizing, but I don't think you understand yet just how distracting it can be."

Teddy shifted and chewed his lower lip.

"I've seen you fight, Teddy," Rainer continued. "You have excellent focus and you've learned from the best, but you've looked at my daughter thirty-six times since we brought you both into this room."

Stella remembered the bolt of pain she'd felt when Teddy made his binding vow to the tournament—and that had only been a cut on his palm. What might it be like if he was seriously wounded?

"How do I block him out?" she asked.

Rainer shrugged a shoulder. "Your bond is different than the one your mother and I have, so at least you have that going for you. Truthfully, I don't know the ins and outs of a heart bond, but you could probably ask your Aunt Desiree. She's been refusing to answer when your mother tries to summon her, but maybe she wouldn't ignore a request from you, Stell-bell."

Stella arched a brow.

Her father laughed. "Fair enough. Now let's focus on this bond. I'm guessing that it's only the strongest emotions that will come through, so it's important that both of you try to stay as steady as possible even when you're surprised in the tournament." Rainer reached over and pinched Stella's arm.

She hissed in pain and wrenched her arm away at the same time Teddy's hand flew to his chest.

"That pain could hit you at any time and you have to ignore it," Rainer said. "Ideally, we'd have time to teach you the scope of pain and shock you might feel, but we have hours, not years."

Cecilia placed her palm over her heart. "Close your eyes. First, focus on just feeling the bond."

"How?" Teddy asked.

"You should have some awareness of what doesn't belong in your chest. What feels foreign, or like it just doesn't quite belong. To me, Rainer always feels a bit off of my own natural rhythm of emotions."

Once Stella closed her eyes and paid attention, it was actually remarkably easy to sense the bond and start to feel what was her and what was Teddy. The bond was tucked in the space just beneath her heart, pulsing with a subtle rhythm.

"For me," Rainer said, "Cece feels more extremes. There's more variability to her rhythms and mine tend to be naturally a little more subtle."

Teddy shifted beside Stella, his thigh brushing hers. "I feel it, but I'm not sure if I know what part of it is her."

"That's okay," Cecilia said. "I want you to both think of the bond as a funnel. Something is always going to be coming through. It's not likely that you two will get to a place of being able to shut each other out completely. We need to work with a baseline expectation that you'll always feel something."

Stella clenched her hands in her dress. The thought of not having her heart to herself for the next few weeks was exhausting. She wanted to slam the door closed on Teddy—to keep him from finding out that every assumption he'd ever made about her was true. She was too soft, too angry, too petty, just too much, and now she wouldn't be able to hide it from this smug prince.

"Our goal," her mother continued, "is to help you limit what passes through the bond. Now that you feel the bond, I want you to take turns noticing each other's particular signature. Stella, think about something that makes you very angry."

Stella blew out a breath and thought of Desiree joining Grace and Arden's hands. She waited for the rage she'd felt—or at least the confusion and dread.

Neither came. All of her anger must have been spent in that moment and the moments after when she'd been attached to Teddy.

Instead, she was hit with an immense wave of sadness. It hurt to think about losing the thing she was so certain about. The grief that the relationship that had always been so effortless for her to slip into was slipping away with that same ease.

Teddy's rough palm slid into hers. Stella's eyes snapped open, and she looked at him, expecting a taunt. Instead, Teddy's eyes were full of disarming gentleness.

"I know," he whispered.

Her eyes burned and she could barely swallow around the lump in her throat.

This wasn't the real Teddy Savero. It was just because she had helped him in a bad moment. This was just a transaction—a way for him to ease the inequity between them.

Stella looked down at her pale hand in Teddy's. "That wasn't anger. I thought it would be."

"That's okay. I could tell what it was," he said.

Cecilia cleared her throat. "Teddy, why don't you try to think of something that makes you angry?"

Stella closed her eyes and tried to make sense of the strange pulsing feeling in her chest. Heated rage sparked through the bond. It was so much more intense than Stella expected, even when it faded from the bond a moment later. It had bled into her body.

"I feel it like an echo," Stella said.

"That's good. Does it feel like yours?" Rainer asked.

It didn't. It felt like Teddy had invaded her chest and left his fury behind. Though it was fierce and bright like hers, there was a pattern to it that felt like a dance move one beat out of step.

Stella's eyes shot open. "I hate that. It feels like it's everywhere."

Her father just smiled. "It will fade in a moment. Take a deep breath."

It was too private. Too intimate. She wanted to scratch out the incessant itch of Teddy. She was so angry she couldn't rip him out of her chest like a weed pulled up from a flower bed.

The candles on the table beside them sparked and the flames burst upward.

"Steady, Stella," her mother scolded.

"I hate it," Stella panted. "I hate him."

Cecilia sighed and held up her hands. "Whatever is between you two that has had you at each other's throats in the past needs to be left behind now. I don't want to know what it is, but you need to be done with it, because some petty childhood grudge is not going to be the thing that takes one of you out in the tournament."

Stella crossed her arms. It was ridiculous to pout when she knew her mother was right, but the bond was already disorienting. Removing the comfortable disdain between them would make everything even more chaotic.

"Figure it out and call us back in once you do," Cecilia said, rising to her feet.

She and Rainer left the room.

Teddy cleared his throat. "Let's go back to the beginning and get it all out at once."

"I told you back at the temple," Stella said. "I'm sorry that I made Juliana cry by saying she would never be prettier than Alexandra. I apologized to her back then, but I didn't apologize to you and I'm sorry."

Teddy pursed his lips. "I'm sorry I put mud on your seat at the Solstice Festival family dinner four years ago."

"It looked like I shit myself, Teddy. I loved that dress and you ruined it."

He smiled smugly. "I know."

"I cried."

The smile fell away from his face. "I'm sorry. It was unkind and I'm sorry I ruined the dress. You look pretty in lavender."

They both froze. The compliment was new territory. As far as she could remember, he had never seriously complimented anything she'd worn. Usually he just said he liked her dress sarcastically and then she'd spend the night second-guessing what she'd worn and wondering if Rosie and her mother were lying when they said she looked good.

His strategy was perfect in its wretchedness.

"I'm sorry that I slipped a laxative into your drink at the winter solstice three years ago. I was trying to get you back for the dress," Stella said.

Teddy leaned back and crossed his arms. "By making me *actually* shit myself?"

Stella burst out laughing. "I said I was sorry."

Teddy arched a brow. "Yes, your sincerity is written all over your face." He shook his head, but his lips tipped into a smile. "I missed my father's birthday party because I was trapped in a washroom until dawn."

Stella muffled her laughter. "Tell me—did I use enough herbs to dislodge that stick up your ass, or should I use more next time?"

Teddy glowered at her as she laughed harder. He leaned against the arm of the couch and waited for her to settle. When she finally composed herself, he grinned again.

"I'm sorry that I used a tongue-tie spell on you to make all of your words twist at the winter solstice party two years ago."

"That was you?" Stella was utterly flabbergasted. "Teddy! My mother sent me to the healer because she thought there was some-thing wrong with my brain. She went through my entire head after that. Do you have any idea what it's like to hide private memories from your memory witch mother when she's hunting through every dark corner of your mind for a problem?"

It was Teddy's turn to laugh. "I hadn't considered that, but now that you mention it, that's very funny."

Stella sat up straighter. "Well, I'm sorry that I cast a scent spell on you when you were meeting with the delegation from Aldrena at last year's summer solstice and wrote the spell so that you wouldn't be able to smell it."

Teddy's eyes went wide. "That was you. I was so confused why all of them would only speak to me for a moment at a time and would keep shifting farther and farther away as we were talking." He scrubbed a hand over his face. "I didn't know until Grace asked me what I'd had to eat to smell so ripe. That was diabolical."

Stella leaned back in her seat and grinned. "Thank you for noticing."

"I'm sorry that I messed with your measurements at the seamstress and had her shorten all your dresses for last year's winter solstice visit," Teddy said.

Stella shook her head. "How on earth did you manage to do that from a kingdom away?"

Teddy smiled sheepishly. "I used Uncle Evan's network."

Stella stared at him, slack-jawed. "Theodore Davide Savero. You used a spy network for a prank?"

Teddy burst out laughing. "Uncle Evan thought it was funny. We just had someone stop at the seamstress and tell her you'd been wearing the wrong shoes when you were measured."

"I had to rip out all the hems myself. I looked like a mess all week." Stella laughed in disbelief. "I can't believe your commitment to being petty."

"I recognize a worthy adversary when I see one—in pranks, I mean." Teddy leaned forward, his elbows resting on his knees. "Is that all of it? Can we call a truce now? To be honest, I feel a little silly given that I started it over something small, but you know how it is when you see one of your siblings upset. You—"

"Have me wipe their memory so they can't compete in a tournament?" Stella suggested.

Teddy glowered at her. "You've made your feelings about that clear, but I swear I have good intentions."

"I know that, but Alex is a grown woman, and she deserves to make her own choices. I understand the protectiveness, but you have to let her make her own mistakes."

"There are mistakes I'd gladly let her make."

"You coddle her."

"I guide her. It might be different if she hadn't been through so much recently, but she isn't focused and I couldn't risk it."

Stella sighed. She understood, but she had a bad feeling about it. "You won't be able to do that forever. If she doesn't get the instinct to protect herself now, she won't have it later when she needs it."

Teddy dropped his head back. "I get it. I don't need another lecture about it, okay? Can we just have a truce?"

He held out his hand. Stella hesitated a moment before shaking it.

"Truce," she said. "For now."

"For now," Teddy agreed.

Stella summoned her parents back into the room, and they picked up where they'd left off.

Much to Stella's chagrin, it was easier to control their connection now that there was less tension between them, but it still wasn't comfortable. Bumping up against the heart of someone you had no business being so emotionally intimate with was strange—like reading the journal of your nemesis.

They traded feelings back and forth for what felt like forever but was really only an hour. Stella was ready to crawl out of her skin by the time her parents finally gave them a break.

She didn't want to know Teddy like that and she didn't want him to know her back. She just wanted to survive the competition and wait for the nightmarish bond to fade and all the senses in her body to be her own again.

Finally, her parents deemed that they had done enough and they sent Teddy back to the castle.

Cecilia excused herself to take a nap, but Rainer stood in the garden window, watching Teddy leave through the back gate.

"You did well today, but it will be another thing entirely when you're in the middle of a fight," her father said. "Gods, I hate this. I wanted a world where you would never have to take a life."

Stella had been doing her best to ignore that possibility. It was foolishness that led her to do so. She simply couldn't think about it too much or she'd be completely paralyzed by fear. Now was a moment for courage, and she needed to focus on one problem at a time.

Rainer sat in a chair by the window, pulled out a half-carved star flower, and began to chip away at it with a blade. Stella crossed the room and sat down in the chair beside him, watching his practiced movements transform a lump of wood into a petal.

After a few minutes of silence, he put the flower and knife back in his pocket and looked at her. "This last year has been frightening for us with the way the Sons of Endros have become bolder. It feels like the kingdoms are backsliding and it brings up bad memories for me and your mother. We had hoped the world would be different by now —better. We wanted to create a world where you could choose the future you wanted."

"That's what I'm trying to do, Papa," she said.

He ran a hand through his hair and sighed. With his face heavy with worry, he looked so much older. "I know. I've seen it before. Do you know what your mother said when she saw you standing in that arena?"

Stella shook her head.

"She said, 'Is that your daughter down there?' And I said, 'No, sweetheart, that's *your* daughter.'" Rainer smiled and shook his head. "You are so much like your mother."

"Then shouldn't you have confidence in me?"

Rainer clasped his hands. "I do. I know that you have her strength of will and, even if I could change your mind now, you're bound to this path. Forgive me for worrying." He looked out at the garden and swallowed hard.

Stella wished she could reassure him, but if it was Leo or Rosie who had entered, she would feel the same.

"I'm ready for this, Papa."

He looked at her with so much grief in his eyes. "I know. That's what frightens me." He cleared his throat. "Just tell me this to ease my mind—when does a warrior put down her blade?"

Stella's lips twitched toward a smile. "When she's dead, or when she's lost the will to fight."

He nodded in approval. "That's my girl. Keep your blade in hand. Never let your guard down. Don't trust anyone."

"What about Teddy?"

"Especially not Teddy," he grumbled.

Stella laughed. "But you all said we should stick together."

Her father rubbed a hand down his face. "Yes. You should trust him not to kill you mid-competition, but he can't lose this tournament, Little Star. The heir to the Argarian throne cannot weather that kind of public loss."

The words twisted knots in Stella's chest. She and Teddy couldn't both win. If she lost, she would lose Arden and this beautiful love story that was just beginning. But if Teddy lost, he would lose Grace and take a humiliating blow to the ego he might never recover from.

But he was a prince. He had power. At the end of the day, if he really wanted to marry Grace, he could probably find a way to make it happen. If Stella didn't win, she would be powerless to stop Arden from being with Princess Eleria. He couldn't call off the engagement without causing an inter-kingdom incident. But if Stella won, she could ask for Arden's hand and the king would have no choice but to grant her a marriage sanctioned by the gods. Even the people of Jeset were incredibly devout to their gods. They would respect the outcome.

Her father leaned forward and squeezed her hand. "I know Endros will make it harder on both of you. Please promise me that you'll remember Teddy is not your savior. He's your competition."

10

TEDDY

The morning of the first challenge, the competitors' tent was already bustling with activity when Teddy stepped inside.

Servants loaded trays of citrus fruits and muffins onto a table in the center corridor, but from the looks of it, no one had touched the food. It was hard to blame them with first-challenge nerves descending.

Teddy hoped he'd be early, but as he strode down the center walkway of the tent, almost all of his fellow combatants were already there, lacing up boots and outfitting themselves with weapons in their individual curtained rooms.

He had slept terribly. The training from Cecilia and Rainer had been helpful, but it was clear by the anxiousness that he and Stella volleyed back and forth as he was trying to get to sleep that they were hopeless with any intense emotions.

His muscles were stiff from sparring with Jalen the previous afternoon and an ache tore up his side as he reached to open the curtain of the same small alcove where he'd suited up for the opening ceremony. He glanced at his name emblazoned in gold on the small wooden placard hanging from the hook outside the room, and then looked down the row of curtained rooms for Stella.

He wanted to get a good look at how everyone was outfitted considering they had no idea what to expect from the challenge, but before he could walk down the hall, someone grabbed his arm.

Teddy turned, his dagger already in hand, and came face to face with Nathan Aiger.

Teddy was so relieved to see his best friend that he sheathed his dagger and threw his arms around him. When he pulled back, Nathan smoothed his linen vest and tugged down his shirt sleeves. It was bold of him to not wear a tunic like most of the men at court, but Nathan was always saying how women noticed when you stood out.

Teddy looked at the flowery embroidery on the vest. He would pass on the latest fashions unless Grace told him otherwise.

"I thought you weren't arriving until next week, Nate?"

"Easy there. I know you missed me," Nathan said. "When I heard that you were competing in the Gauntlet Games, I thought it was surely gossip. I am the reckless, charming friend. Teddy Savero doesn't do things like enter himself into deadly competitions with a bunch of warriors who'd love an excuse to stab him. I had to see it for myself. And here you are, ready to risk life and limb for—" He frowned. "What, exactly?"

Teddy glanced around the room but found no one within earshot. "It's a very long story, but I stupidly went to the Temple of Desiree, hoping she would heart-bond me and Grace."

Nathan stared at him with wide eyes. "I swear I come late to *one* Olney trip and you finally get fun and make havoc for the first time ever."

Teddy punched him in the arm. "Fuck you. I've always been fun."

Nathan eyed him warily. "Looking very official in the princely gear." He gestured to Teddy's heavy armor.

"Official but awfully hot for the climate here," Teddy said. He was already sweating through his clothes beneath the heavy metal breastplate.

"Yes, but the ladies will love it," Nathan said. "I take it you didn't get the bond from Desiree?"

Teddy ran a hand through his hair and lowered his voice. "Oh, I did. Just not to the right woman."

Nathan clicked his tongue. "Are you suggesting that Goddess Desiree doesn't know what she's talking about? Some might consider that blasphemy."

"No, I'm saying the goddess was bored and decided to bond me to Stella for entertainment."

Nathan's face contorted with shock before breaking into a wide smile. He laughed so loudly and suddenly that Teddy jumped. "You're kidding. Gods, that's funny. What did Gracie have to say?"

"Not much. She was busy getting bonded to Stella's boyfriend."

Nathan doubled over laughing. "I can't believe I missed this. So you're bonded to Stella, and her boyfriend—"

"The prince of Olney."

Nathan's eyes went comically wide. "Arden Teripin is her boyfriend? She and Gracie swapped princes. So you're connected to your nemesis? How is she?"

Teddy opened his mouth to speak, but Stella appeared beyond Nathan's shoulder.

"*She* is standing right behind you, Nathan Aiger," Stella said with a smirk.

Nathan spun and bent to kiss her hand with exaggerated reverence. "Lady McKay, lovely as always."

Stella smiled indulgently at him. "It's been a while, Nathan. Good to see you haven't given up on flirting with every woman you come across. Sadly, your efforts are in vain. Have you not heard? My heart is spoken for by one man and chained to another. I'm not sure I can handle a third."

Nathan waggled his eyebrows. "Well, we don't know until we try, do we, love?"

Stella laughed, and the bond in Teddy's chest clenched at the sound. Whatever that feeling was, it was entirely unwelcome.

He'd always admired Nathan's ease with women, but a prince could never get away with casually suggesting a foursome.

Despite the fact that Teddy knew from their bond that Stella had been up late, she looked fresh as ever. Her cheeks were rosy, and her hair was braided into a crown around her head. She wore fine leather armor, including a Novumi vest that held eight blades, and a dagger strapped to her right thigh. Her bow and quiver of arrows were slung over her arm with the practiced ease of someone who shot daily.

"You're very dressed up to watch a bloodbath," Stella said, eyeing Nathan's vest.

Nathan smoothed his hand over his embroidery again. "Thank you, Stella. I'm dressed to catch any swooning ladies of the court that might need a hero a little farther from the action."

She laughed and patted his shoulder. "Happy hunting. It was good to see you. It's been too long."

Nathan watched her go and whistled low when she was out of earshot. "Can't believe you're upset about being bonded to someone with such a fine ass. *Fuck me*. I don't care how much she irritates you. You can't deny she looks great in that leather armor."

Teddy had been trying very hard not to notice. "Truth be told, this is the first time I've seen her out of a dress."

"Hopefully not the last," Nathan said, still distractedly eyeing her backside as she bent to tighten the laces of her boot.

Nathan's admiration filled Teddy with something akin to protective jealousy. That wasn't right. He did not care who stared at Stella McKay's ass. They were *friends* and Nathan had always been a bit of a rake.

"I have no interest in seeing her out of a dress," Teddy grumbled. "She is just a temporary problem that I'll solve once I win this tournament."

Nathan smiled and clapped a hand on his shoulder. "Good to see you looking so confident." He nodded toward the platform at the end of the center walkway where competitors were gathering. "Looks like you better get ready. I'll see you after."

Nathan retreated toward the tent entrance. He paused and turned back. "Ted," he said, the humor suddenly gone from his face. "Be careful out there. This thing is always hard to watch, but I don't want to see you—"

"I will. All will be well."

Teddy didn't feel as confident as he sounded, but that was nothing new. It was the same false bravado he brought to everything in his life.

Before Nathan could say anything else, Teddy turned away from him and walked toward the other competitors.

Outside of the main tent, where the binding ceremony had taken place the day before, there was a small dais, upon which two priestesses in red robes stood, their heads bowed in silent prayer. The competitors gathered in a semicircle around the dais and Teddy took up a spot on the back edge where he could see all the combatants and both entrances to the room.

Fire bloomed bright on the dais and a hush came over the group. The flame receded, revealing the god of war.

There was a hesitation in the crowd. A beat too late, several heads bowed, and others touched their fingers to their hearts and forehead in a salute of reverence to the god.

Endros frowned at the display. "Welcome competitors. Thank you for the truly tepid greeting. Fortunately for you all, I'm not offended."

The crowd shifted, clearly uncertain whether to believe the god.

"You have been weighed and found worthy of the Gauntlet Games by me, your godly gamemaker." Endros locked eyes with Teddy as he continued to speak. "Welcome to your first challenge. A reminder of the rules: at any time during the active challenges, competitors can interfere with or take out their competition, but if you do not complete the required task, you will be eliminated from the Games."

The group of competitors exchanged glances, and Teddy's gaze drifted to Stella. She stood at the back of the group on the opposite side from him.

"The first event will be only twenty minutes and will take place in its entirety within Olney Arena," Endros continued.

Teddy wasn't relieved by that news at all. The Gauntlet Games usually ran one or two weeks depending on how complex the challenges were and how much time was given. Some events took place inside the arena that had been constructed behind Olney Castle, but some of the more complicated tasks took place around the two kingdoms and the crowd would be given certain times to come back and witness the end of a specific event. In between the excitement, the town enjoyed wild parties, storytelling performances, and a street fair in the town square where local and foreign vendors sold their wares.

Endros was either trying to start this year's Games off with a shorter, more violent challenge to get the crowd excited, or he planned to keep the whole Games quick and deadly and it would be over in a matter of days.

"The first task requires a partner, and since it is the wisdom challenge, I should remind you to choose your partner wisely as this is a challenge that requires you to know them and yourself." Endros's words sounded like a threat. "Magic, which includes both elemental summoning and spellwork, is banned from the first challenge. Any contestant using it will be immediately eliminated. Remember, I am always watching and I don't miss anything. Do not think to cheat, or you will pay a high price."

With that, the god nodded to his priestesses and retreated to his place of honor in the stands.

The competitors dispersed into whispers, quickly pairing up as if they'd all been expecting to have to choose an ally. Teddy should have expected it. It happened often in the wisdom challenge, usually with regard to choosing an adversary to compete against. Stella would be an obvious choice since he was confident that her ire didn't extend to actually wanting to kill him.

Teddy made a beeline for her as she shoved several more pins into her crown braid, trying to tame her unruly curls.

He leaned in, keeping his voice low. "Don't let them get you down. Whatever this task is, you know that people will want to make an example of you because of who you are and—"

"I know how to fight," she snapped. "It's patronizing to explain how this competition works as if we both haven't been watching it since we were children."

"We should pair up," Teddy forced himself to say.

Stella scoffed.

"Fine, then, what about—" He nodded to the tall redhead on the far side of the group. "Jeneva Lampry over there. She'd be a good partner for you."

Stella scowled at him. "Because we're both women?"

Teddy groaned. "No, because I watched her in training earlier this week. She worked well with a partner and she doesn't have magic."

Stella cast a glance at the red-haired warrior, who was checking the throwing knives stuck into her chest plate. Jeneva was tall, with a muscular warrior's build. She wore a leather armored vest. Colorful tattoos peeked out from the gap between her shirt and armguards.

"I wonder if her father is losing it over her being in the competition or if he's proud," Stella said. "It could go either way with the huntmaster. I know when my mother entered herself in the Huntgames they used to have before solstice, my grandfather wasn't very pleased, but he was proud. Of course, the Huntgames had way less murder than this tournament."

"Did you imagine your parents would feel the same?" Teddy asked.

Stella laughed. "No. I knew they would be horrified." She glanced at the dark-haired woman next to Jeneva.

"Do you know her? She's awfully small to be rumbling with these warriors," Teddy said.

Stella nodded. "That's Katerina Shank. Her father is one of the best smiths in Olney. Don't let her build fool you. There is not a weapon she doesn't know how to wield, and she's also a witch. Her strongest affinity is water, but she has another talent I'm guessing most people here don't know about."

"Care to share?"

"Of course, *Your Grace*, at your royal command." She pressed onto her toes and leaned in so her lips nearly brushed his ear. "She's good with poisons. I would take care not to even get scratched by any of her weapons."

Teddy shouldn't have been surprised that Stella had done her homework. She was Rainer McKay's daughter, and he would have taught her to know her adversaries well.

"And what have you learned about me as an opponent?" he asked.

Stella smirked. "You'll just have to find out."

He hadn't really thought about the fact that he was at a disadvantage against her. He'd seen her shoot a bow, but he'd never seen her fight with any other weapon, yet she'd watched him train plenty.

Teddy eyed the competition. "We really should pair up."

She laughed incredulously. "No."

Teddy spun on her. "What do you mean no?"

"I mean, I don't want to tie my fortunes to a spoiled prince who has never had to fight for anything until now."

"What happened to me being the only person you were worried about beating?"

She cocked her head and looked at him like he was the dumbest man she'd ever met. "You are. That's why I'm not helping you."

"But you need a partner."

Stella nodded to a man in elaborately decorated leather armor. His dark hair was neatly gathered in a bun at the nape of his neck. He caught Teddy staring and flashed a wide, annoyingly perfect smile. The prick winked.

Teddy whipped his gaze back to Stella. "Fionn Silver is a *mercenary*."

"Which means he's one of the few people in the field whom I know for certain can be bought."

"Loyalty purchased can always be purchased again by a higher bidder," Teddy said, parroting the words his father had drilled into him since youth.

"I'm giving him something he wants—something he can't get from someone else," Stella said. "It's the proper motivation to guarantee he will help me through this challenge. He needs me alive and well to help him."

The same nagging jealousy-adjacent feeling tore through Teddy.

It's just the bond. The only thing he felt toward Stella McKay and her flimsy plan was annoyance, though he supposed it would be distracting if she got herself killed. That, and he'd probably hear it from his father and everyone else if he didn't at least attempt to protect her.

"Are you worried for me, or for you?" Stella asked. "It looks like most people are paired up, unless you want to hitch your wagon to that burly group of brutes over there." She nodded to the four men on the far side of the field. "They seem...nice."

"Be careful with them," Teddy said.

"You know them?"

Teddy nodded. "Wish I didn't. That tall, dark-haired one with the narrow-set eyes and the scar on his jaw is Rett Roachelle. Three years back, he was attacked by twenty Sons of Endros and lived to tell about it. They call him 'The Roach' because they say he can't be killed."

Stella smirked. "And what do you say?"

"I say that there's more than one way to survive the rebels. The easiest one is to be one of them. They get in a few blows and scar up your face and you live to tell about it while looking like a hero. That's a compelling story."

Stella pursed her full lips and glanced at Rett, who winked and blew a kiss. She wrinkled her nose in disgust.

Teddy nodded to the raven-haired hunter beside Rett. "Where Rett goes, Dixon Max follows. He's a hunter like Rett, so he's good in combat, but he has magic. His strongest affinity is fire, but he's also good with earth. Out of their quartet, he's the only witch, so I'm guessing Rett will pair up with him for this first challenge." He nodded to two other hulking men beside them. "The big guy with the copper hair is Christophe Wallthrew. A real piece of work who has a reputation for beating his wife. His father is too powerful in Ardenis for us to really do anything about it unless she chooses to leave him. And the dark-haired fellow beside him is Drew 'The Crew' Barnett. They say he's strong as two men, thus the nickname."

"Those Argarian hunters really love their nicknames," Stella mused.

"I'm just reminding you to be careful with them," Teddy said. He eyed her leathers. They were good quality, but they wouldn't hold up to serious combat and the weaponry Rett and his friends were packing. "You should be wearing more substantial armor."

"Not if I need to move quickly and be flexible," Stella countered, tapping her knuckles to the metal guard on his arm. "This won't help you if the challenge isn't to lay siege to a castle. This is the wisdom challenge, so I assume it will require a level of flexibility." A crease formed in Stella's brow. "Are you well today...after—"

After his very humiliating meltdown before the binding ceremony.

"Just because you helped me in a rough moment doesn't mean you have to coddle me." He sounded harsher than he meant to. "I don't need you or anyone else checking on me."

A smile played over Stella's lips. "Does it give you peace to keep everyone at arm's length?"

Teddy bristled. "I imagine it must be easier to trust people's intentions when you're not a royal trying to stave off rebellion. You are the only person here I'm sure I can trust."

She crossed her arms, and the leather of her breastplate was so new it creaked with the movement. "Really? You trust me?"

"I trust you to be predictably irrational."

"Irrational." She scoffed and shook her head. "Good luck in your first challenge, *Your Grace*. I'm sure you'll pass with flying colors given the immense wisdom you've shown in this conversation. You're used to fighting people who know you're a prince, so I hope you're ready for a real fight. Try not to be a distraction." She backed away and bowed with mock reverence.

Teddy groaned. The last thing he needed was for Stella to get herself killed by trusting a Novumi mercenary. He watched her saunter over to Fionn. The sellsword gave her a long, lingering once-over that made Teddy want to punch him.

Fionn caught Teddy's eye and smirked. "Don't worry, Your Grace. I'll take good care of your friend," he said.

His tone was laced with innuendo, but Stella didn't seem to mind. She smiled brightly as she slung the strap of her quiver over her chest and checked the string on her bow. Then the two of them walked toward the tent entrance.

If Uncle Evan had taught Teddy anything, it was to distrust everyone until you had proof they were trustworthy.

Teddy had prided himself on making wise choices his whole life. Jalen got to be the fun prince, while Teddy was the responsible, rational one. Perhaps it wasn't as exciting, but if there was one challenge where he felt confident his experience would help him, it was this wisdom challenge.

A man with dark hair and tan skin crossed the tent and nodded to him. "I believe you're stuck with me, Your Grace."

Teddy recognized the cut of the man's leather armor as that of his mother's homeland. Teddy owned several such pieces that he used in light combat. Novumi leather workers loved to etch elaborate patterns into their designs.

The man bowed. "Reever Ross at your service—and, given your royal status and the fact that everyone else is already paired up, I won't charge you for my services. I've heard you're a good fighter and you're half-Novumi, so that's good enough for me."

Teddy didn't like the idea of partnering with a mercenary, especially after he'd lectured Stella about it, but he had no other option. He followed Reever toward the corridor leading to the arena, studying the tattoo that peeked out of the mercenary's collar.

"You like it?" Reever asked without looking. He tugged his collar down to reveal the head of a snake. "It's a symbol for the Novumi god of lies. We mercenaries need his gift for persuasion at times."

Teddy only knew about the gods and goddesses of Novum from the stories and songs his mother had shared with him when he was younger. *Delion.* That was the name of the god of lies, but Teddy could vaguely remember something about the god's wandering ways and his jealous wife.

Before he could ask Reever about it, the mercenary was beckoned into the tunnel to the arena.

Teddy strained to hear anything, but there wasn't a hint of sound coming from anywhere in front of him. He couldn't even hear the crowd noise. It made sense that they would take care to use a sound-proofing spell to prohibit any competitors from using enhanced hearing for an advantage.

His stomach grumbled, more from nerves than hunger, but he wondered if he should have eaten something more substantial. Still, experience had taught him it was better to fight hungry than to need to stop and vomit mid-battle. Especially with all those eyes on him.

A priestess beckoned Teddy forward and he walked into the tent, blinking as his eyes adjusted to the dimmer light.

This was not the priestess that had bound him to the tournament. This woman was clad in the blood-red robes of Endros. Teddy did not realize there were still priestesses of Endros. The temples in Argaria had been abandoned for years, but it stood to reason that there might be smaller sects throughout the Argarian countryside.

Despite the history between the Savero line and the god of war, King Xander had not ordered the temples destroyed. He'd explained since Teddy was young that faith inspired loyalty and consequences, and if royalty disrespected the gods, then the people would too.

Teddy had long since learned that the surest way to pique the people's interest was to make something forbidden. It was part of the reason the Sons of Endros had gained so much political traction. They acted as saviors of the oppressed. If they tried to outlaw worshipping Endros, it would have only made things worse.

"Greetings, Theodore Davide Savero. Welcome to the wisdom challenge. Before we begin, you must choose one of the following to aid you in your challenge. Choose either talent or luck. You will need both to complete this task and your partner has already chosen."

Teddy wanted to pick talent, but this challenge was about wisdom, so the twist was to know your partner—or, he supposed in this case, opponent. It was as much about what Teddy would pick as it was about knowing what Reever would prefer.

With Stella, Teddy would have known beyond a shadow of a doubt that she would pick luck. It would be just like her to pick some-thing mythical instead of something practical. But Reever was a complete unknown. Mercenaries had enormous egos, so it stood to reason they'd be just as likely to think they had all the talent required. However, given the unknown nature of the task, it may have also been practical to choose luck.

"Your selection?" the priestess said.

Anxiety buzzed in his chest. His father was always telling him to trust his gut.

"Talent."

The priestess nodded and placed her hand on his head. A warm tingling sensation spread from his crown and down through his body.

By the time the priestess removed her hand, his whole body was buzzing.

She nodded toward the exit. "May it serve you well."

11

———————

TEDDY

Teddy emerged from the tunnel into blinding sunlight and was instantly grabbed by two guards.

"Sorry, Your Grace. It's part of the contest. None of the competitors are allowed to see the arena before it's time," a burly guard in green Olney regalia said. "Forgive me, but I have to blindfold you now."

Teddy nodded, and the men tied a blindfold around his eyes, then began to march him forward. They guided him, with minimal directions, toward the swelling noise of the crowd. Teddy tried not to stumble, but it was difficult while being bounced between their bodies and entirely cut off from his eyesight.

A zap of energy hit him in the chest. *Stella.* The bond lit up. She must have been close. He tried to remember what Cecilia and Rainer had said about finding each other. There was supposed to be a sort of intuitive knowing that Teddy needed to listen to.

He imagined the bond like a rope and tugged on it. A moment later, an answering tug reverberated back. It came from his left. He wished they'd had more time to understand the language of the bond. Rainer and Cecilia could use theirs with ease. How did they check on each other? How did they understand how to communicate

130

with it? He wished he understood more than how to keep Stella from feeling the crushing anxiety that was rising in his body again.

Adrenaline coursed through Teddy, his heart thundering loud enough to nearly drown out the roaring crowd.

"We're going down a ramp, Your Grace. Just be mindful that we're descending," the guard on his right said.

Teddy nodded and focused all his concentration on not falling down the ramp or off the side in what would have certainly been an embarrassment he could not recover from.

They reached the bottom after what felt like an eternity. The wooden ramp gave way to solid dirt beneath his boots and the two guards let go of his arms.

"This is your starting place," the guard on his left said. "Your partner is to your left. When the bell rings to begin the match, you may remove the blindfold. Bells will sound to start the match, at the match midpoint, and when there is one minute left. From the first bell, you will have twenty minutes to retrieve a large ruby from the beast that appears in your section.

"You may use all the weapons on you and anything else from your environment, but you may *not* use any magic. There are witches along the perimeter to ensure no one uses their magic, and if you do, you will immediately be disqualified and removed from the tournament. You may attack your peers as long as you're still competing, but once you retrieve your ruby, your challenge will be complete and you must return to the sportsmanly decorum we expect of competitors. Remember that this is the wisdom challenge, so you should also use your head. You are our second-to-last pairing, so the match will begin soon."

The guards marched away, their footsteps echoing off the long wooden ramp. A moment after the footsteps stopped, Teddy heard the grinding sound of the ramp sliding away from the ground.

There was no way out but through whatever beast was about to be unleashed upon them.

"Reever?"

"Yes, Your Grace?"

"Please, just call me Teddy."

"Yes, Teddy?"

"What did you choose?"

"Talent."

Teddy's stomach plummeted. "Why? I thought for sure you would say you had enough talent."

"The more talent, the better for a mercenary. I am excellent, but it's a moron who doesn't know the ways in which he could be better." Reever laughed. "I can only assume you picked talent as well."

"Yes. Why is that funny?"

"Because a little adversity makes for a better story, and I suppose more entertainment for the crowd."

"But we need both to win," Teddy said.

A meaty hand clapped him on the shoulder. "Kid, I have been making my own luck since I grew up in the poorest neighborhood in Estrellas. This will hardly be new to me."

"Why are you competing? Isn't the whole point of being a sell-sword that you value money over anything else?" Teddy asked.

It was a bold question, but understanding his new ally was the first step to trusting him, or at least trusting what he would do.

"There are more currencies than money." Before Reever could say more, the bell rang out and the noise of the crowd grew deafening.

Teddy ripped his blindfold off and squinted into the midday sunlight. The moment it took for his eyes to adjust was the longest of his life. Even once he beheld the creature, his mind could not make sense of it.

"What *is* that thing?"

Reever stepped up beside him. "It looks like—"

It looked like an enormous lobster with wings. The monstrous red mass reared up on thick humanoid legs, its enormous claws big enough to crush a skull. Black membranous wings stretched out wide on its back.

Teddy didn't know whether to laugh or run. The thing looked absurd. Its large, beady eyes blinked and its massive claws clicked together. The pungent, herbal scent of magic hit him. He'd assumed it would be some sort of animal. He had not expected a strange mythical medley of creatures, both real and imagined. It took a powerful spell to create creatures like this.

The crowd cheered in the bleachers high above them. Teddy and Reever, and likely the other contestants, were on low ground, in a pit that had been carved out of the center of the arena. It was probably designed to corral these creatures and keep them from escaping into the stands. Teddy had been worried about keeping an eye on Stella and now he had such low ground that he couldn't even see her. He could only see the rise of the stands and the bustling crowd bracketing the royal booth where his parents sat looking stoic.

He knew them well enough to see the tension in their hands clasped together on the arm of his father's throne.

Teddy forced his attention back to his task.

Priestesses stood on higher ground at each corner of their pit to judge that no magic was used and that they completed their task in time. One of them held an hourglass, with sand already pouring away as Teddy stared in a stupor.

"What do you know about...lobsters?" Teddy asked, pulling his short swords from his back. They didn't have to kill the beast, but he couldn't imagine getting within striking distance of those giant claws with the beast conscious.

Reever brandished a large, vicious-looking axe. "I traveled with a fisherman who caught them once. Creepy things with their skittering and beady little eyes."

The beast let out a blood-curdling screech. Its wings stretched wide, and it curled in on itself, then launched into the air. It swooped in a high arc and then plummeted toward them with claws clacking.

Teddy stood frozen in place, less out of fear than determination to figure out where the jewel was. The winged lobster closed in on him and the crowd hushed.

"Move your pampered royal ass," Reever shouted, bumping his shoulder.

Teddy ran to the side and wheeled around with short swords flying as the lobster swooped close. His steel blades met a leathery wing, and the beast shrieked, tumbling into the dirt, sparkling brown blood puddling on the ground beneath it. The beast curled in on itself. A pungent herbal scent laced the air and Teddy's ears rang. Whatever magic had created the beast for this contest was powerful and made Teddy's skin prickle up close.

A loud whooshing sound split the roar of the crowd. Water rushed in from all sides of the pit. It was too fast to be natural.

This was why they had started on low ground. Water witches stood on the side of the pit, summoning water from the ground beneath them. Teddy's magic bubbled in his chest, eager to spin the water away.

But magic wasn't permitted in this part of the competition, so he forced it down. Sweat broke out on his brow. He needed to fight the bond, the beast, and his own impulse to rely on his magic.

As if they needed one more thing to demonstrate the urgency. It made sense that the wisdom challenge required knowing your ally and being able to think on your feet.

Normally, the first challenge of the Gauntlet Games was the easiest and the bloodbath came in the second challenge once opponents had a chance to size each other up. Of course, the god of war would choose as many violent obstacles as possible in just one challenge. If they wanted to advance, Endros wanted to make sure they bled for it first.

Water sloshed around Teddy's boots. He'd never admit it to her face, but Stella was right. He was too slow for this type of adversary in his bulky armor, and now it would weigh him down in the water. To make matters worse, he didn't know how to swim since they didn't exactly have easy access to beaches in Argaria. He could have learned in the few summers they spent in Olney, but his father had drilled it into him not to be bad at something publicly and he wasn't sure he'd recover from the embarrassment of needing to be saved from drowning in front of a crowd of Olney onlookers.

However bad that would have been, drowning in front of two kingdoms' worth of spectators now would be worse.

Teddy needed to get the armor off, but that meant opening

himself up to easier wounds from Reever and the monster they were fighting. He unsnapped the hinges on his left thigh guard and let it fall into the mud.

The wounded lobster rolled onto its stomach and skittered toward them. They stumbled back, and the beast climbed onto its humanoid legs. It slammed its tail down and mud sprayed across Teddy's face.

As it arched back, readying to strike, a glint of ruby shone from within the interconnected shell on its torso.

"Fuck me," Reever said, clearly seeing the jewel as well. "We're going to have to kill it to get that ruby. No way it's going to let us just reach in there and I'm not about to have all my fingers clawed off."

He lifted his axe and brought it down on one of the beast's humanoid legs with all his might. The blade glanced off the shell, and Reever narrowly dodged a claw. He tumbled into the dirt and brought the long handle of his axe up just in time to block the lobster from crushing his head in its giant claw.

Teddy dashed forward and swiped a short sword across the back of the lobster's humanoid leg joint. It screeched and slapped him back with one of its wings. Teddy rolled over backward and pushed right back up to his feet, the blood rushing in his ears blending with the sound of water pouring into the pit.

Teddy only had a moment to glance at the water witches again. They could fill this pit in mere moments.

His mind spun wildly as the flying lobster launched into the air. The water turned the pit muddy and Teddy's boots slipped as he searched for the solution.

It made sense why they needed luck and talent. Talent would serve them well enough, but luck would have meant they knew something about the creature they were paired with, or perhaps not being matched with a beast that essentially had natural armor. Lots of men blamed their success on talent, but plenty of great warriors fell. Battle was not a meritocracy, and it was a foolish fighter who wouldn't admit that luck played a hand in who came out on top.

Years of training had taught Teddy every weak spot in armor, but it was hard to fight an adversary whose anatomy you didn't know. He needed to be able to move and adapt faster.

Teddy fumbled with the buckles on the side of his chest plate and it popped free and clattered to the ground. He instantly went to work on his other thigh.

"We need a plan," Reever said, his gaze fixed on the circling beast.

"I'm not allowed to use magic and even if I could, it wouldn't make sense to boil water we're standing in."

"I think you had the right idea before." Reever distanced himself from Teddy. "If we take out the wings, that will keep him on the ground."

"Wings and eyes. Once he lands, I'll—" Teddy cut himself off as the lobster charged toward them.

The beast was definitely laboring with its damaged wing. It was coming right for Teddy. He forced himself to be still, his swords at the ready.

At the very last second, he ducked, and the lobster careened past him into the wall of the pit. It crumpled to the ground, momentarily stunned.

Teddy had his opening. He took a step to charge at it and snatch the ruby.

"Teddy, duck!" It was Nathan's voice cutting through the din of the crowd from above.

Teddy ducked and an arrow just skimmed his shoulder guard. "What the—" He turned and spotted Rett Roachelle on the edge of the wall to their right.

"The fucking Roach," Reever yelled. Apparently, the mercenary was already acquainted with Rett. "He's basically shooting fish in a barrel." The mercenary drew his bow and shot an arrow back. "Dixon must have boosted him out to try to take out the competition. You focus on the beast, and I'll focus on that weasel."

Teddy turned and narrowly dodged a claw to the face. He sliced out with his sword reflexively and jammed it into the lobster's eye. The water sloshed around his knees as he stepped in closer, trying to grab at the ruby.

But the beast shifted, and its shell clicked back into place, covering the gem.

Teddy jumped to the side and the lobster's shorter, razor-sharp legs scraped across his chest. His tunic took the worst of it, but his skin burned where it was scraped.

He forced himself to stay close and crowd the beast, slicing down its other wing.

It screeched and batted him into the wall. Teddy's head hit hard and his vision went dark for a moment as he slid down the wall. His ass hit the ground. He sputtered at the muddy water that splashed up into his face.

Forcing himself to his feet, Teddy backed away from the lobster. It was curled in on itself, making a low groaning sound and cradling its shredded wing.

"Got him," Reever said triumphantly.

Teddy glanced up at Rett. An arrow stuck out of the gap between his breastplate and shoulder guard. But the Roach was pulling another arrow from his quiver.

"Maybe not," Teddy said.

Reever grinned and cupped his hands around his mouth. "Not so fast, Roach. I'd finish your match and go see a healer if I were you. My arrows are coated in a healthy dose of Harlowsberry."

Apparently, there was more than one combatant with poison-coated weapons.

Rett hesitated, his bow half-drawn and his face flushed. "Liar!"

Reever shrugged and nocked another arrow. "I guess we'll finally get to see if you live up to the nickname."

The Roach lifted his bow, hesitated, then turned and disappeared from view with a frustrated shout.

Teddy's head throbbed, and the water was up to his mid-thigh. He needed to lose the rest of his armor, but his clothing was swollen and the buckle wouldn't budge.

He could really have used some luck, but all he had was talent. He glanced up in time to see Reever rushing at him with a dagger drawn. Teddy let his guard down for one moment and Reever took advantage of it. Teddy threw his arm out and the blade deflected off his armguard.

Reever blew out an exasperated breath. "Relax. I'm trying to cut the fastening. We don't have time to save your fancy armor, Your Grace. Get it off, live to fight another day, and buy a new set." He jammed the tip of the blade into the buckle and yanked, and the stuck thigh guard came away with a groan of the hinge.

"Sorry," Teddy mumbled.

A loud cheer went through the crowd. Either someone was dead or someone had succeeded in their task. Fear bubbled in Teddy's chest, but he didn't know why. The beast was badly wounded. Rett was gone, and the water was only up to his thighs.

The lobster rose out of its hunch, shredded wings spread wide, its one good eye blinking at Teddy. The beast had to turn its body fully to see Reever.

"One more rally, Teddy. I think we can do this before the midpoint," Reever said. "You draw it toward you and I will jump on its back. It won't see me coming, but hopefully I can bow it back enough for you to grab the ruby. Just do it fast."

Teddy tapped his short swords together three times, and the beast whipped around and started toward him, Reever forgotten.

When the lobster was just a few feet from Teddy, Reever launched himself up its back. He braced his long-handled axe around the lobster's neck area to yank it back into an arch.

Teddy sprang up the front of its body, using the gaps in its shell as handholds. He caught sight of the ruby and reached up to grab it.

Pain sliced into Teddy's chest and his grip slipped. He fumbled for purchase, wedging his fingers into a joint on the shell of the lobster's chest. He winced against the pain, but there was no cut on his side. He tried to make sense of it as a loud roar from the crowd to his left drew his attention.

Stella. It was *her* pain. Gods, it felt as real as if he'd been wounded.

"What are you doing?" Reever grunted from above him.

It was now or never. Teddy forced himself to reach up for the jewel. They needed to end this before another competitor caught on to the Roach's strategy of trying to take out the stragglers. Were it not for Reever's poison-tipped arrows, Teddy might have been eliminated or killed this round.

He grabbed the ruby and tugged as hard as he could, and finally, it came free. Teddy released his hold on the shell and fell back into the waist-deep water. He held the ruby high and watched as the beast shuddered, groaned, and faded into ashes so quickly that Reever landed on his ass in the water.

A red-robed priestess clapped her hands, and guards lowered a ladder into their pit. Teddy climbed out first. By the time he reached the top, he was wrung out. The trial felt like an eternity, but according to the hourglass it had taken less than ten minutes.

"Congratulations, Theodore Savero and Reever Ross. You have passed the wisdom challenge and have advanced to the memory trial next. Please go enjoy healing and refreshment in the recovery tent," the priestess said, pointing toward the arena exit. She retreated toward her peer.

Reever strapped his axe to his back. "What was that about?" he asked.

"What was what about?" Teddy asked, feigning confusion.

"You lost focus at a mighty critical moment, Your Grace."

"It was the crowd noise."

"It was right before the crowd reacted," Reever countered.

Teddy smiled tightly. He couldn't let anyone know about the bond or they would use Stella against him. "I heard a lady friend's voice through the crowd. A momentary distraction, that's all."

Reever narrowed his eyes. "You should get those scratches looked at."

The mercenary did not seem convinced, but he headed toward the healer's tent. Teddy couldn't show any extra attention to Stella, so he couldn't stay and watch, much as he wanted to.

He forced himself to walk to the healer's tent and not even glance over as he passed the pit where Stella was still fighting.

12

STELLA

The noise of the crowd was at an all-time high and Stella was keenly aware that another competitor had either died or completed the challenge, or perhaps both—a death and a victory at the same time.

"Look alive, princess. That beast is retreating now, but we need a strategy here. This is the wisdom challenge," Fionn said.

Stella glanced from her mercenary partner to the priestess at the corner of their pit, who rang a bell.

Ten minutes left, or she was out of the Gauntlet Games and she'd lose her shot at happiness.

She chanced a look at the royal box where Arden was leaning forward in his chair, his worried gaze fixed on her. Stella forced herself to smile. She looked to the gamemaker's box where Endros sat. A ghost of a smirk played over his lips. Leave it to the god of war to invent the most violent wisdom challenge in years.

Usually, any violence in this challenge was quick and vicious and explicitly a result of not using one's head. But a fight against a monster in a pit that required both talent and luck was sure to produce the bloodshed the god of war savored.

Endros nodded at Stella, his eyes faintly glowing with power. A chill spread through Stella's body, but she refused to be a pawn for him. If he had a score to settle, she wouldn't be the one to pay the price.

Fionn walked toward her, two curved blades in his hands. His hair, which had been perfectly tied back, was now plastered to his forehead and neck with sweat. The intricate design on his Novumi fighting leathers had been slashed by the beast they were fighting.

The sun blazed down and sweat beaded on Stella's forehead. The hairs at her nape had drawn into tighter curls in the humidity, tickling her skin every time she moved.

She sized up their opponent as Fionn stepped up beside her.

The Octobear, as she'd been calling it, stood close to seven feet tall. It had the body of a wild bear, but eight large, tentacled legs sprouted out of its back, each tipped by a bear paw with vicious claws.

The mythical beast was entirely summoned by magic, so loud it made her ears ring. All magical objects had a sort of resonance, but this monster had a more distinct ancient sound that unnerved Stella.

The water in their pit was already up to her calves, soaking into her boots and making her movements slow and slippery.

But soggy feet were the least of her problems. She had a monster to slay in the next ten minutes if she wanted to advance in the contest.

"Is this a bad time to admit I was expecting you to pick talent, not luck?" Fionn said.

Stella scowled at him. "Forgive me for not realizing someone with your ego wouldn't pick talent."

"Offended that you think I don't already have it, princess," he said with a wink. "At least that luck is serving us well." Fionn gestured to the claw gashes on his left thigh.

Stella laughed and winced at the throbbing in her side. The Octobear had gotten her good with one of its long-range tentaclaws. Her shirt and the waist of her pants were soaked in blood, but the leather breastplate had saved her from the worst of it.

She could practically feel the burn of her parents' eyes and she was furious at herself for being wounded. At the exact moment she'd been driving in close to try to snatch the jewel from the green ribbon around the Octobear's neck, she'd felt a shock of fear in her chest. *Teddy's* fear.

The split second of distraction was enough for the beast to claw her, but Stella recovered quickly by slicing off its arm. Unfortunately, it appeared to be generating two new tentacled arms in its place. Now it would have nine, and the wound had only made the monster temporarily retreat.

Stella wished her side would heal faster so that it wouldn't be so distracting. She didn't need another thing splitting her focus. Her stupid bond had nearly been the end of her in the first few minutes of this task.

She stole a quick glance at the hourglass at the top of their pit. Sand was rapidly pouring into the lower half. They needed to win, and quickly.

She pressed a hand to her side, and it came away bloody.

Fionn grinned at her. "Don't worry. You look great in red."

She laughed and winced again. "We have to crowd it. I can try to wound it with my bow from afar, but at least one of us has to get close to swipe the jewel."

So far, they'd only succeeded in deflecting its arms and making it angry.

All her instincts had her looking for the fastest escape route. Stella wanted to flee this danger. Worse, her magic wanted to join the fun. It swelled and pressed against her skin, making her even warmer under the blazing sun.

Her fire magic had always been like this, as swift and temperamental as flames, roaring to life whenever she was hurt or angry. It took tremendous restraint to stuff it down in a fight. When she was younger, she'd trained on the beach until she could master the fits of fire that overcame her when she was hurt or angry. She'd blow all her fire into the sea, letting it turn to steam, away from anywhere it could hurt someone.

Now with fear so wild in her heart, she could barely contain it.

Only her father's familiar refrain rooted her. *Feel the fear. Do it anyway.*

How many times had he encouraged her to try new things with those words? It was okay to be afraid, but she could not let the fear win.

She tried to call up his training. Every opponent had a weakness. The bear's fur was matted along its left side where she'd caught it with her sword before slicing off one of its tentaclaws. She could try to hit it there again.

Eyeing the wound, Stella drew her bow and aimed. Wisdom meant knowing they did not have to slay the beast to get the prize. Wisdom meant playing to the advantage they both claimed. They had excess luck, but Fionn was already a talented fighter and she was already a goddess-blessed archer. Perhaps there was wisdom in taking a beat to consider that this test was meant not to give them a moment to breathe, because the answer suddenly seemed so obvious.

She loosed an arrow. One of the Octobear's arms swatted it away.

The monster let out an inhuman growl, and the crowd gasped.

"Well, shit," Fionn grumbled. "All you did was piss it off."

"Take out the arms and it will have to regenerate. It took almost a minute for them to regenerate last time," she said. "We have to go now. We can't break another charge from that thing."

Fionn grimaced and nodded. "All right. Let's see how lucky we really are. You take the arms on the right and I'll take the arms on the left, but watch out for its shorter, regular bear arms. That's what got me last time."

Stella nodded and followed Fionn as he charged across the pit. She took five quick shots as they charged in the hopes of distracting the beast. All it did was make the Octobear angrier. It slammed its arms down and the water erupted in a wave that nearly knocked Stella off balance.

She looped her bow across her body and drew her short swords to slash away one of the arms. She dodged and ducked the rest, forcing herself to get as close to the bear's body as she dared.

One clawed arm skimmed her shoulder, and another snagged on

her wristguard, but she pressed on. She sliced up and out, severing an arm. She crossed her swords and made quick work of the next two.

Three arms down, two more to go. She moved closer to the next arm as it struggled to double back and fight her off. But the beast bucked and growled as a tentaclaw dropped on the other side of its body. Stella's blade slipped and only sliced into the underside of the tentacled arm.

Dark brown herbal-smelling blood sprayed across her hands. Stella's stomach heaved, and she ducked under its giant bear paw just in time. One claw scraped over the top of her head. The scratch warmed with blood.

She stumbled behind the bear and watched in horror as it swatted Fionn away like a rag doll. He hit the dirt wall hard and leaned against it, looking woozy. The bear bellowed a ground-rattling roar at him.

Stella wasn't quite tall enough to reach the green ribbon fastened around the bear's neck. Another three inches and she could have untied it and snatched the ruby.

Instead, she drove her swords into the wound she'd already made on the bear's side and thrust them upward. The beast screamed.

She twisted. Searing pain lanced her side and she cried out as claws raked the already angry gash below her ribs. If she hadn't moved at the last second, she might have been eviscerated. Perhaps she was lucky, after all.

Her magic surged beneath her skin and it took every bit of her self-control not to lash out and burn the beast to ash.

Panic gripped her. They were running out of time, and she was perilously close to losing control of her magic.

She stumbled away from the beast and ran for Fionn as the bear curled in on itself. Its stumps were quickly sprouting two new arms each.

Fionn shot arrows at the beast for cover, but it retreated into the far corner to regenerate.

The mercenary paused and glanced at Stella's side, which was still bleeding steadily.

A wave of dizziness hit her, and she stumbled into his arms. Water sloshed around her hips and she cursed as it splashed into her wound.

"Easy, princess. You're not looking so good. We need to end this and get you out of here." Fionn steadied her, and she turned and looked at the beast again.

"I couldn't reach the ribbon to snatch the jewel," she mumbled.

"I think we've got one more rally in us. What do you say?" Fionn said.

"I think we've been lucky so far. We don't need to kill it. We just need to remove the ruby. I was trying to get the arms out of the way so I could do this." Stella aimed her bow and breathed out. "To luck," she whispered.

She loosed the arrow and closed her eyes. *Please.* It was a plea not to the gods, but to something deep within herself. *Please be good enough.* She heard the arrow hit the dirt wall with a thud.

The water sloshed beside her. When she blinked her eyes open, Fionn was halfway across the pit. The bear barely noticed his approach. It was writhing in the water as its new arms grew longer. They were nearly fully grown again, several claws beginning to sprout from the ends of each paw.

Fionn sprinted the last yard as fast as he could to her arrow on the pit wall. He jumped to grab the ruby dangling from the green ribbon. The moment his hand closed around it, the Octobear went rigid and then desiccated to dust.

The cheer of the crowd drowned out the pounding of Stella's heart in her ears.

Stella bent forward and bit back a sob of relief as the water level immediately started to recede. She was dizzy and nauseous and had very little fight left. If that hadn't worked, she would have been lost.

She forced herself to roll her shoulders back and turn to face the stands. Her parents were on their feet shouting, as were Leo and Rosie beside them. King Xander and Queen Jessamin were also on their feet, applauding. Jalen and Juliana joined their parents, but

Alexandra stared at Stella with her eyes in narrowed assessment. Did she remember what Stella had done?

Stella shrugged it off. Nothing she could do about it now.

Finally, she looked at Arden. His tan face was paler than usual, but he was on his feet applauding her. The sight of him looking so frazzled made her heart soar. Stella was exhausted and she must have looked frightful, but she beamed at her love.

It was only the first challenge, and she'd almost died. Worse, she'd come perilously close to losing control of her magic, but she refused to let Arden or the crowd see her sweat.

As she turned toward the ladder that had been lowered into the pit, she spotted Endros in front of his elevated throne. He cocked his head, studying her with anger in his eyes, his shoulders shaking. But as flames erupted around him and the crowd gasped, Stella realized the god of war wasn't angry at all. He was laughing.

13

STELLA

The healer's suite was sweltering in the summer heat. All the windows had been thrown open for airflow, but the humidity of Olney summers was inescapable.

Once it was clear that Stella's wounds, though stable, were more substantial than some light healing could fix, she had been brought from the tournament recovery tent to the healer's suite in the heart of Olney City to see the head healer.

According to the frazzled young woman who had dropped her off in the room, three of the sixteen competitors had died in the first challenge.

Stella felt numb to that reality. It felt both real and unbelievable and she hadn't been able to get any more information from the healer before the woman ran off to tend to another ailing warrior. Teddy wasn't one of the fallen, though. The healthy dose of anxiety pulsing in her chest made her confident of that.

The smaller wounds on Stella's head and arms had been healed, but still throbbed. Though pain could be lessened and wounds healed, the ache of the injuries usually lingered for a day or two. Her ruined armor was in a pile in the corner. Her tattered shirt was soaked with blood still weeping from her wound and her skin was sticky with sweat and drying groundwater. It was a bad sign that the cut was so severe and her body so depleted from the fight that it hadn't managed to heal at all on its own. She wanted to bathe desperately, but she'd settle for just a change of clothes at this point.

The healing assistant who had left to fetch her some fresh clothes had been gone long enough that Stella assumed she'd been forgotten.

She lifted the hem of her tattered shirt and glanced at her bloody side. The gory mess made her dizzy. She immediately yanked her shirt down and gripped the edge of the tabletop to steady herself.

The healing suite door flew open and Cecilia ran in. She stopped short, scanning Stella the way she had when she was a child with a scraped knee. Her mother's face was wan, her bright blue eyes puffy. Cecilia blew out a breath and her eyes went glassy.

"We are so relieved you and Teddy are safe," her mother rasped.

"Did he even struggle?" Stella couldn't stop the question.

It wasn't as if she'd wanted him to fail, but he'd been a distraction when she needed focus and wanted it to have been as hard for him as it was for her. After his patronizing advice before the event, she had hoped that, at the very least, he might be marginally humbled.

Rainer appeared in the doorway. He gave her the same assessing look her mother had and nodded once. "You're okay, Stell-bell."

It was more statement than question and Stella could tell that he'd done it for Cecilia's benefit as much as Stella's.

"I'm fine. Don't cry, Mama," Stella said, gesturing to her body.

But her mother's eyes continued to well and Stella knew it was the wrong thing to say.

Her mother reached to pull her into a hug.

Stella ducked her grasp and tried to ignore the hurt on Cecilia's face. "You should wait until I'm not filthy and bloody."

She wasn't trying to be cruel, but if her mother hugged her, Stella would fall apart. She needed her strength now.

Rainer put an arm around Cecilia's shoulders. "She's right, sweetheart. We should let Lyra heal her up."

"I should do it," her mother insisted.

Rainer caught Stella's eye. "I think the tournament requires their official healers work on all contestants, to avoid any accusations of cheating. Isn't that right, Stella?"

Stella was so grateful for the way he always read her so well. She nodded vigorously but her mother didn't look away from the blood crusted on her side.

"You said you just needed to look at her to know she's okay, Cece," Rainer murmured in her mother's ear. "Let Lyra work on her and we'll see Stella when she's done."

Her mother nodded and curled into Rainer's side as he guided her out of the suite.

"Good job, Little Star. We're proud of you. You fought smart, and that was an amazing shot. Not sure your mother could have made it." He smirked as her mother smacked his arm.

"Absolutely could have. I know what you're doing, but I will let it happen because I love you for it," her mother said.

Her father grinned at Stella before they ducked out of the room and left her alone.

A moment later, the door opened and Aunt Lyra smiled and clapped her hands.

"There's my little victor," she said cheerily as if Stella had won the challenge instead of barely surviving it.

Lyra was not her aunt by blood, but she had delivered Stella into the world and had basically helped raise her. With the number of hours Cecilia spent working at the clinic, most of Stella's early memories were of huddling in her mother's office or spying on Lyra and her partner, Mika, as they spoke to patients in their gentle, caring way.

Lyra and Cecilia had that same way of setting anxious people at ease that Stella had always been in awe of. It was not a skill she possessed—other than that rare moment with Teddy before the announcement ceremony. Then, it had seemed quite simple, like she intuitively understood the call of their bond and responded in kind.

Tears burned in Stella's eyes, but she forced them away.

The healer's face softened. "Sweet girl, what have you gotten yourself into? I thought I was going to have to give your mother a sedative."

Stella pressed her fingers to her temples. "Please, no more lectures. I've had all the judgment I can take for one day. I just need my side healed so I can go home and drink wine and sleep."

Lyra frowned and opened the cabinet beside the bed. "Well, I'm afraid I don't have any wine, but Mika keeps some whiskey in here somewhere." She rustled around in the cabinet for a moment before letting out a victorious whistle and holding up a bottle of golden-brown liquid.

She poured them both a glass and handed one to Stella.

"To one challenge down."

Stella smiled and clicked her glass before knocking back the whiskey. It burned pleasantly in her chest as she swallowed. She held out her glass again, and Lyra chuckled and refilled it.

"Last one. I need your senses duller, but I want you awake to heal," Lyra said.

An assistant healer hustled into the room with buckets of fresh water on her arms.

Lyra gestured for Stella to get on the table with one hand while waving the other healer out. "Let's get you cleaned up."

Stella's side twinged as she climbed onto the table and lifted the hem of her shirt. She closed her eyes and listened as Lyra soaked rags and began to clean the wound.

"This is deep, and the skin is shredded. It's clotted but you got very lucky."

"I know," Stella said quietly. She dreaded the inevitable words she knew would come next.

"I can fix most of it but—"

"It will scar. I know."

"I'm sorry," Lyra said.

Stella wasn't vain. Her mother had beautiful scars that were a living story of her past. But without a happily ever after, Stella couldn't help feeling like she'd marked herself permanently for an outcome that was still unwritten.

The longer it took Arden to show up, the more her mind struggled to grasp for reasons he couldn't.

Lyra cleaned the wound and meticulously healed it. The tingling warmth of her magic combined with the whiskey lulled Stella into a calm, half-asleep state.

She wasn't sure how long she lay there as Lyra worked on her. It felt like just a moment, but when Lyra touched her arm and startled her from her daze, sweat had beaded on the healer's brow and the sun streaming through the windows was more slanted.

Lyra held up a mirror, and it took Stella a moment to realize she was trying to show her the scar. The skin was not terribly puckered where the Octobear had scratched her. Faint lines drew out from the middle of the scar, making it look like an exploding star.

Lyra looked at it like it was beautiful, but Stella could only see the ugliness of the wound and the fear she'd felt when she received it. Where her skin had once been pristine and delicate, she was now marked forever by her failure.

A memory rose unbidden.

***

*A*RDEN *SPRAWLED ON THE BED IN ONE OF THE* O*LNEY* C*ASTLE GUEST SUITES. Sunlight cast Stella's pale skin golden as he traced the freckles up her side with his pointer finger.*

"I can tell you're meant for me because these freckles spell my name," he whispered.

"They do not." A thrill ran through Stella at the thought.

"They do," he said, a teasing tilt to his smile. "Now close your eyes and pay attention."

He wrote his name on her side in cursive. When she blinked her eyes open, he hesitated, looking unsure of himself.

Then he continued to trace letters. It wasn't until he got to "o" in "you" that she realized he was writing "I love you."

***

"S*TELLA*?" L*YRA'S VOICE BROUGHT HER BACK TO THE PRESENT.*

"Sorry. A memory," she mumbled.

Stella stared at the star and her shredded freckles. Arden would never be able to write his name in them again.

"I had hoped I could fix it completely, but the ragged wounds are so difficult. I tried to at least make it something faint," Lyra said. "Can I get you anything else?"

Stella smiled sheepishly. "If it's okay, I think His Grace might be looking for me. I'd like to stay a bit longer so he can find me. Would you please make sure the other healers let him in to see me?"

"Of course." Lyra smiled knowingly and ducked out of the room.

Stella stared at the ceiling, and the exhaustion of the day hit her hard.

She desperately wanted to see Arden. If she could just look at him—if he would just hug her—she'd feel better. He'd told her he would find her as soon as he could afterward. But he hadn't come to the healing tent while she was there. Nearly an hour had passed since she'd left the arena. Stella and Fionn were not the last competitors, but there was only one duo left when they'd climbed out of their pit and left the field. He would have had to remain in the royal suite until the challenge was over, but he should have been here by now.

A moment later, the door flew open. But it was not Arden who stood backlit by the late afternoon sun shining in through the windows. It was Stella's best friend.

"Kate—" The word came out as a rasp.

Kate was always full of humor. She had an ease that Stella had never mastered. But now she looked as wrecked as Stella felt. Her usually rosy cheeks were pale and her blue eyes were rimmed in red.

She yanked Stella into a hug and began to sob. "I thought you were going to die, you absolute menace. Why would you join this stupid contest?"

Kate's family had thrown a big party the night the contestants were announced and Kate was expected to act as hostess, which was why she hadn't had a chance to scold Stella yet. She probably hadn't even known until the Games began that morning.

Stella pulled back, trying to master her emotions. Her fire magic pressed against her skin, anxious for release after she'd suppressed it the entire fight. That had always been her issue. The more hurt and angry she got, the more her magic wanted to be free. It was why she always had to be ready to expel it after training with her father. It was why Cecilia had bound her magic when she was little and dealt with her fits of rage at having it suppressed until she was old enough to learn to control it.

Stella stepped away from Kate and snapped her fingers. Fire roared above her palm. Kate didn't even flinch. She'd been expecting it.

Stella began to pace. "I just didn't see a better way to win Arden's hand. They betrothed him to that princess and when Aunt Des didn't bond us together, I didn't have another option."

"Of course you had another option!" Kate snapped. "Let him go. How can you be this blind? You think you know better than the actual goddess of love? I know he is charming. I have seen that magnetism up close. Stella, I am begging you, just this once—listen to me. You didn't give me time to talk you out of this. You intentionally kept me in the dark."

"Why would I do that?" Stella said, but she knew from the look on Kate's face that she wasn't buying the deflection.

Stella hadn't told her because she didn't want to hear what Kate would have to say about it.

Kate crossed her arms. "I have watched you pine after this prince and I've held my tongue."

Stella scoffed. "Your tongue, but not the looks on your face."

"Well, forgive me. It's hard not to voice the fact that you're *settling.*"

Stella looked away, letting her fire blaze higher. The flames sputtered and shrank. She wasn't angry. She was just hurt.

"We have been friends since we were children, so I say this to you with love," Kate said, smoothing her hand over her dress. "I know what it is to be blinded by affection. I have made my share of mistakes. But I have only ever risked my heart for affection. I have never risked my life. Arden is not worth your life. You have had a crush on him since we were children and he has never seen you for the gift that you are. Any man who would make you earn his affection instead of wanting to bask in your warmth is not worth risking your heart, let alone your life."

Stella's fire roared brighter and sweat beaded on her brow. She needed to calm down or she was going to light the ceiling on fire. "You wouldn't understand because you haven't felt it. It's hard to explain. Arden just *understands* me."

"Then where is he?" Kate's cheeks blazed with an angry flush. "He's not here to see you. You were almost mauled by a mythical beast and he can't even risk the ire of his parents to come check on you? I lied to my family and punched a guard in the face to get into the healing suite."

Stella laughed in shock, noticing the bloody knuckles on Kate's right hand for the first time. "I didn't know you knew how to throw a punch," Stella said.

Kate shrugged a shoulder. "I don't. I'm pretty sure I broke something."

Stella looked away. "Arden will see me later. He's trying to avoid an inter-kingdom conflict. He is the heir to the Olney throne. He can't simply come and go as he pleases."

Kate swallowed and licked her lips. "There's nothing to be done now. You're in this stupid contest and you can't get out unless you're humiliated, maimed, or dead. But I'm sure it will all be worth it. Gods. We're twenty-three, Stella. I understand the desire to find your person, but you have your whole life ahead of you and you're in such a rush that you're literally risking your life for someone who isn't even worth the risk of breaking a fingernail."

The words stung. Stella had always been the friend with the temper, and while Kate also had her fury, it had never been directed at Stella. Stella's magic blazed hotter in answer.

"Always with the temper," Kate said, but the anger in her gaze faded to pity. "He invited Grace Farlan to a private dinner tomorrow night. Has he ever invited you to something like that?"

"You're lying." Stella's magic snuffed out all at once.

Kate shook her head, looking too weary for her age. "Wish that I was, Stell."

Envy twisted in Stella's chest. Stella had never needed to worry about being beautiful enough. She had goddess-blessed beauty and, as Kate relentlessly reminded her, Rainer McKay's perfect smile. But she was the first to admit that Grace Farlan had regal beauty. She was steady, temperate, tall, and curvy, with blonde hair that was always stylishly coiffed.

Grace looked like a queen. Stella looked like a wild forest witch.

Stella had been friends with Grace for a long time. Not the way she was with Kate, whom she saw daily, but she'd grown up looking forward to the McKays' month-long visits to Argaria every spring and to the Farlan sisters' month-long visits to Olney every summer. She'd seen the way that Grace turned heads, but she'd never felt envious of the attention until now.

"As your friend, I need to tell you the hard truth that no one else will," Kate said softly.

"Get out," Stella snapped.

Kate opened her mouth to speak, but instead turned away and closed the door behind her.

Stella's fire guttered with the slam of the door. She grabbed her ruined armor and stormed home without looking back.

ALL STELLA WANTED WAS TO COME HOME AND REST AFTER THE FIRST trial, but she hadn't had time for anything other than a quick bath and a meal before the next obstacle had appeared before her in the form of Grace Farlan in the McKay Estate sitting room.

It was too much to see perfect Grace when Stella had made such a mess of herself that day. When her body would forever bear the scar from this tournament.

Stella hovered in the sitting room doorway, wrapping the sash of her dress around her finger. She always felt underdressed around Grace. Now she was wearing a simple cotton day dress while Grace looked like she was ready for an elegant dinner party. Intricate embroidery ran along the bodice of her chiffon dress and shimmered as she moved.

"Grace?"

Grace looked away from the window and smiled tightly. "I know I'm probably the last person you want to see."

Stella shook her head. "Of course not. I know it's not your fault. I should probably be apologizing to you. You got caught in Aunt Desiree's game when she was just trying to teach me a lesson."

Grace had always been an echo of Aunt Sylvie in how she was always perfectly styled, with the most current dresses and neat, shiny hair, but more like Uncle Evan in the quiet, observant steadiness of her personality.

Grace folded her hands in her lap. "I've been thinking about possibly exploring things with Arden. I know we all said that we would accept the outcome of the ceremony at the temple. Truthfully, I didn't think I'd get paired with Teddy, but I was certainly not expecting to be paired with someone else. Especially someone I've known for so long. It got me thinking maybe I've been missing something."

Stella stared at her, dumbfounded. "You don't want to be with Teddy? You went to the temple with him. I thought you were in love."

"That's not what I'm saying. Of course I love him. Teddy is my best friend, and he is a kind, thoughtful partner, but—" Grace licked her lips and took a steadying breath. "I've never been with anyone else. We have known each other for so long and I have no doubt that he's a good man, but I find myself wondering—"

Silence stretched out, and Grace shifted in the chair.

"Wondering what?" Stella prompted.

Grace finally met her eye. "I wonder if there's more out there and I'm selling myself short by pairing up with the first man I've felt real affection for. My mother is always reminding us that she tried to create a world where women had more options and I'm going to— what? Marry the first man I've ever had feelings for?"

Anger burned in Stella's stomach. So what if she was talking about stuffy Teddy? Grace had the very thing that Stella had always wanted, and she still thought she'd find something better.

Stella huffed a disbelieving laugh. "You think you're selling yourself short with someone who is so devoted to you that he literally entered a deadly competition to earn the right to marry you?"

Grace winced. "I know how it sounds. I tried to talk him out of entering, but that's what I'm saying: Since he's come closer to taking over as king, Teddy doesn't *listen* to me. The closer he gets to the throne, the more rigid he is. He's decided what we are, and it feels like there's no room for me to actually become someone else. I'm so young. What happens if I don't match his vision for our future?"

Stella shook her head. "This is none of my business. It sounds like you should be talking to Teddy. Not me."

Grace stood suddenly. "No, what I'm trying to say is that *you* can make him see."

Stella stared at her. "That he doesn't listen to you?"

Grace took one of Stella's hands in hers. "No, you can make him see other possibilities. Surely you must feel what I've been feeling." She pressed her other hand to her chest. "This magnetism. I'm drawn to Arden, or maybe just—I understand him better. What I'm saying is that I think I owe it to myself to see what this is—to see who I could be with a little space."

"So, what are you asking for?" Stella asked.

"*Your* permission. We've been friends for a long time. I know you care for Arden and I've been holding back from spending time with him, but my mother said it might be best to just ask you directly instead of avoiding him completely." Grace smoothed her dress and met Stella's gaze again. Her clear blue eyes were so pleading. "I feel selfish for even asking. Your friendship is important to me, and if you say so, I'll walk away and forget about it and ignore this feeling in my chest for the few weeks until it disappears. I'll decline his private dinner invitation and not speak to him until this passes. But if there is even a part of you that understands how much this whole thing has tilted my world and compelled me to take a second look at a possibility I hadn't considered, I hope you'll grant me your blessing."

Kate had been telling the truth after all. It was unlike her to lie, but she was so angry, and Arden had never invited Stella to a private dinner. He'd insisted that nothing in the castle ever stayed private long and he didn't want her reputation ruined by gossiping servants.

The excuse that had once made sense felt so flimsy now. Kate's implication had hurt, but the reality was worse.

Stella swallowed the lump in her throat. "If it's fine with Teddy, it's fine with me."

Grace's rigid posture relaxed slightly. "I know he'll be okay with it. You should both try, too. They say if you love something, you must let it go and see if it returns to you. Then you'll truly know it was meant to be."

"If you think you need to lose someone to appreciate them, then you deserve to lose them forever," Stella snapped.

Grace looked down. "I'm willing to risk it." She turned to leave.

"Why?" Stella called after her. She wasn't asking for Teddy's sake so much as her own.

Grace turned back, looking warily from Stella to the garden outside the sitting-room window. Grace was a talented earth witch. Perhaps she felt Stella's magic bursting to escape her body.

She met Stella's gaze. "I'm willing to risk it because if I have to choose between losing him and losing myself, I will always choose myself."

Stella watched her friend leave.

All epic love stories required adversity. Arden would come back to her and they would be stronger for it.

14

TEDDY

The last place Teddy wanted to be after the day he'd had was in a crowded bar, trying to blend in with the drunk patrons while he was sober.

Every muscle in his body ached. Even his hardest training paled in comparison to fighting for his life while trying to avoid drowning. Now all he wanted was the quiet of his guest room at Olney Castle.

The Poison Vixen was not the kind of bar that Teddy would have picked. He would have preferred somewhere quiet with a good whiskey selection. That was why Nathan never let him choose their celebratory spots.

Nathan always insisted on the loudest, most boisterous pubs with the best music and the most beautiful women—two of whom were perched on either side of him, hanging on his every word.

The fiddle music kicked up again and Teddy sighed, leaning back in his chair.

"Have another drink. For the love of the gods, man, you almost died today," Nathan said, waving over a barmaid.

The woman leaned over the table, her breasts nearly tumbling out of her obscenely low-cut dress.

"Another round for my two lovely companions and whatever that handsome fellow over there wants," Nathan said, nodding to Teddy. He slipped the barmaid a tip, and she tucked it into her ample cleavage as she ambled away.

Teddy wrinkled his nose. He really shouldn't be here.

Nathan caught the look on his face and sighed. He turned to the women beside him. "I'm sorry, ladies. I know I promised more tales of my bravery in battle, but I'm afraid I have some business with His Grace that requires private discussion. We appreciate your discretion, and we're sure you won't let anyone else know that the prince is here."

Teddy fought not to roll his eyes when Nathan looked at him for confirmation. This was an old game that Nathan loved to play with women in pubs.

Teddy waved a hand half-heartedly. "Yes, Nathan is a very valuable asset to the crown and I'm afraid he's privy to things that aren't for a lady's ears."

The blonde woman who had been practically sitting on Nathan's lap leaned over and whispered something in his ear. He nodded, and she rose to her feet and flitted back to the bar with her friends.

"She seems *nice*. What'd she have to say?" Teddy asked, sipping his ale.

"She just told me where and when I could find her later if I wanted to blow off some steam from working so hard. Says she also knows how to work hard," Nathan said, a shit-eating grin on his face. He glanced around the bustling room. "Speaking of later—where is Jalen? He said he would meet us, but it's getting late. What could he possibly be doing that's more important than this?"

Teddy couldn't help but laugh at Nathan. He was so ridiculous, and for a man who wasn't royalty, he'd certainly mastered the ethos of thinking of himself as the center of the universe.

A figure darted out of the crowd toward their table so quickly that Teddy's hand went to the dagger on his belt.

The cloaked figure set a glass down on the table and shoved back her hood, revealing neatly braided black hair and golden eyes just like Teddy's.

"Alex, what are you doing here?" Teddy snapped, releasing the hand from his dagger.

She grinned and winked at him as she poured herself a glass of his whiskey. "Jumpy tonight, brother. I don't blame you after the day you've had."

Nathan held up his glass to clink with hers and waved at her leather armor. "Alexandra, you look gorgeous and ready for a fight. I'd say I wouldn't want to run into you in a dark alley, but that would be a lie."

"Nathan, save the flirting for someone you have a snowflake's chance in an Olney summer with. If I wanted a medium-dicking from a lazy lay, I could probably pick, oh, I don't know—" Alexandra looked around the room. "Any man in this bar."

Teddy rubbed a hand over his face. "Can you not speak that way when I'm sitting right here? Both of you."

Alexandra turned her glare on him. "Am I offending your noble sensibilities, brother? Too bad. I'm a princess and I do what and *whom* I want."

Nathan clapped and poured her a drink. "It's good to see you, Alex, but I'm afraid you're throwing off our clandestine meeting vibe," he whispered conspiratorially.

"Sorry to say that I have unfinished business with my brother," Alexandra said.

Teddy swallowed a gulp of whiskey warily. "None I'm aware of."

She cocked her head and sweat broke out on Teddy's lower back. She couldn't possibly know what he'd done before the binding ceremony. Stella had been rushed, but he'd seen the sincerity on her face. She wanted to help, and she had.

And yet...her judgment nagged at him. She'd been adamant that she couldn't promise Alexandra wouldn't remember.

"Cut it a bit close today, Teddy," Alexandra said, watching him over the rim of her whiskey. When he didn't respond, she tugged on her linen vest and sat up a little straighter. "Not as close as Stella, though."

Teddy tried to look disinterested, but all he had been able to wrangle so far without being obvious was that Stella was advancing in the Games. He didn't *care* about her, but he didn't want her to die. The feeling of immense relief was just because she survived, and he didn't have to feel her death or see her family upset.

He cleared his throat and leaned back in his chair. "Oh?"

Alexandra's eyes lit up. "I knew you were interested."

"Well, of course I am." Teddy tapped his chest to indicate the bond.

She scoffed. "Yes, I'm sure you're just concerned about your own well-being."

Teddy scoured his brain for something to say to deflect. Stella hadn't grown on him. If anything, it was just a magical bond that made him care. "I'm just worried about the fairy princess getting herself hurt in a tournament for warriors."

Alexandra arched a brow. "I wish she'd heard you call her that. I'd love to see her clock you for being an ass. Stella is as well-trained as you are and you know it. Don't be sexist."

"I'm not sexist. I'm just saying that she is untested and too whimsical for this kind of brutality," Teddy said.

Alexandra opened her mouth to counter him, but Nathan gasped and sat up straighter, his gaze fixed on someone at the bar.

"Who is that? In the lilac?" he asked.

Alexandra craned her neck to see who he was looking at. She turned back to follow Nathan's gaze a second time, as if to check if he was joking. "You mean Rosie McKay?"

Nathan choked and sputtered on his whiskey. "*That* is Rosie McKay? Wasn't she just a child?"

Teddy rolled his eyes. Nathan had always been in such a rush to seem older and more mature, but he was only two years older than Rosie.

Rosie sat on a stool at the bar with two friends. Intricately woven flowers adorned her lilac dress, and when the light fabric shifted with her movement, it looked like a living garden. That, combined with the flower crown atop her neatly braided golden-brown hair, gave her the look of a forest goddess. She was tanner than Stella and her eyes were brown instead of green, but of course, the two weren't related by blood. They did, however, share some of the same mannerisms, like the way Rosie glanced around the room every few minutes and the way she sipped her wine.

"Pretty sure you were children at the same time," Alexandra said to Nathan, echoing Teddy's annoyance. "But if you mean that Rosie has grown into her beauty, you're certainly right about that. Not that she'd bother with someone like you."

Alexandra met Teddy's gaze over the rim of her glass, a hint of mischief in her eyes.

Nathan cocked his head to the side and glared at her. "What do you mean, someone like *me*?"

Alexandra feigned a casual shrug. "You know, she likes romantic guys. She's an artist. She wants someone more cultured and less... slutty."

Nathan scoffed. "Alex, are you saying you think that's a woman I couldn't win over?"

Alexandra leaned her elbows on the table, her hands clasped under her chin. "I think you'd be suicidal to go after the youngest McKay. If her mother doesn't chase you off, her warrior father will, and if either of them aren't enough, let's not forget that Stella and Leo would cut your dick off for even sniffing around their little sister. I'm afraid for all your charm, there are some women who are just not for you, Nathan, love."

Teddy pinched the bridge of his nose. Alexandra may as well have put a target on Rosie's back.

Nathan was on his feet and halfway across the bar in a second. Alexandra just laughed into her drink.

"My baby sister is a fucking menace," Teddy grumbled.

"Your baby sister is *bored*," Alex said. "It's like Isla always says: Make yourself a menace or else some man will come along and try to make you his."

She stared into her glass, as if the mere mention of those words made her sad. Perhaps repeating them now, when Isla was gone, gave them a new, sadder meaning.

"She'll come back," Teddy said.

He shouldn't have said it when he was uncertain. But he'd always taken this role with his siblings. It was his job to protect them, even if only for a little while. Especially when it came to Alexandra. Better a hopeful wish now and a hard truth later than something that would inspire more reckless behavior.

Alexandra cleared her throat and sat up straighter, tugging at her vest. "If you say so."

"Tell me about the challenge," he said, desperate for a deflection.

"You did a shit job, if I'm honest," she said. "Not your best showing, though I must admit that the moments I wasn't afraid you were going to get yourself killed were genuinely entertaining. A giant flying lobster." She laughed suddenly and loudly. "Where do these witches come up with this shit? That was just about the last thing I expected. I suppose that's the point. Anyway, I've been telling you that you don't train enough. Too much time on politics and it shows."

Teddy scowled at her. "Alex, I'm asking—what happened today? I know you have a full scouting report on everyone."

She leaned back, sulking into her whiskey.

"*Please*. You're my favorite sister."

She looked unconvinced.

"Fine, you're my favorite *sibling*."

She rolled her eyes. "Who else would you pick? Jules is so busy trying to become a flawless echo of our mother and Jalen is too busy trying to fuck his way to being likable. And you're too busy being perfect. I am the only one with any character."

Teddy laughed in spite of himself. Alex was so cutting, but her brutal honesty had always made her reliable in her own way.

"I know the Roach and Dixon finished first. Who was second?" Teddy asked.

"Jeneva and Katerina."

Teddy's jaw dropped. "No way."

"Don't be sexist," Alexandra snapped.

"I'm not. I'm just stunned they were so quick with everyone else in the field. And given the size of the beasts. I had to scale an eight-foot lobster, for fuck's sake."

Alexandra laughed. "With considerable difficulty, I might add. What happened to you?"

Teddy sighed and tapped his chest.

Recognition stole over Alexandra's face. "When the bear got her. It was just a split second before you slipped."

"A bear? I fought a flying lobster, and she fought a *bear*?"

Alexandra pressed out her hands as if to brace against his questions. "Not a normal bear. It was like a bear-octopus combination with arms tipped in claws. Very vicious. She was smart. They told the crowd who had what gifts. All of you who chose the same advantage struggled the most. Stella and Fionn both chose luck, and that was clear. Stella was nearly ripped in half."

Teddy's blood went cold. He should have at least checked on Stella after the fact. Her pain, fear, and anxiety had been fizzling in his chest all afternoon, mixing with his. It had been so bad that he'd ignored the protests of his body and had gone for a run in the sweltering heat, which he was regretting now that the whiskey was hitting him hard.

"So, Jeneva and Katerina—how did they pull it off?" Teddy asked.

"Poison-tipped arrows. They were fighting an enormous viper, but whatever they used on those arrows brought it down very quickly. I think maybe some type of paralytic."

Teddy considered it. He wasn't planning on writing them off, but this certainly changed the rankings in his mind. The first challenge was already showing how ruthless all the competitors could be. Perhaps that was inevitable with Endros as the gamemaker.

"So Reever and I were third. Who was after us?" he asked.

"Drew and Christophe. They did the same thing Rett did. They managed to tie their beast up. They were fighting the same lobster thing as you, but they clipped its wings right away and Drew cracked its shell. It was really struggling to move well after that. Drew boosted Christophe up the wall and he took out Aaron Harper, who was in the arena next to them. Once he was down, Scott McCadly didn't stand a chance. He is a fearsome fighter, but they were fighting a giant viper and it bit him."

Teddy shivered. He'd been around death and he knew it was an inevitability of the competition—but it still felt so soon for so many warriors to have fallen.

"You're holding back," Teddy said. "I know you. You never have so little to say about a fight."

Alexandra eyed him suspiciously. "Now why would I hold back, dear brother?"

Teddy froze. He couldn't tell if she remembered what he'd done.

A light buzz reverberated through his chest. *Stella.*

Teddy lifted his gaze as she stepped into the bar.

Gone was her leather armor. It had been replaced with a pale aqua dress. The light fabric dipped low, offering a glimpse of the inner curve of her breasts. It was the type of gown that would have made tongues wag in Argaria, but was nothing scandalous in Olney's hot climate. A healthy flush colored Stella's cheeks. Her dark hair was swept up on top of her head, and she'd tucked a crown of flowers around the pile of curls. It was jarring to see her looking so gentle when she'd looked so fierce just hours ago.

Nathan, who was sitting on a barstool next to Rosie, caught Teddy's eye and arched a brow.

Teddy forced his gaze back to Stella, and she was staring right at him, something sad and urgent in her eyes. His mouth went dry. He should—

"*Ted.*" Alexandra's voice cut through the fog in his head.

He snapped his head around to face his sister.

Her mouth was fixed in a crooked smile. "Oh, you are so fucked. You should see your face right now. You look like you just spotted a siren in the middle of the sea and you're ready to bash yourself on the rocks just to get close to her."

Teddy waved a hand. "It's just magic."

Alexandra slouched in her chair, casually sipping her whiskey. "I don't know. You've always had a bit of tension with her. Why is that?"

"Why are you holding back?" he countered.

Alexandra cocked her head, her hazel eyes thoughtful. "Have you ever had a dream that felt so real it made you distrust someone you typically trust implicitly?"

Teddy sipped his whiskey to try to steady the rapid beat of his heart. He needed this to be a passable lie, and if Alexandra heard the skip in his heart's beat, it would only confirm whatever suspicion she already harbored.

"I can't say I've had a dream that convincing, no."

Alexandra rolled her eyes. "I suppose you do lack imagination."

"Tell me what you saw today, Alex."

She grinned at him—the same smile she'd always flashed him whenever he asked that question after they watched a fight, ever since she was a child.

"The Roach has a reputation as a fearsome fighter, but it was Dixon who took the beast down. Just from watching them train, I can tell the Roach has an old injury in his left leg. I'm guessing it's his ankle, but it makes all his attacks on that side more tentative. Dixon is an accurate marksman, but he takes too long to target. Not like your girl." She nodded toward Stella. "She hardly even needs to look. You know, Father told me that he once watched Cecilia shoot every target at the range blindfolded. I asked Stella if she could do that, and do you know what she said?" She paused for effect. "She said if you shoot from here," Alexandra tapped her chest, "your aim will always be true."

Teddy scowled. "That's whimsical."

"No. I think she's right. It's confidence, not whimsy. She meant if you shoot with trust in yourself, you shoot better, and she's right. She's blessed by the goddess of the hunt, so of course she's a great archer, but she also doesn't overthink it."

"And what of her fight?" Teddy asked, trying to sound casual.

Alexandra poured herself more whiskey.

Teddy eyed the bottle. "Is that a good idea?"

"Calm down, *Dad*. This is a bar. Did you think I'd call for a proper tea?"

"You're a princess. You should conduct yourself with some moderation."

She rolled her eyes. "Life is too short for moderation. This fine whiskey is the price of your post-battle report. Now where was I?"

Teddy sighed in exasperation. "Stella."

He felt Stella's eyes on him as if she sensed that they were talking about her.

Alexandra ran her finger over the rim of her glass. "Stella is good. She stays extremely calm even when she's hurt. She knows how to follow through, even when her plan doesn't go as expected. She's adaptable. She and Fionn actually made a great team. They had a natural sense of each other as if they'd been fighting together for a long time."

Teddy sneered. "I don't like him."

"Why? Because he's handsome and talented and Stella picked him over you? How'd you manage to fuck that up?"

Teddy gestured to Stella. "She's willfully defiant. I suggested we work together, and she turned me down. She'd already made a deal with him. Foolish of her. Gods know what a man like that wants from her."

Alexandra waggled her brows. "I can think of a thing or two he might want."

Teddy's stomach plummeted. "What about Fionn?"

"He didn't shoot his bow, so I didn't get a good look at that, but he's fast, talented, smart—though I guess you don't become such an infamous Novumi mercenary without being smart. He understood how to rally her, never lost his head in the fight even though they were both badly wounded. He's excellent with short swords. No notable weaknesses that I could read in that fight except maybe over-confidence. But they did both choose a luck advantage, so it's hard to tell if he was just counting on that to save him."

"And the rest of the field?" Teddy sipped his whiskey, listening intently as Alexandra fed him a report on the surviving competitors.

When she finished, he leaned forward. "So three down in the first challenge."

Alexandra nodded. "Thirteen of you left. I suppose that eliminates any risk of needing to pair up again."

"Not sure it does. It was very distracting and I think—"

"Grace, lovely to see you," Alexandra said loudly, talking over him.

Teddy whipped his head around to find Grace standing behind him. "Gracie, what are you doing here?"

He looked past her. Evan was not in the bar as far as Teddy could see, but he knew enough about the man who'd trained him to be vigilant to know that his Uncle Evan would never let one of his daughters out this late without some sort of backup. Not that she didn't know how to handle herself, but with the Sons of Endros being so bold, she couldn't be too careful. There had to at least be a guard waiting for her outside, if not Evan himself.

"I was hoping we could speak." Grace smiled tentatively at Alexandra. "Privately, if that's okay. I'm sorry to interrupt."

Alexandra waved a hand and swiped the bottle off the table a moment before Teddy could beat her to it. "Of course. I wouldn't want to get in the way."

Grace gently pulled the bottle from her hand and poured a bit into a glass. "Just need to borrow this for a moment." She knocked back a shot and shuddered. "Gods, that's dreadful."

Teddy stared at her, slack-jawed. Grace had never been much of a drinker; when she did drink, she preferred sweeter cocktails or bubble wine. She poured more into her glass.

Alexandra arched a brow and snatched the bottle back. "Well then. Have fun."

Teddy watched her retreat to the bar, where she threw herself onto the stool next to Nathan.

Grace settled into the seat beside Teddy. "She seems in good spirits."

"Of course she is. There are lots of pretty foreign men and women here who are easily held in the thrall of Princess Alexandra."

"Royal attention can be very compelling. I should know," Grace said. She was trying to sound casual, but her posture was too rigid, her hands clasped and white-knuckled.

A group of men on the far side of the room broke into raucous laughter, and Grace jumped.

"Gracie? What's wrong?" Teddy asked.

She touched her hair, a nervous habit that came out on the rare occasions when she didn't know how to approach a subject. "I've been thinking about what happened at the temple. Arden invited me to spend some time with him and I'd like to do that."

Teddy didn't want to have this conversation in a crowded bar, but perhaps that was exactly why Grace had picked this place. She knew him well enough to know he'd need to stay calm and listen, even when he didn't want to.

"I'm competing in the Gauntlet Games for you."

She smiled tightly, her eyes darting around the crowd before coming to rest on Teddy. She leaned in closer and he saw a rare hint of anger in her eyes. "No. You're competing in the Gauntlet Games *for you*. Or maybe to make a point to your father. I explicitly asked you not to take this risk, but you had your heart set on it."

The liquor had gone to Teddy's head, and his thoughts were muddled. He wanted to counter her argument. If he could just think clearly, he was certain he could win her over.

Grace cupped her glass in both hands and stared down into the whiskey. "I tried to talk to you before this trip, when your parents first began bringing up a political marriage. But you didn't listen. I thought maybe going to the temple would make you understand. But it's as if the more you're met with obstacles, the more you want to prove the world wrong. I didn't expect—" Her voice broke.

A cold ache spread through Teddy's chest. "You didn't think we would be paired?" Breathless disbelief wrenched the words from his stupid, drunk mouth.

"I did not expect to be paired with you or anyone else. At first, I thought that the goddess was just messing with Stella, but when she whispered to me after she paired us, she said that life is full of surprises and sometimes our greatest loves hide in plain sight."

"Fuck that," Teddy said. "Fuck the gods and their meddling. She doesn't know you and your heart. She doesn't know the way you are the safe place for me to be myself."

Grace held up her hands to brace against his anger. "It got me thinking that someone could love me for me, and not just for the way I make them feel." She licked her lips. "Lately I have wondered if we serve each other not in growing stronger, but in staying rutted in our ways. I have loved you for so long that it became the singular focus of my days. I think that I've lost myself. I would like the chance to see who I am now."

Teddy's mouth went dry as he fumbled for anything to change her mind. "I can fix this—"

"You can't," Grace said softly. "I love you for always wanting to fix everything. But not every problem can be solved with more effort or perfection on your part. It is a credit to your character that you care enough to change for me, but this is something I need to do."

The words were like a body blow that left him struggling for air. He had to be able to fix it. There had never been a problem he couldn't fix by trying harder—by being better.

But this wasn't fixable. She wanted time and freedom, and he was terrified of losing her.

"I realize the timing is bad and I feel selfish for even asking, but I'm worried I would always wonder if I didn't at least try to see what it would be like to spend time with Arden. I'd like to do it with a clear conscience. Hurting you is not my intention—" Her voice broke again. Grace blinked her eyes and looked at the ceiling.

Panic spread through Teddy's rib cage until it was hard to draw a full breath. He was furious at himself for not noticing. How could he have been so consumed with his own worries that he hadn't realized how unhappy she was?

"I think we've grown too much together and I would like to see who I can be unburdened by the weight of your expectations," she said, her voice a hoarse whisper. "I think it could be good for us. Perhaps this will be clarifying and we will find our way back to each other feeling more confident than ever."

Gods, he was not expecting the way those words would sting. He was bringing her down—the only woman he'd ever loved.

Teddy wiped his sweaty palms on his pants and leaned forward. "Well, it sounds like you've decided what's best for both of us. Or did you just hope I'd offer you absolution for leaving me in such a critical moment?"

He was surprised by the sharpness of his anger. He hadn't meant to sound so cutting. Truthfully, he was envious. Grace could walk away. She didn't feel an inevitable future hurtling toward her—or at least she had found a way to dodge it.

Teddy didn't want to admit he'd spent years praying some secret trapdoor escape from his life would make itself known. He felt a sudden and fierce jealousy that Grace had found one. He had no such luxury, and his denial had come to an end.

"Is that all?" he asked flatly.

She searched his face, her expression awash with confusion and hurt. "I'll leave you to your drink, then."

Grace rose, floated through the bustling crowd, and disappeared along with the hopes he had for his future.

He'd been so focused on Grace that he'd tuned out the world, but now the cacophony of the room rushed back in. The bar felt suddenly too hot and crowded. The stench of ale and sweat was suffocating.

He poured himself more whiskey, splashing a good bit of it on the table in his rush for the relief of a stiff drink to wash away the last few minutes.

Alexandra poked her head out from a nearby booth. She held up a fresh bottle as she returned to her seat across from him.

"You look like you could use another bottle or two." The joviality in her tone was so forced, but he let her fill his glass from the fresh bottle as he tried to rein in his panic.

"I've found there are few problems that can't be fixed by a stiff drink and a pretty girl to flirt with," she said, clinking her glass to his.

She was good enough to ignore the tremble in his hand.

"My world is falling apart, Alex."

But his sister did not look at him with pity. She looked angry. "The worst thing that will happen to you is that you'll be king," Alexandra said. "Forgive me for not feeling bad for your tremendous fortune. You focus on the choice you can't have instead of the many, *many* you do. You do realize that Jalen being an outstanding warrior means that I will probably be shipped off to marry some foreign prince or lord to secure alliances."

"Our mother wouldn't do that," Teddy said.

Alexandra scoffed. "She may not have a choice with this rebel madness."

The thought of her playing wife to some foreign prince or lord was incomprehensible, even if it was likely. What a waste of a warrior. Alexandra was so talented and her withering on some foreign throne was not something he could abide.

She spun her glass in a circle on the wooden table. "It's unbelievable that our father has spent years trying to strip away his own power and hand it back to the people, and they still want to throw it in his face. Their arguments don't even make sense. No one is making them worship any other gods, and yet they're the ones trying to force their insane Endros doctrine on everyone else. They insist on a return to *traditional* values, but they mean a world at war where only the wealthiest people thrive—where women are property who should only ever aspire toward being wives and mothers. They see the common folk being lifted out of poverty and offered the same opportunities as a threat instead of a good thing. It's unbelievable how delusional they are and how quickly they have been able to spread panic instead of seeing reason."

"This is part of ruling, Alex," Teddy said. "Politics is more than just doing what's best. It's about getting people to buy in to what you're doing. People hate change and, while I loathe their methods and their messaging, the Sons of Endros have done a spectacular job of reinforcing the idea that they shouldn't have to change at all."

"At least you get to rule over the crazies," she said, taking a long gulp of whiskey.

"You think I want to be king, Alex?" The words would not stop coming. He'd had too much to drink and that combined with Grace's rejection had left him feeling there was nothing to lose and no reason to perform anymore. "You think this is fun for me? To always be an impeccable version of myself? To not ever have a chance to be more than just what is expected of me? It's so easy for you to judge, but you are the youngest and a woman. The expectations for you are just not the same at all. You wouldn't be so keen to rule if you understood the personal costs."

For a moment, his sister appraised him with quiet shock. Fuck, he was drunk. He had not been drunk in public. Ever.

Alexandra stood. "Well, *Your Grace*, I suppose I'll never get the chance to understand. I'll leave you to your pity party."

She disappeared into the crowd without another word.

Teddy sat at the table for several moments, barely even registering the loud music and dancing around him, and then stood with a start, eager to get back to the castle and away from the crowd. He took a step away from the table and the world tilted. He caught his hand on the booth beside him until it righted. This was bad. He was very drunk.

He tossed some coins onto the table and pulled on his cloak, tugging the hood up to shadow his face. It took every bit of concentration to cross the room and dodge all the dancing couples and barmaids without falling. Finally, he reached the door and pressed into the cool night air. The worst was over, and he'd be back at the castle and away from the public in no time.

15

STELLA

The moment Stella stepped out of the bar and into the bustling street, she felt uncertain about her choice to follow Teddy. She'd left Rosie inside with Alexandra and Leo. While she was sure that they could handle fending off Nathan, she didn't like that she wasn't there to deflect his sudden and inexplicable interest in her sister.

It had to be a bet. She'd known Nathan Aiger since they were teenagers and Teddy started bringing him to Olney for the Solstice Festival. Nathan didn't do genuine interest.

It was part of the reason Stella had always tolerated him, despite his lousy choice of best friend. Nathan was harmless and he would be sure that Leo got Rosie home safe. That was all Stella cared about.

Stella turned to her right and hesitated, straining to hear footsteps over the muffled music from the bar behind her. She should just go back inside and let the prince brood. But Teddy had been a little unsteady on his feet. Perhaps no one else would notice. He held it together so well, but she sensed the fuzziness in their bond.

She looked both ways, scanning the damp cobblestones of the street. The rain had stopped, but the humidity was just as wretched as it had been all day.

"Where did he disappear to so quickly?" she grumbled.

A thread of panic shot through her. Perhaps someone else had noticed and already made off with him. She drew up the memory of watching him leave the bar and scanned it for anyone suspicious. There were a few people who bowed or curtseyed when he walked by, despite his waving hand dismissing the gesture as unnecessary. No one had seemed especially interested, but that didn't mean someone hadn't been waiting for him outside.

She closed her eyes and pressed her palm to her chest the way she'd seen her mother do when they were at the market and she was searching for Rainer. Cecilia had described it as tugging on a rope and waiting for a tug on the other side, or feeling a slight buzz across the bond whenever she got close.

Stella imagined it like a rope disappearing into oblivion. She tugged on it, but nothing happened. With a sigh, she started down the street until she felt a sudden pleasant hum in her chest. Torch-lights reflected off the puddles between the cobbled ground, making the night feel more magical and sparkling, though Stella wasn't usually allowed out so late in the evenings, so perhaps Olney City always looked so whimsical when the evening torches were lit.

The large flames had sparkling crystal clusters at their center and were spelled to ensure that the city stayed well-lit through the night and no loose embers would escape the magical fire, even on the windiest nights. In the morning, the flames died, and the crystal center charged all day in the glow of the sun, so they were ready to burn through the night again. On cloudy days, the torches sometimes needed to be recharged by fire witches. Since fire was her strongest affinity, Stella was well-read on the spellwork and ingredients used to make the torches work.

Last year's Gauntlet Games had been plagued by rain and Stella had gone through town each day refilling the torches with her magic. Normally, it wouldn't be a big deal for a few parts of the city to be darker. But during the Games, when so many people were in town just looking for a fight, the huntmaster felt it was best to ensure there were no dark corners for anyone to sneak off to fight in.

Stella paused in front of a bakery, took a few more steps, and the hum came again, stronger. She kept going a few tentative steps at a time until the buzz was so strong it sent a shiver through her body.

Teddy's voice cut through the humid night. "Godsdamnit."

She followed the sound to the alley beside the bakery and paused. Teddy was speaking emphatically to someone she couldn't see. She was torn between stepping closer to hear what he was saying and running before he saw her.

Torchlights from the street at the other end of the alley wreathed him in a golden glow.

"Get it the fuck together," he whispered, his voice low and vicious.

Stella was eternally a victim of her curiosity. She edged closer, straining to see who he was speaking to, but when she cleared the corner, there was no one else in the alley.

He was talking to himself.

She stifled a laugh at the drunk prince giving himself a pep talk to walk home. "Teddy?"

He whipped his head around, his expression morphing from confusion to annoyance. "Of course you're here. You're everywhere. No escaping you—like a fucking haunting." He waved his arms in a wide, graceless circle.

"Are you drunk, *Your Grace*?"

It was a cruel jab to use his title like that when he was clearly drunk, but she was as angry at him for not holding on to Grace as she was at Grace for finally realizing Arden's potential when Stella had loved him for so long.

Teddy stared at her for a long moment and a strange grief slid into her chest. It took her a moment to realize it was his.

"Do you think they'll be happy together?" he asked.

The vulnerability on his face unnerved her. Stella had no right to it. Whatever their bond did that made them both feel this way was uncomfortable, and he was drunk on top of it. Sober Teddy would never ask her something like that.

She licked her lips, uncertain why her mouth was suddenly so dry. "I think it's easier to be idealistic about a possibility. Grace and

Arden will have to see if they can reckon with the reality of a long-term commitment. I think it's natural to stare down your future and feel like running. Haven't we all felt the tug of oblivion from time to time?"

When she met Teddy's gaze, she only found confusion. "No, Stella. Can't say I have."

She cocked her head. "You've never stood at the top of a cliff and thought for just a second about jumping into the sea? You've never wanted to take a swing at someone bigger just to see what would happen? You've never been close to someone and thought about kissing them?"

He stared at her, and then his gaze almost imperceptibly dropped to her lips before he looked away. "I guess I know what you mean. I've just never been able to indulge that."

They began to walk, and Teddy stumbled. Stella caught his arm, but he had already righted himself.

"Why?" she asked.

"Because the heir to the throne must be impeccable all the time. Never reckless. Never temperamental. And never drunk in public."

"I suppose two out of three isn't bad," Stella teased. "Care to share why you're breaking your sacred, boring rules?"

"I don't want her to feel stuck with me. But what if it's easier to be with him? Arden has always been so easy-going. What if she likes him better? I can't bear to say no to her, but I also hate feeling like I'm losing the only woman I'd ever loved. Worse, I feel like I've done an awful job loving her. How can I be surrounded by people so wonderful and supportive and yet I have missed the mark with the one person I most wanted to please? I..." He trailed off, staring down at his boots.

Stella was torn between shock and relief. He had always been stoic, but this version of him was disarming. He had never seemed capable of any type of softness, but perhaps this was the version of him that had captured Grace.

The tension released from her shoulders. It was nice to talk to someone who understood her plight, even if Teddy was a spoiled, uptight prince.

Stella didn't want Grace and Arden to spend time together, but since they'd been bonded, Stella couldn't get over the persistent fear that, if they didn't see this through, she would always worry that Arden was secretly pining for Grace. As painful as the thought of them spending time together was, she knew her parents' story, how they'd needed the clarity of distance. Perhaps that was exactly what Arden needed, too.

"Let's get you safely back to the castle," Stella said. She wrapped an arm around Teddy's waist, trying to ignore the citrus and cedar scent of him. "At least she spoke to you about it," she whispered bitterly. "At least she checked on you after the challenge. Gods, at least she checked on *me*."

Teddy drew away. "Your injury. I forgot." He narrowed his eyes at her stomach as if the healed wound would start bleeding again at his remembrance.

"I'm fine," she said. "Just sore."

He nodded, holding her gaze longer than he ever did sober. "Alex said you were good. She said you shoot from the heart, so your aim is always true." He shook his head. "Arden didn't check on you? At all?"

Stella shrugged casually. "He's been taking over a lot of new responsibilities. He sent flowers."

"Your favorite flowers?" Teddy asked.

Stella stared at him. "What?"

"Did he send your *favorite* flowers? Does he even *know* what your favorite flowers are?"

The cruel jab was a relief. This was the Teddy she knew, and it was better to be back in familiar territory. She'd had all she could take for one day.

"Why do you care what flowers he sent me?"

"I care because if you're risking your life for someone's affection, I think you deserve for them to at least know you," Teddy said.

"Don't pretend to care and don't judge him. You don't know what we have."

Teddy smirked in an annoying, self-satisfied way. "But I know he should have sent you daisies."

Stella almost stumbled. "How do you know that?"

He didn't meet her eye as he spoke. "Your father used to bring you bunches of them from the royal gardens when you were homesick over the winter holidays."

"That's quite a memory you have."

"A prince and warrior must be observant."

Stella struggled to swallow the lump in her throat. Not all princes, it seemed.

Teddy finally looked at her and arched a brow.

She didn't like his prodding. Didn't like that it felt as if he could see how she'd waited in front of the garden windows, certain Arden would appear at any moment.

"He will come," she'd said to Rosie. And Rosie had smiled because she was patient and kind and thought the best of everyone.

Though her sister's optimism often drove Stella mad, she was grateful for it then.

Stella shoved the memory out of her head and glared at Teddy. "He will show up. He always does, in time."

"But should you have to wait?"

"Does Grace wait for you?" She wanted so badly to deflect away from this. She hadn't had much to drink because of the blood loss and because she was already feeling bad enough about herself without adding alcohol. Now she wished for the oblivion of a tall glass of whiskey.

Teddy smirked. "Not anymore, but she did. And I waited for her. She takes forever to get ready."

Stella laughed. That was the truth. She'd never met anyone as meticulous about her appearance as Grace.

"It should be that way. Compromise means you both have to wait sometimes," Teddy said.

Stella tried to think of a time when Arden had waited for her, but he had so many more demands on his time than she did. It never felt fair to waste his time. It wasn't difficult to make herself available when she had so little else going on.

Her anger flared at Teddy's scrutiny. "You don't know what Arden is to me. I may tease you, but I would never doubt your devotion to Grace. I've seen it enough."

His face fell. "But I guess you'd doubt her devotion to me."

Stella sighed. "I wouldn't have before today. She came to speak with me."

Teddy whipped his head around to look at her and nearly fell over. Stella pulled his arm over her shoulder and wrapped hers around his waist.

"What did she say to you?" he asked.

"I imagine about the same thing she said to you that has you this drunk."

"I'm not drunk. I'm just not sober, strictly speaking."

Stella laughed. "Honestly, this version of you is preferable. Perhaps we should make this your new baseline."

He yanked out of her grip. "This is none of your business. How did you even find me?"

Stella held her hands up. "I'm sorry. For what it's worth, I was as shocked as you seem to be. I didn't have the heart to say no to her either."

Teddy looked away and ran a hand through his hair, leaving the dark strands sticking out in all directions.

"I wish I'd never gone to the temple that night," Stella said. "Regardless of what happens with them. We need this heart bond severed before the next challenge."

Teddy nodded. "Finally, we agree on something. I know this preliminary bond will wear off in a few weeks if we don't fortify it, but I don't think I can handle another challenge with it. It almost cost me the match."

"And you almost cost me the same," she said. "It's settled. The second challenge is in four days, and we need to go see Desiree and get her to stop messing with us." She nodded toward Olney Castle in the distance. "Shall we?"

"I can see myself home," he said.

"I'm sure you can, but I'll feel better if I see you get there safely myself." She glanced down a nearby alley. She'd been ignoring the creeping feeling of being watched, but now the small hairs on the back of her neck lifted.

Teddy gave a petulant roll of his eyes, but he held out his arm, and she threaded her hand through.

She pushed the pace as they walked in silence, the eerie feeling chasing her even as they approached the main street leading down to Olney Castle's courtyard. A soft rush of spirit whispers filled the air.

It took Stella a moment to realize what they were. She'd only heard them a few times when helping in the healing clinic with patients who were close to passing.

"Death whispers." She met Teddy's wide eyes. "Teddy, I—"

A voice like a knife scraped across a whetstone came from the dark alley several paces ahead of them. "Well, if it isn't the goddess-blessed children of our fearless king and the great Rainer McKay. You really struggled today, *Your Grace.*"

Rett Roachelle stepped from the shadows into the torchlight with a smug grin on his face. This was the man Teddy had called "The Roach," and with the way he skittered from a dark alley, the nickname felt appropriate. His lackeys, Dixon, Christophe, and Drew, appeared in formation behind him.

Stella felt a strange protectiveness. She was the only one who could use Teddy's title as a barb. Their history dictated that. The Roach using it felt wrong and entirely unearned.

Teddy straightened and leveled a glare at Rett. "Looking to go a round on even footing instead of when you have high ground and a long-range weapon?"

The Roach scoffed. "I imagine it wouldn't go so well for you right now."

"Oh, I don't know. I think I'd put my money on His Grace even a few drinks in," Stella said.

"Your father may be a legend, Savero, but you are not him. Not by a long shot," Rett said.

Stella watched Teddy's jaw twitch out of the corner of her eye. She'd always noticed how he looked up to his father. Much as he hated her, Stella imagined she was the only person who could understand what it felt like to try to follow in some very large footsteps. King Xander was as charming and at ease in public as Teddy was stiff and broody. If anyone knew what it was like to fall short of their family's folklore, it was Stella.

"And you, Lady McKay? Going to defend his honor?" Rett taunted. "Wouldn't mind getting down and dirty with you. It would be an honor. Or is that a privilege only reserved for princes? I hear you aim high."

Stella was not an especially violent person—she'd never even seriously injured someone—but the entitled, menacing look in Rett Roachelle's eyes made her feel violent. She imagined grabbing the dagger on her thigh and jamming it into his groin. She imagined how easy it would be to rip the air from his lungs and leave him gasping on the ground. She wouldn't do it because it would disqualify her from the competition, but it was satisfying to think about what kind of sound he would make.

It wasn't a good sign that he knew about her involvement with Arden. Only her mother, her siblings, Kate, and she supposed Teddy and Grace knew. But if people realized that they could hurt her to get to Arden, he'd be in danger.

The death whispers swelled louder and more threatening. The sound of them set Stella's teeth on edge. She'd never heard them like this. Despite the fear that was slowly turning her insides cold, she forced herself to focus on one specific spirit.

Stella couldn't see them the way her mother could, but she could hear them and sometimes she caught flickers of them out of the corner of her eye. She narrowed her gaze on one and smiled.

"What are you smirking at?" Christophe asked.

"Just a ghost over your right shoulder," Stella said, winking at him.

Teddy went rigid beside her, but Christophe and the other men all twisted as if they'd be able to see it.

"Can she even see them?" Rett asked, a hint of panic in his previously confident gaze.

Dixon shrugged. "Kingdom lore says that her mother could. I don't know."

Stella gave them her fakest smile. "Can we pass now, gentlemen? Teddy and I have a few more bars to hit before closing time."

Rett wrinkled his nose. "A lady should be home at this hour."

"The lady would be if you would get out of her way," Stella countered.

Christophe sneered at her. "If she was my woman, I'd slap some sense into her."

Stella cocked her head. "If I was your woman, I'd slap some sense into myself. Can't imagine the sheer amount of brain damage that would be required for me to end up in such a dire circumstance."

Dixon chuckled, ignoring the loathing glare Christophe sent his way.

The louder and more urgent the death whispers became, the more Stella's magic reared up, itching for something to burn.

"You're pathetic and not even that pretty for someone with so much magic in her blood," Christophe grumbled.

Stella pressed a hand to her heart in faux pain. "I'll try to come to terms with the disappointment that you thought I was the type to care what you think. Now *move* or I will move you. If you get hurt doing something dumb out here, the healers won't heal you from non-tournament-related injuries."

A creepy smirk played over Rett's rat-like face. "Don't you want to play, Lady McKay?" He nodded to Drew. "Grab her. I want to have a private chat with her down that alley."

Drew stayed put. "Isn't she—you know—a goddess? What if she curses me or something?"

Christophe started toward her.

Rage warmed Stella's chest and she could feel Teddy's as well, its distinct signature mixing with hers.

Stella waved her fingers at Christophe as if casting a spell, and he flinched. "What's the matter, Christophe? Afraid of a woman who can hit back?"

Stella was going to light the night on fire, but she didn't want to hurt Teddy. She leaned close enough that only Teddy would hear her. "Can you wield fire?"

Teddy gave her an indignant side-eye. "Of course."

"Good. Do it now."

Teddy snapped and, mercifully, fire sparked at his fingertips. Summoning fire would make him temporarily immune to burns.

She let her magic rise beneath her skin. The fever spread through her blood. Sweat beaded on her forehead and lower back.

"Going to burn us up, prince?" Christophe taunted as he stepped closer.

"I know you've committed, but I hope you'll reconsider. It would be very unwise to continue with this plan. Don't touch me or you'll be very sorry," Stella said.

Drew charged at them and grabbed Stella's arm. She tried to wrench away, so he'd have to use both hands and grip her tighter. Once he had a firm grip with both hands, she crossed her arms and fastened her hands around his. Then, she summoned as much heat as she could.

Drew frowned. "What is she do—"

She watched the realization dawn on him and he felt the unnatural warmth of her skin. It only took a split second before he started trying to pull his hands away. She let them burn, ignoring the smell of burning flesh until she saw the panic in his eyes and felt his palms blister.

Drew bellowed a pained, inhuman sound. Finally, Stella let him go.

He stumbled back, waving his blistering palms. "You can't do that?"

"Do what? I was just standing there when you grabbed me without permission. If you were burned by my fever, that's hardly my fault. I did warn you not to touch me," Stella said.

Rett glared at her. "We'll tell the Games officials."

"Please do. I'd love to hear what they have to say about your activities away from the arena," Stella said. "Have a nice evening, boys."

She wove her arm through Teddy's like he was walking her home and not the other way around.

Dixon stepped out of her way as she walked by. Stella paused and listened to the soft hum of spirits. She locked eyes with Dixon.

"Your Grandma Nina is *so* disappointed at the lot you've fallen in with. Says she wouldn't be making you any cherry tartlets with this kind of behavior."

Dixon's mouth fell open.

Something like respect hit her in the chest. *Teddy's* respect. It was thrilling.

They continued down the street and it took every bit of Stella's will not to turn back and make sure the Roach wasn't following them. Her adrenaline was so high that she couldn't hear anything but the wild beat of her heart in her ears as her skin cooled.

After walking a few blocks in silence, Teddy leaned in close. "We're alone. Wouldn't want to run into you on a dark street corner."

Stella laughed. "Thank you, Your Grace. Wouldn't want to try to go shot for shot with you at a bar."

He laughed, and it softened his whole face. She couldn't ever remember seeing him laugh so genuinely at something, and the effect was mesmerizing. He looked so handsome when he smiled like that.

Stella cleared her throat, searching her mind for anything to distract from unwelcome thoughts about how good-looking her nemesis was. "So tomorrow afternoon? The Temple of Desiree?" she said. "I know Desiree is usually only in residence in the evenings other than on moon ritual nights, so it's probably best that we plan to get there after dark. We can have her break the bond. We'll stay the night in the guest suites, and it will give us time to get back before the next challenge."

They approached the castle gates and the hunters outside the courtyard straightened from where they leaned against the wall, talking to each other.

"Good evening, gentlemen," Stella said. "I hope you don't mind, but I insisted Prince Teddy celebrate our victories today, and being the honorable man that he is, he drank both our servings of bubble wine to keep me from being hungover tomorrow. That said, he's a bit in his cups right now, so if one of you would be so kind as to see him to his room."

She savored Teddy's glare, thrilled for their relationship to return to its baseline of mild contempt.

The guards dropped into panicked, exaggerated bows.

"Your Grace," they said in solemn chorus.

"Up you go," Stella said, patting Teddy's ass as he took the first step.

He scowled at her over his shoulder. "Enjoy your vigil."

It took her a moment to realize what he meant, but when she did, all her previous loathing returned. She spun, ready to stalk away, praying that Arden would be waiting for her when she got home so she could shove that satisfaction in Teddy's face when she saw him in the morning.

A shrill scream sliced through the night. Stella froze. Another scream rang out.

Stella didn't think; she just ran toward the sound.

"Stella, don't run toward the fucking danger!" Teddy shouted, lumbering after her with an unsteady gait.

Stella had assumed the death whispers had faded because she'd put Rett and his friends in their place, but now she wondered if she'd been hearing them for a different reason entirely.

She sprinted toward the frenzied screaming, keeping the castle courtyard walls to her right, her injured side protesting the exertion the whole way. She finally reached the end of the wall, turned, and saw a crowd gathered near the western courtyard gates. The screaming had stopped, transformed into muffled sobbing.

Stella slowed her pace as several hunters shepherded the crowd away from someone slumped against the outer courtyard wall. She pushed her way to the front of the group. A panting Teddy came to a stop next to her.

"Are you out of your mind? You could have—" Teddy stopped talking when he saw the reason for the commotion.

One of their fellow competitors, Victor Schwoebleman, was propped against the castle wall, his throat slit from ear to ear. His elegantly embroidered yellow tunic was drenched in blood that looked almost black in the dim light. Little rivers of red flowed between the cobblestones. It had happened right there outside the palace walls.

Several hunters circled the body, looking at the bloody mess. Several more were searching nearby alleyways and one stood holding a weeping woman. The rest were gathered around a hunter holding a torch, staring up at a still-dripping bloody painting above the body. A ring of fire around the open jaws of a viper—the symbol of the Sons of Endros.

Beneath it were the words *"Strength Above All."* Their nonsensical motto was sprinkled in propaganda all over town, but it was different to see the words in blood.

Stella shoved the hunter aside and stepped closer, squatting so she could see better.

A dagger was jammed into Victor's chest. It had been used to pin a piece of parchment there, but the shadow of the hunter's body made it too dark to read it.

Stella snapped her fingers and summoned fire. The hunters halted their movements as if expecting her to light the body, but they stilled when they saw the note.

Recognize the Sons of Endros as a part of the ruling body of Olney and Argaria immediately. Give us a seat at the royal table of advisory. Our demands will no longer be ignored. You have until sundown the night before the next challenge to meet our demands or we'll kill the Gauntlet Games competitors one by one, until there's no one left to play in your petty war games.

– SOE

The words chilled Stella. Victor Schwoebleman was a talented Olney hunter. He'd survived the brutal first challenge only to be made a macabre centerpiece in a threat from the Sons of Endros.

She'd been afraid earlier today, fighting for her life in that pit. But at least in the pit, she could see the threat.

"Stella." Teddy's voice broke her trance.

She rose to her feet and met his eyes. He looked almost concerned. But then she remembered what he'd said before they'd found the body, and she didn't want his pity.

"Yes, Your Grace?" she asked, intentionally loud.

The closest hunter captain took notice and immediately stepped up to Teddy's side. "Your Grace, you should really be inside at this hour. It's clearly not safe in the streets this evening, especially for you."

"I can handle myself," Teddy grumbled.

Stella could tell he was trying to keep it together, but the hunter was close enough to smell the booze on him, so it wouldn't be terribly convincing for someone with enhanced senses.

Teddy grabbed Stella's arm as she made to push by him. "Where are you going? You're in shock."

"I'm fine, and like you said, I'm off to begin my vigil," she snapped.

She took off at a brisk walk, but by the time she rounded the bend in the courtyard wall, she began to run again.

Stella prayed that Leo and Nathan had taken Rosie home before the commotion broke out. The whole sprint home, her mind bounced between the message from the Sons of Endros and Teddy's words. She should not have felt shocked by his cruelty after she'd been so kind to him in the face of his vulnerability.

As the businesses and apartment houses of the city gave way to larger sprawling estates, Stella slowed to a brisk walk. She labored to catch her breath, wanting to blame the stitch in her side on the cramp and not the fact that she felt abandoned by one prince and wounded by another.

As soon as she reached her family's estate, she dashed through the front door and up the stairs. Her pain faded when she saw Rosie, already sprawled out asleep in her bed.

A creak in the hallway startled her, and she paused. She turned to see Leo leaning against the doorframe of his room.

"What's wrong?" he whispered.

"Is everyone asleep?" she asked.

"I think so. Mama might still be up reading."

She nodded. "Everything's fine. I'll tell you about it tomorrow."

He hesitated a moment, then nodded. "You did well today, but you could tell me if something was wrong."

"Just a long day."

The lie came with alarming ease. The harder lie would be the one she had to tell herself in order to get to sleep: *Everything will be less scary in the light of day.*

16

STELLA

Arden was not waiting for Stella when she woke up the next morning, or after she'd braided her hair and prepped for her swim.

In the cool seawater, she tried to avenge herself against the growing anxiety in her chest with every stroke of her arms.

Arden didn't love her anymore. Arden didn't even care that she'd been hurt. Arden didn't know what her favorite flower was.

It couldn't be true. If he didn't know her favorite flower, then why had he brought her daisies when he first started walking with her in the mornings? But ever since Teddy had said it, Stella could not shake the fear that it might be true.

Fuck Teddy Savero. She would not have some bitter prince spreading poison in her mind.

Each twist of her body through the water was agony, her side still savagely sore from the already healed wound. Though her goddess bloodline meant she healed faster than normal people, even without actively using her magic, it didn't prevent her from feeling pain. The fact that it still hurt so badly and that she had needed help from a skilled healer was a clear sign of just how close she'd come to dying.

On her walk home from the beach, the visual she'd been trying to avoid all morning refused to stay buried any longer: Victor Schwoebleman's bloody body. She wondered about the timing and if Rett and his friends could have had enough time to kill Victor after seeing her and Teddy. She replayed the memory in her head of when the death whispers had started and peaked, but she'd been burning Drew's hands when they were loudest.

She shivered as she remembered the feeling of being watched. The Sons of Endros could have been lying in wait for her. Walking Teddy home might have saved them both. Gods, running into the Roach and his friends may have protected them.

Walking in the front door of the McKay Estate, Stella entered the living room and paused in front of the wall of portraits. Her favorites were the one of Cecilia standing next to her huntmaster father with a bow in her hands, one from Rainer and Cecilia's wedding with her mother clad in a dress that looked like the night sky at dusk, and her favorite, a picture of a young Cecilia surrounded in a swirl of color, painted by the late Rosalee Reznik, Stella's grandmother.

Stella closed her eyes and tried to imagine a portrait of her and Arden there next to the rest. She held the vision in her head as if she could make it happen with her will alone. What was a spell if not something woven from vision and words and will? She *would* make it happen.

She dashed upstairs and washed the salt water from her skin and hair with new resolve. Then, she ravenously ate the breakfast Rosie brought to her room. Healing was hungry work and she'd used her magic to fend off Rett and his friends.

Rosie watched her in quiet assessment from where she was sprawled on Stella's bed, her fingers never leaving the silk thread and dried flowers in her lap. Her sister was always creating—always so visionary and happy in her solitude.

"Do you want me to bring you something else?" Rosie asked. "I know Papa made more. I'm almost finished with this string." She knotted another flower into the line and then held it up.

"What's it going to be?" Stella asked.

Rosie shrugged and smiled, a far-off look in her eye.

For a moment, she looked like her mother, Rosa. Stella was so young when Rosie's mother lived with them that it was hard to remember much, but she remembered little things like the way Rosa's eyes sparkled when she smiled and the way she always had paint on her hands and fingernails and a glow about her when she started a new project.

"You look like your mom when you talk about your art," Stella said.

Rosie's cheeks pinked. "Really?"

Stella nodded. "I never thought about it before because I don't have my own full memories of her, just the ones Mama has shared with you. But there are these little things, faint moments that are mine. She would light up like you do when you're thinking about what you're working on."

Rosie smiled and her eyes sparkled. Stella felt nothing but guilt for ever making her feel like their blood mattered. Love ran so much deeper.

"You never talk about her," Rosie said.

"I don't like to because I don't like to remind you—"

"That she's dead?" Rosie smiled sadly. "I know she's gone and sometimes I feel so guilty that she had to die so I could be here. But I always want to remember her."

Cecilia had met Rosa at the healer's clinic when she was coming in for prenatal visits. The two became fast friends because Rosa's husband was a fisherman and she always scheduled the last appointment of the day in the hope he'd be able to come with her. He was rarely able to make it, which meant that Rosa was left with three-year-old Stella and Leo to entertain her.

When her husband was lost to a storm a few months later, Rosa was a pregnant widow with very little money to her name. Cecilia and Rainer had taken her in and let her stay in the family's seaside cottage.

In Stella's memory, it was a strange time because they moved from the cottage where she'd spent her childhood to the family estate. It seemed massive in comparison to the tiny house where she'd been born. But every day, Cecilia would take Leo and Stella to visit Rosa and they would get to see what she was working on.

"We spent a lot of afternoons with her. I remember she used to sneak me and Leo extra biscuits."

Rosie laughed. "So you always had a sweet tooth like Mama."

"Of course. I was so confused after she passed and you came to live with us and Mama used to take us down to the cottage to sit with you and it felt so empty without her. I think she'd love what you've done with it. It feels alive again. You've really made it your own," Stella said.

Rosie preened. "I think she'd like it too." She cocked her head and eyed Stella. "You're being suspiciously nice. You don't have to feel bad about what you said the other day. You already apologized and I know you only said it because you were angry. You've always had a temper but I know you don't mean it."

Guilt settled in Stella's stomach. "Fine. Would you prefer to talk about Nathan Aiger?"

A blush stole up Rosie's neck and cheeks. "There's nothing to talk about. You don't need to protect me, Stella. I've known Nathan a while, too. I know better than to get attached. It was just nice to have attention. It made me feel pretty."

Stella frowned. "You *are* pretty. Beautiful, really. If you weren't, Leo wouldn't hover so much."

Rosie smiled brilliantly and jumped to her feet. "I should go get these strung up." She hesitated. "Will you be okay? I know last night was upsetting, and you were hoping to see Arden."

Stella waved a hand. "It's fine. I'm sure he has a good reason for being absent."

Rosie frowned and, though she was much too kind to say it, Stella could practically hear her unspoken *"Doesn't he always?"*

Rosie had always been Stella's confidant in all things romantic and whimsical. She idolized their parents' relationship as much as Stella did, but she clearly had patience that Stella lacked.

"I know you're not sold on him, Rosie, but it's like Mama says. There are things you can only see when you're inside the relationship. No one knows the quiet things that happen away from prying eyes," Stella said.

Rosie waggled her eyebrows, her mouth drawn in a teasing smile. "I bet they don't. Though I wonder how quiet they are."

Stella chucked a pillow at her sister. "Rosalee Maura McKay, was that a sex joke?"

Rosie deflected the pillow and grinned. Her cheeks were blazing, and she held up her hands in surrender. "All right, all right! I'm leaving before you ruin my hours of work."

She gathered her flowers and thread and skipped out of the room, her pale blue dress billowing around her as she went.

Finally alone, Stella lay back in her bed, stared at the ceiling, and let the dread she'd been shoving down roll over her. Had there been an inquiry into Victor's murder yet? Had they apprehended the men responsible?

It must have been chaotic. It would be impossible for Arden to get away now, but at least the upheaval might scare off his foreign fiancée and her family.

A light tap on the open door startled Stella from her daze.

Her father leaned against the doorframe. "Hey, Stell-bell? Why is the prince of Olney in our living room with two dozen roses?"

Cecilia appeared at his shoulder. "Oh? Are they white? Perhaps he murdered a friend of hers and thought some flowers an appropriate apology."

Rainer rolled his eyes. "I was out of my mind, Cecilia. Flowers seemed a safe starting place. Will I never live it down?"

Her mother just laughed heartily as her father rubbed a hand down his face. They were always like this—full of quick, intimate teasing for which no one else had context.

Gods, Stella wanted that. She wanted a person with whom she could communicate only a few words and make them laugh that way.

Stella shot up in bed and smoothed her dress. "Is there something suspicious about a man bringing me flowers?"

"There's something suspicious about a prince who shows up with two dozen roses from the queen's garden," Rainer said, crossing his arms.

Her mother laughed loudly. "Oh, is that what you're worried about? History repeating itself?"

Rainer pinned her with a glare. "You should be worried about it, too."

"Oh, stop. There's no need for anyone to worry. I already had a nice talk with him," Cecilia said in a way that very much made the word *talk* sound like a threat.

Stella pushed past her parents and took the stairs two at a time. Arden stood in the living room, looking handsome and exhausted. His dark hair was mussed, his eyes shadowed in circles, and there was a deep crease in his brow as he looked her over. The sunlight streaming through the windows to the garden made his golden-brown skin luminous.

Seeing him standing in her living room made Stella feel like she would explode with either relief or tears. Relief won.

"You're in my house," she said, still not quite believing it.

He thrust the roses toward her and finally smiled. "I am. Got a talking-to from your mother." He read the panic in her eyes immediately. "She was fine," he said. "Nothing I wouldn't expect from the mother of a woman I'm courting."

Stella stilled, looking from Arden to the roses and back again. "What about Princess Eleria?"

"Her parents have dissolved the betrothal contract, at least for the time being. They are staying in town and could change their minds, but for now, it's on hold. My father thinks that was the entire point of that little stunt last—"

Stella shot her hand out to press a finger to his lips. She shook her head and mouthed, "*They don't know*," nodding toward the other room where she could sense her parents lurking.

"They will soon," Arden countered.

"Just give me a few hours of peace."

"That's part of why I'm here, though."

Stella's stomach bottomed out. "You're not here to check on me?"

Arden took the flowers from her, placed them on the table, and gestured for her to sit on the couch. He sat beside her and took her hands in his.

"I'm here because I was worried sick all day yesterday and all night. I didn't sleep at all from worrying for you, which was only made worse when we were woken at that ungodly hour and told that you had seen the body and the message. Stella, I—" His voice broke, and he placed her hand over his heart. "I'm here because of the inquiry but also because when I saw you bleeding in that pit, fighting that beast, I could not breathe. I almost passed out. Issa pinched me at one point because I'd been holding my breath and my face had gone purple. I hate that you're in the Gauntlet Games and I hate that it's my fault, and now, with the Sons, you have even more of a target on your back."

Stella was so moved by his sincerity. He'd never been so vulnerable with her. Charming, yes. Funny, absolutely. But it was rare that he let her see him so serious.

"Does she know about us? Your sister?" Stella asked.

Arden shrugged a shoulder. "I think she suspects. And I've been feeling so guilty about you entering to save me from this wedding."

"It's not your fault—any of this. You didn't know they were going to betroth you to that princess," Stella assured him. "You thought we would announce our relationship and your parents would be pleased, just like I did. It's just a bump in the road—this contest and the wretched Sons of Endros making a mess of everything."

"I felt so confident in you before the Games started, but seeing you hurt terrifies me," Arden said breathlessly. "With Endros as the gamemaker and you and Teddy in the Games and the Sons of Endros literally murdering contestants, I—" His voice cracked. "I'm not worth this kind of risk. I wish I could get you out of this."

Stella frowned at him. It was sweet that he wanted to protect her, but she needed to win the favor so that she and Arden could have an undeniable gods-blessed union. She hated to stir things up when he was trying to protect her, but she had to say it.

"I don't want out."

Arden waved a hand. "I know. But I don't know if I can watch another challenge like that, Stella. I've done everything so that you can at least know your options. I asked my parents if there was a way and I went through some old books in the library—"

"You went through books?" Stella asked, stunned.

Arden winced. "I had the royal scholars pull the original Games records, and I spoke to my father since he was there with your parents at the creation. But no luck. The only way out is through."

"So why are you here?" she asked.

"There's an inquiry today at the castle. I thought it would be a good time to formally announce our courtship. There will be lots of important people around, and that way, if my parents bring up the betrothal again, they will already know about you and I won't have to keep you a secret. It's what I should have done from the beginning. I just didn't want this beautiful private thing between us to be ruined by all these outside opinions."

Stella knew what he meant. He was the prince of Olney, and she would have been under tremendous scrutiny. While it had its downsides, she had liked the intimacy of having something private, away from the world.

She was so relieved and overwhelmed to finally have what she wanted that it took a moment for the practicality of it to hit her. "Arden, we can't do that."

He smiled like he thought she was joking. "What? Why?"

Stella lowered her voice to a whisper. "Because it will put even more of a target on my back than I already have. I have an uncontrollable heart bond with Teddy that almost took me out in the first challenge, and my mother killed Endros back when he was a god living in this realm. If the Sons of Endros realize they can hurt or threaten me to get a seat on your father's royal advisory committee, it will only make things worse. Rett Roachelle and his friends already know about us somehow. I denied it, but I don't need it to spread farther than that. The Sons of Endros were able to kill a man right outside the castle walls. They are bold and looking for any advantage. I know this is what I've been asking you to do for months, but this could not be worse timing."

She watched the realization settle over him. He slumped into his seat. "I'm sorry. I didn't think."

"No, you didn't." Stella felt like she was seeing him in a new light. Perhaps it was spending time with someone as uptight and anxious as Teddy, but Arden seemed almost naively carefree. How could he not have considered how his decision would affect her? Especially after last night's violence.

She didn't want to push, but his careless suggestion made her angry.

"What about Grace?" Stella asked.

Arden stilled and met her eyes. "I've been waiting to speak to you about that."

"Until after you spoke to her?" Stella asked, her tone a little sharper than she meant it to be.

He looked down at his hands and she felt suddenly and violently furious at him.

"You didn't come to see me when I was terribly wounded or for hours afterwards and I would have let all of that go, but do you know who *did* come to see me? Grace. The person you had already made time to invite to dinner."

Arden squeezed her hands. "When you put it like that, it sounds bad, but all the families were together after the match and we got to talking. I was supposed to be speaking with Eleria, but she was not feeling well after all the bloodshed and retired to her rooms. That left me with Grace and her sisters and my siblings, but I couldn't leave and see you because Eleria's parents were still there and expecting our attention."

"And you and Grace just hit it off."

He pressed a hand over his heart. "Don't say it like that, Stella. Gods know I love your temper, but this connection is confusing. Obviously, I've always thought Grace was a beautiful woman. I would have to be blind to not recognize that, but you know how it is. We have always just been friends because I was pining over you and she was pining over Teddy. I'd never really considered it until she was so at ease talking with me and Eleria's parents and I have just never experienced that feeling of having a partner. And you know Grace—she's so very comfortable in those situations."

It was so unfair of him to compliment Grace for doing something Stella had never been in the position to do. It was unfair to compare her to Grace at all. No woman should be compared to someone who had a perfectly symmetrical face, stunning hourglass figure, and supernatural poise. Stella thought she'd done a decent job of holding her own with him at court parties and when their families were together, but this was clearly different.

"I realize the ridiculousness of asking you for your permission at a time like this—when you're risking so much for me," Arden said. "It's all come as such a surprise. I know that you and I are meant to be. But there's a part of me that worries if I don't at least spend some time with Grace, I'll always wonder if it was just your Aunt Des messing with you, or if I somehow missed something with a woman I've known my whole life."

That was supposed to be *her* connection. Stella wanted to scream at him, or Desiree, or just in general. But she knew he was right. Her mother had been in love with someone else before she ended up with her father. They had always said that their early struggles made the joy of the rest of their lives that much sweeter. If they went through a war and so many trials, Stella could weather a courtship that would probably amount to nothing.

She dropped her head back and blew out a breath. How could she really be mad at him when she had the same fear? How could she hold him accountable for her own lack of faith? Great love stories required immense trust.

"I worried the same thing," she said softly. "I trust you."

Arden straightened, looking immensely relieved. "But this is why I also wanted to announce that we are courting. Because you are important to me and I want everyone to know. This is just a bump in the road and I'm relieved that you understand this is just something I have to see through so I can know for sure." He looked down at his hands. "Have you spent time with Teddy?"

Stella laughed and the tension unclenched in her chest. "Only when he was being a drunken ass last night."

Arden grinned. "You're kidding. I've never seen him drink more than a whiskey an evening."

"Well, I suspect he was having the same conversation we're having and is less adaptable to changes in his plans. You know how he is. We're going back to the temple to ask Desiree to break the bond. It's too dangerous during the Games. So at least you won't have to worry about my commitment to you."

Arden looked down at his hands. "That's wise. Do you think she'll do it?"

Stella shrugged. She wanted to ask him if he'd considered doing the same, but she was afraid of his answer. It wasn't as if it was the same kind of impediment to Arden and Grace going about their normal lives as it was to Stella and Teddy, who were competing in a deadly contest.

Arden studied her for a moment. "How are you, really? I know you heal quickly, but you had me pretty worried."

Stella thought of the star-shaped scar on her side. She wasn't ready to tell him that she'd been permanently marked by the contest yet, but he must have read it in her face.

Arden's eyes narrowed. "Are you still hurt?" When she said nothing, he stood and went to the window. He stared out at the garden, his hand rubbing the back of his neck.

"Just a flesh wound. A scar is not a big deal."

"Of course it is. How would you feel if someone scarred me?"

She'd been so worried he would miss the freckle constellation he used to write his name on her side that she hadn't thought of the guilt she'd feel if the roles were reversed and he was so badly wounded that he'd forever bear the scar.

"I'm sorry. I shouldn't tell you how to feel, and I keep saying the wrong thing," Arden said. He glanced out the window. One of his guards was in the garden, beckoning for him to go. "Damn. I've already been gone too long." He pulled Stella into a hug.

It wasn't appropriate, but it felt so good to be held and her parents wouldn't object after all she'd been through yesterday. She tucked her face into his neck and breathed in the familiar salt air and fresh laundry scent of him.

"I love you," he whispered. "You're going to win the Games and get your favor. I just know it." He pulled back and met her gaze. "I know you said we can't announce our courtship until after the Games, but since you need to come in to answer some questions about last night for the guards, do you want to walk back to the inquiry with me?"

Stella wanted to, but she shook her head. "Probably better that I don't."

He nodded and stepped away. "Stay safe, Stella." He turned to leave.

"Arden?" she called when he reached the doorway. "What's my favorite flower?"

He turned, his gaze flitting from the roses on the couch to her. "Do you not like the roses?"

Stella paused, torn between telling the truth and doing what she had always done—telling him what would put him at ease.

He walked back to meet her, and she caved.

"Of course. I love roses."

He frowned like he'd caught her in the lie, but when she said nothing, he bent to kiss her hand. "I'm lucky to have you. You always go with the flow."

Stella used to like when he said that. She'd taken the ease between them and the way their lives just fit together as a good thing. Before, it had made her feel frictionless and easy-going, but now it made her feel a touch foolish.

She watched Arden and his guards leave through the garden gate and waited a full ten minutes before she snuck out the same way and crossed town to Olney Castle. It was best not to tell her parents. The last thing she needed was them marching into the castle alongside her and riling everyone up. She would just pop in, be interrogated, and be back home before they were the wiser.

Her father's stress level could be measured by how many flowers he carved in a week and he'd already given her two daisies since the binding ceremony. She didn't need to add any more stress to his plate.

The guards at the castle gates let her in and, as soon as she stepped into the courtyard, she was escorted inside and into a sitting room on the ground floor. It faced the queen's gardens and Stella stood there watching the morning light shine brilliantly off the vibrant summer florals.

A guard entered the room a moment later, dressed in green Teripin regalia. He handed her a cup of tea. If it was being given to her by anyone other than a gruff-looking hunter, Stella might not have hesitated.

She held the steaming cup to her nose and sniffed.

"You have to drink it before the inquiry starts, my lady," the man said when she didn't immediately sip it. He nodded to it. "It's not going to harm you, but I have instructions to stay until you finish it."

"Before the inquiry?" She sniffed the tea again and the faint spicy aroma clicked a memory into place.

Truth tea. They were giving all the competitors truth tea so they would be more forthcoming for the interrogation. It didn't so much force the truth as it loosened the lips. Stella took a bracing breath and knocked the tea back in one gulp.

The guard took the empty cup and left the room.

Stella stared out at the garden, trying not to panic. She immediately drew up all her memories of truth tea: how to brew it, the herbs used to make it more potent, and how to mask its scent. But she had no memory of any way to prevent or lessen its effects.

Panic rose in her chest as she pulled up memory after memory, searching for any way out of this mess. But the more useless experiences she called to mind, the more anxious she felt.

The door creaked open, and she turned, only to come face to face not with a hunter captain or one of the king's advisors, but with the god of war himself.

Endros crossed the space in a few short strides. He reached for her hand with a knife-sharp smile on his face. "Welcome, little goddess. We've not formally met, but I knew your mother. I think it's time you and I speak."

17

TEDDY

Whiskey was a mistake.

It took Teddy a while to realize that the pounding in his head matched the pounding outside of his head. Someone was at his bedroom door. Someone who clearly wanted to be punched in the face.

He groaned, squinting into the bright morning light that poured through the curtains he'd forgotten to close the night before.

"I'm coming." His voice was ragged from sleep, his mouth too dry to say more. He stood, his muscles screaming with the remnants of the previous day's battle.

He stumbled across the room and cracked the door open.

Jalen leaned against the doorframe, looking impatient. His face split with a smile when he took in Teddy's appearance.

"Oh, Ted. You look rough. Are those yesterday's clothes? Did you sleep with your shoes on? Alex said you would be feeling it this morning, but I'm not sure I've ever seen you in such a state," Jalen said.

Jalen's effusive energy this early in the morning was overwhelming even when Teddy wasn't hungover. It was certainly way too much for the state he was in.

"What do you want?" he snapped. "What time is it?"

Jalen grinned wider. "It's half-eight. You slept in."

Teddy groaned and rubbed his temples to ease the ache.

"I'd let you sleep later, but there's an inquiry. You need to come downstairs for questioning," Jalen said, stepping into Teddy's bedroom. "Gods, you reek. Did you drink the whole bottle?"

"No. Alex drank half." Teddy was joking, but by his mental accounting, he realized it might have been true.

When he was young, his parents had taken him to a healer who magically enhanced senses. Her work had granted him sharper hearing, eyesight, and senses of touch, smell, and taste, but it also meant that he healed faster. Not as fast as Stella, who had godly magic in her blood, but faster than a typical person.

He also metabolized alcohol faster. And yet, he still felt rotten.

"It's so rare that I'm the prince who has it the most together and I'm kind of enjoying the self-righteousness that comes along with it," Jalen said. "No wonder you're so insufferable all the time."

Teddy grimaced at his brother. "I could still kick your ass."

Jalen laughed. "If I didn't enjoy seeing you delusional, I might be offended. You're clearly hurting, but Endros wants all the competitors questioned to check their involvement with the death of Victor Schwoebleman."

Teddy glowered at him. "Endros, the god these maniacs worship, would like to question us, the contestants in his murder games, to see if we are killing each other outside the arena."

Jalen nodded. "You got it on the first try. Maybe you're not in such bad shape."

"What does our father say?"

Jalen frowned and tapped his fingers together in an uncanny impression of their father. "'Teddy can handle himself.'"

While Jalen's skin tone was darker, more golden-brown than olive like their father's, he had the same hazel eyes and smirk. He'd long ago mastered the king's mannerisms and loved to impersonate Xander, especially if he'd been recently chastised.

"Also, our mother is expecting you downstairs in fifteen minutes," Jalen said with a gleeful smile.

Teddy cursed and stumbled to the washroom, ignoring Jalen's laughter as he slammed the door.

Queen Jessamin Orum Savero stood in front of a sunlit window at the end of the royal wing of Olney Castle with her consort and guard, Maren, at her side. Teddy could tell by the jeweled dagger at the waist of her elaborate gown that she was anxious.

His mother always carried blades, but she only displayed them so obviously when she wanted other people to know she was ready for a fight. Jessamin had been raised in the Queendom of Novum, a large island in the middle of the Adiran Sea. Since her older sister, Karina, was the heir to the throne, Jessamin had been raised to lead the Novumi army. It was a twist of fate and shifting alliances that saw her sent to Argaria to marry Xander Savero.

Maren leaned close to the queen and whispered something in her ear, and his mother's shoulders relaxed.

Teddy's chest clenched. That was what Grace had always been for him—the steadiness and humor, the comfort in his most stressful moments.

Teddy hesitated and Jalen stepped on his heel, nearly running into him.

"Hedging, brother?" he teased.

Teddy didn't have time to respond. His mother had seen them.

Her face lit up as he walked closer. "There's my handsome boy."

"Good morning, Mother," he said, kissing her cheek.

She froze and sniffed as she drew back. "Long night, Theodore Davide?"

"Uh-oh, the full name. I'll see myself out," Jalen said, taking the first chance to escape any official duty, as always.

"Traitor," Teddy grumbled.

His mother tilted his chin up to look at his eyes and clicked her tongue. "So unlike you. Is this about yesterday?"

He jerked his head away and was rewarded with a throbbing spike of pain. "Sure. Let's go with that. Just blowing off some steam after a fight."

"A dangerous time to choose to get drunk in public," she said, slowly studying him.

He wasn't about to tell her about Grace. This wasn't the time or place. There were too many eyes and ears inside the castle.

"Walk with me." It was a command if he'd ever heard one, but he held out his elbow and his mother threaded her arm through.

She was only a few inches shorter than him, but she leaned her head against his shoulder.

"Your father is with Marcos," she whispered. "They can't find a way to stop this from happening. We think it's best to let Endros question you. It's clear you were too drunk to have done anything and at least there will be plenty of witnesses to say you weren't there, but whatever is happening now is bigger than all of us and it's best if we pretend to go along with it for now."

Teddy nodded.

"Evan believes this is truly the work of the Sons of Endros and not one of your competitors. Almost every single one of them has whereabouts accounted for—"

"That doesn't mean anything," Teddy interrupted. "They could have had someone else do it for them and just used the rebel group as a coverup."

His mother smiled approvingly. "That's what I said."

"So what does Evan suggest?"

"He's having each one of them followed to see who they interact with and then we will try to trail those people, but at some point, that won't be sustainable. I believe he's trying to focus on the most likely candidates—so those who have wealth and access that could pay for assassins and to cover it up."

Teddy squeezed her arm a little tighter. "We had a scuffle with the Roach and his friends leaving the bar last night."

His mother smiled and waved at a well-dressed lord and lady who walked by them. "We?"

"Stella and I."

Jessamin's eyebrows shot up. "Oh? You were leaving together?"

Teddy rolled his eyes. "Not like you're thinking. She walked me back to the castle because I was drunk and she was not and—" He tapped his chest and lowered his voice. "She just didn't want to feel me make a fool of myself."

"I don't know. I think that girl has a good bit of her mother in her," Jessamin said. "Cece has always been concerned with everyone else before herself."

"Except Father." The words were out of his mouth before his sluggish brain caught up.

His mother stopped short and glared at him. "I won't hear that from you. You are young and don't know what you're talking about. You can hate her all you want for being the hero when you think your father should be, but I have taught you better than to ignore the deeds of women in history in favor of what men decide is important."

Teddy looked down at the ground, chastised. "I'm sorry."

If his father was the one constantly reminding him to be impeccable, his mother was the one who was always praising him for his wisdom and temperance and allowing him a place to express his frustration and anxieties. She was also the one to remind him that his father hadn't mastered everything all at once. It had taken Xander a long time to come into his own as a ruler. Jessamin was a woman of grace and gentle encouragement, unless he needed a firm push.

But Teddy was so tired of the pressure already and he wasn't even king yet. He didn't know how either of his parents had managed to not be completely burned out on court life by the time they were his age.

His mother took his chin in her hands and forced him to meet her eye. "It's fine. You've had a stressful few days. Now, you must prepare yourself for this interrogation. You can't act out. You can't react at all. I hate to pressure you, especially when you're in a state, but if ever there was a time to be perfect, this is it. Endros will try to bait you with everything you expect him to. You can assume he knows the truth about our family, but it's best you play dumb."

Teddy rolled his shoulders out and took a deep breath.

She cupped his face in her hands. "I know that you are your own man now, but this is a moment when I need you to be *my* son. Be as still as the mirror surface of a lake. No matter what is going on beneath the water, you must remain placid. We don't know what game Endros is playing, and until we do, things need to remain business as usual."

"Yes, Mother."

He knew she was right. His mother was an amazing strategist, and he had enormous respect for how calm she could remain while listening to men take credit for the success of her ideas. He'd watched his father smirk at her across war strategy tables for years, a silent conversation passing between them, Xander animated and obviously annoyed, Jessamin reminding him not to show it. Though their relationship was unconventional, they made an excellent team.

As good of a team as Teddy and Grace would make. His stomach dropped as he tried to shove the sadness to the farthest corner of his mind.

Teddy frowned. "One question, though—how is Endros managing to run the interrogation himself? He can't possibly expect to stay corporeal here long enough to speak to all twelve of us who remain in the Games."

Jessamin glowed with pride. "Good catch, darling. Evan and I suspect that's exactly the point he's trying to make. They believe the faith of the Sons of Endros has strengthened his ability to stay in this realm for longer periods of time. We think he's trying to show off— intimidate us with his looming presence."

Teddy swallowed hard. That was an unnerving possibility. All the living gods had been killed and had ascended to the Otherworld, the realm of the gods. Their power could be felt in small ways in the living world, and they could stay for short periods of time to visit with their subjects, capable of using a limited amount of their magic on the world. But conducting a full-day interrogation of the remaining twelve competitors should have been beyond Endros's capability.

The god of war and discord thrived off instilling fear, so this was probably just another tactic.

His mother led him down a candlelit corridor. She squeezed his arm and his chest warmed. "You should be up next. I'm not sure where Rainer and Cece are, but Endros is in there with Stella now."

"Endros? Is in there? With Stella?" Teddy didn't think. He charged toward the doors.

Rainer and Cecilia weren't out here waiting because Stella had most definitely not told her parents she was being interrogated by the god of war.

His fingertips brushed the handle, and the door swung open.

Stella stared at him, her face awash with surprise and relief. Endros appeared over her shoulder. Teddy lost his composure. Seeing the god looming over her filled him with protective rage.

"Your *Highness*," Endros said, the title meant as a taunt more than anything else, but Teddy's focus was immediately drawn to Stella.

Their bond buzzed with warmth. That's what he'd felt a moment earlier. Not his mother's comfort, but the nearness of Stella.

Stella's eyes flickered with surprise and then hatred.

Well, that settled that. She was still mad.

Enjoy your vigil. What an unbelievably cruel thing to say. Teddy didn't even know why he'd said it.

No—he did know. He'd started to realize he'd been wrong in some of the assumptions he'd made about her. He'd started to see an unnerving kindness in her and so he'd said the meanest thing he could to shove her away.

Now he regretted it because he could tell by the distrust in her eyes that he would have to pry the information she'd shared with Endros from her. Drunk Teddy was so shortsighted.

Stella brushed by him. "Good luck, *Your Grace*."

"Thank you, *my lady*," he countered.

Out of the corner of his eye, he caught the menace in her tight smile. Whatever momentary lightness had come from fighting together last night was chased away by the familiarity of being at odds again. Her anger was almost a comfort. This, at least, was a place that he knew how to work from.

Endros gestured Teddy into the room, but he didn't step out of the way. Teddy was forced to brush shoulders with the god. It was a power move, meant to display he was just as corporeal as a mortal.

The god closed the door as Teddy crossed the room and slumped into a chair. He tried to look as pained as he felt. This was actually a scenario where his senses being dulled was a good thing. It would slow any reactive impulses.

Endros gestured to a cup of tea on the table. "Drink."

Teddy lifted the cup and sniffed.

"No need to test it. Poison is a woman's weapon," Endros said.

Teddy sipped the tea instead of saying what he wanted to say, which was that poison was an *efficient* weapon. There was no point trying to convince a man of brutality that poison could be as much an art as swordsmanship.

He studied the god of war and discord through the steam rising from his cup. Endros looked every bit the warrior—broad and muscular, with a crisp linen shirt and leather vest that strained against his chest. His dark hair was threaded with gray and brushed back into neat waves. A scar several shades lighter than his tan skin ran down the right side of his jaw, and his silver eyes glowed faintly with something otherworldly, just like his son Cato's. Though, where Cato's were usually lit with curious mischief, his father's held only predatory menace.

Endros had no weapons, but he exuded the kind of powerful aura that made it clear he didn't need one. He probably knew ten ways to kill a man without breaking a sweat.

Teddy knocked back the rest of the tea, his stomach gurgling loudly in protest. He should have at least had some toast before coming in here. He set the cup down with a clatter as his stomach roiled. Maybe Endros had lied, and it was poison.

"It's truth tea," Endros said.

Teddy's stomach plummeted. He'd had a whole cup of truth tea and now he was about to be interrogated. What had Isla said about truth tea? His magic was sluggish, buried under the weight of his hangover.

Her voice floated into his mind. *Skirt the truth. Say things that are true but not the exact answers to the question, or offer slight deviations. Instead of saying "I don't remember," when you do, say "my memory is fuzzy." It's vague enough to be true.*

Seemingly satisfied that the tea had enough time to work, Endros sat down across from Teddy. "What kind of man are you, Theodore Savero?"

Teddy stared at him, trying to look as bored and hungover as possible. "How do you mean?"

Endros grinned in a feral way that let Teddy know he'd stepped right into a trap the god had laid for him. "I mean, are you the type of man who is eternally in competition with your peers? I can't imagine why else you would be interested in so many women who want Prince Arden instead."

Teddy's eyebrows shot up, and he laughed out of sheer surprise. Not neutral like he'd promised his mother, but hopefully it read as apathy.

Endros cocked his head like a predator studying prey. "That's funny."

"A bit. Yes." Teddy leaned back, tilting his chair onto its back legs. "No. I'm not eternally in competition with my peers, nor do I see Arden as competition. When you're the best, you don't feel compelled to prove it relentlessly."

"Perhaps you are like your father, after all. He thought he was invincible once." The god pursed his lips and shook his head. "He learned, though."

Teddy allowed the silence to stretch out. Isla had taught him everything she knew about interrogations, and silence was his new best friend.

"Surprised your ego is still intact after your fight yesterday. Not sure that it's warranted," Endros said.

Teddy was comforted that there was nothing the god could say that would be worse than the way he'd already taken himself apart piece by piece, retracing every mistake he'd made down to the way he'd first drawn his blade. Endros thrived on creating fear and conflict, but Teddy would be shocked if the god could find something meaner to say than the constant running monologue of inadequacies in his head.

Teddy wasn't foolish enough to believe he had no weaknesses. He loved far too many people, and he knew his family history. Love was an easy pressure point to exploit.

But he'd been so conditioned to temperance—too aware of the danger that waited for him or anyone else in his family to lower his guard. It was exactly why they were all so well trained. His parents had seen to that. Even Juliana, whom people often underestimated because of her beauty and poise at court, was a fierce fighter.

"Nothing to say?" Endros prodded, looking for a weak spot to apply pressure.

"You haven't asked another question," Teddy said.

"I wonder. Do you have your father's same preference for pretty little goddesses?" Endros asked.

Teddy laughed again, this time out of sheer shock at the question.

Endros went rigid and his eyes narrowed. "I'm not usually known for my humor."

"No, it's just that I can't stand Stella McKay."

"Oh? Perhaps you're not your father's son."

Teddy frowned.

"Don't make that face," Endros said. "That's a compliment. Your father was weak and sentimental. All impulse and no patience. You seem to have more of your mother in you."

It took all of Teddy's concentration not to fidget under the god's assessing gaze. Fear crept into the corners of Teddy's mind, the hairs rising on the back of his neck. There was nothing wrong, yet a creeping dread washed over him.

He met Endros's eyes again, and it hit him. This was Endros's magic. His power was known to bring fear into the heart of even the bravest soldiers.

A sharp tug in his chest snapped him out of his daze. Stella must have felt his fear.

"I think you'll find my whereabouts were well accounted for last night. I was with Stella McKay, Nathan Aiger, my sister Alexandra. Most of the patrons of the Poison Vixen can confirm I was there until mere moments before the body was discovered."

Endros pursed his lips. "Yes. Stella told me about bumping into some other competitors and hearing death whispers just a few minutes before you arrived at the castle gates. Quite convenient."

Teddy forced a frown. "Not terribly convenient for me, since I was drunk. I would have a hard time taking down most of the remaining competitors sober. I certainly couldn't have done it in the state I was in last night."

Endros eyed him for a long moment. "You may go."

Teddy hesitated. It couldn't be that easy, but he wasn't about to stay and give the god a chance to pick him apart anymore.

He rose to his feet and walked across the room with casual slowness, even giving the god his back for a moment when he opened the door. Teddy turned and bowed before stepping out into the hallway.

He walked down the hall without looking back, barely breathing until he reached the end of the corridor, where he was surprised but relieved to find Stella waiting for him just inside a sitting room. Teddy stepped inside and sat down next to her.

"Don't read into it, Your Grace. I figured it was best to stay close to the other combatants, just in case. That way, I'd have witnesses if someone tries to take me out or decides to get handsy again." She nodded to Drew, who was glowering at her from where he sat on the far side of the sitting room. His hands were wrapped in bandages that made it look like he was wearing enormous mittens.

"No healers?" Teddy asked.

"Not from the contest," Stella said. "I suspect Dixon tried to fix them, but burns are slow work. I found out the hard way when I was younger and learning to control my power. I had such a bad tantrum once that I burned my father by accident. It took a week for Lyra to fix what I'd done. A healer has to keep working layer by layer of skin and let the swelling go down. It's a very delicate skill and I think Dixon's talents are more utilitarian—how to keep someone from bleeding out, set a bone, pull pain from an injury."

Teddy had never thought about it. Fire had always been easy for him to control, but witches with fire affinities were known for their quick tempers, just like witches with storm affinities like him were known for being mercurial and memory witches were known for getting lost in thought. It was unclear whether affinity was influenced by personality or vice versa.

"That was smart, by the way—last night. You made sure he'd only be hurt if he touched you first." Teddy tried to sound sincere but he could tell by her sneer that he'd done an effective job of ensuring they stayed adversaries.

"Try not to sound so surprised," she snapped.

Teddy shouldn't have been shocked that she'd been strategic. He just didn't understand the way she switched so swiftly from rational to impulsive.

Stella rose from her seat and shoved the leather satchel that had been sitting next to her into his arms. "Jalen packed this for you."

"You're ready to go see your aunt?"

She nodded, a crease forming in her brow as she started toward the hall, her hands clasped tightly in front of her. Teddy wanted to ask her what had happened, but there were far too many ears inside the castle. He needed to wait until they were out of the city.

In the wild, they could finally speak freely.

They walked through the castle hallways and out into the sweltering midday heat.

"If we leave within the hour, we can make it to the temple before it gets dark," he said.

"I just need to change into riding clothes," Stella said. "My bag is already packed."

When they cleared the castle courtyard, she picked up her pace, as if she could sense him gearing up to apologize.

"Stella, I'm—"

"He came this morning, so fortunately my vigil didn't last long," she said, walking faster.

Gods, Teddy felt like such an asshole, but he was relieved Arden had finally done the bare minimum.

"Good that he could finally make the time." The words slipped out, a remnant of the truth tea's effects.

Stella spun on him so fast he almost ran right into her. "Oh fuck *off*, Teddy. Not everyone can be a paragon of princely devotion by completely ignoring their partner's unhappiness."

Her words were like a slap across the face.

She crossed her arms and continued. "He brought flowers and apologized for taking so long. In fact, the reason he was delayed was because his betrothal had been called off. He wanted to make our courtship official."

"But that would put an even bigger target on your back."

"I know. That's what I told him."

Teddy wanted to think the best of his old friend, but Arden was making it hard. Jalen had always been closer to the prince of Olney since they were closer in age, but Teddy had still grown up seeing him every summer his whole life for the Godsball, the Solstice Festival, and the Gauntlet Games. He never would have expected Arden to be capable of such thoughtlessness.

"So we're keeping it quiet for now, but once the Games are over, we will make it official," Stella said.

"Does that mean he's not courting Grace?" He was torn between anger that Arden had Grace's attention and was rebuking her and relief for the same reason. He wanted Grace to be happy, but it would be so hard to watch her be with a lifelong friend.

Stella pushed her pace faster, as if trying to outrun his question. Teddy jogged to catch up, his head still throbbing along with his pulse.

They turned down the long, shady lane that led to the McKay Estate. The morning was unbearably hot. Sweat dripped down Teddy's back as he hurried along behind Stella. At least there was a breeze blowing in off the sea, carrying the scent of salt and summer florals.

Stella stopped short as her family home came into sight.

Fionn Silver was leaning against the garden gate.

Teddy shepherded Stella behind him. "What the fuck is he doing here?"

Stella shoved him aside and kept walking. "He's not here to kill me, you idiot. Not before I've paid him what he's due and not if he wants to win the competition."

The mercenary smiled warmly as they approached. Teddy scowled back at him. No hired sword should have a smile that straight or skin that unflawed. Though Fionn's nose had clearly been broken a few times, it gave him a sort of roguish charm to go along with his otherwise remarkably symmetrical face.

"Hey there, princess. I'm calling in my favor," Fionn said.

"What favor?" Teddy asked at the same time Stella said, "It's not a good time."

Fionn offered a humble shrug and sympathetic smile. "I'm afraid it can't wait. You're not welching on our deal, are you, princess?"

The use of the pet name twice in as many sentences made Teddy roll his eyes.

Stella sighed and looked toward the back of her house. "It has to happen right now?"

"I'm afraid so." Fionn sounded apologetic, but the sincerity was lost in the way he smirked at Teddy.

"Will it take long?" Stella asked.

"Indeed. This is delicate work."

Teddy looked between the two of them. What sort of deal had she made? He guessed something to do with memory. Though it wasn't her primary affinity, he knew she was still extremely skilled at memory magic, just like her mother.

Stella took one last longing look at her house before she turned to face Teddy. "I'm sorry. We'll have to finish our business tomorrow."

"Absolutely not," he said. "You can't just run off with a trained killer when we are all being hunted by a trained killer. Even if he's not the one doing it, two of you being together will just increase the like-lihood that the assassin will take an interest. Perhaps a two-for-one."

"I'd like to see him try," Fionn said, looking only mildly insulted at the insinuation that he couldn't handle himself.

Teddy knew he was being irrational, but he couldn't control himself. The bond was possessive. It wanted to be near her. Even in the few moments they'd spent together, he felt like his headache was lessening, as if the connection and nearness of her were revitalizing. That was annoying.

"You didn't seem concerned when it was the two of you spending time together," Fionn said. "What are you two, anyway? Lovers?"

Stella's expression shifted from annoyed to horrified insultingly quickly.

"Don't look so stunned. You make a handsome couple."

Stella faked a gag.

"Am I so repulsive?" The words were wrenched from Teddy's stupid mouth by the truth tea. At least that was what he told himself. It was that or a simple need for reassurance after Grace had dumped him and bruised his ego. He was just hurting, hungover both emotionally and physically, and he wanted assurance.

Stella placed a hand on his shoulder and with deep sincerity said, "Of course you're not objectively repulsive. You're just repulsive *to me.*"

Fionn laughed so loudly and suddenly that Teddy jumped.

"Gods, she is refreshingly honest, isn't she?" Fionn said.

Stella rolled her eyes. "Am I dressed appropriately for whatever this favor is?"

Fionn gave her a slow once-over. "Yes, I'd say so unless you want to slip into something more showy."

Stella cocked her head. "Though I did not explicitly say so, I am a lady and I'll not risk my virtue. Any favor between us will not be sexual."

Teddy ran a hand over his face. Of course she hadn't clarified that before making a godsdamned deal with a mercenary. As if they were the most virtuous lot. His blood boiled that Stella had been so apt to spite him that she'd entered into a foolish bargain with someone who could use her however he liked.

Teddy took her arm. "This is a bad idea."

She glared up at him. "This is none of your concern. Go sober up."

"I don't think so, *princess*," Teddy said. "Until this killer is apprehended, I go where you go."

Stella stared at him for a long moment, heat flaring in her cheeks. "You can't control me," she whispered.

Teddy chuckled. "Oh, that much is clear. But I can try to contain you."

"Do you want to take a moment to freshen up?" Fionn asked.

The crease in her brow returned. "No, why?"

Teddy bit back a smile. Her hair *was* a bit unruly. Most ladies kept their hair neatly pinned up, but Stella's looked like she had twisted it back into a ponytail, started to pin it up, and then had given up halfway through either from lack of time or overwhelm at the sheer volume of dark curls. It somehow looked right on her, though. She looked like she belonged in Olney. Like she'd just returned from a morning of riding on the beach and was running to the market for some errand.

Fionn shrugged and held out his arm to lead her away from the house. "All right then, princess, let's go get my money's worth out of this trade."

Teddy fell into step behind them.

"Don't look so worried, Savero," Fionn said without turning around.

Did the man have eyes in the back of his head? How did he know what Teddy's face looked like?

Fionn pulled his arm in, drawing Stella slightly closer to his body. "I'll take good care of your girl."

That was exactly what Teddy was afraid of.

18

———

STELLA

"Liar!" Stella slammed her hand down over the cards, sending ale sloshing from several glasses around the table. She hopped to her feet and twirled in a celebratory dance as the rest of the men at the table groaned and cursed. One by one, they tossed their cards onto the top of the pile.

Fionn, who had just been caught, gave her an indulgent smile. "It's *from the lips of a liar*, princess, but we'll let it slide." He leaned back in his chair and applauded her celebration.

The other players looked less than thrilled. Around the table sat an older, retired fisherman named Merl, a sailor named Jackson, a Novumi merchant named Harcom who was in town to sell intricately beaded gowns during the Gauntlet Games, and Teddy's partner from the first challenge, Reever.

Stella covered her mouth in mock embarrassment. She was trying to skirt the line between staying sober and drinking enough to be believably drunk.

Fionn's gaze was hawk-like. The mercenary's watchfulness rivaled her father's. If she acted too over-the-top, he'd know she was pretending.

"She's hustling us," Jackson complained.

"Beginner's luck," Fionn assured him as he passed Stella another glass of bubble wine.

The glass was her fourth. She'd knocked one over with feigned clumsiness and dumped another in the plant on the windowsill behind her when Fionn left to get them another round from the bar, but she'd had to drink at least two glasses and she already felt the pleasant buzz in her system.

The more she had, the more the bond in her chest hummed along with the haze of alcohol. It was so strong now that her ability to block Teddy out was clouded by proximity and drink. All the more reason to get Fionn's favor over with so she could go to the temple, have Goddess Desiree break the bond, and end her nightmare.

Teddy's gaze burned into her. He really thought Stella was dumb enough to drink everything she was handed without checking for sedatives. Any witch worth her salt knew to check—any female witch, at least. She supposed men didn't worry so much about someone dosing them with a sedative.

She reached her hand into her pocket and pulled out a handful of dried truth root. It was the same herb used in truth tea, but it also made a good herbal exchange for spellwork.

All magic required an exchange. Channeling her elemental magic used her body's energy sources, which meant she felt hungry, tired, and depleted after using it and would downright collapse if she used too much. Witches who burned out that way spent days in bed recovering.

Spellwork was different. It only required setting your will, knowing the incantation, and an herb or other material for exchange. Since this spell tested if a drink was spiked with something danger-ous, truth root would make the answer more obvious.

Stella subtly dipped a finger into the wine, her lips moving silently through the words of the incantation. A moment later, she released a small handful of ash onto the floor. She waited for the tell-tale prickle at her fingertip that would indicate something was off with the drink. Instead, her fingertip grew numb.

It was just alcohol.

She caught Teddy looking and leaned in. "You didn't think I'd be so foolish as to not check my drink, did you? I'm not like you."

Teddy stared down at his whiskey, realization dawning on his face. He'd been annoyed when she stole his whiskey under the guise of taking a sip, but she was checking that his drinks weren't spiked either. He was clearly under the impression that he'd come along for *her* protection. It was just like him to think he was being helpful when he was actually a liability.

His tagging along was patronizing. He'd been so focused on her and their surroundings that he'd forgotten all about his own drinks, not that he'd had many.

Stella took a long sip of delicious wine, swallowing as she held Fionn's gaze. The mercenary really had excellent taste.

She placed her glass on the table slightly harder than she should have and leaned back into her seat. "Is this truly the only favor you wish from me? If so, it's the easiest one I've ever traded away."

Fionn grinned. "For now."

She couldn't press any harder. No matter how restless Teddy was, they would have time to go to the temple tomorrow. Surely this favor couldn't last longer than one day and night. If they left by noon tomorrow, they'd make it to the temple by dark and they could stay the night and be back by midafternoon the following day. That would give them enough time before the second challenge started.

Stella was concerned about the gap between events. She wondered what fresh nightmare Endros was setting up for them that required so much preparation. The tournament could only last two weeks, but he seemed content to draw things out.

Teddy's irritation grew more urgent in her chest. Fionn seemed to sense it, too. He smirked and shuffled the cards with the skill of an avid player.

"Tell me, Your Grace," Fionn started. "Do you play this game often, or did you just make an exception to play chaperone to the young and impressionable Lady McKay?"

"I'm not that young," Stella said at the same time Teddy said, "She's not remotely impressionable."

Fionn laughed heartily.

Stella pinched Teddy's face in her hand and pushed his lips into a pout. "You'll have to excuse His Broody Highness. He was *over-served* last night."

Merl barked a laugh. "Over-served! As if it's the barmaid's fault for being so accommodating! I've never used that one, but I'll have to try it. It's a terrible thing to be wasteful with booze this good." He held up his glass and waited for them all to clink it. "Hair of the dog that bit ya. It's a solid strategy. In my experience, the best strategy."

"Seems like it's your *only* strategy, Merl," Reever taunted.

The patrons at the surrounding tables broke into a chorus of laughter that suggested Merl was a regular.

"It only postpones the inevitable," Stella said.

She looked around the pub. She'd not been to Nightmare's Muse before because of its ominous name, but the pub's wine selection was excellent.

"You two have been friends for a long time?" Harcom asked, nodding at Teddy and Stella.

Stella wrinkled her nose. "Oh no, we're not friends. His Grace is just obsessed with me and follows me everywhere I go."

Teddy choked on his whiskey, and the men burst into laughter.

Fionn winked at Stella. "Can hardly blame you, lad. She's a beautiful woman. Even more so with a blade in her hand."

"Yes, of course. Stella has plenty of admirers and friends. Though I must say I haven't seen Katherine Crawley for a while," Teddy said. "I thought for certain you would have summoned her for this. She's not one to miss a party."

A pit formed in Stella's stomach. *Kate.* With all the stress of the murder, inquiry, and Arden's offer, she'd managed to put their fight out of her head.

Kate's words stung in the way only a best friend's could. But she was wrong. Arden had shown up and explained himself. He'd wanted to make things official. Kate was the one who owed her an apology, not the other way around.

Stella sipped her wine slowly. "I'm sure Kate would have been delighted to join us had I the time to ask her before being forced to fulfill my end of a bargain. As you'll recall, I didn't realize we were coming to a bar when the favor was called in."

Teddy studied her, rubbing his chest absentmindedly. He could probably feel her hurt through their bond. "Perhaps another time."

"Perhaps," Stella parroted. She focused on trying to narrow the funnel of their bond the way her mother had taught her. She refused to break her glare, though she felt the way the men at the table were making eyes at each other over the growing agitation between her and Teddy.

Finally, she dragged her gaze from Teddy's and nodded to the cards. "Another hand, or have I won enough of your money, gentlemen?"

Fionn said this was only a stop on the way to her favor.

"Is this our final destination?" she asked.

Fionn shook his head. "No, we needed to wait a bit, but now that it's dark, it's safe to say you can finally pay your debt."

Adrenaline shot through her blood, a thread of anxiety bursting through her bond with Teddy. Sayla's bow, that was annoying. He really needed to control himself better. She'd already gotten so much better at the meditation exercise her mother had taught her to temper her emotions. Teddy had clearly not been as studious with learning how to manage.

Fionn signaled to the barmaid and paid their tab as Stella shook hands with the gentlemen around the table before collecting her winnings and shoving them into the pocket of her dress.

Then Fionn shepherded her outside.

"You can go, Your Grace. Probably best that you're not involved in this next part anyway," Fionn said to Teddy once they were outside.

"I go where she goes," Teddy said firmly, a hand resting on the dagger at his hip.

Stella hated that he just decided for her. He could have at least asked her if she wanted him to tag along first.

"You're making me look weak," she whispered.

"I'm making you look like someone has your back. Besides, you shouldn't be seen alone at night with a man of questionable character. It wouldn't be good for your reputation. Especially considering how public a figure you are now and could be in the future," Teddy replied, his voice barely audible.

She turned back to Fionn, resigned. "Where I go he goes."

Fionn shrugged. "The more the merrier, I suppose, but it will be a little harder to be discreet as a larger group, not that I don't love a challenge."

Reever stepped out of the bar, chased by the sound of music and merriment.

"You're coming, too?" Teddy asked.

"I go where he goes," he said, pointing to Fionn.

Fionn just glared at him. According to the documents Uncle Evan had brought Stella from the harbormaster, the two men had arrived together a week before the start of the Solstice Festival. There was a strange tension between them that Stella hadn't noticed before. Fionn was such a flirt. Stella hadn't quite figured out how to tell how much of it was natural charm and how much was genuine interest.

"Where are we headed?" Stella asked.

"The docks," Fionn said as they started down the street that led toward the sea.

The docks at night were not at all an appropriate place for a lady. Despite hunter patrols, it was a place of pop-up gambling dens, frequented by some of the least scrupulous people in Olney City.

Stella hurried along behind Fionn and Reever, watching as Fionn affectionately elbowed his friend.

They turned onto a narrower lane, darker than expected. The torches were spaced farther apart and the two nearest flames had burned out.

"That's odd," Teddy said, noticing at the same time she did.

Stella felt the same prickling on the back of her neck that she'd felt the previous evening a moment before she heard footsteps behind them. A rush of death whispers filled the air.

She felt the movement behind her before she saw it, ducking just in time to miss the swipe of the dagger. The assailant read her well and changed angle and Stella was forced to throw up her forearm to block. The blade cut right down to bone. She yelped as she jabbed out with her own dagger.

The man was cloaked in black, his face covered except for his eyes, but Stella made out a crest of a viper surrounded in flames on his shirt.

The Sons of Endros.

Bold of them to attack four competitors at once. The Gauntlet Games competitors should have still had a few days before their lives were under threat. Though, maybe the Sons had only said that in the hope of creating a false sense of security.

Steel clashed beside Stella as Fionn and Reever engaged with two other assailants.

She turned just in time to duck a sword swipe from a fourth attacker.

Teddy stepped forward and slid his dagger into the man's side.

Stella refocused on the assassin in front of her. She put her hands up, clutching her blade and ignoring the burning pain in her forearm. Her attacker favored his right leg. Perhaps it was an old injury to the left, but Stella could use that advantage.

When she twisted past him, she slammed her heel down on his left ankle, and he grunted. He landed a punch to her ribs, and she sliced her dagger along his left side. Bright red blood splattered across her gauzy lilac dress. The assassin darted away from her, laboring on his left ankle. A muffled laugh came from behind his face covering.

"You don't have it in you, girl," he said. "You've got the skill, but not the will to take a life."

Stella was terrified that he was right. She could injure him gravely, but she could not bring herself to kill him, even when she could tell he'd happily do the same to her. She'd played as defensively as she could, hoping he'd get discouraged or tired and make a mistake that would allow her to injure him enough that he'd flee. But he just kept coming.

Hot blood dripped down her arm, and she tried to keep her hand elevated so it wouldn't get sticky. She knew the wound would heal, but it was deep, and it was still a slippery mess.

A body hit the ground hard behind her. Out of the corner of her eye, she watched Fionn take down one of the men he was fighting. If she had short swords, she could have made quick work of all of these men, but with only a dagger and her half-drunk hand-to-hand fighting skills, she could hardly handle one assassin at a time.

A fist connected with her temple, and she stumbled, cursing. *Pay attention.* Suddenly, her reflexes felt too slow. Panic squeezed the air from her lungs. She was going to die on this darkened street corner as a message to the people of Olney, who just wanted peace.

The attacker came at her again, and Stella jammed her fingers into the soft notch at the bottom of his throat. He flinched. The second of surprise was enough for her to knock the blade from his hand and try to knee him in the groin.

He moved at the last second, and she hit his thigh instead. He hooked his arm under her lifted knee and swung her into the wall of the building beside them. He pinned her there. One of his hands gripped her throat and squeezed.

She jerked her dagger toward his ribs, but he caught her wrist and slammed it against the wall. He dug his thumb into the laceration on her forearm. Pain whited out her vision and she dropped her dagger.

Her father's words flared in her brain. *There are only two reasons a warrior drops her blade: when she's lost her will to fight, or when she's dead.*

The assassin's other hand came to her throat, choking off her air. She kicked his shin, but he didn't even flinch. Fumbling with her blood-slicked hand, she clawed her nails across his eyes.

Her attacker stumbled back, bending forward to shield his eyes and cursing. Stella swiped her dagger from the ground and slammed her knee into his stomach as she rose to her feet.

She had a clean shot at his throat, but she hesitated. It was one thing to train to kill someone. It was another to actually do it. She'd plunged a blade into an opponent's side or arms. But to go for someone's throat...

It was only a split second of hesitation, but it was enough for him to recover.

She watched in slow motion as he grabbed a blade tucked into his boot and shoved it up toward her chest.

Stella froze. She waited for the pain, but it never arrived.

A blade came out of nowhere and slid across her attacker's throat. Blood spurted from the wound, spraying across the cobblestones and Stella's boots. She gaped at the man as he slid to his knees, his hands frantically trying to stop the flow of crimson. He collapsed onto his side, looking up at the night sky, and then his chest went still.

Stella watched the blood form rivers between the stones, unable to look away.

"Stella." A broad chest appeared in front of her, blocking her view of the body. Teddy's hands came to her arms.

Warmth pulsed through the bond. *Teddy.* Teddy, who couldn't stand her. He had saved her.

Stella was as relieved as she was mad at herself for needing to be saved. She didn't want him to be right about her that she didn't have the heart to kill someone.

She shook her head. He couldn't be right. Not now. Not when she would need to be capable of this, and worse, to win the Gauntlet Games.

But what did it say about her if she couldn't even bring herself to take a life when her own was in peril?

Teddy lifted her chin, and she met his luminous golden eyes. "You can't freeze like that in the competition. That's the difference between life and death." His voice was soft but insistent.

"You think I don't know that?" she snapped.

She was grateful for the dark hiding her humiliation. She was the daughter of one of Olney's greatest warriors and she'd never killed a man. The assassin was right. She didn't have it in her, and that was a terrifying revelation. She didn't need Teddy to remind her of how short she was falling of her legacy.

Teddy lifted her arm, wiping her blood on his sleeve. His touch was gentle, his hands callused and warm against her bare skin as he held the still-seeping wound up to the torchlight. "It's deep."

She was vaguely aware of Fionn and Reever watching them. "It's fine. It will heal," she whispered. "Don't overreact or they will read into it. They can't know."

Teddy nodded. "Do you think they noticed?"

She licked her lips and shrugged. "You got injured right after I did, so it's hard to say, but you aren't subtle."

Teddy looked away. "I'm sorry."

He turned to look at Fionn and Reever. "I think that concludes the evening. Whatever favor is owed will have to wait. I'm taking Lady McKay home."

Fionn nodded, and Stella was relieved he didn't argue.

"You had quick reflexes after all of those drinks," Fionn said, a hint of suspicion in his tone.

Stella shrugged. "What can I say? The fight is in my blood."

Reever watched the exchange with a smirk on his lips. "If it's all right with you, we will just see you two back safely before we head back to our rooms."

Teddy nodded and tucked Stella under his arm, guiding her away from the bodies. They walked down the street and waved over a hunter patrol to deal with the mess they'd left behind.

Stella was still in shock, hardly able to pay attention to the words that Teddy said to the men because her full attention was focused on seeming fine.

Teddy guided her home, a hand on the small of her back. He was silent the whole way. As they stepped through the garden gates, Reever and Fionn came to a stop to offer them some privacy.

Teddy was trying to send comfort through the bond. Unfortunately, it just felt like he kept pushing on her chest, and that was enough to snap her out of her daze.

"I'm fine. You can stop prodding me. And don't come into the house with me. If my parents find out what happened, they will just worry more and my mother doesn't need the stress right now," she whispered.

Teddy blew out a breath as they came to a stop in front of the back door. He waited for her to meet his gaze. "Just because you couldn't do it then doesn't mean you won't be able to another time. Don't make this mean more."

"I know." She didn't, but she appreciated him saying so. His shift in mood was disorienting. "Thank you."

The words seemed too small for saving someone's life, but she didn't know what else to say. Teddy nodded, pulled a handkerchief from his pocket, and wiped the tacky blood from her arm.

The wound had already knitted itself perfectly back together.

"That's very handy magic," Teddy said. "Thank you for testing my drinks."

"You're welcome." She gestured to the blood stain across her dress. "Hopefully, I can get in and up to my room before they notice the blood." She touched her hair tentatively. "How do I look?"

Teddy smiled softly, a faltering sort of affection in his eyes. "A little wild, but no worse for the wear. Your hair always looks like that."

She frowned at him, and he laughed.

"Just being honest, *Minyha*. It suits you."

She frowned. The word sounded Novumi, and while she'd learned an abundance of curse words in the language thanks to Alexandra's colorful vocabulary, she didn't recognize this word. His tone was part-teasing, part-exasperated.

"What does *Minyha* mean?"

Teddy clicked his tongue. "Not a scholar of languages, I see."

Stella rolled her eyes. "Never mind."

She made a mental note to look it up in the Olney Royal Library when she had a spare moment.

Stella glanced over his shoulder at Reever and Fionn, who were still waiting at the garden gates. "You trust them to see you back safely? It's curious we were attacked when I was supposed to be delivering on Fionn's favor."

Teddy shook his head. "If he was involved, it would make more sense for him to wait until after he gets what he wants from you, not to mention that four competitors together made us an obvious target."

Stella chewed her lower lip. "Are you sure you trust them to walk you back to the castle safely? You could stay in one of our guest rooms for the night."

"It's good to see you worried about me," Teddy teased.

Stella laughed, and it snapped all the tension in her chest. "You're an ass. Now will you please get them out of here? I'm going to use that trellis to climb in my bedroom window and change before my parents see the blood."

Teddy gave her one last look and then nodded and stepped away. She watched him and the mercenaries retreat before climbing up the thorny trellis and into her bedroom window.

She was careful to step over the creakiest floorboards, but nearly jumped out of her skin when she turned and found Rosie staring at her wide-eyed from the bed.

"What are you doing in my room?" Stella asked.

Rosie looked her over, her eyes snagging on the blood spray on Stella's dress. "I could ask you the same, though from the look of your dress and your creative entrance, it seems you're trying to hide the signs of a scuffle from our parents."

"I'm okay," Stella said, half-believing the words.

"It would be understandable if you weren't, though," Rosie said.

Stella nodded and looked away from her little sister, a lump forming in her throat. "I was ready for opponents to come for me in the arena, but not on the streets."

Rosie stood, turned Stella around, and began to work on the buttons on the back of her dress. A moment later, the stained lilac fabric slid to the floor.

Rosie gasped. In the looking glass, Stella could see her sister's gaze on her side.

Stella instinctively brought her hand to the star-shaped scar. "I know it's ugly."

Rosie's eyes filled with tears. "That was a very bad wound. You didn't say it was that bad."

"It *wasn't* that bad," Stella said. She just wanted to forget the scar was there, pretend she was as whole as she'd been before she almost died in the arena—before she'd almost died in the street tonight.

Stella yanked on her nightdress. Her heart rate finally slowed when Rosie began to unpin her hair and braid it so it wouldn't be a mess in the morning.

She'd been so confident when she headed out for the day. But now, in her room, with her sister fixing her hair, Stella felt just how close she'd come to losing everything for the sake of love.

She thought of the way Arden had looked when he said he loved her—the way he wanted to announce their courtship.

"It will be worth it."

The fact that she even had to say it aloud made it clear how much she was beginning to doubt it.

19

TEDDY

The sunshine glaring through the intense spray from the waterfall next to the Temple of Desiree created the illusion of rainbows cascading over the white marble roof. Teddy closed his eyes and let it wash over his face, happy for the refreshment after the hot journey. His clothes were plastered to his skin. He'd happily plunge into the clear pool beneath the falls if he was certain he'd be able to stand, but he made a point not to go into an unknown body of water in front of people, lest they realize he didn't know how to swim.

Stella walked a few paces ahead of him, shoving pins into her hair, most of which had come loose of its haphazard updo on the swift ride. He could begrudge Stella McKay many things, but she was an exceptional rider. He'd expected to have to prod her along due to her lack of training, but she pushed the pace the entire way.

That settled some of his concerns, but what nagged him was the way she'd hesitated last night and had nearly gotten herself killed. There were no marks from the fight left on Stella's body thanks to her goddess blood. But he could read her disquiet in how jumpy she was. The moment she dismounted, she'd nearly leaped right back up on the horse when a mouse scurried by her boot.

During the fight, he'd watched her out of the corner of his eye, but she'd had everything in hand until she had to deal the killing blow. All her fear and desperation hit him so fast.

What bothered him more was how unnerved he was by her hesitation—by the wild fear that had gripped him in the split second he thought he might be too late to save her. Gods knew what the next challenge would bring. If Stella couldn't handle blood on her hands, that made the need to break their bond even more important.

Standing outside of the imposing white temple walls, he felt suddenly hesitant. Without the bond, she would be on her own with her inability to do what was required to survive the competition. If she couldn't kill an assassin, she wouldn't be able to kill a competitor. He'd been right in his assessment of her. She was too soft for this.

"I think we should work together in the next challenge," he said as they walked up the dirt pathway to the temple entrance.

Stella turned to look at him, removing the final pin from her dark curls. "What if it's a challenge that pits us against each other?"

"Must you fight me every step of the way? I'm just thinking about last night and your—"

"Dress? Quick wit? Legendary card-playing?"

Teddy rubbed a hand over his face. "Your inability to kill that assassin."

"I don't lack the ability. I just needed another second," Stella said. "You saved me the effort."

Teddy pushed past her. The lush ferns bracketing the trail brushed over his boots as he stepped toward the front doors and the waiting priestess.

He'd expected to feel a pang of grief at the sight of the intricate gilded design on the doors that Grace had liked so much. But he felt more determined than anything else.

The priestess outside of the temple, clad in pale pink robes and a flower crown, held up a hand as they approached. "State your purpose, please."

"I need to speak to my—" Stella stopped to correct herself. "We'd like to speak with Goddess Desiree urgently."

The priestess eyed them as if she'd never seen them before, even though she'd checked them both into the temple ceremony just a few days ago.

It felt like a lifetime ago now. How foolish Teddy was, thinking that he'd be paired with Grace when she'd been trying to break up with him. It was a relief to finally be putting this whole thing behind him. This was just one task checked off of his exhaustive list, but it would allow him to have his focus back so he could win the Gauntlet Games.

Winning was still the priority. He'd given up too much already. Even if he couldn't marry Grace, he still wanted the right to choose his partner in the future. He hadn't realized that envisioning his entire future intertwined with Grace's meant he'd have no vision for himself alone. Now he was at a loss for most of it, but he knew his chance at happiness would rely at least in part on not being forced into a political marriage.

The priestess stared blankly at Stella as she flipped through the thick guest book. "Let me check. What are your names?"

Stella sighed, exasperated. "Stella Selene McKay and Theodore Davide Savero."

The priestess paged through the book with excruciating slowness. Finally, she found their page and held it open for them to sign. "You have to sign here and acknowledge that you understand the rules—"

Stella huffed and signed the book. "Yes, yes. We know the rules. We just did this a few days ago." She signed her name in the book sloppily and passed the pencil to Teddy.

He leaned over the book to read what they were signing.

"Teddy, come on." She tugged on his arm. "You must be joking. Has anyone ever told you that there's not a right way to do every single thing? Let's just go get this over with."

"Didn't you learn your lesson last time?" Teddy asked, arching a brow.

She crossed her arms and leaned against the wall.

Teddy scanned the page. "What does this say here?"

The priestess leaned over and squinted at the place where Teddy's finger rested. "That you accept the outcome."

"So it's the same as last time?"

Stella laughed. "It's not like it could get worse, Teddy. It's all up from here. Now, if your curiosity is satisfied, can we please go? I'm so sweaty and I need a bath. I just want to eat something and cool down."

Teddy hesitated a moment before signing the book. The priestess waved them inside.

As soon as they stepped into the entryway, the energy of the hall felt different. It wasn't just the lack of people gathered for the moon bonding ceremonies; it was a quiet hum that stirred in Teddy's chest as he entered the space, like the bond knew it was returning to its source.

A beautiful priestess greeted them. "Welcome back, Your Highness. Lady McKay. We are happy to host you, though surprised to see you so quick to return. Are you eager to affirm your bond?"

Teddy opened his mouth to speak but closed it when he saw the disgust on Stella's face at the mere suggestion.

"Could you try to look less horrified?" he grumbled.

"Not really, no." Stella turned her gaze back to the priestess. "No, we are here to speak with my—with the goddess—if she's in residence today, of course."

The priestess's full lips lifted into a smile. "Of course. We are happy to host you and she is here, though she's in private company at the moment. Perhaps you would prefer to help yourselves to some dinner and freshen up in our suites."

"Yes, please," Stella said.

"Perfect. You'll find soaps and oils in the baskets by the cooling springs just outside of your suites. You may help yourself to any of them. We will send clothes to your rooms," the priestess said as she shepherded them down the hallway away from the entrance.

"But we have our own clothes," Teddy said.

The priestess smiled at him indulgently. "I'm certain you do, Your Grace, but for private audiences, the goddess prefers her subjects wear clothing of her choosing and she is quite particular. She won't take an audience without it."

Teddy wanted to argue that they hadn't done that the night of the moon ceremony, but he kept his mouth shut. This was a goddess flexing her power for the sake of doing so.

He followed the priestess and Stella down the white marble hallway, past tall vases full of bright pink roses and pale peonies.

The priestess guided Stella and Teddy into suites beside each other.

"We will drop off refreshments momentarily," the priestess said.

Then, the door closed behind Teddy and he was finally, blessedly alone. The room was small but beautiful, appointed with cream linens on a large bed, a pitcher of water with sliced lemons in it on the nightstand beside a vase full of a dozen pale pink roses. Orange early evening sunlight poured in through the sliding glass doors that led out to a stone patio and a private bath.

Teddy peeled off his clothes, dropped them in a pile, and immediately walked outside and descended into the bathing pool. He was so eager for the relief of the cool water that he didn't even test to see how deep it was. He crossed the pool, heading straight for the small trickling waterfall on the far end of the alcove, letting the water pour over his head.

The relief was instant as it rinsed away the sweat and dust from the road, leaving Teddy feeling refreshed.

Something moving between the large leafy foliage to his left made him jump.

The bond in his chest hummed to life. *Stella.*

Their suites were right beside each other, so of course their bathing pools would be too.

She caught his eye and offered a completely unselfconscious salute.

Water slid down her neck, along her collarbones, disappearing between the upper swells of her breasts. The large leaves between the two pools were just high enough to block her chest. He was grateful for the greenery between them, though some small part of him loathed it. He needed the bond gone and that irrational interested possessiveness with it. Stella McKay was not his, and he didn't want her to be.

She hummed softly as she lathered her hair.

Teddy tried not to look, but even as he busied himself choosing a soap, his gaze relentlessly slid back to her. *Just the bond*, he chided himself. The pull to her was undeniable.

She plunged under the water to rinse. Then, she popped up and poured some sort of conditioner into her hair, working her fingers through it thoroughly.

Teddy tried not to watch her every movement, but she kept humming and drawing his attention.

She plunged under again and rinsed her hair. Finally, she surfaced and poured some sort of oil into her hands. She ran it through her waist-length hair and the scent of something soft and floral hit Teddy.

Stella loosely twisted the wet curls up on top of her head and pinned them into place. Then she descended on the plate of fruit and cheeses the priestesses had left her as if she hadn't eaten in days.

From his current angle, he could only see her from the collarbones up, but if he walked closer, he would see everything. She smiled at him as she bit into a slice of melon. Juice dripped down her chin and onto her chest before slipping out of sight. Teddy imagined licking it off. How would she react? Just thinking about it sent a surge of heat through his body.

He chided himself for thinking something so lewd about a woman he barely tolerated.

Stella lifted a cherry and her tongue darted out as she pulled the fruit from the stem. "Gods, that's good." She moaned obscenely and the bond in Teddy's chest flared to life.

"Must you eat so loudly?"

He closed his eyes, scrubbing his hair to try to drown out the sound of her so thoroughly enjoying her meal. But with his eyes closed, all he could see was juice dripping onto her chest, and all he could imagine was wiping that smirk from her face by licking her clean. He'd give her something to moan about.

Teddy fisted his hands. That thought was entirely unwelcome.

He ducked below the water to rinse his hair and block out her groaning. Normally, the thought of going underwater in something other than a bathtub would be terrifying to him, but the intrusive thoughts sparking through his mind were more frightening.

The water muted everything, and the tightness in his chest released. He blinked his eyes open and pushed back up to the surface. Stella sighed and all the blood in Teddy's body rushed south. He took another breath and dunked himself again.

This time, he looked at the light rippling over the perfectly clear water and the stone floor of the pool. He tried to calm the heat pounding through his veins.

It wasn't as if he hadn't explored things with Grace. They had a great time in bed, but he'd never been that riveted simply by the sounds she made. The stupid heart bond was destroying him. Why had he ever thought it was a good idea to be this connected to anyone? It was ruining his self-control entirely and making him fantasize about truly insane things.

Teddy pushed back up to the surface and drew in a few gasping breaths. As he slid his hand over his head to squeeze the excess water from his hair, he hazarded a glance at Stella. She was eating some type of cream-filled pastry.

She took a bite and the white cream spilled onto her hand. Teddy was riveted. She held his gaze as she lifted her fingers to her lips and sucked each one clean. His cock twitched as she swirled her tongue around them and watched his every reaction. Despite the cool water, his whole body was on fire. He was helpless to the pull of her.

"Hungry, Your Grace?" Her voice was so sultry. "I didn't think you had a taste for sweets."

Clastor's fucking sword. Teddy dunked himself again, trying to regain even the smallest semblance of control. He turned, studying the patterns of light on the rocks that divided the two pools, only realizing for the first time that it was less of a wall and more of an arch, designed so lovers could visit each other, he supposed.

That was when he saw her ass. He gasped and water rushed into his mouth. He pushed back up to the surface, coughing and sputtering water.

When he finally got control of himself, Stella had flattened the leaves between the pools. She leaned into the wall, her breasts just below the edge of the stone. Seeing her like that, all he could imagine was being behind her with her firm ass pressing against him. He needed to dunk himself again, but if he went under now, he'd be looking directly at her pussy.

His cock was painfully hard, and he'd done more sweating than cooling down.

"Are you well?" she asked, her eyes full of both curiosity and lust.

He held perfectly still as her gaze raked over him. Her cheeks pinked as her eyes traveled over his abs, then lower. This close to the wall, she could see everything through the perfectly clear water.

Teddy had always been a bit vain—not in the same way Jalen was, but he spent hours training. He liked the mixture of shock and interest on Stella's face.

"My eyes are up here, *princess*," he said.

Her gaze shot to his and her cheeks flushed bright red. She liked the nickname just fine when Fionn used it. Teddy was thrilled to ruin it for her.

Stella crossed her arms and stood to her full height. "Just surprised to see so many muscles on a man whose most practiced exercise seems to be judging other people. I'm shocked you can find the time for anything else."

Teddy smirked. "Happy I could impress you."

He fought to keep his gaze on her face and failed. Her hair was still pinned on top of her head, but water dripped from the ends of several loose tendrils along her neck, over her crossed arms, and down the lines of her firm stomach. Her figure was lithe, not quite imbued with a warrior's strength, but she was clearly a woman who trained regularly. Teddy stopped following the droplets' descent at the water's edge. He would *not* look any lower.

Lust warmed the bond in his chest. Did she *like* that he was interested?

"Much as I appreciate your gawking, I was hoping you'd give me some peace," he said slowly.

Stella kicked her lower lip into a pout. "Oh, I'm sorry. Am I disturbing you? Is the prince used to bathing alone in exclusive fancy washrooms?"

Teddy scowled at her. "No. I just find your incessant moaning very irritating."

Stella smiled wickedly. "Oh?"

She was doing it on purpose, trying to wield the power she had over him like some kind of game.

It had been too long since he'd had sex. Teddy wasn't opposed to a casual fling, but he also wasn't the type of man to go long stretches without intimacy.

The past few weeks had given him little alone time. From traveling to Olney to being dodged by Grace during the festival until now, he had been so busy and exhausted every day that he'd hardly had time for self-gratification.

He regretted that now, with a beautiful, wet, naked woman in front of him trying to drive him out of his mind.

"It's just this place," she said softly, her face somber. "It's just the energy of the temple and Aunt Desiree. It makes things feel a certain way. I used to notice when she visited. It feels lovely and compelling, but you don't need to worry. It's not permanent."

Of course—the goddess was doing this on purpose. She was probably trying to force them to spend more time together.

"She's probably watching us from a temple window somewhere."

"You don't think she was actually busy?" Teddy asked.

Stella shrugged. "I can't say for sure, but I think it's a fair guess. She's known to be quite nosey—always getting involved where she isn't needed."

She turned back toward her room and climbed out of the pool

slowly, as if making sure she had purchase on each mossy rock before continuing. That slowness granted Teddy a long look at her backside.

"Your Grace, I can feel you staring at my ass," she said without turning around. She wrapped a linen towel around her waist and grabbed a second one to dry her hair.

"It's a nice ass," Teddy said.

"Nice?" She scoffed. "*Nice*? Nice is how you describe a new type of tea or an afternoon stroll."

Teddy couldn't fight a smile. "Oh, I'm sorry, *my lady*. Allow me to adjust my compliments to your requirements. You have a *legendary* ass. The bards should write songs about it, the likes of which would be sung in pubs for years to come, so all in the two kingdoms can forever bask in the glory of it."

She grinned at him over her shoulder. She was still topless, facing away from him, with the towel wrapped around her waist. Water dripped from the curls atop her head, trailing down her smooth back to the dimples at the base of her spine.

She smirked. "And to think you were horrified at how inappropriate it was to bathe next to each other and now you're openly gawking."

Teddy ignored the jab, his gaze catching on the edges of a shiny scar on her side. He could only see the barest hint of it, but he felt angry that she'd been permanently marked while trying to win a contest for a man who didn't appreciate her.

She noticed his assessment and tugged the towel higher protectively.

Teddy looked away, feeling chastened. He shouldn't have been looking at her at all, but it was a reflex. He had only seen one woman naked for the past few years and it was simply curiosity that made him look.

But Stella probably felt ashamed of the mark. It was bad enough sharing this forced intimacy with each other—Teddy had no right to her pain.

So he turned and let her retreat without a word spoken.

20

——————

TEDDY

The outfit the priestess had left for Teddy was nothing he would normally wear, but he wasn't about to upset a goddess in her own temple. He'd dressed in the thin, pale pink linen shirt and perfectly fitted pants. It was a bit unnerving that they fit so well, as if the priestess had taken one glance at him and knew his measure.

He ran a hand through his hair, stepped out of his room, and followed the white stone hallways to the main temple. Candles in various shades of pink and cream and roses and peonies covered a white marble altar.

Behind the altar, Goddess Desiree lounged on a plush chaise, an attendant pouring her wine. She looked regal and stunning in an uncanny way that made it hard to do anything but stare at her. Her brown skin glowed in the firelight and her dark fuchsia dress hugged her curves. Her black hair was braided elaborately, twisted around her head and topped with a diamond-encrusted diadem.

When she saw Teddy, her face brightened. She passed her cup to the servant and stood, descending the few altar stairs to be on his level.

Teddy pressed three fingers to his forehead, lips, and heart in a sign of reverence and bowed to the goddess.

"Your Grace," she said, her voice a sultry caress. "How lovely to see you looking refreshed. My colors suit you."

Teddy nodded, keeping his eye on the goddess of love's face and not the barely-there fuchsia gown that showed off large swaths of warm brown skin and accentuated her full hourglass figure. Her blue eyes glowed brightly as she looked him over, lingering on his chest as if looking at the bond itself.

"Thank you for your hospitality, goddess."

Desiree clapped her hands and grinned. At first Teddy thought it was at his praise, but then he turned and saw Stella walking into the room.

If he'd thought the bathing situation was inappropriate, the dress Stella wore was downright indecent.

The dusty rose color was beautiful against her fair skin. The neckline plunged between her breasts and the fabric was so sheer that, were it not for some strategically placed ruching and draping, he'd see everything he'd been trying so hard not to look at when they were bathing.

Teddy's mouth went dry as she walked toward him.

He felt the goddess's assessing gaze, but he could not drag his eyes away from Stella.

Finally, when she stepped up beside him, he managed to stop gawking.

Desiree's full lips pushed into a pout. "Look at her. She has still not been well-fucked. What are you waiting for, Your Grace?"

"Aunt Des!" Stella shrieked. "I have, too!"

The goddess gave her a patronizing smile. "My lovely girl, you don't know what you're missing. I can see the lack of vitality in you. I gave you the perfect opening this evening out in the baths. Why did you not take it?" She stepped behind Stella and looked at Teddy over her shoulder. "A man like that is so pent-up. You don't know what you might discover if you can let him loose."

Teddy didn't like the reflection of himself through the goddess's eyes. He knew how to have fun and he certainly knew how to please a woman.

Grace was not his first. He'd had his fair share of fun before they got together. He was certain no one would have called that version of him pent-up, at least not in the bedroom. But that version of him felt remarkably distant now, as if it had happened in another lifetime and he was only now remembering the faint whispers of it.

When neither of them spoke, Desiree crossed her arms. "And you both wish for me to break this bond?"

Teddy and Stella nodded in unison.

"Okay, prove it. Just one kiss and I will stop my nagging," the goddess said. "Honestly, Stella, the fact that you don't have any faith in your favorite auntie is very disappointing. I am telling you that the potential between you is something *extraordinary*."

Stella hesitated for only a moment. "I'm not kissing him. We came here to have you undo this. Teddy is controlling and petty and only cares about himself and his five-year plan for self-improvement or whatever it is he fantasizes about," she huffed.

Teddy gaped at her. Did she really still think that of him? Even after he'd saved her from having to kill someone? Perhaps his chiding her about it was the reason. Teddy understood that conflict. He used to feel that way, but his parents had trained that hesitance out of him —not to be cruel, but to make a point. When he was younger, he'd hated it, but as he'd grown, he understood they only did it for the sake of his survival.

Now if a man was coming for Teddy, he wouldn't even flinch. And yet, some protective instinct—probably their bond—wanted him to save Stella from needing to be that way. Not to keep her in some state where she was dependent on him, but to preserve the wild whimsy about her that was growing on him. She didn't belong in the Gauntlet Games—not because she wasn't skilled or because she couldn't win, but because she didn't have it in her heart to kill. Every other competitor was there to do what they must, and while death was not a guarantee, it was a clear and ever-present possibility.

Desiree sighed. "You are your mother's daughter."

"Thank you," Stella said sweetly.

"Not a compliment," the goddess said.

Stella glared at Desiree, but the goddess just waved a dismissive hand and started toward the hallway. "Fine. Suit yourselves. If you are so content to waste your potential, I cannot make you see that which you're blind to. I'm off to find better company." She turned to face Teddy, her eyes glowing in a subtle threat. "Keep her alive."

Teddy waited for the goddess's footsteps to retreat down the hall, the echo of her silk slippers growing fainter until a door closed and he and Stella were finally alone.

"You really think I'm cruel and petty, *Minyha*?" Teddy asked.

She sighed and crossed the room to pick at some wax that had spilled onto the altar. "I think you decided to hate me for years over some imagined slight of your sister, and perpetuated our prank war so you could keep me at a distance. Easier to see me as a charmed fairy princess instead of a real person." She met his gaze. "*Minyha*. It means magic?"

Teddy smirked. There was no way she knew Old Novumi. "It means you should be better studied in languages if you're going to be queen of Olney."

Her anger hit him in the chest. *Good*. He was angry, too.

"I saved you from having to kill that man last night. The least you should be is grateful."

"Grateful?" she spat. "I didn't need you to step in and play savior, Theodore. I am quite capable of saving myself. I know you're used to Grace, but some women just want the chance to fight for themselves."

Teddy crossed the room to stand right in front of her, pointing to her neck. "He was strangling you. Gods help me. You are fucking maddening."

She stepped closer, her nose mere inches from his. "And you are a spoiled prince with a savior complex and—"

He thrust his hand into her hair, yanked her head back, and kissed her. It was a reflex in response to the sudden pulsing need to rid himself of this energy. Their connection set his teeth on edge and electrified every nerve in his body with wanting.

He waited for her to shove him away, but Stella tugged him closer and that was all the invitation he needed. He walked her backward, shoving aside the candelabras so he could press her against the marble wall without setting her indecent dress on fire. The candles crashed to the floor, and all the flames on their side of the room snuffed out, filling the air with fragrant rose-scented smoke.

Teddy tore the pins out of Stella's hair violently and yanked her head back for better access. He slid his hand down her neck, his thumb resting over her pulse. He'd thought about his hands on her throat before, but for the sake of strangling her, not for the thrill of seeing how her heart raced as he kissed her.

He was starving for an outlet, and it seemed Stella was too. All the stress and grief of the past few days came out at once.

She bit his bottom lip and bunched her hands in his tunic. There was no tentativeness about it. Everything in the kiss was hungry and incendiary, just like her magic. Teddy shifted to cup the back of her head, his other arm curling around her waist.

She ground against his thigh. Fuck, that was hot. He wanted her to get off, wanted to see her get herself off using him, wanted to hear the sounds he brought out of her by his mere presence. Being prince and wielding storms had never made him feel as powerful as this.

He'd always had power he didn't want—influence at court, rule of a kingdom, rule of storms—but this wildness was something he wanted the ability to coax out or tame at will.

Stella gasped into his mouth, her tongue tangling with his. She tasted sweet and tart like cherries.

He wrapped her hair around his fist, tilting her head back, and nipped at her jaw. She arched into him, her soft breasts pressing against his chest. He kissed along the length of her jaw and ran his nose down her neck, breathing in the sweet floral scent of her skin. Gods, it was intoxicating. He didn't just want to taste her; he wanted to consume her, to see what would happen if he slid his hand up her dress. He dragged his teeth over the spot where her neck met her shoulder, and she cursed.

She dug her nails into the back of his head, urging him on, and rubbed herself harder against his thigh.

Teddy felt like he was going to combust. His skin was hot and tingling, his whole body lit from within by some supernatural fever stoked by her touch. He kissed his way back up her neck until he finally met her lips.

He pressed her back against the wall, his hips rolling to meet her rhythm. His cock was painfully hard, straining against his pants.

Stella shuddered and sighed, tipping her head back.

Gods, he wanted to lay her on the altar stairs and spread her thighs and make her come so hard she'd feel it for days. He wanted to wipe that smug smile off of her face for good. She was so certain she knew him. But she had no idea how happily he'd ruin her for any other man.

Teddy jerked away, equally disturbed and elated at that thought.

A shockwave raced through him, like a hundred little sparks lighting at once behind his sternum and spreading through his limbs. Goosebumps rose on his skin, but the sensation wasn't unwelcome. The glowing feeling in his chest grew downward like roots and upward like branches. The sensation was pleasant and too much, and he wanted more.

Stella stared at him, her green eyes bright in the candlelight, pupils blown wide. Her face and neck were flushed and every place he'd kissed was bright red. A gentle thrum of satisfaction pulsed through him. It was like he'd left his signature behind on her skin.

He shouldn't have liked it.

She ran her hands down her goosebump-riddled arms and pressed her palm to her heart. "What was that?" She touched her other hand to her swollen lips and looked up at him with wide doe eyes. "*What did you do?*"

Teddy opened his mouth to speak.

"You sealed the bond."

They both jumped and spun to see Desiree standing in the temple doorway. She took stock of the candles and puddled wax spilled across the white marble floor.

"I knew you could do it," the goddess said with a smug smile.

Teddy shook his head. "No, no, no. Take it back. I didn't agree to this. I—" He tugged at his shirt, his chest suddenly so tight he couldn't breathe.

"I don't want to be connected to him *forever*," Stella said. "I never wanted to be connected to him at all. We didn't agree to this."

"You did when you came here a second time—when you signed the book to enter—"

Stella stared into Teddy's eyes, and he saw his own shock and horror reflected there.

Mercifully, the goddess seemed to realize that they were already poised to explode and took a step back. "Well, I was going to offer my congratulations."

"You were going to offer smug satisfaction and nothing else. You've done enough," Stella said sharply.

The goddess arched a brow. "Don't forget whose temple you're standing in, Stella. I'm a gracious host, but I abhor rudeness in my house."

Stella clasped her hands in a white-knuckle grip. "Thank you for your hospitality, goddess. But we'd like to be alone, if you don't mind."

The goddess smirked. "I bet you would. You may return to your rooms when you're finished being in denial."

Desiree offered one last smug grin and left them alone in the half-dark temple.

Stella's chest heaved as she tried to catch her breath. "Why did you do that?"

"Why did *you*?" Teddy countered.

The air between them was still charged, like the atmosphere before a storm. Teddy wasn't sure whether to stay or run. He had kissed her, but she'd pounced on him just as eagerly.

He took a step toward her and all the candles in the temple flared.

She held up a hand. "Just give me a second. This bond is messing with my magic."

Teddy arched a brow. "The bond? I thought fire was your strongest magic."

"It is, but my magic follows my emotions."

Teddy looked at the flaring candles on the altar. "And you're feeling—"

She cocked her head and glared at him.

Anger. Good. That was safer. Whatever line they'd just accidentally stumbled over was dangerous and volatile. They needed to stay in safer territory.

"It doesn't have to mean anything," he said.

"It doesn't," she agreed, but a swift shock of hurt slid through their bond.

Did she want it to mean something? Teddy studied her, but her face betrayed nothing.

"I never thought you'd do that," Stella said.

"It was just the bond. I still love Grace."

Stella scoffed. "What? Are you worried I will tell her? Your secret is safe with me, but I'm not sure that she cares."

Teddy scowled at her. "Of course she would care."

"I know breakups are hard, but I didn't think you were the type to stay in denial."

Teddy clenched his hands into fists. "I'll show Grace I can change. I can be better."

Stella scoffed. "You can't always be better."

"*I* can."

She shook her head and blew out a breath. "I pity you that you think that."

Every time they found common ground, it was as if she was resolute to take them right back to where they'd started. Teddy could take all of her irritable jabs and all her naive sunshine hopefulness, but he would absolutely not take pity from Stella McKay.

"You don't understand. You are beloved. You are the treasured daughter of the fairy-tale lovers of Olney. I am the son of a rumored bastard. I come from an untraditional family system. And for the past five years, the Sons of Endros have been mercilessly making our lives hell. There is no room for error." He shook his head and scrubbed a hand down his face. "There's no room to even breathe. All for a job I don't feel equipped for or capable of. How could I possibly when I'm constantly reminded of the ways I'm falling short?

"The problem with keeping a kingdom full of people happy is that everyone wants something different. There are those who aren't happy without their status. They aren't satisfied unless there are people beneath them. They only thrive in oppression. But we don't want that. My father was hoping the monarchy of Argaria would have less power now, but every time we have tried to cede some, the Sons of Endros have made havoc. There is never a moment where I can be seen as weak or even human. You think I'm cold? Set apart from everyone else? I have no choice, Stella. I have to be." He shook his head. "Being out in that bar the other night was the first time I've been out in six months and the first time I've been drunk in years—the first time ever in public. A king must be above reproach."

Stella stared at him.

"I can't be too cruel, or too soft, too quick to anger, or too patient. I am always perilously perched on a cliff, blindfolded and told to walk the edge without falling. I'm always one false move from slipping and ruining everything for my family."

"But the twins and Alexandra are not nearly as—"

"They are not the heir to the throne."

She licked her lips and smiled sadly, her face so full of pity he had to look away. "They will always find something," she said softly.

"I know that," he snapped.

She held up her hands. "No. I mean they will always find something. It's not possible for you to be so impeccable that no one will take issue because, to your point, everyone wants something different in a king."

A lump formed in Teddy's throat. That was the sentiment he'd been fighting against for years. He had to be enough. He had to prove to his father that he could do it, that the immense sacrifices Xander had made would be worth it. That the kingdom wouldn't slide into anarchy at the hands of men who wanted to set their culture back hundreds of years, just so they could feel powerful.

His mother, Jessamin, had worked so hard to ensure that the practice of men trading off their daughters into marriage contracts was largely a thing of the past. Women had autonomy now, and they'd used it to choose partners for love, to build careers for themselves to help elevate many of them from poverty. It was her life's work.

That was part of the reason the Sons of Endros were so frustrated to begin with. Men of Argaria and Olney had lost their power over women and, rather than modify their behavior to attract women, they wanted to strip women of the autonomy they'd gained so that they could go back to feeling valuable for merely existing. He could hear his mother saying those words after council meetings. She'd come to Argaria and married his father to make a difference in their world and these patriarchal lunatics were threatening her life's work so they could feel in control.

Stella stepped closer, clearly reading his frustration and stress through the bond. She squeezed his hand.

He was so disoriented. So off-kilter with this new knowledge of her. The softness of her skin, the springtime scent of her so strong and heady at the crook of her neck that he wanted to bury his face there for days.

Teddy looked away, trying to master himself. Twenty-four years of self-control had been completely wrecked by one heart bond.

"This changes nothing," Teddy said, more to himself than her. "I still want to win Grace back."

"Why?" Stella looked almost angry.

"Why what?"

"Why win her back? Why be with someone you have to win over in the first place?"

"Because I love her. Because she's right. I've been too controlling, too—" He searched for the right word. "Rigid. I've been too stuck in my ways, and I haven't been a good partner to her. I can change."

Stella placed a hand softly on his shoulder. Her green eyes met his. "Yes, but Teddy, should you have to?"

The question was a splinter lodged into the deepest, rawest wound in his heart. He'd spent years curating himself. He'd become a creature of meticulous preparation, of schedules and constant improvement. He trained away his flaws, shoving any reservations, any weaknesses into the deepest, darkest corners of his mind, and he only ever let them out when he was alone—with the exception of that moment before the Gauntlet Games binding ceremony when Stella had seen him break down.

He'd been as perfect as possible, but all that perfection had not saved him from constant scrutiny. The more perfect he was, the narrower the measures of success became. He was trying so hard, but the pressure was getting to him.

"If she can only love you if you're different, then does she even love you at all?" Stella asked softly.

She'd made such a succinct and brutal study of him. Those words coming from her gave new meaning to "knowing your enemy." It was unnerving to be seen by her, and he'd had enough surprises for one night.

Teddy felt overexposed, burned to the core by her recognition. There was no judgment behind it; he felt in that moment how much they had in common.

"What would you know about love?" Teddy snapped. "You're so obsessed with your stories, but real love isn't all so neatly tied up."

Stella did not look nearly as put off by his sharp words as he'd hoped. In fact, she looked almost relieved by them.

"Such a skeptic," she said with a sigh. "But cynicism doesn't make you mature. It just makes you boring."

Teddy crossed his arms and scowled at her, but he was happy to return to that dynamic. The kiss had shifted the landscape between them. Her taunt brought them back to common ground.

Stella held her hands out in a truce. "Look, things obviously did not go as planned tonight. We're both on edge. We have to be back in time for the next challenge. Let's go get some sleep. I'll even tell you one of my stories that you hate so much."

His lips twitched, but he appraised her with skepticism. Other than his moment of panic before the tournament binding, it had been a long time since he heard her tell a story. His sisters had always enjoyed the McKay family's storytelling rituals and came home raving about Stella's stories every solstice.

She rolled her eyes. "*Your Grace*, you will love it. It has blood and violence and a walled-off city in the middle of a monster-infested forest. If you're not at least entertained, I'll let you give it a full realist's critique at the end. I'll even tell you how you're right about everything."

Teddy bit his cheek to keep himself from smiling.

She cocked her head and winked at him. "You're right—I'm trying to de-escalate things and I know those words will just get you all hot and bothered again."

Teddy smothered a laugh. "Fine. Spin your fluffy story."

She threaded her arm through his and Teddy let his heart-bonded nemesis lead him away from the mess they'd made in the temple.

21

STELLA

One kiss ruined Stella McKay's life.

She hadn't slept all night, and she was paying for it as she warmed up for the second Gauntlet Games challenge. Fatigue weighted every swipe of her blades.

The sun beat down on her as she slashed her short swords across the chest of the practice ring dummy.

Teddy had kissed her. *Teddy Savero*. Lifelong prank nemesis. Incessant royal snob. Broody Prince of Argaria.

Teddy was painfully handsome, but she'd always been too put off by his seriousness to think of him as desirable.

And yet, she'd tossed and turned all night, thinking about the urgency with which he'd kissed her. She hadn't realized someone so composed could also possess that kind of passion. He had managed to do the one thing she'd thought him impossible of doing—surprise her.

Arden was a great kisser, and from their first kiss they'd slipped into a rhythm together with such ease. He had kissed her with urgency, passion, and sweetness, but he'd never kissed her with the violent, wild abandon Teddy had.

What had Teddy said when he was drunk? *"You're always here. Like a fucking haunting."*

She understood what he meant. That was how she felt. Haunted by the memory of his hands on her skin, the rush of his breath on her neck, the vibration of his groan in her mouth. It was an unfortunate time to have magic that perfectly preserved memories. She couldn't stop turning it over, analyzing every touch, picking apart his every movement, his every sigh.

Each time, she felt the same flutter in her chest like butterflies taking flight around her heart. Really it was more like moths driving mindlessly toward a flame.

She'd known immediately that it was a mistake. She'd expected Teddy to be methodical, scientific in his approach, but he was almost reckless in his commitment to unnerve her.

She hated that it felt so good to kiss him. The new connection in her chest seemed to swell and shudder like a sigh of relief just from the memory of it.

The bigger mistake wasn't letting him try to crush her with a kiss. It was trying to match him movement for movement.

Heat spread through her body still, blooming up like roses reaching toward the summer sun and down like autumn roots trying to hold fast through winter. Her skin felt fevered, made new by all the places he had touched her, as if the pleasure was a blessing and now she was reborn.

She kept poring over the memory, tracing it repeatedly, hoping the repetition would dull its effect. Instead, it scored it into her brain, into every nerve ending in her body, her skin prickling with the need for him to do it again. Stella clenched her thighs together against the building ache.

"Sayla's bow!" she huffed.

She came at the dummy with full force, blades flying, slashing against the matted straw chest. Sweat beaded at her hairline when she finally stopped moving.

Much as she wanted it to, waling on the dummy wouldn't exorcise the ghost of the kiss from her body. She wasn't cleansed. She was cursed. The more she tried to force the new knowledge from her mind, the deeper it rooted.

They'd solidified the bond. Now she was stuck with him. *Forever.*

If someone had told her months earlier that she would have this kind of connection, she would have been thrilled. It wasn't the same as what her parents had, but it was the modern world's closest estimation. She'd thought having someone who was always there—always connected to her—would feel comforting, but now she felt unnerved and entirely on edge. Of course, she would have also assumed the person would be Arden and that the bond would be requested instead of thrust upon her.

She huffed in frustration and went through one last sequence of footwork and advances until she felt her energy waning. She stilled and took three deep breaths.

It wasn't the time to lose her composure. Everything was fine. She would adapt to this new normal. Teddy was a good kisser, but it didn't have to mean anything more.

Still, she couldn't stop seeing the look on his face when she'd asked him if he should have to change. A few honest words from him had tipped the balance between them. For years she'd wanted to know how to put him on his heels, but now she wished she didn't know the constant pressure of perfection he felt. His coldness toward her had ensured that he'd always stayed at a comfortable distance. Suddenly he seemed too human.

A bell sounded from the direction of the competitors' tent. The fifteen-minute warning.

Stella shook her head and forced herself through her pre-fight routine to settle her mind. She checked the laces on her breastplate and tightened her armguards. She'd struggled in the first event, but this challenge was all about memory and that was something she had well in hand.

However, her confidence didn't settle her nerves as she walked toward the competitors' tent for the second challenge. They'd been told nothing about the event except that they should pack to travel for seven days. The thought of being away for so long made Stella very nervous. She was already exhausted from fighting with Teddy, fighting for her life, and fighting with Kate.

Stella was so angry that her friend hadn't left word for her, knowing she was walking back into the arena again.

It was a relief, at least, that Arden had sent more roses to wish her luck. They'd arrived with a note that simply said, *"Be safe."* He was clearly respecting her request for secrecy.

The sun beat down on her as she walked through the bustling temporary market set up by the arena. The scent of candied nuts and spun sugar filled the air, and children screamed in delight as they handed coins over and snatched their sweets.

Stella's mind wouldn't settle as she rounded the back of a refreshment tent.

As the competitors' tent came into view, a hand clamped over her mouth and yanked her backward. She tried to bite the fingers covering her mouth, but her captor just tightened his grip.

Something cold and metal clamped around her wrist. She recognized Dixon's voice as he whispered a spell before Stella managed to wiggle an arm loose and punch him in the throat. He stumbled back, gasping.

It felt like she'd been plunged underwater, the whole world dulled, bled of color and sound. She stared at the bracelet on her wrist and the recognition snapped into place. An Unsummoner bracelet, an item spelled to block a witch's elemental magic until it was removed by the person who put it on.

Stella didn't know how he'd acquired such an artifact. Though they were once barbarically used in training for witches pursuing the Gauntlet when her parents were young, their use had been outlawed except in extreme cases. In Olney, they were only used for dangerous criminals awaiting trial for using their magic to hurt others. They weren't the kind of items freely available.

Stella yanked on the cuff. She hadn't been cut off from her magic since her childhood, and she was bereft by the loss of it.

A shadow fell over her and Stella looked up as Rett stepped out from behind the tent beside them.

"No burns for us today," Rett said. "It's temporary. We just want to test something and we can't do it if you're boiling our skin off."

Irritating that they'd learned their lesson from their previous scuffle.

"Hold her hand out," he said.

Dixon restrained her and clamped his hand over her mouth again as Drew grabbed Stella's arm and wrenched it to the side, petting it tenderly.

Stella's blood ran cold, but she didn't have time to worry about what he had in mind. He bent her finger back, and she gasped in agony. He waited. Then, he did it again a moment later with another finger. Stella's stomach turned over, the pain so bright and sudden that her body seemed poised to get it out by any means necessary.

She swallowed the bile and bit the hand covering her mouth, trying to yell for help. She wasn't a damsel, but even she knew that she couldn't fight off four elite warriors without her magic or a weapon. Not when they'd had the element of surprise, at least.

They weren't supposed to attack her outside of events. But if no one was around to see her wounded, who would punish them?

"I was having a drink at a bar in town last night and I heard the most interesting piece of local gossip," the Roach said. He pulled out a dagger and tested the point on his ring finger. "A young man was there celebrating being heart-bonded to the woman he loves. It was quite romantic."

Stella stilled her squirming. He couldn't possibly know. Only their families knew, and they wouldn't tell anyone.

"I congratulated him. Bought him a nice whiskey to celebrate, even though he was already a bit in his cups. Then he leaned in close, and do you know what he said to me, Stella?"

Stella cocked her head and tried to give him her most bored look. She focused on the throbbing in her hand.

Rett leaned closer to her. "He said that his lady was delighted to be at the temple at the same time as Prince Teddy Savero and even more excited to see him heart-bonded." Rett shook his head and laughed. "Now, you have to imagine my surprise, Stella. His Grace is not exactly the type you'd peg as a romantic. So I asked if he and Lady Grace were happy. And do you know what the man told me?"

Dixon wouldn't move his hand, so she gave a quick shake of her head.

"He said that was his favorite part. That it was very romantic to see the prince paired with the daughter of Olney's most famous soul bond. He felt it had a certain fairy-tale quality to it." Rett grinned. "Wouldn't you agree?"

Stella struggled against Dixon's grip. If they knew they could hurt her to get to Teddy and vice versa, they could use that to their advantage in the next challenge. She was certain that Teddy had felt her pain. She needed to get away before he reacted to it.

Christophe rounded the corner with a wide smile plastered to his face. He nodded, and the Roach turned and patted Stella on the shoulder.

"Would you look at that? We have confirmation. Lady McKay has been a very naughty girl, running off to the Temple of Desiree to get a bond."

Stella's only saving grace was that she was in so much pain her panic blended right in. They couldn't know. Especially before the second challenge. She could think of a good lie. It would be fine.

But her hope evaporated as Teddy rounded the tent, his gaze passing over her before coming to rest on the Roach.

"Rett, what the fuck do you think you're doing?" Teddy asked.

Rett cracked his knuckles and Stella winced, the memory of her own bones cracking so fresh in her mind that she almost vomited.

"I'm unraveling a little mystery. It seems you got yourself bonded to Lady McKay and now you're both in the contest together. Do you know what they call that, Savero?"

Teddy crossed his arms. "It's 'Your Grace' or 'Your Highness.'"

Stella almost laughed. She'd never met a man with more contempt for his title, but he still wanted to pass along the humiliation of making Rett address him properly.

If she wasn't careful, she might actually start to like Teddy for his personality. She wrinkled her nose at the thought.

"You have a huge liability, *Your Grace*," Rett said with a mocking bow.

"It's an interesting theory, but I'm afraid it's not true," Teddy said.

Stella felt his rage simmering through their bond.

"Nice try, Savero. We knew better than to believe the words of a happy drunkard at a bar. But we know it's true now," Dixon said.

"The second I snapped her fingers, you winced and found us. I'd say that's pretty clear," Drew said.

Stupid fucking bond. All Teddy had to do was not react. It was a broken finger. Stella wasn't bleeding out.

Rett clicked his tongue in admonishment. "She certainly gets around. Is it that smart mouth of hers, Savero? Is it as good at sucking cock as it is at snarky comebacks? Can't imagine how else she'd manage to hook two princes."

Teddy straightened, his hand flexing at his side.

Stella hadn't seen him look like that before, his eyes full of unleashed fury. An electrical charge passed through the air.

"Careful, Roach. I don't like when people touch what's mine."

Mine. The word sent a shiver through Stella.

Just the bond. Just magic. But Teddy was looking at Rett's hand on her arm with murderous intent.

Death whispers burst to life in the air, and Stella froze. She looked from Rett to Dixon to Christophe and Drew. All of them seemed equally menacing. The whispers crescendoed suddenly and Stella held her breath, waiting to see who would move first.

Rett ran his hand up Stella's neck and over her cheek affectionately. "Olney hunters are a chatty bunch. I hear she heals so quickly thanks to that goddess blood. We could have a good time with her. I bet it will take her hours to die. And you'll feel it the whole time, Savero."

"Keep your fucking voice down," Teddy snapped, looking over his shoulder.

They were far enough from the tent that it was unlikely the other competitors could hear them. Still, with so many warriors possessing enhanced hearing, Stella wasn't certain that some of the more astute of them might pick up on the fact that half of their group was missing and come poke around.

"I don't think I will," Rett said. "I wish I had realized sooner that you were a two-for-one deal. I could have knocked you both out in the first round." His rat-like face pinched in delight as he pulled out his dagger and pressed the flat of the blade to Stella's cheek.

Teddy held perfectly still, but the first tingle of storm magic crackled through the air. "You'll be disqualified from the Games. You probably already will be. You attacked a competitor outside of a challenge."

"Who will tell?" Rett asked.

His intent was suddenly clear. Stella and Teddy couldn't tell the Games officials without Rett and his friends sharing loudly about their bond.

She brushed her fingers over one of the throwing knives tucked in her vest. The death whispers grew shriller and more insistent. Then, they abruptly cut off.

Stella glanced around their circle. Clearly, the whispers hadn't been for them, but she felt no relief at that.

"It looks like we are at an impasse," Rett said smugly.

Teddy's gaze turned lethal as Rett nodded. Dixon released his hand from her mouth and grabbed the cuff on her wrist again. He whispered an incantation and the Unsummoner bracelet slid free.

She jerked her arm from Drew's grip, but not before Rett nicked the skin along her jaw.

Stella clapped her hand to the cut. It was shallow. It would heal perfectly and not leave a scar, but the fact that he'd gotten away with the cheap shot after his friends had broken two of her fingers made her blind with rage.

"We're going to have so much fun in this challenge." Rett laughed as he and his minions retreated.

Teddy was on her in seconds, pulling out a handkerchief and wiping the blood from Stella's face.

She swatted at his hand. "It's fine. It won't even scar."

Teddy took her face firmly in his callused hand and tilted her chin up. He ran his thumb gingerly over the place where the cut had been just a moment earlier. But he wasn't looking at the mark. He was staring at her lips.

Heat flushed Stella's body, a thumping pulse of desire beating through the bond.

"Teddy." Her voice was a breathless rasp.

She couldn't decide if she wanted to shove him away or pull him closer. Everything was so confusing. All the emotions flying back and forth through their bond and the adrenaline still coursing through her blood made her desperate to release the pent-up energy in her body.

There were too many people around to be looking at each other like this, and yet Stella couldn't tear her eyes away.

"I'm sorry," Teddy whispered. "I should have been more strategic, but it was so much pain hitting me at once. I thought you were—"

"It's fine." Stella gritted her teeth as she set her fingers. It would take the bone longer to heal and it would hurt all day, but she was still in one piece.

The bell rang in the arena, startling them both. Five-minute warning.

Teddy pulled away. "Stay close to me. We don't know who Rett might tell about this and they're for sure going to be coming for us now that they know."

She nodded, adjusted her quiver and bow across her body, and brushed her hands down her leather vest. There were eight blades tucked into the soft leather, a gift of fine Novumi craftsmanship from Queen Jessamin and King Xander on her twentieth birthday. It fit snugly over her leather breastplate and fastened around her waist.

Stella remembered the way her father had looked at that vest— like he hoped she'd never have a use for it. When he saw her in it that morning, he'd gone out to his workshop immediately to work off his anxiety.

Stella felt guilty for worrying him, but after the last challenge, she'd adopted a "the more weapons the better" approach.

The roar of the crowd swelled as Stella and Teddy entered the arena. Gone were the pits from earlier in the week. Now the ground was sunbaked and cracked, dust trailing them as they crossed the field to line up next to the rest of the competitors.

Stella squinted at the bustling crowd. Ladies sat fanning themselves beneath the early summer sun. Vendors walked through the stands, handing out glasses of lemonade.

Stella felt Arden's gaze before she saw him. She smiled with what little reassurance she could muster and was relieved when she saw that he had a pink rose pinned to his lapel as if he was carrying her favor.

It was a romantic gesture—a way to let her know she was still on his mind and in his heart—even if she'd kissed his Argarian counterpart the night before. She wanted to appreciate it, but the sight of it left her feeling terribly guilty. She'd managed to ignore the sneaking sense that she'd betrayed him by kissing Teddy since it happened, but looking at him now, she felt rotten.

However, she had more pressing problems to handle. If Rett and his friends had access to an Unsummoner bracelet, they could use it on anyone in the competition. She needed to stay far away from them, and she needed to make sure Teddy didn't do anything stupid like try to pay them back.

They'd talked about it at length on the ride back to Olney that morning. Their goal for this challenge, assuming they didn't have to be at each other's throats, was to steer clear of the rest of the field and let them pick each other off.

Stella scanned the royal booth and met her mother's eyes. Cecilia visibly relaxed when Stella smiled at her, then drew a finger across her throat and tapped her ear. The death whispers. Cecilia had heard them, too.

Stella shrugged, feeling suddenly selfish that she hadn't even worried someone else might have been hurt. When Rett and his minions didn't do anything, she'd assumed all was well. She glanced down the line of competitors.

Eleven of them. Stella counted again and came up with the same number.

"Teddy," she whispered. "Who's missing? Did someone end up being too injured to compete after the last challenge?"

Teddy looked down the line. "Not that I know of." He scanned the group. "Reever. He was fine when we saw him at the pub the other night."

The mercenary's absence made Stella uneasy, but there was no time to worry about him. Not when they were about to embark on the one challenge that could give her an edge.

Endros was already poised on his throne on the gamemaker's dais. He rose from his seat of honor. "Welcome back, competitors. It seems we're one short. I've sent several hunters to remedy that, but rest assured that his blood is probably burning by now. I'm sure he'll show up soon, but time is of the essence, so we'll get started. This is the memory challenge and I'm quite excited about this one. In honor of the origin of the Games, I have decided to send you on your own short quest."

Three women stepped into the sunlit arena. Stella squinted, shading her eyes as they walked closer. She didn't recognize two of them, but she knew the third from seeing her mother's memories. Though she hadn't been seen in almost twenty years, Raven Whitewind looked exactly as she had in the memory Stella prized of the first time her parents had met.

Stella gawked at the woman and the crowd broke into a flurry of loud whispers.

"Who is she?" Teddy whispered.

"That's Raven Whitewind. She's the seer who used to bond guardians and witches for the Gauntlet. She—"

"Bonded your parents," Teddy finished.

Stella nodded. "People thought she was dead. She's been gone for most of my life."

Endros held up his hands, and the crowd quieted. "The point of this challenge is to honor and remember our history lest we make the same mistakes again. And so, I'm granting you this chance to go and take your own Gauntlet journey as they did in the old days, but with a twist. The challenge is simple. You'll each be given an enchanted memory stone with which you can retrieve the memory even if you do not possess memory magic. You must go to the Muddled Mind Bar and Boarding House and retrieve a map from my son."

Urgent whispers rushed through the crowd at the reference to the god of influence and manipulation. Stella had never met Cato, and her mother had always refused to speak about him.

Endros allowed the murmurs to die down before he continued. "You'll then go to the cave marked on your map and retrieve the memory stored there. The original creators of the Gauntlet have been kind enough to grace us with their magic once more, so even those of you who do not possess memory magic will be able to secure the memory in your stone just by bearing witness. The trick is not losing yourself inside the illusion of it."

The tone of his voice and the way Raven wrinkled her nose in response made it clear that the witches' cooperation had been less than enthusiastic.

"What kind of memory?" Fionn asked.

Endros narrowed his glare at the mercenary. "As we all know, memory is an integral part of Olney culture. As the saying goes—we must remember our mistakes so as to not make them again, right?"

The crowd tentatively applauded in agreement.

Endros held up a hand. "That is why I have enlisted the help of the loved ones of each competitor here today. The witches retrieved memories from your friends or relatives who had particularly hard-earned lessons from their lives." Gasps went through the crowd and Endros smiled indulgently at them. "Yes, yes, everyone must pay a tithe to these Games. Otherwise, they won't bring us together. They'll just tear us apart."

Teddy fidgeted beside Stella.

"Now, I'm sure our lively crowd is disappointed to not be able to watch this entire challenge, but I do have a treat," Endros continued. "There will be a daily screening of the returned memories at sundown each day. So you will get your entertainment."

The crowd offered a mix of applause and apprehensive murmurs.

"All contestants will pack and be at the northern edge of town on the main road in a half-hour. Remember that once you cross the line out of town, the challenge rules are in play," Endros said. "And a reminder that you may use all types of magic during this challenge, including elemental summoning, spellwork, and magical objects."

"Great, it's going to be a fucking bloodbath," Teddy whispered.

Stella looked at her parents. Her father was whispering in her mother's ear, their hands intertwined. Her mother looked haunted. She met Stella's gaze again and mouthed, "*I love you.*"

Stella forced herself to focus on what Endros was saying, trying not to worry about what memory he might have demanded from her parents.

"Any family members or friends who attempt to explain anything about the memories they've shared will be hit with burning pain until they stop attempting to break the deal they've made with me, so you will not get any hints out of them." He smiled over his shoulder at Cecilia. "Good luck to all our competitors and I can't wait to see how you all handle yourselves in the field."

A bell rang, signaling the start of their half-hour to retrieve their horses, and Stella and Teddy bolted from the arena.

TWENTY MINUTES LATER, STELLA WAS IN HER FAMILY STABLES, STRAPPING her saddlebag to her horse, Shark. The horse, for his part, would not stop nudging her pocket, looking for the apple slices she'd hidden for him.

"Shark, stop it. We have to get across town in a few minutes," she said, and he nipped at her vest. "Behave yourself."

She was nervous about the challenge, especially now that Rett and his friends knew about her bond with Teddy. Especially now that their bond was stronger and more insistent. She could sense his proximity with alarming precision, her gaze constantly drawn to him.

She felt him now, looming just outside.

"Your horse is named Shark?" Teddy called.

"Yes," Stella said as she led the horse out of the building.

"Why?"

"Because he's gray, and I named him when I was ten and obsessed with sharks."

Teddy laughed, and it occurred to Stella how rarely she heard him laugh. He smiled just as infrequently, but it was similarly riveting with his perfect teeth and full lips and the way it lit up his golden eyes.

Shark nudged Stella's hip.

"Behave, you," she chided.

"Like horse like rider," Teddy teased.

"Yes, we both prefer other company."

Teddy gave her a look that said she'd enjoyed his company just fine the previous night in the temple. At least he wouldn't say it, knowing she could say the same to him.

He mounted his horse gracefully, and Stella followed suit. They trotted out of the stable grounds and up the trail to town.

Stella nodded to Teddy's horse. "What's his name?"

"I suck at poker."

She frowned. "Odd time to admit that, but I'm surprised. You're usually so stoic."

"No. That's the horse's name," Teddy said. "I lost a bet with Alex and she picked the name. It was this or Alexandra the Great. I couldn't let her have the satisfaction. I just call him Poker."

"So Alex is good at poker?" Stella asked.

"No, she's just good at cheating."

Stella laughed. "You two have always seemed close."

Teddy nodded as they rode up the main cobbled road through Olney City. "We are, but she's a pain in the ass. She is talented but far too confident for her skill level and, as you've seen firsthand, indiscreet with her dalliances, of which there are many. I wish she had just a tad less love to give."

"Don't begrudge a woman her fun," Stella said.

Ahead of them, the road clogged with a crowd of competitors and onlookers. Only a narrow path through remained. Stella pulled

Shark to a stop and Teddy and Poker stopped beside her, content with their place at the back of the line.

"Jalen and Juliana have always seemed more of a unit," Stella said.

Teddy nodded. "Jules is smart and so good in social situations, but we just don't interact as much as we did when we were young. And Jalen, he's busy with the hunter army."

Screaming erupted behind them, rushing through the crowd in a wave. Stella wrenched her head around, already reaching for her bow. Hooves pounded against the ground and a horse tore up the street toward them, but there was no one on its back.

It wasn't until it was almost on top of them, when the brown horse slowed to a trot, that Stella realized someone *was* actually on its back.

"That's Reever's horse," Fionn said from somewhere ahead of Stella.

A hunter guarding the line managed to grab the reins and slow the panicked horse to a stop.

Stella gasped at the sight.

A deep red line like a smile was cut across Reever's throat. The wound gaped open but the blood on his clothing and the saddle was already drying. Reever's eyes stared sightlessly up at the sky. His body was secured to the horse by several ropes, a dagger jammed into his chest, pinning a piece of paper in place.

Stella's stomach heaved. She looked away and drew in deep, slow breaths to keep herself from vomiting.

The hunter pulled the paper free and held it up to read. The back of the sheet had the symbol of the Sons of Endros drawn on it in blood.

"'You were warned, but you did not listen. As these players hunt each other, so too will they be hunted, one by one. Until there are none. Or until we get a seat at the king's table,'" the hunter read aloud.

The crowd broke out into murmurs and the competitors' horses shifted restlessly. The beasts were clearly reading the anxiety of the crowd.

The spectators turned their attention to Endros, who waited at the front of the line of competitors, astride a large black horse. Sunlight glinted off his salt-and-pepper hair and his golden armor. He looked every bit the god of war, ready for battle, and that was probably the idea.

He lifted his arms. "Quiet, please!"

The murmurs of the crowd died down.

"The Games must go on," Endros said. "I'm sure your monarchs don't want their inability to control their own people to interrupt this sacred tradition."

The god leveled a smug smile at Kings Marcos and Xander in their makeshift royal booth on the balcony of the Winding Way Pub. To their credit, both kings looked entirely unmoved, but Stella could only imagine the chaos that would unfold once they were behind closed doors.

Endros nodded to the hunter holding the starting flag. "You have seven days to complete this task and return to the arena with your memory stones. Good luck," he said.

Endros signaled the flag bearer, who waved the white flag.

The competitors took off immediately, but Teddy threw an arm out toward Stella.

"Give me a moment," Teddy said.

Stella wasn't so sure that opening themselves up to being ambushed by letting everyone ride ahead was a good idea, but the horror of seeing Reever had taken some of the edge off of her sass.

Teddy watched their competitors ride ahead with singular intensity. A crackle passed through the air.

"How is Shark in a storm?" he asked quietly.

Stella turned to look at the prince as his meaning dawned on her. "He does well with storms. My mother broke him in and she conjures storms when she's upset." She looked down the road. "Don't hurt the horses."

"You're too soft for these Games," Teddy grumbled.

He gave no other warning, simply let his storm gather. A rush of wind bowed the trees and lightning struck just ahead of most of the competitors. Horses reared and riders fell.

The crowd behind them shouted in awe and shock, but Teddy ignored them. He split the storm, pummeling the riders on the trail and brushing them off to the side with ease.

"Ready?" Teddy asked.

She nodded.

"Reever is an elite fighter. He saved my ass in the first challenge," Teddy said, taking one last glance in the direction the hunters had led the mercenary's body.

Stella took a bracing breath. "Then we will have to be better."

She kicked her horse into a gallop and raced forward as if speed alone could leave her doubts behind.

22

TEDDY

Far below the hill where Stella and Teddy sat watching, the lanterns outside of the Muddled Mind Bar and Boarding House swung in the evening breeze. The heat and humidity were less oppressive so far north, and a chill crept into the night air.

Stella picked up a few more loose pine needles from the forest floor and began to braid them into the string she'd been working on to pass the time. "We've been watching for an hour. If someone was waiting to murder us outright, we would have spotted them by now. Besides, we were far enough ahead that we're probably just giving everyone a chance to catch up by waiting."

"There could still be assassins," Teddy whispered.

"We only have a week. Not taking advantage of the lead was a mistake," Stella argued.

Teddy tipped his head back and squeezed his eyes shut. Gods, this woman was so impatient. "We were attacked the other night, or do you not remember me saving you?"

Stella stood, stretching her legs. "Well, I'm going to get a drink, a map, and a room. You can suit yourself out here."

Teddy stared at her in the dusk light. "We are not staying at the Muddled Mind."

"Then where are we—" Recognition tore over her face. "Absolutely not. I'm not sleeping on the forest floor a second night in a row when I don't have to. We'll be just as likely to be eaten by some wild animal as we will to be attacked by our competition."

She turned and untied Shark from the tree behind them and led the horse down to the crossroad stables.

Teddy watched her from a distance for a few minutes. Then, he groaned and rose to his feet, untied Poker, and led the horse to the stables.

The stable hand grinned at him, taking Poker's reins and holding out an expectant hand. "Good evening. Your lady said you would handle the boarding payment for the evening."

Teddy laughed in disbelief and handed over enough coin for both of them. It was almost endearing the way she knew he would follow her.

As he approached the front door, the muffled music grew louder. He took a long look down the trail they'd come from, then at the few patrons talking in hushed tones and smoking, and finally pressed through the front door.

It was like stepping into another world. Outside, it was quiet and peaceful, but inside, a fiddler played loudly as a bard sang a lewd drinking song.

Teddy was greeted by a woman with pale, freckled skin, neatly styled black hair, and eyes so blue they looked almost violet. Teddy was not up on fashion, but he could recognize that her stylish purple silk dress didn't belong in a country rest stop. It was cut like all the finest gowns at court, with jeweled embellishments and golden embroidery. She looked about ten years older than him, but there was something uncanny about her eyes and the simmering, ancient-feeling pulse of magic coming off of her.

Stella stopped short beside him, staring at the woman as if sensing the same.

The woman smiled, and the skin around her eyes crinkled. "Welcome to the Muddled Mind Bar and Boarding House. What can I do for you, travelers?"

"You work here?" Stella asked.

The woman nodded. "I work where I want."

"You're a witch," Stella said. "But you're also more."

"And so are you, dear. My name is Skylar—now, what can I do for you?" the woman said.

Stella took a wary look around the boisterous bar as if finally second-guessing her idiotic plan to storm in here. "We're looking for a meal and two rooms for the night," she said finally.

Skylar nodded. "Afraid we only have one room, loves. Quite a lot of you coming and going. But you're welcome to share and to have a meal. I think you'll find what you're looking for at the bar. Follow me."

She zipped into the crush of people without checking that they were following. Stella hurried behind her, shoving drunks out of the way as they crossed the room.

The bar was larger than Teddy had realized. It looked cozy when they walked in, but now he had the disorienting sensation of walking a great distance. He glanced behind them and it appeared as if they were mere feet from the front door.

The place was spelled. The tables and patrons stretched out in front of him for what looked like a mile. Teddy continued to follow Stella, waiting to spot one of their competitors or for someone to recognize them, but not a single person even glanced at them in the ten minutes it took them to walk across the space. Finally, they reached the bar that had looked just a few feet away initially.

Skylar stopped in front of two miraculously free barstools. "Here you go. The lazy ass of a bartender will be with you shortly."

Teddy took his seat, but Stella stayed standing, staring after the woman.

"It's the manipulation magic," Stella said. "Looks small and unassuming from the outside, but it's actually a pocket dimension on the inside. Very intricate and old magic to create something like this. It would require someone with great power, or a lot of experience."

"You think she did it?" Teddy asked, nodding to Skylar.

"I think she cloaked us through the whole room and that's not an easy spell to maintain that long if you don't need to. Did you notice not a single person looked at us?"

Teddy nodded. "Why, though?"

Stella shrugged, but she was clearly on edge, scanning the room in the same way he'd seen Rainer do hundreds of times. The same way Teddy did in every room. He was relieved she had the instinct to always seek out the quickest escape route and the most likely place from which an attacker could enter.

"I know you're not happy to be here, but I don't think anyone is going to expect us to stay here for the exact reason you didn't want to come in daylight," Stella said. "It's stupid to stay here, but as long as our cave locations aren't more than a short ride, it makes sense to get a good night's sleep before we have to be on our guard in the wild. At least here we know the way in and out."

"I don't like it."

Stella rolled her eyes. "Of course you don't. You're trying to play badass for a week and I'm trying to get you to spend a night in a real bed. I'll let you in on a little secret, Your Grace. If you're actually tough, you don't spend your time trying to prove it to other people. You just live your life. Let's just sleep in the bed this one night. You'll thank me tomorrow."

He'd been so focused on safety that he hadn't thought about the fact that one room meant one bed. It meant sleeping close to her. He'd be able to smell the wildflower scent of her hair and see her sleep-rumpled and soft in nothing but a nightgown.

The bond in his chest seemed to have a mind of its own. A primal, possessive tug shot through him and her gaze snapped to his, then dropped to his mouth. Suddenly, all he could think about was the way she'd kissed him, the way she'd ground against his thigh and groaned into his mouth. A fever tore through his blood and he leaned closer to her.

Her lips parted in a sigh, like she was feeling the same thing. The bond drew him forward. He was about to reach up to cup her cheek when his senses snapped back into place. He drew back like he'd been shocked.

"This fucking bond is going to be the death of me," he grumbled.

Stella winced. He hadn't said it to hurt her, but as a man whose life required an enormous amount of composure and control, the magnetism of the bond was making it harder and harder to maintain his stoicism.

Teddy glanced back toward the door, trying to ignore the buzzing bond. It looked deceptively close, just like the bar had when they were standing there. Skylar leaned against the wall by the front door and gave him a wave. "Doubtful I'll sleep well with that witch or whatever she is milling about."

"You look like your father," a voice said from behind his right shoulder.

Teddy startled and spun to face Cato, former god of manipulation and influence turned mortal bar owner. Despite his humanity, the air still vibrated around him with the remnants of his power.

The god walked by him and rounded the bar, ignoring his gawking.

Teddy's parents had spent his whole life telling him to stay away from Cato, so while he'd met the god in passing, he'd never truly interacted with him.

"Thank you," he said.

Cato grinned widely. "Ah, I see you got his confidence."

Stella stood at the end of the bar, staring at the god warily.

Cato glanced at her, mopping up a spill with a white rag. "And you look just like your mother, except for the eyes, the height, and that frown—that's all your father. It's like traveling back in time looking at the two of you." He glanced at Skylar across the room, but the witch seemed to be avoiding looking their way.

"Figures that Skylar made space and sat you here. Did she say anything when she dropped you in my lap?"

"She called you a lazy ass of a bartender," Teddy said.

The god nodded. "Could be worse, I suppose."

"Are you two—"

A stormy look passed over Cato's face and Teddy immediately

regretted opening his mouth to ask. He was here for a map, not gossip.

"What did you do to her?" Stella asked.

Cato looked down at the bar. "I told her the truth. Everyone thinks they want the truth, but they don't want *the* truth. They want what they expect the truth to be."

The cryptic answer was exactly the type of thing Teddy expected from the god after years of hearing about his talent for skirting the line of deception and manipulation without people noticing.

"We're here because of the Gauntlet Games," Stella said. "Your father sent us to retrieve our cave maps from you."

Cato brushed his hair back from his forehead, revealing a bright white scar through his right eyebrow. Teddy couldn't help but stare at it. Although he was mortal now, the scar was depicted in all the art of the god of manipulation back in Argaria. Every time Teddy saw it in paint, he wondered what sort of weapon could permanently mark a god.

"Ah yes, he's certainly enjoying his chance to have a little vengeance," Cato said. "I'm sure he meant to demean me by making me a tool in his challenge, but the joke's on him. I love a bargain." He knocked his hand on the bar three times and his gray eyes lit with a silver glow. "The task is simple except that it's not at all. You have to trade with me for something I actually want."

Teddy tipped his head back and blew out a frustrated breath. Of course. Of course he would have to bargain with the very god his parents had warned him constantly to never make a bargain with.

Long ago, his ancestors had made a deal with Cato—so long as a Savero didn't make a deal with the god, he would never be able to influence them. His entire youth had been filled with warning stories from his parents to never, ever, under any circumstances, trust Cato.

Teddy was about to break that news to Stella when she reluctantly sat down on the stool beside him and rested her hand on his.

"I'd like to bargain for both of our maps," she said.

Cato's eyes danced with delight. "Now, what could you offer that might be that valuable?"

"My mother asked me to give you this." Stella pulled a wax-sealed piece of parchment from her vest and handed it to him.

Cato opened the letter and read it quickly. From what Teddy could see, there were only a few lines on the paper, but Cato stared at it for a few long moments.

The god walked away and returned a moment later with two scrolls. He handed one to Teddy and one to Stella.

Teddy was stunned into silence. He had expected to have to do something wild to get through this challenge. He hadn't counted on Stella taking care of it for him. He was so relieved. If she hadn't, he would have had to break another promise to his parents and he'd already shattered their trust in him by entering this stupid contest.

Cato pulled two pints of ale and set one in front of each of them. "Your mother has not spoken to me in twenty-five years. I fear you're about to find out why."

Teddy saw Stella prepping to test the drinks.

"No need, baby dove," Cato said. "Poison isn't my style. I just know you two will need a drink in a day or two when you retrieve those memories."

He nodded at them and ambled off down the bar to wait on another patron.

"What could your mother have offered him in that small letter that was worth two maps in this contest?" Teddy asked. "Did she tell you?"

Stella took a long sip of ale, her bright green eyes vibrant in the candlelight as she said a truly unexpected word. "Forgiveness."

A FULL STOMACH AND A PINT OF ALE LED TEDDY TO BELIEVE THEIR quest was on an upswing, but his hope was dashed immediately when they stepped into their small room in the boarding house.

It was worse than Teddy had expected. There was no plush chair for him to pretend to sleep in. There was hardly any furniture at all—

only a nightstand with fresh candles, a hutch to store their clothes and gear, and, of course, one bed.

He paused on the threshold until Stella shoved him inside.

"Let's go. I want to bathe before bed and you need to, also." Her gaze lingered on the bed for a moment. "It's not a big deal."

"Speak for yourself. I'm used to sleeping alone."

She muttered something that sounded like "frigid."

"Are you not used to the same?" he asked.

"No. I'm not." She smirked as she unzipped her satchel and pulled out what looked like a scrap of blue silk, a linen towel, a bar of soap, and two small jars, one that contained an oil and the other some kind of cream.

Teddy stared at her for a long moment, trying to master the strange jealousy swirling in his chest.

The corner of Stella's lips quirked into a smug smile. "Don't be jealous, *Your Grace*. Rosie has bad dreams, and she often sleeps in my bed. She kicks something vicious."

He wanted to offer a clever comeback, but she slipped into the hall before he could counter. He followed a moment later to bathe in the washroom at the other end of the hall. He took his time to scrub the grime from his skin and clean beneath his nails in the hopes that, by the time he came back from such a thorough bath, she would already be asleep in bed.

He dried himself, changed into linen pajamas, and padded back down the hall to their room. Stella was not asleep in bed. She was still bathing.

She stepped into their room a moment later. Her skin was flushed from the heat of the bath and her wet hair dripped onto the silk, plastering it to her breasts. Teddy had been trying to forget how much of her skin he'd seen when they were bathing at the temple, but it all rushed back to him.

Stella stretched her arms up and pushed her wet hair behind her shoulders. Her nipples strained against the delicate blue silk.

She caught him looking and smirked as he snapped his gaze away.

"Are you well, Theodore? You look a bit flushed." The pleasant, teasing edge to her voice sent a surge of heat through his blood.

"Never better." He gestured to the bed that was pushed against the wall. "Do you want the inside or outside?"

She glanced at the bed. "Outside. I don't need you pinning me in."

His mind filled with an unwanted vision of caging her beneath his body. He climbed into the bed, trying to shake that daydream from his head.

Stella crawled in after him and snuffed out the candle on the bedside table. She nestled under the covers.

Teddy was certain she wasn't trying to be so close. There just wasn't much space in the single bed.

The bond was like another entity tucked between them. Teddy waged a private war with the desire to hook an arm around her waist and tug her against his body. Her hair was pinned up on top of her head to keep it out of her face, but the soft vanilla scent of whatever she'd put in it smelled so good that he still wanted to breathe her in all night.

He was relieved at least that she was facing away from him so that he wouldn't constantly have to drag his gaze away from the wet silk stuck to her breasts. The pale curve of her neck looked soft and inviting—the skin begging to be kissed.

"Why do you always smell like wildflowers?" he whispered.

"It's a family spell. I smell like the day I was born in late spring. My mother bound the scent of the season to me. Why? Does it bother you? It smells the strongest at pulse points."

Gods, hearing that made him want to bury his face in her neck. His cock twitched.

"No, it doesn't bother me." He sounded pained and not at all believable.

She was quiet for so long that he thought she'd fallen asleep, but then she spoke again. "I think it bothers Arden. He keeps buying me perfumes and commenting when I don't wear them."

"But you don't like them?" Teddy asked.

She sighed. "They are such lovely gifts, and they all smell nice, but it feels like I'm wearing something made for someone else."

"They don't feel like you," Teddy said.

She glanced at him over her shoulder. "Exactly. See. You get it. When I told him that, I think he was insulted."

Teddy wanted to punch Arden Teripin in the face. What was she even doing with the Olney prince when he clearly didn't appreciate her? Arden bought her perfume and flowers she didn't like and he hadn't even noticed.

Teddy sighed. Just like *he* hadn't noticed that Grace was unhappy. He didn't have room to judge.

In the dark, the rest of Teddy's senses were sharper and Stella overwhelmed every one of them—the sound of her breathing growing more shallow and steady, the salt air and wildflower smell of her skin, the warmth of her body that was not quite touching him.

He sighed and stared past her at the wall on the other side of the room, waiting too long for sleep to claim him.

A WARM TUG IN TEDDY'S CHEST WOKE HIM FROM HEAVY SLUMBER. HE blinked his eyes open. Gray light poured in between the gap in the faded red curtains. It took him a moment to remember where he was. The Muddled Mind.

Stella was still asleep beside him, her ass pressed against his hard cock. Sometime during the night, he'd draped an arm over her side. His hand was tucked against her stomach.

She shifted and sighed, and his cock twitched as she rubbed against him.

If her breathing wasn't so soft and steady, he would have accused her of pretending to be asleep so she could torture him.

She burrowed closer to him, grinding her ass against him.

Teddy was so hard. An unwanted vision filled his head—Stella pinned beneath him, screaming into the pillow while he fucked her from behind.

He tried to force the thought away, but instead, it just kept becoming more detailed. His fingers threaded through her hair, the flush of her skin, the way she trembled for him.

Stella shifted, pressing her ass into him harder.

Teddy could not escape her. His back was up against the wall. Her scent was everywhere, and every place their bodies touched felt lit up with sparks.

Logically, he knew sharing a bed was a terrible idea, but his body seemed entirely on board with it. It was just the stress of the past week pent up inside him that needed some kind of release.

Her hand slid on top of the one he'd placed on her stomach and she started to guide it lower.

Apparently, he wasn't the only one feeling it.

"Fuck," he rasped. "Stella."

She startled awake. "What's wrong—oh." She released his hand immediately. "I'm sorry, I didn't realize I—"

"Must have been a good dream," Teddy teased.

Her cheeks flushed pink. "Were you having the same dream?"

"No. Why do you ask—"

She pressed her ass against his hard cock. "That's why."

"No, that's just a natural occurrence when I wake with a beautiful woman in my bed."

They both froze as they realized what he'd said.

Teddy fumbled for anything else to say, but by the grace of the gods, Stella rolled out of bed and onto her feet. The boarding house floor creaked underneath her as she padded across the room and started to dress. Teddy stared up at the ceiling and tried not to think about the fact that the body that had been pressed against him a moment ago was now naked and no more than ten feet away. The bond tugged on him, beckoning him to peek. That's how it felt—like his gaze was constantly being pulled toward her—like the light in every room was making her glow.

It was exhausting. He pressed a pillow over his face and sighed.

"It's safe for your delicate eyes now, Your Grace," Stella said.

Teddy threw the pillow aside and glowered at her. Stella curtseyed as she buckled her dagger vest.

"Gods, don't tell me you're a morning person," he grumbled.

She cocked her head to the side, her dark curls falling over her shoulder. "Did I not see you running on the beach first thing in the morning when you arrived in Olney weeks ago?"

"Yes, but just because I'm up early doesn't mean I'm happy about it," Teddy said, pushing to his feet. He grabbed the back of his shirt and tugged it off.

Stella watched with rapt attention. Her gaze dragged over his bare chest and then lower, coming to rest on his still-hard cock tenting his pajama pants.

"Do you mind?"

She licked her lips as she braided her hair and continued to stare. "Shy all of a sudden, Your Highness?"

He ignored her and changed his pants.

A piece of parchment slipped under the door, and Stella crossed the room to pick it up.

"What does it say?" Teddy pulled on a fresh shirt and his leather vest.

"'Leave the horses. Beware the bugs in the woods. The river is safest. Skylar.'"

Teddy sat down on the edge of the bed and pulled on his socks and boots. "What does that even mean? There's not a river near here."

She frowned and stuck the note in her pocket. "But there is one near the caves." Pinning her braid around her head in a crown, she slung her bag over her shoulder. "Why would we leave the horses?"

Teddy frowned and considered it. "It's rainy season. There were a few mudslides on our journey to Olney that slowed us down. Or—"

Stella arched a brow. "Or?"

"Or that witch is trying to get us killed."

She crossed her arms. "It will take longer on foot."

"Then it takes longer."

"So you trust her now?"

"Why give us the maps if they wanted to kill us? They could have just poisoned our dinner."

Stella sighed, but she didn't argue further. "Then you better move your royal ass. We have a lot of ground to cover today."

Stella pushed the door open and stepped out into the hallway. A blur of green whizzed by the door and tackled Stella to the ground. Katerina Shank shoved up, pushing off of Stella's back, and sprinted toward the stairwell.

Teddy made to give chase, but he was shoved into the wall as Jeneva Lampry barreled into him, knocking the breath from his lungs.

He spun, catching her in the ribs with an elbow. Teddy shoved Jeneva into the opposite wall. The hallway was too narrow for a fight. A dagger sailed past his face and he whipped his head around to see Katerina waiting for her friend at the top of the stairs. One inch in the wrong direction and he would have been cut by what was surely a poison-coated dagger. That's what Stella had said about Katerina— that it was wise to not even get a small cut from one of her blades.

Jeneva slammed the heel of her palm into Teddy's chin, and his head snapped back. His teeth bit into his tongue, the pain in his head momentarily bright and glittering.

The distraction was enough. Jeneva turned and ran toward the stairs. Stella tossed a blade after her. It clipped her red braid and embedded itself in the wood wall with the ends of her hair.

Their two adversaries escaped down the stairs, a door at the bottom slamming behind them.

Teddy should have given chase, but instead, he stared Stella down. The same fear that he'd felt when she hadn't stabbed the assassin coursed through him. Stella had missed on purpose. She'd let them get away.

"Don't look at me like that. I scared them off." Stella crossed the hall and yanked the blade from the wall, sliding it back into her vest.

"You let them go."

Stella ignored him, looping her bow and quiver across her body and picking up her fallen satchel.

Teddy's heart was still pounding. He wasn't afraid their opponents wouldn't be scared off. He was afraid they'd know that Stella didn't have the stomach to kill and they'd come back soon to finish the job.

23

STELLA

They'd been on the run most of the day, trying to put distance between themselves and Katerina and Jeneva, though Stella felt confident they wouldn't follow. The women were strategic, taking a shot when the opportunity presented itself, but they had their own caves to visit and their own memories to retrieve. Katerina and Jeneva were allies—no doubt a pair of women would be underestimated in the competition, and that made them targets. They didn't have the luxury of hunting when everyone else was hunting them.

Still, Teddy had driven Stella on, insisting they leave the horses boarded at the crossroads and travel on foot to attract less attention, but after a day of hiking, even in the slightly cooler weather, Stella was regretting listening to him. Her feet were screaming from the tough terrain.

But Teddy was right. The summer had brought thick mudslides to the lower hills and they would have had to leave the horses in a less hospitable environment. Stella was glad that Shark was somewhere he could be taken care of, even if it meant they would have to go back to pick him up later.

In what was either a stroke of good fortune or a very obvious trap, her and Teddy's caves were only a couple of miles apart, so they could make most of the journey together. She was glad for the company, even if Teddy was quiet and broody and constantly doubling back to cover their tracks. Their progress was slow, but if they kept this pace, they would reach the first cave—Teddy's cave—by nightfall. If all went well, he would retrieve the memory while she stood guard, and then they could camp in the cave for the night and head to hers in the morning.

Stella had wanted to prove that she could do this herself, but now she was glad to have someone watching her back and she'd grown to almost like his quiet company. Teddy was serious, but also attentive. He knew the forest well, knew which berries were safe to eat, and had a talent for foraging mushrooms. As far as traveling companions went, he was very resourceful. Perhaps he had simply realized that she complained far less when her belly was full.

He'd also taken to asking her to tell a story to pass the time, and while it was annoying that he asked strangely specific questions about the most innocuous parts of each tale, the conversation was a good distraction from her blisters.

The afternoon was hot but not nearly as hot as it was farther south in Olney, and she was grateful for that. Still, all the hiking made her wish she was in something other than leather armor.

"Can we stop for a break soon? I need some water."

Teddy sighed. "I'd like to go a few more miles before we stop, but—"

He drew his blades and spun toward the forest to their right.

A blur of color came sailing out of the thick foliage so fast it took Stella a moment to realize it was Dixon and Drew.

The sky went suddenly dark, clouds blotting out the bright sunlight as a swirling tempest took form overhead. The tree branches groaned.

Dixon looked up, his magic surging, ready to defend Drew from whatever Teddy was summoning.

Stella could wield storms, but not like this. Her storms were chaotic and wild. She could sense an organized rhythm in Teddy's magic, like he was carefully weaving threads on a tapestry.

Teddy sprang into action immediately, his swords moving like an extension of his body. He called down lightning and directed it with his blade. Dixon and Drew had the element of surprise. They had attacked *him*, but they were the ones immediately on their heels. Teddy came at them so hard that there was little for Stella to do but stand there and watch his back.

She'd always known Teddy was powerful—could sense it when he was close, like an electrical charge running over her skin—but now she could begrudgingly admit that Teddy Savero was mesmerizing in action. She'd never seen his father fight, but her mother had talked about it like it was a thing of legend. Teddy commanding lightning and wind with one hand while he wielded a blade with the other was some of the most precise magic and fighting technique she'd seen in her life.

How could anyone stand against him?

Dixon fought against the storm, sending the bolts of lightning scattering into the nearby trees. They sparked into flames. Stella yanked the fire from the branches, rolled them into a fireball, and lobbed it back at Dixon. He barely deflected in time, pulling a blast of cold rain on it just as it singed his leathers.

Teddy was fighting Drew. Dixon was covering them. Stella searched the woods around them for any sign of Rett or Christophe. They had to be there. That must have been what Skylar's note meant. The bugs in the woods were the Roach and his friends.

She drew her bow, aiming into the trees beside her. She listened closely, trying to tune out the clashing steel and swirling wind behind her and just focus on what felt out of place in front of her.

An arrow shot out of the trees and she only had time to shift her weight enough that it skimmed the outside of her arm.

"Bleeding gods," Stella groaned. It wasn't deep, but it was enough to draw blood.

She fired back, half looking at what she was doing, half going entirely on instinct. The satisfying grunt as her arrow struck flesh came a second later.

"Fucking slut witch!" Rett came barreling out of the brush despite the arrow stuck in his thigh.

He tackled her to the ground.

Stella kneed the arrow lodged in his leg and he howled and rolled off of her.

Before, when Stella had been fighting some faceless assassin, it had been hard to wrap her mind around killing someone. But, surely, confronted face to face by the man who had promised to hurt her so Teddy would feel it, Stella would be able to finish the job.

Pain flashed through the bond. She heard Teddy grunt, but didn't dare look at him.

"I'm fine," he shouted to her over the storm, but the clouds were pulling apart, sunlight shining through. Whatever had happened was enough to momentarily break his connection to his magic.

Stella sprang to her feet and drew her short swords as Rett scrambled to stand. He yanked the arrow from his thigh with an animalistic growl.

Stupid. Now it would bleed like crazy until he was healed.

He drew his short swords and charged at her again, forcing her to block a blow that rattled down her arms.

Sweat pooled on her back and neck, the loose curls from her braid clinging to the clammy skin. She was tired and hungry and she just wanted to get to her cave and complete this stupid challenge. Most of all, she was so sick of people trying to kill her.

Her satchel and bow and quiver rattled against her back as she went on the offensive. She charged at Rett and knocked him back until she could see Teddy in her periphery. Rett's blade cut into the skin just above her armguard and she grunted as she pulled away. Blood sprayed across the dirt at her feet, but it was a surface wound. It would heal in a minute.

She needed to get her and Teddy out of there. As she began to fight Rett, she called to mind the map of the area and the rest of Skylar's note. *The river is safest.*

They were close to a river crossing. They could cross the bridge, but that would add at least a day to their journey; while that was doable, she preferred not to cut it so close.

She broke a strike and kicked the wound on Rett's thigh again. He countered by slicing one of his blades across the top of her hand. Stella's shirt sleeve was damp with blood. Odd that the wound on her arm was still bleeding. Superficial cuts healed in moments for her thanks to the remnants of goddess magic in her blood.

She twisted away from Rett and pulled her sleeve up. The cut looked the same as when it had first been inflicted.

When she looked up, Rett was hunched, catching his breath, but he smiled smugly. "Not healing in the way you're accustomed to, eh? Treated my blades with a little something special for you. Let's see how you do fighting like the rest of us mere mortals."

Stella parried him, but he was stronger, and she was tired from the hike. She managed to knock away one of his short swords, but he just drew his dagger and kept coming.

Stella ran toward him, swiping her blade across his shoulder. Rett caught her wrist and plunged his dagger into her side. Her leathers were finely made but still no match for the wickedly sharp blade.

The pain was momentarily blinding, bright and white, sparks exploding in her vision. She instinctively slammed her forehead into Rett's nose, and he stumbled back, wrenching his blade free.

Blood poured from the wound in Stella's side, and she stumbled.

"Stella!" Teddy's voice was panicked, but he was still fighting Drew and Dixon, so he didn't turn to look at her.

"It's fine," she said.

Rett coughed, wiped blood from his mouth, and laughed menacingly. "She's not all right. I got your girl good. Told you I'd stick her with one tool or another. Maybe both if she's a good girl."

He grabbed Stella's arm and squeezed, but she could barely feel it over the blinding pain in her side.

Teddy's rage was like a forest fire burning through their bond.

The storm came on so fast and furiously that the wind almost knocked them both over.

"Get your fucking hands off of her." Teddy's voice was the ominous low rumble of thunder that came before a lightning strike. "Call a storm, Stella."

Stella summoned her storm magic the second before a bright lightning strike slammed into the center of their fight.

Everyone went flying in different directions. Stella hit the ground hard, her side protesting the impact, blood pouring into the dirt beneath her. Summoning the magic had saved her from being killed by the shock, but it didn't save her from the impact of being thrown ten feet from the blast. For a second, she stayed there, hugging her satchel across the front of her body and staring up at the sky.

Then she remembered the urgency. She groaned as she pressed up to her knees. She crawled to her short swords, which had landed a few feet from her, and then to her bow. She fastened her short swords at her hips and looped her bow across her chest. With great effort, she forced herself fully upright just as Teddy sprinted to her side.

"Let's go!" he shouted.

"Are they dead?" Stella asked.

"Probably not all of them, but you know the first rule of elemental combat. Don't burn through all your magic when you don't know what else you might face. Better to retreat."

"To the bridge?" she asked.

"To the bridge." He grasped her arm and tugged her down the trail.

They ran for a few minutes until Stella needed to stop. Her entire side was covered in blood, her wound still bleeding profusely. An arrow whistled past her head and Stella took off running down the trail again.

The sound of her heartbeat in her ears was nearly drowned out by the sound of the rushing river. Every deep breath was agony, her side screaming for her to stop, but the arrows still flying around them were a clear sign that they couldn't. They rounded a bend, and she unhooked her bow and drew an arrow from her quiver.

Shooting was an instinct. She had a goddess-blessed gift for it from her Aunt Sayla, the goddess of the hunt, but Stella had been shooting a bow since she was old enough to hold one. It was one of the first and most useful things her mother had taught her and something they had bonded over.

She drew her string back, ignoring the pinch in her side, and loosed the arrow, then turned and continued to run.

A loud curse rose behind her. She knew she'd hit Drew's shoulder, and he'd have a very hard time shooting until it was healed.

Her footsteps synced with Teddy's as the narrow plank bridge came into sight. They ran out onto it as swiftly as they dared, but the wind whipped so high up and the bridge swayed beneath them. They slowed to a walk, holding the ropes on both sides as they hurried across.

Nearly halfway across the bridge, Teddy stopped short and Stella slammed into his back.

"What's wrong?" Stella glanced over his shoulder and saw Christophe Wallthrew standing on the other side of the bridge, waiting for them.

"It's a trap," Teddy said.

She turned around to go back the way they came, but she could just make out Drew and Dixon descending the trail toward the edge of the long bridge.

Teddy turned to look at her, his hand brushing her bloody side. "I thought you healed quickly. Why are you still bleeding so much?"

Stella had wondered the same. "I don't know. Maybe they—"

Rett's words flew through her mind again. *"Let's see how you do fighting like the rest of us mere mortals."*

Teddy grabbed her arm. "What is it?"

She brushed her fingers to her side, staring at her blood. "I think maybe they used Godsbane."

Teddy's eyes went wide. "Does that mean you can't use your magic?"

She snapped a flame to her bloody fingers. "No. I think it just means I won't heal the same way or be able to do intricate memory recovery until it's out of my system."

"How long will that take?" Teddy asked.

Stella shrugged. "Longer than the next two minutes. It looks like our best way out is down."

The river rushed far below them.

"The fall could kill us," Teddy said.

"Not if you break it with a gust of wind while I ease the water up a bit."

He looked at her skeptically. "That's a lot of coordination."

"We have about thirty seconds until we have to jump either way."

Teddy stared down at the water and fear seared through her chest. "Might be a bad time to mention that I can't swim."

"What?" Stella stared at him in disbelief. "How is that possible? You've spent a month every summer in Olney."

"A prince cannot be bad at things."

"Bullshit. Jalen is a terrible archer."

Teddy laughed, both from the stress and at the truth of that assessment. "He is. But I never learned to swim, and the older I got, the more awkward it would have been."

Stella grimaced down at the current. "All right. Hold on tight and do not let me go. When we jump, you need to send a gust up to slow our fall. I'm going to try to steady the current, but it's going to be rough and very cold. Whatever happens, do not let go of me. I cannot fight the current to get to you if you do."

She felt the first prickles of a storm as she glanced to where Rett and his friends charged onto the far end of the bridge. The whole structure swayed with the added weight.

She met Teddy's golden eyes. "Trust me."

He nodded and lifted her onto his back. Stella wrapped her arms around his neck and her legs around his waist and jumped.

The wind tore at her hair and she swallowed a reflexive scream as they plunged toward the water. They fell for what felt like an eternity.

Stella reached her magic wide. Water summoning had always been so sluggish for her; the violence of it was similar to fire, but it was slippery, harder for her to channel and control. It tore through her energy stores so much faster than fire and required the sort of attention that she didn't have while free-falling in the arms of a prince who would drown if she let him go.

Teddy's sudden windstorm arrested their fall just enough for her to draw the water up.

"Hold your breath," she shouted, her words instantly lost in the wind.

They plunged into the column of water. The jolt rattled her bones and stung her exposed skin. Stella gasped out half of her air at the shock of the frigid water.

Teddy instantly let her go as they descended into the vicious current. She had to claw her way back to him.

They went down and down and down, until finally the descent arrested. Stella released her legs from Teddy's waist and kicked hard, propelling them back to the surface.

Stella gulped in air as Teddy flailed beside her.

"Stop panicking," she said, yanking him closer as the current tugged them swiftly away from the bridge.

Teddy did not stop. His fear was a living thing in her chest. Stella fought the swirling current. Hooking her arm across his chest, she curled herself around his back and pulled him long to float with his back resting against her body.

"Breathe," she said in his ear.

He relaxed the slightest bit, but his hands held a death grip on the arm she had across his chest. The water battered them from all sides, driving them downstream. Stella tried to ease the passage with water magic, but there were so many rocks and eddies. Each time they clipped a boulder, she lost focus, and they both went under. Each time they swallowed water, Teddy trusted her less.

She glanced back at the bridge. It grew smaller and more distant by the second.

"Stella!"

She whipped her head around at the terror in Teddy's voice.

Rapids. They were heading toward rapids.

She kicked hard, but the current was so strong. She heaved her water magic out, trying to propel them toward the shore. Pain tore down her side from the movement. She gritted her teeth and pushed harder, kicking wildly. But they were entirely at the mercy of the river.

She held on to Teddy tightly as they plunged into the violent rapids. The roaring water blocked out all other sound and blended with the roaring of her heart.

Her shoulder slammed into a rock, and she cried out. They started to sink, water splashing into her mouth.

They slammed against a large bolder, Teddy's body taking most of the brunt of the impact. Water pinned them there.

Stella was burning through her magic at an alarming rate. She was violently shivering, still bleeding, and summoning her least efficient magic to try to ease a raging river, all while trying to keep a lump of a prince from drowning.

She was walking a fine line between using too much and not enough. If she burned through her magic, she'd pass out in the middle of the river and they would both drown. But if she didn't use what she could to ease their path, they'd surely be bashed on the rocks.

Teddy coughed and sputtered, his body rigid with fear, but she felt him pushing out his magic, weaving it with her own.

Unfortunately, it seemed it was not his strongest summoning, either. It made sense. The mountains of Argaria had many gentle streams from snow melt, but the rivers and lakes were frozen half of the year. He wouldn't have had a chance to practice water summoning.

Together, they steered the current to propel them around the largest obstacles. Stella's muscles burned under the strain of keeping them both afloat and the sheer exhaustion of fighting nature. She glanced downriver for a good place to stop, but the current kept picking up.

That's when she realized the roaring was getting louder.

"Is that—" Teddy started to flail as he put together what she already had.

They were headed toward a waterfall.

He shoved his magic out, trying to arrest the current. Instead, the water in front of them bowed momentarily and the current behind them slammed their bodies into the wall of water. The impact ripped Teddy out of her arms. The jolt of it rattled her bones.

Stella flailed for him, her frozen fingers grasping at nothing. She caught a flash of his scarlet shirt and, for the first time all day, was happy he'd worn such a conspicuous color. She dove into the current, using it to propel herself forward with strong, practiced strokes.

It was reckless to swim this way in a river, but if she didn't get to him now, he would die and it would be her fault. Death whispers rose with the roaring of the waterfall. Insistent panic hit her so sharply in the chest that she gasped. Surfacing, she tugged on their bond. A terrified jolt echoed back. She turned her head and caught sight of him pinned against a rock. The rapids surged around him.

His head was stuck under the water and the bond in her chest pulsed with panic, fear, and grief. Stella threw a wild flare of power at the rapids behind her, pouring every bit of magic she could into it.

Her body dropped instantly, hitting the rocky riverbed so hard she almost let her magic slip.

The current slammed against the shield of water she'd formed. Her body flashed hot and cold, the effort of holding back the river heating her chilled skin. She jumped to her feet and turned her shield into a tunnel curling around them.

The control was difficult, but it lessened the pressure and let some of the current go over their heads. Stella felt herself approaching the end of her magic. She ran to Teddy, stumbling over river stones, her legs burning with the effort.

He wasn't breathing. His lips were blue. The death whispers turned to shouts.

She shoved down her fear. Sweat beaded on her skin, steaming in the cold air. She collapsed beside him, rolled Teddy onto her back, and pressed to stand. She staggered the ten feet to the riverbank.

The second her feet touched dry land, the river crashed back into its normal rhythm behind her.

Stella's magic sputtered, her eyelids growing heavy. She was so tired.

She dumped Teddy's limp body on the ground and knelt beside him. She pulled hard on their bond, but nothing happened. She placed her hands over his chest in the way her father had taught her years ago and pressed hard against his sternum in a percussive pattern.

"Please," she rasped. "You can't die. I won't let you."

She was so exhausted. Every muscle in her body was burning, the pain so bright she knew she was close to passing out. She stopped, pinched his nose, and blew air into his mouth. Then she continued her compressions on his chest.

She used the last thread of her magic to reach down his throat and into his lungs, and she tugged as gently as she could manage. She pulled all the water from his lungs. It was difficult to trust herself with such delicate magic when she was so panicked.

If he slipped away, he would take a part of her with him.

Finally, Teddy coughed. Stella frantically rolled him onto his side as he sputtered water. She continued to pull with her last thread of magic until she was certain there was nothing but air left in his lungs.

A sob tore up Stella's throat as he rolled onto his back and looked up at her. His eyes were luminous in the late afternoon sunlight, but his lips were still purple.

"It's annoying that you look this handsome when you're half-dead," she rasped.

Teddy's eyes softened, and he took her hand.

Stella's eyes burned as she gasped for air. "You weren't breathing. I hate you for scaring me like that."

But she didn't hate him at all. She hated that he made her care. Hated the unbridled terror she'd felt when she thought she wouldn't be able to save him. Hated how she couldn't stop shaking now—not from the adrenaline still pumping through her blood, but from the fear of losing him.

For so long, she'd thought Teddy was cold and judgmental. But he wasn't either of those things. Away from courtly eyes, he was incandescent—lit up by the lack of critical assessment—focused, attentive, and funny. She was startled by how much she liked spending time with him—how something that had seemed impossible when they set out had become almost intuitively easy after just a few days.

"I'm fine now," he soothed as he tried to sit up.

Stella tried to help him, but a sharp pain tore through her. She gasped. When she pressed her hand to her side, it came away bloody.

"Stella—"

A wave of pain rolled through her and the world went dark.

24

TEDDY

The wound on Stella's side was bleeding again. Warm stickiness coated the arm that cradled her against Teddy's body.

Teddy was exhausted from nearly drowning, but Stella's shirt was soaked in blood. She'd saved him, and if he didn't find shelter, she might die for her efforts.

Even with the Godsbane in her system, the bleeding should have stopped by now. The fact that the wound wasn't clotting was a very bad sign.

The forest was silent. The only sounds were the breaths sawing in and out of Teddy's lungs and the chirping of birds in the pines high above them. Teddy's muscles burned from exhaustion and shivering. It was unseasonably cold for not being very high in the mountains.

"Stella, I need you to try to stay awake," he said.

She groaned and snuggled closer to him, mumbling something into his neck.

"I know it hurts, but I'm going to find somewhere for us to stop and rest soon, and I'll wrap your wounds and get you warm."

She shivered, her cold fingers slipping inside his torn shirt to press against his chest.

Teddy wasn't sure how far downriver they'd come. While the water carried them faster than they ever could have gone on foot, it could have carried them too far beyond the caves. He had no idea where they were.

He tried to shove down his panic so Stella wouldn't feel it, but the sun was dropping low on the horizon and it was getting colder. His breath came out in little white clouds as he climbed the steep hill.

When he reached the precipice, he caught a glimpse of light reflecting through the thick pines. It had to be some kind of structure. He stumbled toward it.

Stella groaned at being jostled, but she hadn't fully woken since she collapsed beside him at the river. He'd been walking for at least a half-hour.

He carefully approached the small cabin. Chopped wood was stacked neatly by the dark green door, to the right of which was a well pump that Teddy prayed was functional.

He stayed close to the wall, peeking in the cabin's window, but, as he suspected from the lack of smoke coming from the chimney, it was dark inside.

He jostled the doorknob and, mercifully, it opened. The cottage was stuffy and dusty, but not overrun by cobwebs. It looked like someone had been there recently. The wood bin by the fireplace was well-stocked, and the bed was covered in a white linen dust sheet, but the rest of the furniture was uncovered.

Teddy crossed the small room in quick strides. He awkwardly tugged the cover off the bed, laying Stella gently on the quilt. She didn't stir, and when he saw the state of her split armor and the side of her shirt, he understood why. She'd been bleeding much more than he thought. Her undershirt was soaked and even the waistband of her pants was drenched in dark blood.

Panic threatened to overtake him, but Stella needed him. He stacked logs in the fireplace and summoned the dregs of magic he had left to get a fire started.

He pulled the few things he could find from the pantry. There was a jar of honey, some dried tea, potatoes, carrots, an onion, jerky, and nuts. He set them all in a line on the counter.

In the cabinet beneath the counter, he found a heavy cauldron, a kettle, and a large metal bowl. Teddy stepped outside and filled each one with water. He set the cauldron and the kettle over the fire, then ran to Stella's bag. It had opened during their time in the river and all of her clothing was drenched. He wrung it all out just outside the cabin door and draped her shirts, pants, and undergarments over the drying rack by the fire. Then he yanked off his soaked vest and shirt and hung them over the kitchen chairs in front of the fire.

He rifled through his bag in search of anything dry. Most of his clothes were wet, but finally, at the bottom of his bag, tucked inside the enchanted pouch his mother had gifted him for his birthday two years ago, he found one dry set of clothes and a small satchel of chamomile. He quickly stripped out of his wet pants and pulled on the dry pair as he cast a glance at Stella. She was still out cold. Her skin was so pale that she blended in with the ivory linen pillowcase and her lips were almost blue.

He needed to get her out of her wet clothes, but he also didn't want her to stab him for seeing her naked, not that she seemed to mind when she was teasing him at the Temple of Desiree.

Still, it was different when she wasn't conscious.

He crossed the room and pressed a hand to her cheek. Her skin was cold and smooth under his callused palm, but she didn't stir.

"Stella, wake up. I have to change your clothes."

She didn't move. Teddy unlaced her boots and pulled them off. He tried to shake her awake, but she remained unconscious. Carefully, he unbuttoned her trousers, closing his eyes as he hooked his hands into the sides of her pants and undergarments and peeled the wet fabric down her legs. Fortunately, they came free with a bit of shimmying.

He hung the clothes over the arm of the plush chair by the fire and grabbed his dry shirt. He went back to the bed and sat Stella up, shifting his body behind her. The leather of her armor vest creaked as he unbuckled it and slid it free. It hit the ground with a metallic clang thanks to the stays tucked inside it.

"Stella," he said, a little louder than before. But her head lolled against his shoulder.

Teddy crossed his arms over her chest and grabbed the hem of her shirt. He pulled the damp linen away from her skin, catching the edge of her bandeau. It took more effort than expected to peel the wet clothing off of her limp body and wrestle her into his dry shirt.

He moved out from behind her and laid her down on the bed, rolling her onto her right side and pushing the shirt up so he could look at her wound. The skin was red and angry and crusted in blood. The cut was small but deep—a puncture wound. It had stopped bleeding, but he wasn't sure if that was a good thing. He knew she could still bleed out internally, and gods knew what kind of sediment she'd been exposed to in the river.

He needed to find something to protect against infection. His mind was sluggish, and the forest was almost dark outside. He frantically tore through his memories. Isla had drilled into him the importance of having basic field herbalism memorized, but his exhaustion and anxiety were weighing on him. He didn't know exactly where they'd landed after their trip down the river, but it was safe to say they were somewhere south of the Border Lands.

Calla root was common enough around here and the bright orange stalks would be easy to find even in the dusk light. He vaguely remembered seeing some when he was walking back from the river.

He held his hand to Stella's forehead and checked her pulse. It was steady.

Teddy hurried out of the cabin and into the woods, retracing his steps. The cold air stung his bare chest, but he ignored it, focusing on putting one foot in front of the other. Half a mile down the trail, he found the bright orange stalks sprouting from the roots of a large oak tree.

He used his dagger to pry a few stalks loose, since the base was the most concentrated part of the herb. His breath burned from the cold air as he ran back to the cabin.

Stella was still asleep when he returned. He poured some boiling water from the kettle into the metal bowl, cut off the top of the root, and dropped the bottoms into the bowl. After letting it boil for a few minutes, he removed a few stalks from the water and placed them in a smaller bowl he'd found in the cabinet above the counter. He left the rest of the stalks in the water to make a healing tea. He took the bowl with the drying roots outside to cool.

The minutes ticked by too slowly. His heart rioted in his chest. Despite his best efforts to hate Stella, she'd gotten under his skin. He cared about her. He'd come to like her confronting personal questions and the way she talked in her sleep. He'd even come to enjoy the way her constant complaining about being hungry distracted him from the worry loop in his head.

She had saved him. If she'd let him go in the river, she would have survived on her own. She wouldn't have had to use all of her magic to ease the way for him, and she probably could have healed herself once she got out of the water.

But Stella had protected him. As much as he wanted to blame it on the bond alone, he knew her. Stella wanted to protect everyone. That was just who she was. It made her both fierce when it came to standing up for the people she loved and gentle in how she always hesitated before a killing blow. That same softness plagued him with the persistent fear that she was going to get herself killed in this competition.

Gods, she might die if he couldn't figure out a way to help her heal.

That thought filled him with terror, not because of how his parents or hers would react, but because the more he'd gotten to know her, away from their families and their old patterns, the more he was charmed by her.

He liked Stella McKay. He'd always been irritated by her extremes, but the more he was around them, the more he realized that his irritation was born entirely out of envy. Those same extremes had always felt stuck inside him, clotted in his chest, with no way out.

And yet, just hearing her share so freely made it feel like he could eventually get them out.

He pressed a finger into the mushy calla root. Finally, it was cool enough to use.

He walked back inside and tried to get the right angle to mash the root, but the bowl kept tipping. In his frustration, he resigned himself to chewing it down to make a poultice for the wound. It was slow work, but after a few minutes, he had enough to pack into the wound on her side.

Teddy sliced several clean strips of fabric from the sheets, dropping one in warm water and using it to clean the blood from her skin. Then, he gingerly spread the bright orange herb into the wound and wrapped several strips of linen around her waist until the wound was packed and protected.

Stella groaned as he tied the bandage. "So much movement."

"Nice of you to join me finally," Teddy said. "You need to drink some of this tea I made you."

She sighed but didn't open her eyes. Teddy grabbed the calla root tea and helped her sit up. She kept her eyes closed and leaned her head against his shoulder as she sipped on the tea.

She didn't speak or open her eyes for a few minutes. Finally, she blinked her eyes open. "Where are my pants?"

"You were too cold to keep wearing wet clothes. I put you in my only dry shirt," Teddy said. Her fingers skimmed his side, and he shivered. "Sorry to be inappropriate."

"No, you're warm," she said, snuggling closer and taking a long gulp of tea.

"I can pump some bath water up for you to rinse off and mix in some water heated from the fire so it's not quite so cold," Teddy said. "I think you lost some clothing from your bag in our swim, but your soap is still in there."

Stella sighed. "Please."

Teddy was relieved to have something to do to keep his mind busy. He extracted himself from her grip and grabbed the washbasin from the corner of the cabin. Outside, he pumped water into it, stopping when it was half-full. The cold water sloshed against his bare chest as he hustled it inside. He poured the remaining kettle water into the basin.

He'd been lucky to get the fire started after the amount of magic he'd spent in the river, so he didn't have anything to offer. He looked up at Stella and she smiled weakly.

"It's okay. I'll be quick and then I'll get under the covers."

Teddy nodded and tossed her a linen towel from the pantry. "Are you okay doing it yourself?"

She blushed and nodded.

"Let me know when you're finished, and don't get that bandage or the wound wet."

Stella waved him off.

Teddy stepped outside, grateful once again for the cold evening air against his heated skin. He felt hot all over, thinking about how good Stella looked in his shirt—the same shirt she was now stripping out of.

"Fuck," he grumbled.

The minutes dripped by until finally he felt a strange tugging sensation in his chest.

Teddy pressed his cold fingers to the door and cracked it open. "Stella?"

"Did you feel it?" she asked. "I was calling you with the bond."

Teddy stared at her. She had done a terrible job of drying after her bath and his shirt was stuck to her skin, translucent in spots.

He cleared his throat and looked away. "Feel better?"

She slumped onto the bed and picked up her mug of tea. "Yes, but I'm so tired."

"The tea should help," Teddy said. "And once you're feeling a little more awake, I found some food in the pantry. I think this is a fishing cabin, so there's not much, but there's enough to help revive us."

She gulped down more tea. "I'm so thirsty. As if I wasn't nearly drowning earlier today. How long was I out?"

"An hour? Two, maybe? It's hard to say. Long enough for me to find this place, start a fire, find some calla root to pack your wound, and make you healing tea."

She froze with the mug halfway to her lips. "This is calla root tea?"

"Yes. Why?"

She tilted her chin up and met his gaze. Her green eyes were doe-like, her pupils blown wide. "How much did you use? It was smart to use it because it has almost supernatural healing effects, but you only need to use a small dose. You have to be careful not to take too much because of the strong aphrodisiac effect."

Teddy froze.

"Teddy, how much did you use?"

He moved away from her, letting her sit on her own, trying to prepare himself for her reaction.

She fanned her flushed cheeks with her hands. "How much?"

"All of it. I didn't know how much to use so I used three stalks."

She groaned. "Men! Why do you always think more is better in all things?"

Teddy arched a brow, and she looked at the mug.

"Oh my gods. I've probably had a full stalk. No wonder I feel so —" Stella shivered and rubbed her hands down her arms.

A mixture of panic and fascination crept through Teddy's mind. "What do I do?"

She gestured to the empty pitcher on the table. "I'm probably going to be—"

"I know." Teddy rubbed a hand down his face. He couldn't believe he'd been so stupid.

"It's supposed to get really bad unless you can—" She cleared her throat and looked away. "Unless you can find release. Usually more than once."

Teddy stared at her. "No."

She winced, hurt blooming in her eyes.

"You misunderstand," Teddy said. "I would, but I'm not comfortable touching you when you're under the influence."

"I'll be in pain."

"Can't you just...touch yourself?"

Her cheeks went fiery red, and she looked away. Gods, that was fun. He hadn't anticipated that Stella McKay was shy in bed.

He held her gaze. "Have you never touched yourself, Stella?"

Her cheeks burned brighter. "Of course I have. I just haven't—" She abruptly stopped talking and stared into the cup.

Teddy grinned. "You normally have so much to say."

"I've only ever been with Arden and I've tried to—oh, forget it. This is private," she snapped.

Teddy placed a finger under her chin and guided her gaze to meet his. "I'm not making fun of you. I think you're cute when you're embarrassed because you're usually so bossy. Please tell me what you meant."

She took a deep breath. "I've never been able to make myself finish. It's like I hit a wall. It gets too intense and then I can't keep going."

Just thinking about her alone in her bed trying to solve the complex puzzle of her body heated Teddy's blood. This was not how he thought this was going to go. He thought he'd heal her, and she'd sleep it off, but now she was a few minutes from completely being under the spell of a powerful aphrodisiac.

She reached her thumb up and brushed something from the corner of his mouth. "Did you drink some, too?"

Teddy froze. "I tested to make sure it wasn't too hot, but I chewed the root to make the poultice. It was too hard to try to mash it with my knife. I didn't know it only took a bit, and I figured it would only help me recover from my near drowning." He was suddenly aware of how fast his heart was beating. "Oh, no."

Stella huffed a surprised laugh. "You might not be as affected, but I imagine you will feel it."

Teddy stood abruptly, grabbed the rickety metal pitcher from the table, and stalked outside. He tried to ignore the heat building in his body as he pumped water from the well. It poured into the metal pitcher in spurts.

Teddy took three deep breaths of chilly air to steady himself. When he felt calm, he pressed back inside.

He tried to ignore the buzz in his chest and the need tugging on him as he crossed the room and poured water into a clean mug. Stella took it wordlessly and drank it all down, holding his gaze the whole time.

Stella placed the mug on the nightstand. She shivered again. The shirt was still damp and stuck to her skin, her pink nipples pushing against the thin fabric.

"I'm hot all over," she said. She twisted her wild hair up on top of her head and jammed a few pins in it to hold it in place.

Teddy sat down on the edge of the bed and pressed a hand to her forehead. She was burning up.

When he drew back, her gaze was hooded and entirely focused on him. She crawled across the bed to where he sat and pressed him onto his back.

"Stella, what are you—"

She straddled his lap and kissed him.

The whole world disappeared.

Gods, he was so weak. Teddy let her blot out every memory of the terror of the day, her mouth moving insistently against his. Let her make him feel alive again. Let her wind her fingers through his hair and sink her teeth into his bottom lip. But when she started to roll her hips against him, his brain caught up to what was happening.

"Stella," he rasped.

She pulled back and met his gaze, her lips bitten, her neck and cheeks flushed, and her pupils huge—a reminder that she didn't want him. She was just under the influence of a heart bond and a very strong aphrodisiac that he should have known not to give her so much of.

"I need—" She brought his hand up to cup her breast. "I need to be touched. I *ache* everywhere."

Teddy cursed, tossing her off his lap and onto the bed. The bond in his chest felt like a tether drawing him to her.

"I need you," she whined.

The tug in his heart was insistent. His cock strained against his pants, his whole body buzzing with desire, the herbal high, and Stella's need through the bond.

Clastor's sword! Was this how it felt to be bonded—like you had to fulfill every need of the person you were attached to? It felt less an option than a necessity, but he'd be damned if he'd do something when she was high.

Stella licked her lips and stared up at him in excitement. His shirt was riding up her thighs as she writhed on the sheets.

Fuck. He could imagine those strong legs wrapped around his waist as he drove into her. Could picture her calves hooked over his forearms, his hands fastened to her waist as he thrust into her.

He needed a cold bath or a drink, or both. He was worried about everything outside these cabin walls, but this woman was the thing with the true power to destroy him.

Now he could finally admit that he wanted to touch her, wanted to see her come undone at his hands, but he wouldn't do that unless she wanted it with a clear mind. He wouldn't have her blaming anything but her own desire for whatever happened between them.

"Stella, I can't touch you when you're in this state."

"Please," she whined, grabbing his hands and pulling them to her thighs.

"You're high."

Things were getting out of hand. Teddy needed a way to stop her from touching him because he was weak and pathetically susceptible to her enticement.

He stood abruptly and grabbed his belt. Stella whined until he came back to the bed and climbed on top of her. She spread her legs and hooked her thighs over his hips. Teddy cursed, burying his face in her neck to groan as she bucked against him.

He was fighting a losing battle against his desire, but he forced himself to pin her hands above her head, wrap his belt around them, and tie them tightly to the bed frame.

Stella looked up at him, her face and neck flushed, her eyes hooded.

She was beautiful like that, and she needed *him*.

"No way," he said, jerking himself away from her.

"Come back," she whined.

Teddy crossed the room and went straight outside. He stood in the cold for an hour, listening to her muffled whining through the door.

Finally, when she was quiet and the heat in his body had cooled from an inferno to a bonfire, he stepped back into the cabin.

Stella was asleep. Her head lolled against her arm, Teddy's shirt rumpled around her thighs. Her face was soft, but her cheeks were still rosy, and he was relieved that she looked so vital.

Teddy slumped into the plush chair by the fire and finally gave in to his exhaustion.

25

STELLA

The first thing Stella was aware of when she woke was the ache in her arms. Her hands were tied above her head. She yanked on the binding before her eyes were even open, and it was only when she heard the clatter of the buckle against the wood that she remembered why she'd been restrained.

Mortification froze her in place. She had thrown herself at Teddy. She'd begged him to touch her.

She stared at the ceiling, waiting for the feeling of utter humiliation to dissipate. Her cheeks burned at the memory, even as her body still hummed with desire.

The fever in her blood had broken and the effects of the herb had mostly dispersed. Her muscles were knotted with effort and anticipation, but she'd slept heavily and her mind was finally clear. Her sense of magic was still weak—a clear sign of how dangerously she had depleted herself to save Teddy.

The blankets had been pulled up over her legs. While she was still sore, her muscles ached less than they had the night before.

She had a vague recollection of Teddy's warm body next to her— of him strapping her to the bed because she wouldn't stop grabbing him. She remembered him leaving her to wear herself out, and then she had a foggier memory of him returning and lying down beside her.

Had he really done that or was it some fever-dream fantasy? The memory of writhing against him and his voice low and breathy, telling her to sleep now and he'd give her what she wanted later.

"I know you're awake."

She turned her head slowly to delay the humiliation.

Teddy sat in the chair by the fire. He was still shirtless, but his hair was damp and the cabin smelled faintly of his citrus and cedar soap. He smirked at her, as if reading the pattern of her thoughts.

"Sleep well?"

"How long was I out?" she asked.

"I think a few hours. I slept for a while too, but it's still full dark outside. I've been up for a bit. I wasn't sure how long the calla root would stay in your system, and I didn't want to deal with you begging while I bathed."

Stella's cheeks burned, and he grinned wider and stretched, his muscles rippling as he moved.

"Not that I blame you." He took a long sip of tea as if savoring her glare.

"I'm feeling much better. Clear of the influence that made me delusional," she said.

Teddy arched a brow. "Oh, trying denial, are we?"

Stella huffed a breath. "There's nothing to deny. I was under the influence."

"Were you under the influence when you were gawking at me changing in the boarding house? When you were rubbing your ass against my cock and trying to get me to touch you when you woke up?"

Heat rose up Stella's neck.

He crossed the room in a few long strides. "You're really going to pretend that was all the work of the calla root and you feel nothing for me now?"

He yanked the blankets down, his ravenous gaze sliding up her bare legs to the hem of the shirt that skimmed the top of her thighs.

Stella chewed her lip and squeezed her legs together. "I feel nothing." Her voice was airless.

Teddy cocked his head. "Well, if that's the case, I'll leave you to rest instead of finally giving you the relief you begged me for earlier."

Stella's mouth dropped open as he turned away and started back toward his chair.

"Wait," she rasped.

He was back across the room in a second.

Teddy prowled over her, caging her in so that she was staring up into his eyes.

"I'm going to need to hear you say you're clearheaded, *Minyha*. You really burned through my self-control earlier, so I need you to say you understand."

He shifted, and his hardness pressed against her. Stella was suddenly aware of every nerve ending in her body, of the pulsing need that was less of a reaction to an herbal overdose than to the man whose good looks she'd been trying to ignore for the better part of her life.

Up close, it was impossible to overlook how compelling she found Teddy, especially shirtless. He was the exact right combination of handsome and roguish. His nose was straight, but a thin, pale scar on his lower lip and another on the left side of his jaw signaled a history of combat. The brown skin of his chest was muscled and smooth but for a couple of faint scars along his left ribs—his weak side in combat, from what little she'd seen of him fighting.

He leaned closer and his dark hair, normally so perfectly styled, messily fell over his forehead. Dark lash-framed eyes, a deep hazel that lightened to a golden ring around his irises, hooded with lust. The effect was devastating.

The air was tense with possibility. Teddy's breath ghosted over her lips, smelling faintly of mint from his tea.

"Understand what—"

He kissed along her jaw and scraped his teeth down her neck. The man literally had his teeth to her throat and all she could do was offer him a better angle.

He yanked on the ties at the top of her shirt, then pulled back to meet her eyes as he unlaced the shirt.

"Understand that if you say yes, I get to do whatever I want. I've been crawling out of my skin with anxiety. I have nothing but steam to blow off, and I want to make you scream and come until you cry."

Stella shivered.

Teddy's lips tipped into a smirk. "Oh, do you like that, *Minyha*? When it's so intense that you cry—so intense you can't breathe because you need it so badly. So intense it blocks out everything else in the world. Something physical to match up to all those other big feelings."

Stella was too embarrassed to say that she had no idea that was possible, but he seemed to read it on her face.

Teddy clicked his tongue. "I like you like this. Tied up and helpless to me. *Fuck*, Stella. There is so much I could teach you." The hoarse desperation in his voice sent a pleasant shiver through her. "You're killing me. Say yes."

"Yes. I'm clear-headed."

He barely let her finish the word before he kissed her. He tasted like mint and honey, and she'd never tasted anything so perfectly fresh and sweet. Teddy sighed into her mouth and it was as if he'd breathed fire into her. She rolled her hips, grinding against his hardness.

Teddy's hand instantly moved to pin her in place.

"Slow down. I bet you just need a little more time. A little more patience with yourself." He brushed his fingers up her right thigh, leaving a trail of goosebumps. "So soft. How do you like to be touched?"

He didn't wait for her to answer. He brushed his fingertips over her clit. It was so gentle, but it might as well have been a lightning strike. She felt that touch through her whole body.

Teddy did it again with more pressure and she moaned.

He propped himself on one arm so he could study her every reaction. She'd seen this same intensity on his face when he studied an opponent. It was very compelling to be the subject of such focus, but it also frightened her. What would he see when she couldn't hide anything from him?

It shouldn't have felt so comfortable to have someone look right through her, and yet it did.

Teddy slid a finger inside her with agonizing slowness and she clenched around it immediately, like she'd been waiting for just that. He pumped his finger in and out in a smooth, practiced rhythm, adding a brush of his thumb over her clit as he moved.

"I knew you'd be ready for this. *So ready*. Gods, you're so wet for me, Stella."

His praise twisted the tension in her body a little tighter.

"More," she rasped.

Teddy hesitated a moment before pushing a second finger inside her. The pressure increased along with his pace and he kissed a line along her collarbone, looking appreciatively at her breasts.

"Have to admit, I like seeing you all undone and wearing my shirt." It was more a subconscious admission than actual praise for her, but it still made her shudder.

He kept up the steady, insistent rhythm, adding a little more pressure on her clit with the heel of his hand, until Stella's heart was racing, her breath coming in and out in shallow, rapid gasps.

She was so close—right on the edge of her climax. If her hands weren't still restrained by the belt, she would hold his hand in place right where she wanted him. She lifted her hips, desperately chasing a little more pressure, but Teddy stopped.

Stella let out an outraged cry, and Teddy chuckled against her neck. "Not so fast, Stella. I have to take you up slow."

"*Fuck* slow," she whined. "I don't want to go slow."

She felt Teddy smile against her pulse point. "I'll make it better."

He yanked the opening in her shirt wider and kissed down her pale skin, his teeth nipping at the soft curve of her breasts. Finally, he started to move his fingers again, and pleasure sparked to life across her skin.

He sucked her nipple between his lips and dragged his teeth over the peak. Stella's whole body clenched. Teddy hummed his approval, and she was pathetically desperate to hear the sound again.

Stella was frightened of how good it felt—of how eager she was to sink deeper into this consuming pleasure. Teddy touching her felt equally novel and normal. This was territory she'd never even thought of exploring with him, but now that he was touching her, it seemed like they'd somehow always been heading here.

He started to kiss lower, dragging the hem of his shirt up her skin. His fingers skimmed the rough terrain of the new scar on her right side, and Stella went rigid.

Teddy scraped his teeth over her hipbone, and she twitched. He drew back and pressed her legs wider, continuing to pump his fingers lazily in and out of her and brushing his thumb over her clit.

Teddy was always so uptight. She hadn't expected him to be so wild now, but he descended on her like he was ravenous. She writhed away from him reflexively, but he pinned her hips to the bed with an arm as he licked her clit. He sucked hard, and she gasped as chills raced over her skin.

She'd never seen someone so unrestrained and singularly focused on her pleasure. He was as skilled with his tongue as he was with his fingers, and she didn't know something so filthy could feel so good.

Teddy varied his pressure and rhythm, using his mouth and fingers until her muscles were clenching seemingly at his will and she was gasping and muttering curses.

It was too much. Too intense. There was so much pent up in her body. The fear of the fight, the anger at Kate and Grace, the desperation to survive. It all broke at once, the climax bursting like sparks behind her eyes.

A hoarse cry scraped up Stella's throat, something guttural, as if the pleasure was pulled from the deepest part of her. It rolled over her in wave after wave until her thighs shook violently and her feet cramped and tears streamed down her cheeks.

Teddy kept his fingers moving even as she twitched and tried to escape his grip.

He clicked his tongue. "Poor Stella. Is that too much?"

She nodded frantically, but he sucked her clit harder and her body felt fractured between too much and not enough. She tried to squirm away, to get just one moment of reprieve, but Teddy was in the grips of their bond or the remnants of the calla root. He had no mercy—only hunger.

"Teddy," she whined.

He bit her inner thigh and grinned up at her. "I like you like this. No clever comebacks. So wet and needy for me."

Stella tipped her head from side to side. "No one has ever touched me like this."

He froze, heat flaring in his eyes and rushing through her chest. "Grim's gates! You're killing me, *Minyha*." He bit her other thigh, and she gasped. "One more. Give me one more and I'll let you rest."

Part of her wanted to say no, to rip her hands free and shove him away and have one blessed moment of feeling nothing, but a greater part of her wanted whatever was building. She was afraid of this— afraid of the way the first climax had shaken loose all of her emotions. Another might break her into someone who could not survive him.

The bond hummed in her chest. She pressed her heels harder into Teddy's shoulders and gripped the leather of his belt tighter. Teddy's arm across her hips pushed her into the mattress more firmly.

He added another finger and pumped them faster as he scraped his teeth over her clit and the tension in her body snapped so suddenly that she couldn't even make a sound. The orgasm tore all the air out of her lungs. Her body was suspended, arched off the bed as she gasped and clawed at the belt around her wrists.

He watched her with hooded eyes, his fingers moving at their same insistent pace, his tongue flicking against her. Her chest was so full of pleasure—both the feelings in her body and Teddy's through their bond. He was enjoying this as much as she was, and that made her even hotter. She shouldn't have cared how he felt, but she really, really did.

Finally, after what felt like an eternity, the waves of ecstasy settled into ripples and she collapsed to the bed. Teddy knelt between her thighs, unbuttoning his pants.

Stella watched in stunned stupor, straining against the binding on her wrists. "Let me—"

"No, I just need—" He stroked himself with his soaked fingers. It was so filthy but so hot to see him helpless for her. He slid his drenched hand up and down his length a few times until a guttural groan tore out of him and he cursed as he came on her stomach.

He fell forward onto one arm, breath sawing out of him. He cursed and stared at her spread wide for him and Stella flushed and started to close her legs.

Teddy pressed a hand to her inner thigh. "Don't be shy now. Seeing you like this is doing something to me."

Stella knew what he meant. She felt a strange, wild possessiveness. She liked that he'd marked her in such a primal way—liked that he couldn't contain himself. She even liked the way he'd groaned and cursed when he came on her.

He brushed a thumb over her cheek, swiping away a tear. "Guess I got those tears out of you after all."

She didn't like that he saw something in her that she'd missed in herself. It made her feel exposed and raw. She'd craved that level of intensity, the complete lack of mercy he'd shown when she needed to be pushed, but she hated that Teddy had been the one to give it to her.

Stella didn't know her body could feel so good. Sex with Arden was fun, but it never felt like this—this feeling of being a slate wiped clean. Her body was suddenly a revelation. She'd never felt transformed by pleasure, and she had the strangest feeling of lightness from it.

Now Teddy looked like he wanted to do it again; if Stella wasn't so wrung out with pleasure, she would have let him, but as it was, she could barely keep her eyes open.

Instead, he released her hands from the belt, gently wiped her clean with a rag, and settled into the bed beside her. He tugged the blankets up to cover them and threw his arm across her waist, nuzzling into her neck.

It felt at once both strange and like the most natural thing, but she was too exhausted to question the new shift in her feelings for him. What she was feeling was alarmingly close to affection, and not just because he had made her climax harder than ever.

It was because he'd trusted her in the river. Because he'd carried her miles to the cabin and had chewed a poultice for her wound. Because he'd murmured comforting things to her as he worked and because he'd curled up beside her so she wouldn't be cold or afraid when she woke.

Stella's limbs were heavy as rocks. "Teddy?"

He hummed softly.

Stella could barely keep her eyes open. "What does *Minyha* mean?"

He was quiet for a long moment. "Go to sleep," he whispered.

Stella wanted to argue, but she was fighting a losing battle with her exhausted body.

26

STELLA

Wind whistled through the boughs high above Stella. Gray clouds peeked through the lush summer canopy. A storm was threatening.

Teddy walked ahead of her, his pace so quick that Stella practically had to jog to keep up with him. "I don't like the idea of splitting up," he said. "Especially after yesterday."

"You saw the map, *Your Grace*. The caves are close enough. It won't be a big deal for us to split up. It's only a couple of miles between the two. Besides, we don't have enough time to wait until you're finished with your trial. Our swim cost us enough time already and the memory trial could take hours. We both need to finish as soon as possible so we can make it home before the challenge deadline." Stella stumbled over a root, barely catching herself before she bumped into Teddy. "You're walking awfully purposely for being in the middle of the woods."

"There's a bad storm coming. I can feel it. And there's an old hunters' hideaway up ahead," Teddy said. "From the war."

Dry leaves in the underbrush kicked up and Stella's braid whipped against the side of her face as the sky swirled with heavy charcoal clouds. She loved the scent of the northern forest in a storm —like pine and damp moss and the smell before rain.

Stella heaved a breath, quickening her pace to keep up with Teddy. Her side was perfectly healed thanks to Teddy's hard work, but even with healing magic, the ache of the injury would linger for a few days and she felt it every time she took a deep breath. She looked forward to paying Rett back.

"How do you know where you're going?"

Teddy glanced at her over his shoulder. "I'm not sure our alliance goes as deep as sharing kingdom secrets."

Stella rolled her eyes. "As if my parents didn't help yours keep your precious kingdom."

Teddy stopped so suddenly that she almost ran into his back. He curled an arm around her hip, avoiding the ache on her ribs.

The bond in her chest flared with warmth and Teddy shifted like he felt it too. Since the night before, she felt hyperaware of him and his proximity, of the hint of his woodsy-citrus scent that lingered on her skin.

A shiver ran through her body as she remembered the heights to which he'd brought her body. The whiplash of being so gravely injured to feeling more vibrantly alive than she ever had was disorienting. She'd been out of step all day, and the fact that the score was unsettled between them made her even more uneasy. He'd saved her from the assassin in town; she'd saved him from the river. Then, he'd saved her from the wound Rett had delivered and kept it from getting infected.

She couldn't quite name the gnarled feelings inside her chest. The messy tangle seemed less a result of their bond and more a result of his actions. Teddy was brave and decisive in a fight, gentle and soft when she needed it, and alarmingly sexy without trying. Her old contempt had morphed into affection, and she wasn't sure what that meant for her—for them.

Teddy's hand skimmed her hip and her mind went back to being woken early that morning, to his gentle hands on her side—to the soothing feeling of him healing her wound. To wishing he'd done more.

Stella shook off the thought. The new intimacy between them was so disorienting.

Teddy pointed to a tree, and she followed the line to a dark brand a good ten feet up the trunk.

"Anyone can read a map if it's stolen. The Argarian hunter bases were always marked in broad areas on maps. But to be able to find them, you follow the crest burned into the walnut trees."

"There are tons of trees," Stella said.

Teddy grinned. "But very few walnut. They are intentionally pruned back near these sites, and they are the only trees with markings." He turned to meet her gaze. "Now that I've shared a secret, perhaps I should get one in exchange."

His tone was teasing, but Stella didn't know what to do with this playful version of him. They hadn't spoken at all about the previous night, and she wasn't sure if she wanted to put the memory completely out of her head or relive it over and over.

He smirked as if reading the direction of her thoughts. "I hesitate to say the next part. I don't want you to fall any more in love with me than you did after last night."

She shoved him away. "Don't flatter yourself. I had an okay time."

He scoffed. "An okay time. Stella, I think I have permanent indentations on my shoulders from your heels digging in when I made you—"

"Enough!" Stella held up her hand as if she could block the memory.

Teddy offered a smug grin. "This base has a bathing chamber."

Stella couldn't hide her relief. She hadn't had time to bathe that morning and, despite the cooler temperature as they hiked, it was hard work. Her body was still exhausted from channeling so much magic and energy the day before. The blood loss alone was enough to make her want to lie down on the forest floor and take a nap.

Teddy strolled away, moving through the trees as if returning somewhere he'd been a hundred times before.

Finally, he came to a stop next to a huge outcropping of boulders. "The bath is back there."

Stella glanced around but could not see a single building or structure large enough to hide a bathing chamber. "But where is the actual shelter?"

Teddy pointed up.

Sure enough, a good thirty feet above them was a small structure tucked into the branches of a sturdy oak tree.

"A treehouse!"

Teddy grinned at her delight. "It's a small hideout, but there are a few like it throughout the region. This one is my favorite."

"You learned this in training?"

He nodded, something like pride shining in his eyes. "Isla encouraged my father to have me go through hunter training. She thought the army would respect a king who went through the same training as his soldiers more than one who didn't. My father agreed."

"Wise of them," Stella said. "That must have been hard."

Teddy shrugged a shoulder and pointed to a rung hammered into the tree's trunk. "When you finish bathing, just climb up these rungs. They wind around the tree, so they aren't as easy to spot. Just be careful climbing up."

Stella nodded and watched him easily ascend the tree before she ducked around the rock alcove. The bathing tub was tucked away and covered in a sheen of dust, but was in remarkably good shape. It must have still been occasionally used by huntsmen on patrol. She pumped water into the basin and rinsed away the dust, then unplugged the drain that let the water funnel out the side of the tub. When it was empty, she pumped in fresh water.

Her side protested the work of drawing the bath, but she wanted to be clean more than she wanted the pain to stop.

When the tub was full, she called up her fire magic. It was weaker than usual and required more urging than she was used to, but soon her hands were scalding, and she stuck them in the tub. Slowly, she moved her hands through the water until it was steaming hot. It was an unnecessary indulgence, but her body had been through so much in the past day and she wanted just a few moments of luxury after being cold and sweaty.

Stripping off her clothes, she lowered herself into the hot water, groaning at the divine feeling of being pleasantly warm for the first time all day.

The sun was setting, and soon it would be cold enough to see her breath. Much as she wanted to stay in the tub until the water was cold, she quickly washed her hair and body. Rising from the bath much sooner than she hoped, she patted herself dry with a linen towel they'd stolen from the cabin and wrapped her hair.

Stella hesitated, trying to decide what to dress in and opting to wear the shirt Teddy had loaned her. It wasn't that she wanted to wear something of his, but more that she didn't want to dirty another set of her clothes yet. She'd already slept in the shirt the previous night, so it just made sense.

It had nothing to do with the fact that the shirt smelled like him and that she liked the way Teddy looked at her when she wore it— with possessive satisfaction in his eyes. She didn't want to belong to him, but she liked how wanted that look made her feel.

Stella slipped socks and boots on, hooked her bag and weapons over her shoulder, and started to scale the tree. It was slow going as she climbed and learned the constantly shifting rung pattern. It was harder to see the new rungs as she ascended into the dark canopy.

Finally, she reached the opening to the treehouse. Her side ached as she reached up and pulled her body onto the platform.

She glanced around the space. The ceiling was at least seven feet high at the center of the room, but it sloped down at the sides. The wooden planks of the roof formed a pattern that made her a bit dizzy. A large bed sat on the far side of the room and four smaller bunks lined the walls.

Rain began to drum against the roof. The storm came on all at once and the soft patter turned into a roar.

The sound was soothing. Stella yawned and stretched, her side pinching in pain.

Teddy grinned at her from the edge of the larger bed. "Tired already? I thought you were in better shape."

Stella scowled at him. "I was in fine shape in the river yesterday. Forgive me for being wrung out after all of that."

His brows shot up. It was the wrong choice of words. He seemed to notice her attire at that exact moment; his gaze slowly dragged down her body like a caress, coming to rest on her bare legs. "Quite an outfit."

"I didn't want to dirty fresh clothes until tomorrow. I only have one set left."

He arched a brow. "If you say so. I thought they all got a good cleaning in the river." Teddy stood and unbuttoned his shirt, tossing it onto the bed. "Sorry, I claimed the captain's quarters. You'll have to take one of the bunks."

Stella rose to her feet and tossed her bag onto the closest bunk. "I'm sure I'll manage."

Teddy laughed, opened the trapdoor, and descended into the nearly dark forest.

The treehouse was small but neat. On the far side of the room, there was a large glass lookout window that had a beautiful view of the valley below them through the branches. A small table was pushed beneath the window with a cabinet of dry food beneath it and several books tucked onto the shelf next to the meek provisions.

Stella set her short swords on the table and rifled through the pantry. She wasn't hungry, as they'd had a big lunch of two large rabbits Teddy had managed to catch and wild mushrooms he had foraged, but she was hoping for sweets. She'd only been away from Olney a few days, but she was already missing her father's baking.

She glanced at the large bed Teddy had claimed. There, in the center of it, was a piece of paper and a pile of wild berries. Stella crossed the room and lifted the paper.

For your sweet craving.

Stella stared at the note as she popped a berry into her mouth. The juice was sweet and bright and she savored the treat.

He knew her well enough to read her cravings and to choose

blackberries—her favorite. Teddy was so attentive. Alarmingly so. She'd like to blame the bond, but then she remembered how he'd known that daisies were her favorite flower, and how at lunch he'd left all of the mushrooms he knew she'd liked best for her.

The storm rattled the treehouse window. She wondered if Teddy liked being out in the chaos of it. He seemed to like being in this space, almost like he was reliving something nostalgic.

It was disconcerting, the way that the vision of Teddy she'd carried in her head for so long did not match who he was in real life. She had assumed that Teddy's life was very charmed, but it must have been difficult to go through training with people who were looking for any chance to humble him. He'd been sweet when they were young, but that seemed so long ago. He'd been so cold to her the past few years, and between that coldness and their incessant volley of pranks, her own judgment crept in. After spending so much time with him, she had a new appreciation for the way the burden of expectation had shaped him.

Stripped of the prying eyes of court, he was thoughtful, resourceful, and warm. All qualities she'd thought him devoid of. He had seemed the black sheep among his less serious siblings, but now it was easy to see that he fit in with them perfectly and that his sternness around them was born out of protectiveness and concern for their reputations. He'd never had the option of not worrying about appearances. Of course he didn't know how to relax.

Stella pulled her clothing out of her bag and took inventory. Everything had been dried and neatly folded, undergarments included, when she woke up that morning. Something about seeing her clothing neatly organized by a prince made her feel uneasy. The familiar territory between the two of them was now uncharted, and she couldn't decide if she wanted to go back to how things were or charge into this new, unknown place.

Beneath the raging storm, Stella was suddenly aware of something more than the wind howling.

Death whispers.

Stella stilled, and a terrible, cold knowing settled in her bones.

She jumped to her feet, yanking on her dagger-filled vest, only taking the time to fasten one strap, and belting her short swords at her waist.

She took the rungs down at a reckless speed, ignoring the tearing of the wind and the terrifying heaviness of the dark. Her heart was in her throat as she felt blindly for foot- and handholds. When she finally jumped the last few feet to the ground, Teddy's panic hit her in the chest.

It could be the Roach and his friends finally coming to finish the job. Of course, that would only make sense if they also had to retrieve their memories from nearby caves. Otherwise, they'd be wasting precious time.

She squinted against the icy driving rain and forced herself to move slowly so as not to trip or make extra noise in the dark.

She paused at the edge of the stone for a moment and listened. The death whispers were swelling by the second, becoming more insistent and drowning out everything but the storm.

As Stella rounded the corner, she caught sight of a man dressed in black, a red Sons of Endros symbol embroidered on the back of his armor.

Sheets of rain blew underneath the stone overhangs, but the man didn't move. He was focused on a second man who had a cord around Teddy's throat.

Teddy flailed, his legs splashing in the bathwater, his hands wedged between the cord and his skin.

Stella drew a blade from her vest and sent it sailing toward the chest of Teddy's attacker. She didn't have time to see if it struck. The struggle stopped, and in the split second of silence, Stella heard a third assassin behind her. She drew her short swords and spun toward him.

The man's face was half-covered, just like the assassin she'd fought in the streets of Olney several nights earlier.

"Lady McKay," he said menacingly. "A two-for-one deal, is it? Royal prick and his whore."

"Nice that you know my name. Care to share yours?" Stella asked, slipping her sword up to slice at his face covering. "Perhaps the name of whoever sent you?"

"What makes you think it wasn't the god himself?" the assassin taunted.

"Endros doesn't answer prayers," Stella said.

Stella was vaguely aware of the other assassins watching them closely. These men were just waiting to pick her off. It didn't matter if she was tired of fighting. They'd left her no choice.

The assassin came at her hard. He was broad and strong. She blocked a sweeping overhead attack. The strike rattled down her arms and she felt every bit of the previous day's blood loss, but for all the fighter's bulk and skill, he was too slow. His movements were precise in the way of someone who understood moves and counter-moves but had practiced a perfect sequence over and over without trying variables.

She tested him with slight deviations in movement as they parried a few times. He had a habit of looking where he was going to move next. It would have been less obvious if the bottom half of his face wasn't covered, but the only places she could search for tells were his eyes. It was a common battle habit, one her mother had trained out of her.

While her father's training had been full of precision and skill and strength, her mother's had consisted of how to fight someone who was bigger than you and how to trust senses other than sight. She'd made Stella spar blindfolded until she learned to read movements through touch and sound.

Stella twisted away from the attacker. Just as she'd hoped he would, he stepped forward. She spun the blade in her hand and plunged it backward, right through her attacker's breastplate. She shoved the blade up and twisted, meeting so little resistance that she worried she'd done it wrong. But when she pulled her blade free, blood poured out of the assassin's mouth and chest. He made a choked sound as he fell to his knees and then onto his side. By the time he was on his back, his sightless eyes stared back at her.

She couldn't breathe. All the air rushed out of her lungs. Her heartbeat pounded loudly in her ears.

It was exactly as her mother had once told her. The most dangerous person in the room was the one who was willing. Most fights were about size, strength, and skill, but for the first time, Stella understood that it wasn't just survival that was the great equalizer. It was a threat to someone you wanted to protect.

She felt the air shift with the slide of the next assassin's sword before she heard it. She rolled her shoulder back at the last second and the blade skimmed her vest, leaving a gouge down the front of the fine leather. This fight needed to end fast.

It was only some innate animal instinct to survive that kept Stella moving, that sent her charging toward this new adversary as if she laid waste to villains regularly. She crossed her short swords and blocked the swipe of his left blade, slicing across his wrist.

Stella slammed her shoulder into his chest, and he stumbled back, throwing up his right blade. She anticipated the movement, the cause and effect of battle like a complicated puzzle that came together in her mind a second before it happened in real life. Moments like that always felt to her like she was animated by something other—some uncanny and innate talent for violence that she hadn't quite earned.

She parried with her left sword and spun toward him as she turned, cutting his throat with her right blade. Blood sprayed across her face and hands, but she kept turning as a fourth man charged at her from the bushes.

There was no thought left in her head, just pure instinct. She finally understood what her father had meant when he'd called it a complicated dance. Her body knew every movement, but instead of following as she did on the dance floor, she led. She crossed her short swords to block a heavy-handed cut, then shoved her elbow up into the man's chin. His head snapped back, and she spun, sliding her crossed blades up to deflect his blow and drawing them both across the man's throat.

He dropped in a bloody heap, and Stella stared at him. There was no one else coming at her. Something in her chest released, and she was finally able to draw a deep breath again.

She turned and glanced at Teddy, who stood panting with nothing but a bright red line on his neck where the thin rope had been. The man who had been choking him was in a heap at his feet.

Stella stared down at the bodies crumpled around her.

She thought it would be hard to kill, but it had been remarkably easy. Survival was an instinct, but still, she couldn't draw her eyes away from the carnage. Killing was as easy as breathing, and she felt nothing.

She was vaguely aware of Teddy's voice, of the rain pelting her face, of the wind lashing at her hair.

"Stella! Don't look at them. Look at me. Look at my eyes."

The world was half-dark from the clouds, but Teddy's eyes were still bright and golden—a beacon in the storm.

"Good. Now listen to me. Those men were assassins, and they would have killed you if you'd given them the chance. You did what you had to do."

A hysterical laugh bubbled up her throat. "What I had to do? I had to kill three out of four of them without breaking a sweat."

"It was a sight to behold, if I'm honest." His eyes flicked down to the drenched shirt plastered to her skin. It was entirely transparent and speckled with blood.

She frowned. "It was horrifying."

"It was *necessary*." Teddy's voice was deep and firm and full of certainty. He took her swords from her hands and awkwardly fed them back into their sheaths at her hips.

Stella stared at her palms as the pouring rain turned the bright red blood a paler pink by the second.

She felt at once like she'd lost something vital and gained something awful.

Teddy's hands were warm on her cold cheeks. "You were so beautiful. I have never seen someone fight like that."

Stella had always thought she was more like her mother, and she was angry at being so soft. But looking at her blood-stained hands, she wondered if she had more of her father than she'd thought and she'd just never experienced the circumstances that brought out that side of her.

She'd seen her father fight in several swordsmanship tournaments, but the stakes of those contests were just bragging rights. It was always obvious he was holding back—swiping to maim and not to kill.

Once, she'd heard a man describing Rainer McKay in battle as supernaturally efficient in his ability to read the shifting tides of a fight and tilt the field his way. He'd called her father a skilled and efficient executioner.

Do I have that same killer instinct?

She hadn't expected it to be so *easy*. She'd known it was a possibility—even a probability—when she entered herself into the Gauntlet Games, but she thought she'd see it coming.

Stella was aware of the storm raging around them, but she could barely hear it. She was focused on Teddy's face and on the pounding of her heart, which didn't seem to register that the fight was over.

"You're going to be fine. You're just in shock. We need to get you inside and warm you up."

"Can't you stop the storm?" she mumbled.

He shook his head. "It would take too much magic and I just spent the better part of what I'd replenished. I'll need it if any other assassins come along."

Stella looked around the forest for any other attackers. Lightning flashed in the sky above them. She tipped her head back, letting the rain wash over her like it could wash away her sins. Her magic prickled restlessly at the tips of her fingers. Fire wouldn't work out here, but she could pull on the storm or rage alongside it.

"*Stella.*" Teddy's voice dragged her back from the cliff of her mind. "Climb back up to the treehouse. You can do that, right? I will take care of the bodies."

Bodies. Bodies she had made with her two swords.

Stella turned away from him and trudged through the mud to the base of the tree. She pulled herself up rung by rung, happy to have something rhythmic to focus on.

When she got to the top and dragged her chilled body over the ledge into the treehouse, she lay on the floor, staring up at the beams of the roof. She lifted her hands to look at them in the lantern light and was stunned to see that the rain had washed all the blood away. It was like it had never happened.

Stella lay there looking at her palms for several long breaths, listening to the rain pounding against the treehouse roof and the tell-tale rhythmic dripping of a leak somewhere in the far corner of the room. Finally, she forced herself to crawl over to her bunk. She pulled the shabby quilt around her body as the trembling began anew.

27

TEDDY

Mud squelched under Teddy's boots as he shoved the assassin's body down the steep incline. He turned back to face the treehouse. From this angle, he could only make out the faintest glow in the treetop. It was the kind of thing you'd only see if you were looking for it.

He lifted the last assassin, hauled the dead weight over his back, and set to weaving through the thick trees to get rid of the body.

Teddy had often heard it said that when a warrior was about to die, their life would flash before their eyes. But Teddy had been outnumbered, with a rope around his throat, and he had not seen his life.

He'd not seen the last few years as a comfort. Instead, he'd seen the past few days. He'd imagined a future looking into bright green eyes.

Teddy had thought of Stella.

He'd worried about who would protect her in the competition. How she'd be burdened with the guilt of his loss. She was like that—like him in that way—so responsible for everything all the time.

Even when they were in the river, he hadn't felt fear like he felt seeing her walking into the bathing chamber in his half-soaked tunic.

He was terrified the assassins would hurt her—that they'd make him watch. That he'd die choking on his complicated feelings for her.

Stella had looked like something out of a myth. Her blades were an extension of her limbs, her movements exact, efficient, and mesmerizing. She was beautiful and ethereal, like a rain-drenched goddess of vengeance come to deliver him from death's clutches.

She must have felt him panic, but she was there so quickly. Perhaps she'd seen them coming, though he didn't know how. It was so dark in the forest at night and, with the lantern on in the tree-house, it would have been almost impossible to see anything below.

Truthfully, Teddy was mortified he'd needed to be saved. Again.

It was hard to admit, even in the privacy of his own mind, that he didn't want the score settled between them. An outstanding debt left their business unfinished. It gave him a reason to seek her out. It gave him time to figure out what this was.

He'd assumed so much of it was the bond, but when he watched her fight the assassins, he hadn't felt afraid that the bond would break and he'd feel the pain of it being torn out. All his terror had been wrapped up in the thought of Stella being hurt. Of what those monsters might do if given the chance.

When he woke that morning wrapped around Stella, his face buried in her neck, he'd told himself it was just the bond, just the intimacy of an intense near-death experience and two lonely people who desperately needed to blow off some steam.

But he wasn't thinking about fucking her now—well, that wasn't true. He was still thinking about that. She'd fought off those assassins in just Teddy's soaking-wet shirt and her dagger vest and he'd never seen anything so sexy in his life. But he was mostly thinking about how the fuck he was going to help her through this. He still remembered the cold feeling that had settled over him after his first kill.

It was a dividing line between the hypothetical and reality. It was a dividing line in his life between when he thought he might have what it took to be heir and when he was certain. He could trace so much in his life back to that moment.

He'd been so young. At sixteen, the thought of being responsible for an entire kingdom was unimaginable. But once he'd slid his blades between the ribs of someone who was trying to kill him, it had suddenly seemed much more attainable.

If he could take a life, surely he could be responsible for many more. If he could feel the numbness that came after, the shock of realizing exactly what he didn't know he was capable of, then he could be capable of greater things—and maybe even worse ones. He'd been fighting for the former ever since.

Stella seemed somehow diminished, as if the swipe of her blade had rent her of something vital and she would forever be tarnished by this brutal lesson in survival.

Teddy had wished it upon her—the vicious knowledge that came with taking a life. He'd wanted her to lose her shine. Now that she had, the loss felt personal.

It was just because she had evened the score. He had liked her owing him. It made him feel a little superior, but also connected to her by something other than the magic of their bond.

But he knew what it was to face down death and realize you have the instinct to fight for your life enough that you'd take another's. Stella was different—not soft, exactly, but certainly gentler—or maybe fiercer, in a different kind of way.

His father had once told him that no one loved as fiercely as Cecilia Reznik. Now Teddy felt like he knew what Xander meant. Love was something people thought of as soft, but love could have claws and sharp edges and a desperate desire to protect.

He hadn't felt that before—the fear that he wouldn't be able to soothe something—that there was no way to make Stella feel better. He had always been able to find a way to be smarter, calmer, better in some way. But now he worried there was nothing he could do to transform this hurt into something healing.

This desire to do something wasn't just a want. It was a need—an incessant impulse in his chest. He'd wanted her before, but now he wanted to do anything to dispel the coldness of losing that shred of innocence.

Teddy felt wretchedly guilty for wishing away her whimsy and wanting her to have to face harsh realities. He felt more guilty for being relieved that she had.

Rain blurred his eyes as he tossed the last assassin's body over the edge of the nearby ravine. Then he turned back toward the treehouse.

As he walked, he scoured his brain for how to make her feel better. But that was just it—there was no feeling better.

This was a loss of innocence that left a person cold and isolated, even if they'd been around people who had experienced the same thing. The revelation of discovering that you're a person who can do what you must to survive is haunting.

He trudged back to the tree and climbed through the branches, trying to imagine what he could do to help her.

28

STELLA

The trapdoor creaked open and Teddy climbed inside just as Stella was beginning to worry something had happened to him. He closed the hatch and ran a hand through his hair, wringing out the rainwater into a puddle on the floor.

It wasn't until Teddy walked over to her, grabbed the discarded towel from her head, and began to pat the ends of her hair dry that she realized she'd created her own small puddle on the floor behind her.

He knelt in front of her. "May I?"

She stared at him blankly.

"Wipe your face."

"There's blood on my face?" Stella's voice was a breathless whisper. Panic surged through her body. She wanted it off—wanted to rid herself of every reminder of what she'd done.

Teddy wiped the damp towel across her cheek and jaw, following the rag with the brush of his thumb. "There you are. Though I admit the blood was kind of sexy."

Stella stared at him, waiting to feel anything other than a bone-deep cold.

He placed a cup in her hands, keeping his palm beneath it

when he realized how badly her hands were trembling. "Drink some water. It's not a good idea to make a fire now, so I can't make tea. This is the next best thing. Now, drink up and give me your hands."

For once, she didn't want to argue with him. She still felt half-dazed, but she was happy for his calm, commanding tone. Trying to process what had just happened felt impossible, but she could follow instructions.

She drank the entire cup of water as Teddy rifled around in his bag and returned a moment later with a clean pillowcase from one of the bunks and one of the small wooden stakes that she'd used to cook mushrooms over the fire earlier that day.

Teddy sat down in front of her and took her right hand in his. He flipped her palms face-down with shocking tenderness. To her horror, she realized that, though the rain had washed the blood from her skin, it lingered beneath her short fingernails.

He carefully went to work, using the pointed tip of the stake to scrape her nail beds clean.

"Look at my face, not what I'm doing," he said.

Stella frowned at him. "I don't want to look at your face."

"Why not? You're always telling me how handsome it is."

She gasped out a laugh. "It is. It's irritating."

He arched a brow but kept his gaze on his work. "Is it?"

"Yes. It's distracting. Especially that scar on your lower lip."

He met her eyes, then his gaze dropped to her lips. "Well, then, it sounds like we're even, because I also find your mouth very distracting. That little bow on your upper lip. Can't stop staring at it."

Warmth spread through Stella's cheeks, the first she'd felt since she'd come in from the rain.

He continued his ministrations, stroking a thumb over the top of her hand as he worked. "I was sixteen," he murmured. "The first time I killed someone."

Stella stared at him, dumbfounded. "Why?"

She meant why because the war was over. Why? Because he was a prince and had people to do his dirty work for him. Why? Because

Xander and Jessamin had always seemed regal but warm, parents who would do anything to protect their children.

Teddy sighed and licked his lips. "I was very young and so cocky. You know how it is—your parents are warriors, you think that it will be easy. As if it passes down through blood and it will be as simple as the swipe of a blade."

Stella knew exactly what he meant. When violence was theoretical, or just for the fun of knocking Leo on his ass and getting bragging rights, it was easy. But when faced with the bloody reality, she felt wholly unprepared.

Teddy paused for a moment, wiping the tip of the stake on the towel. The lantern light guttered, sending shadows scattering across Teddy's face. The wind whistled through cracks in the treehouse walls.

"I suppose it is easier when it's necessary," he said softly.

Teddy was cleaning up the remnants so she wouldn't see them later and relive it, and he was telling her this story—this very private story—to distract her. He was doing everything possible to make this easier for her.

A lump formed in Stella's throat, and the shocking numbness in her chest started to dissipate.

"In Novum it's a rite of passage," Teddy continued. "My mother, Isla, and Aunt Maren were all entered into tournaments where they were expected to get their first kill at sixteen." He shook his head and moved on to cleaning the nails of her other hand. "My father hated the idea. It is one of the few fights I've ever seen my parents have, and it was bad. In the end, my mother won, as she always does. Having Isla's support sealed my fate, I think."

Stella studied him with rapt fascination. He'd always been so contained. Was it pity that made him share something so personal?

"They took me to Novum, to a first kill's tournament. I was so nervous. Everyone was watching. My parents, my grandmother, Isla and Maren. Everyone I looked up to. Everyone I knew was strong. And, of course, all of the competitors were hoping to get a crack at me. Prince of Argaria and grandson of the queen of Novum."

Stella couldn't imagine having someone she loved and respected witnessing her first kill like that.

"He was eighteen. His name was Alvin Arlume. He'd just completed the final forging from Callemoore. I was terrified to face off against someone who had finished the Novumi warrior training program, but my grandmother thought it was important that I fight the best."

"How did you win?" Stella asked.

Teddy paused his work and was silent for a long moment. "I am used to shutting down the feeling part of my brain. I just shoved it all away. It was him or me and I was willing. I didn't know for sure until the moment my blade slid between his ribs. I remember what that felt like. It changes you, and I'm sorry that you have to know that."

His gentleness frightened her. All she could do was watch as he scraped the dried blood from beneath her nails, wiped her hands down with a bit of water and whiskey from his flask.

He met her gaze, his eyes soft in the dim lamplight, and she knew all at once that this wasn't a secret shared out of pity.

It was in the way he was looking at her, in the tender way he squeezed her hands. He'd shared this story with her because he wanted her to feel less alone.

"You almost died," she rasped.

"But I didn't. You saved me."

"What if we die in this tournament—or from the assassins sent by the Sons of Endros? What if I die before—" She caught herself just in time. Right before she admitted the mortifying truth.

She was terrified she'd die before she had experienced her fairy tale love.

"My father isn't going to let the Sons on his council and neither will King Marcos. There's no way that they will respond to this kind of manipulation by giving those tyrants what they want. As soon as you start negotiating that way, you can never stop. That way lies madness and chaos." He ran his thumbs over the tops of her hands in a soothing rhythm. "Now, what were you about to say?"

"I don't want to die before I have a chance at the same kind of love my parents have. I know I—" She blew out a breath, feeling properly mortified by the honesty. "I know you think it's stupid and frivolous, but they are a literal fairy tale. It takes time to build that. I want the chance to know someone like that and to be known."

Teddy brushed a tear from her cheek.

Stella shuddered, blowing out a breath to avoid sobbing. "I want the chance to actually *live*. I have to. I cannot give up now. *Especially* now. This is what stories are made of. They're nothing without conflict." Her chest was so tight that she could barely breathe, but the words would not stop tumbling out of her. "But what if I've picked a conflict I can't survive—or, worse, what if I've picked a conflict that turns me into someone unlovable?"

"You haven't. You were so brave tonight. Any man who isn't impressed by your courage in the face of danger isn't worth your time, anyway." He hummed low. "Watching you wield those blades. Gods, Stella. I was mesmerized."

"Don't patronize me. I'm not going to break. I'm just going to fissure a little. I'll be fine in the morning," she whispered. But even as she said it, she wasn't sure. She felt so different, like the old version of her had left her body, like some part of her was gone.

"We should get you out of those wet clothes so you can warm up."

"You know there are easier ways to get me naked than almost getting yourself killed," she said.

His face lit up with a wicked smile, and warmth surged through the bond. "There you are, *Minyha*. You had me worried for a few minutes there." He nodded at her shirt. "Seriously, though. You should take it off. I can give you another shirt."

She could have waited for him to turn away, but Stella stood and undid the buckles on her vest, letting it fall to the floor. Gripping the bottom edge of his shirt, she pulled it off and tossed it aside. She stared at him where he still knelt on the floor—daring him to look away.

Teddy's gaze raked over her slowly.

"Does that please, Your Grace?"

Teddy's throat bobbed. "It does. Would please me more if you let me touch you."

Stella hesitated. Just a few days ago, this scenario was unimaginable, but now it felt inevitable. She didn't just want him to touch her. She wanted to feel him everywhere. She wanted him to blot out what she'd done and untangle the knotted mix of emotions inside her with pleasure. After what they'd done in the cabin, she felt confident he could.

"On one condition."

Teddy looked up at her from his knees. "Name it."

She liked seeing him like that—supplicant and waiting for her permission. She felt a strange satisfaction seeing a prince humbled only for her.

"Promise you're not doing this because you feel like you owe me."

"The only thing I owe you is the follow-through on what I didn't get to do in that cabin," Teddy said. "Now get on the bed."

Stella sat down on the captain's bed and watched as he stood and unbuttoned his pants.

Teddy was glorious, vital, storm-blown, shirtless, damp hair curling ever so slightly. He stood over her and she laid back, letting him look his fill.

She wasn't normally so comfortable being stared at, but with all they had been through in the past few days, she felt like he already knew her, like there was nothing he would find that he didn't somehow already know.

His gaze was hooded, hungry in a way that made her clench her thighs together.

Stella didn't want to worry anymore. Her body was taut with fear and her heart so heavy with grief that she worried if she lay on the treehouse floor, she'd never get back up.

Teddy crawled over her and cupped her face with one hand. "Tell me what you need, because if you keep looking at me like that, I'm going to think it's something similar to what I gave you last night."

"Make me feel good."

He kissed down the valley between her breasts but paused at her stomach. His fingers skimmed her side, and she went rigid when she realized why. Her scar.

She'd forgotten it was there. She was so desperate to feel his hands all over her. She hadn't kept any clothing on and now he could see the mark her foolishness had left on her.

His callused fingers scraped tenderly over the ugly skin before he kissed each of the points of the mark.

"Don't—" she gasped.

He frowned. "Why?"

"It's ugly. It ruined my constellation." She traced the freckles on her side without needing to look. She'd felt that pattern traced into her skin so frequently that she could retrace it by touch alone.

"No, *Minyha*. Your constellation isn't ruined. It's remade." He brushed his lips over the jagged scar. "I didn't see it before the scar, but this is beautiful. Look at what you've conquered. I only see your strength written on your skin."

Stella looked away, tears pricking at her eyes. Surely he was just saying that. Of course scars could be beautiful. The matching crescent scars on her parents' hands, or the golden ones over their hearts—those were beautiful scars made from love. This was an ugly reminder of how much she'd miscalculated and of what her failure could cost.

He kissed the mark. "Tell me how to help."

"I want." That was the complete thought. She didn't want one thing. She wanted all the things. She wanted to forget, to feel everything and nothing, to feel pain and pleasure, to feel cared for and used. She was made of want.

And Teddy instinctively understood.

He wrapped his arms under her thighs and pinned her hips to the bed. He held her gaze as he slowly licked up her center. The eye contact alone was obscene, but the sensation and the way he flicked his tongue over her clit sent a shiver through her body.

Teddy feasted on her, fucking her with his tongue like a man possessed. He didn't slow down when she clawed at his wrists, didn't mellow his pace when an orgasm shook through her. She arched, and he lifted her hips off the bed, holding her suspended, her shoulders still on the bed as he fought to keep control of her squirming body. He didn't stop until she was practically sobbing and every bit of pain in her body was transmuted into pleasure.

He slowly lowered her back to the bed, kissing her inner thighs, then her stomach, the scars on both her sides, her breasts, and finally her mouth.

Teddy caged her in, looking down on her with smug satisfaction on his face that was very much earned. "Are you satisfied?"

"I want more," she rasped.

Teddy groaned against her inner thigh. "Thank fucking gods."

He stood and shoved off his pants, fisting his cock in his hand.

She hated that it was so perfect. He was perfect everywhere else; he didn't also deserve to have a perfect cock. He was big and thick, but not so much so that she didn't think she could take it.

He spit into his hand and stroked himself roughly a couple of times before kneeling on the bed and notching himself at her entrance.

Painstakingly slowly, he pushed inside her. She wanted him to speed up, to slow down, to stop looking into her eyes like he was enamored, to stop being so handsome and kind because it made her feel terrified and safe at the same time.

She felt every inch as he stretched her.

She whimpered, and he paused. "Too much?"

She shook her head. "Not enough."

He pushed deeper, until he was fully seated inside her. Stella felt completely grounded with that sensation, the feeling of his body warm and firm on top of her, and the pulsing hum of their bond. The calm affection running back and forth between them through their connection was overwhelming. Her lust, his joy. His need, her anxiety.

She waited for him to move, but he stayed there, unmoving, kissing her for a long time.

"Gods, you feel so good," he whispered against her mouth. "The bond is killing me. I know you want me to move, but I'm trying to keep myself from fucking you through the bed, *Minyha*."

She wanted to ask him what it meant for the hundredth time but was also afraid to know now.

"Please," she moaned.

That plea was all it took. He drew his hips back and thrust into her. They both gasped. He was so deep, but she wanted him deeper. His hand came beneath her lower back and tilted her hips to give her more friction on her clit each time he moved.

Her eyes rolled back, and her groan dissolved into a string of expletives. Teddy chuckled and dragged his teeth over her nipple. She arched into him.

It was alarming how quick of a study he'd made of her pleasure. Stella could already feel the first bit of pressure mounting. She had not even mastered her own body so well.

He moved faster, hips rolling, churning, his hands holding her firmly in place so she had the best angle. The combination of his mouth on her breasts, neck, and jaw, the thick glide of his cock, and the friction of his body against her was driving her out of her mind. She dug her heels into his ass and urged him deeper.

She felt like she was drowning, and also like she would die if he let her up for air. Her body was alive in a way it had never been— burning with a fever she had never known and didn't understand.

He stared down at where their bodies were joined. "You're so perfect, *Minyha*. You're taking me so well."

Stella shuddered at the praise.

"All you needed was to feel me right—" He changed the angle of her hips and his cock nudged something inside her that ratcheted her pleasure even higher. "There. Right there. I knew you needed that because this is what only I can do for you."

It was so possessive and hot. He kept her hips at that angle, moving faster and then slowing each time she got close. Her whole body was rigid, muscles clenching and unclenching.

"Teddy, *please*."

That was all it took. He steadied his rhythm and fucked her harder.

The climax came over her so hard she screamed—a guttural, wrenching sob of a scream that came from the same place that felt numbed over since she'd killed the assassins.

Tears streamed down her cheeks, and it felt like every emotion had been wrung out of her body at once. She tucked her face into his neck and urged him faster, praying he wouldn't notice the way he was breaking her apart and putting her back together with only his body.

She scraped her fingernails down his abs. Gods, he was sexy. She'd seen plenty of men spar shirtless, but she'd never seen anyone who looked like this—like he was sculpted by the gods themselves. She slid her hands to his hips, urging him on.

She needed him to finish now, because if he made her come again, she was going to fall apart and become a sobbing mess.

It was like he read it in her body—maybe some understanding of their bond let him feel it, because he slowed down and drew back, forcing her to meet his gaze.

"Stella."

He said her name with such softness as he kissed away her tears.

"You're so beautiful. It's exhausting trying not to look at you all the time."

"That's just the bond," she rasped.

"It's not. I have always thought that. I think it's part of why I was mean."

Stella laughed. "Because you were mad that I'm pretty."

"Because I thrived on control, and I can't control myself around you."

She wanted him to stop saying sweet things and fuck her. She wanted it hot and dirty, like it had been in the cabin. This had turned into something too vulnerable, and she felt like a raw wound.

"But you are gorgeous." He brushed his finger over the scar on her side as he said it to emphasize the point. "Even more so with these marks of your courage. And I know you want me to be rough right now, but what you need is what I'm giving you."

He pumped his hips slowly and kissed her. Stella met his rhythm, curling her legs around his waist. He groaned and buried his face in her neck, mumbling incomprehensible praise into her skin.

Teddy's fingers were bruising on her hips. He was trying to hold out, as if he was certain there was more pleasure left for him to squeeze out of her, but Stella was exhausted, emotionally raw, and afraid that, if he kept looking at her that way, she would completely fall apart.

Even now, the bond tugged in her chest like a hook connected to his heart; like she would never get enough of this—whatever this was.

Just sex. Just comfort, a voice in her head said.

But she knew that was a lie. He wasn't looking at her like this was just physical. What she felt deep in her chest was not just physical.

She pressed her heels against his lower back, holding him deeper inside of her, and he moaned and found his release with a few jerky movements of his hips.

He drew back, meeting her eyes. She found her confusion and muddy emotions reflected there. Mercifully, he said nothing. Instead, he flopped onto the bed beside her, allowing their breathing to settle.

Stella lay on her back, feeling wrung out and shaken, her whole body alive with pleasure.

They were quiet for a few long moments, listening to the storm raging outside and the creak of the branches around them.

"You know, I always thought you liked being heir. It seemed like it came so easily to you."

He sighed. "Well, now you know it doesn't."

"I'm ashamed to say I didn't even really think of you as a person. More a sort of icon—a living ideal," she said.

He scoffed. "I'm not really a person most of the time. I'm a title."

She was quiet. "I'm sorry I gave you such a hard time about it. I never really thought about the way people talk to you. The way *I* talked to you. Has anyone else asked you what you want?"

Teddy sighed and looked up at the ceiling. The rain had slowed to a drizzle, a percussive tap on the treehouse roof.

"I'm not sure I even know what I want. I only seem to know what I don't want."

Stella smiled, running her fingers through his hair.

He tilted his head so he could kiss her palm. "I don't want to get up early. I don't want to dress in fancy clothes. I don't want to be proper and act like a figurehead instead of a person. My parents are performers, but I am not. I did not inherit their ease the way Jalen, Jules, and Alex did. Everyone else in my family is so at home in their roles and I am just eternally exhausted by mine. It's like I'm another species shoved into the wrong family."

"Alexandra doesn't exactly blend," Stella whispered.

Teddy laughed, the sound deep and rumbling and so rare that Stella couldn't help but smile.

"She doesn't," he said. "But she is at ease in herself. It's the rest of us who are wrong in her estimation and she who's at home in her role."

Stella grinned at that. Alexandra Savero had always been quite composed, wearing her leather armor instead of dresses, even as a little girl. She was a woman who knew what she wanted and wouldn't let anyone, not even a king or queen, tell her what she ought to wear, say, or do.

"I always admired that."

Teddy smiled softly. "As do I."

Stella drew her fingers down his chest, tracing the ruts that defined the muscles of his abdomen. Goosebumps rose on his skin, but he didn't stop her.

"What would you want? If you could have anything?" she asked.

"Some fucking peace and quiet. I want to lie in bed all day reading nonsense stories instead of history or battle tactics. I want to learn to swim without being afraid, for fuck's sake. And the only crown I want to wear is the kind made of daisies like the ones you used to make me when we were young."

Stella blinked at him in disbelief. He'd hated her for so long that she'd forgotten the way they'd been when they were children spending summer days on the beach, ripping flowers from the cliffside trail to try to make crowns as grand as the ones her father used to make her with his dexterous carpenter's hands.

"But it doesn't matter what I want. It may as well be a wish. The kingdoms are too unstable for me to be so selfish. As much as I'd like to run off and be free to live on my whims, I love my kingdom and my people, even if they don't love me back. I can't abandon them when they need me. My father told me once that being a great king is like being a parent—that you love your people unconditionally, whether they love you or hate you. I've never felt that so keenly as I do now."

They both went silent, and Stella wondered if they were thinking about how close he'd come to being relieved of that role just hours ago.

Stella shook her head, trying to blot out the memory, but her magic wanted to pull it up over and over. Memory magic could be like that; a mind turning over and over, constantly drawn back to the past, always slipping into daydream and memory. Her mother was like that, but Stella was normally much better at staying present.

The guilt left her with the haunting uneasiness that the assassins might not be the last lives she took.

Teddy, clearly sensing the direction of her thoughts, pushed her onto her side and yanked her back against his front so his body was curled around her.

"Stop thinking and go to sleep," he murmured into her ear.

Make me. She was so tempted to say it aloud, but the comfort of someone protectively holding her while she slept was a luxury she'd never experienced.

He pressed his palm over her sternum and the bond felt warm and bright, calmed by Teddy's proximity. It was like this hollow in his arms was the space she was made to fill, and the moment she was tucked safely into it, sleep came to claim her.

29

TEDDY

Stella's pale skin took on an ethereal glow in the morning light cascading through the treehouse window. Teddy knew he should wake her. They had more ground to cover today, and they needed to complete the memory retrieval and start the journey back if they wanted to make the deadline.

Still, he couldn't bear to disturb her. He knew what it would be like. She'd wake and for one blessed moment she'd forget what she'd done and then he'd have to watch her remember again. It was part of the reason he'd barely let her sleep. He didn't want to let her have a single moment alone with her thoughts.

He'd been a comfort to her. He'd helped her through what was probably the worst night of her life, and he felt guilty for enjoying it.

It wasn't just the sex, though, that had been mind-blowing. It was the way he'd intuitively known exactly what to do—the way she'd let him help. The softness of her looking at him with so much relief and trust. Gods, he did not even trust himself that way, but when she looked at him like that, he thought maybe he should.

He was too aware of her now—her proximity, her scent on the air like fresh rain on wildflowers mixed with salted sea air. He could get addicted to that—and to the way she slept pressed against him all night.

She sighed and shifted, her green eyes fluttering open. She smiled, and it was half-shy, half-wicked. Her skin had already healed, no remnants of the bite marks he'd left all over her when they got into things. He would have felt bad, except when he'd done it, she came so hard that she'd needed a full minute to lie still and recover.

Stella was pent up in the way he was, in the way that only the two oldest children of the most famous families in the two kingdoms could be. He liked that she needed it as badly as he did.

Teddy slid his hand down her side and lust warmed their bond, along with the dregs of grief and disappointment. Last night was supposed to be an ending. It felt too soon, but it was for the best. He knew he should just get up and start his day, but his cock was already hard from the memory of the previous night, and he wasn't ready for it to be over.

"Did you need something this morning, *Minyha*?"

Mischief flared in her eyes. "I can still feel you inside me."

"Fuck," he groaned. It was so stupidly possessive, but he loved it. He loved how quickly she understood what to say to make him crazy.

He flipped her onto her back. He wanted to make sure she felt him in every movement, all day—that she was so thoroughly fucked that, even though she didn't want to be with him, she would at least feel his presence in her body for a day or two.

He shoved her knees up toward her shoulders, bearing her to him. He stared at her for a moment, feeling half mad for her. Then he pushed into her slowly, watching the pleasure on her face.

She moaned, and the sound vibrated through his whole body.

The night before, she'd been desperate for a distraction and then wild for release, but in the light of day, she was slow, clearly studying him in the way he'd studied her.

He moved his hips, hard and insistent, kissing her neck, nipping at her skin, running a thumb over her nipple. He needed this violent affection as much as she did. He wanted to touch her everywhere, consume her, breathe in nothing but the scent of her.

Her clenching became more rapid, her nails scoring his back. She was close. He pumped into her one more time, then pulled out.

Her eyes snapped open, and she glared at him. "Not yet, *Minyha*. I don't just want you to come for me. I want you to feel the aftershocks of this climax for days."

She whimpered as he slowly pushed back inside her. She was still twitching. Her pussy was so tight and wet, gripping him like she wanted to take him deeper into her body.

He didn't understand what came over him, but he felt possessed by this need for her. He clicked his tongue in admonishment, and she shivered.

"You're so greedy for me now. Do you feel that?" he murmured into the skin of her neck as he bottomed out inside her. "Do you feel how deep I am? If you were mine, I would remind you of this all the time. I would make you feel this good every night and every morning."

She clenched so hard around him that he worried he might go over the edge. He dragged himself back at the last second.

"Not yet. You don't come until I let you."

He fucked her hard, pumping in and out of her, dragging his teeth over her nipples, listening to her whine and protest when he slowed his pace. He brought her to the brink twice more before she flipped him onto his back.

It was so unexpected that all Teddy could do was lay there, staring up at her. Her dark curly hair was wild, some of it partially covering her perky tits, some draping down behind her back so far that when she arched, the ends tickled his thighs. Her neck and breasts were red from him nipping at her skin, and the sight made his cock twitch.

Stella sank down on him and started to move. Her left hand came up to tweak her nipple, and the right rubbed her clit in time with the pace of her hips. She was miraculously unselfconscious and so beautiful.

Teddy had never been so happy to be used. He was going to fuck her even harder when she was done, just to remind her who was in charge of her pleasure, in some sick attempt to prove himself once more.

He gripped her hips, helping her keep pace as she rode him. Then her whole body seized, her mouth falling open in a rasping groan.

She climaxed, her back arched as his thumb stroked her clit. He loved the sound she made—like someone rent from her old self—like someone he'd made new with his touch.

When the aftershocks finished rippling through her body, she stopped her rocking and gave him a lazy smile.

"I was tired of waiting."

Teddy's laugh was cut off when she lifted off him and began to kiss down his stomach. Then, she took his cock in her mouth and he was entirely at her mercy.

Good gods, the wicked things he had no idea she could do with her tongue. He fought not to thrust his hips, to seek out more of her hot mouth. She must have read it in his movement because she took him deeper into her throat, and Teddy's eyes rolled back.

He had to pinch himself to keep from coming instantly. He used to have the same meticulous focus in the bedroom that he did everywhere else, but now he'd been humbled by their bond. It made everything so much more intense to feel the pleasure she got out of making him feel so good.

She brought him to the brink three times with the kind of knowing that only came from being directly and magically connected to someone.

Then, he couldn't take it anymore. Teddy knew he should move slowly, savor this, but the frenzied fever of her was still burning through him. He pushed her off of him, flipping her onto her hands and knees, facing away from him. Stella just braced her hands against the headboard as he slapped her perfect ass.

Teddy took her hips and pushed into her hard. She moaned loudly. He was happy they were in the middle of nowhere, so no one could hear the way he was going to make her scream and cry. He wanted those sounds to himself. He wanted *all* of her to himself. He wrapped her hair around his fist and yanked her head back, nipping at her ear.

"Tell me what you want," he rasped.

"I want to feel it."

"Thank gods," he groaned, then thrust into her harder.

He had not been quite so rough with her before, but this was for him. This was what he needed—for her to know that this was the thing only he could do for her. Only he could help her find this kind of intense release.

She pushed back against him. Gods, he wanted to teach her filthy things. He slapped her ass again, and she cursed and clenched around him.

His time was running out. Stella was frantically meeting his thrusts, bearing down so hard on him that he could barely do more than rock against her.

He slapped her ass harder. "Stop moving and just let me be in charge. Your only job is to take what I give you and come on my cock."

He fucked her savagely, with every remaining remnant of fear that lingered from the previous night driving him. He lost himself in her body until she gripped the headboard and screamed. She clenched so hard that Teddy had to stop moving. Her thighs trembled and her head fell back.

Finally, her muscles relaxed enough that he could fuck her through the end of the climax. As soon as it was over, she fell forward, her torso resting on the bed, hips still in the air, thighs spread wide for him.

That was all it took. He gripped her hips with bruising strength and came with a grunt. His body moved in a frenzied rhythm, the climax so intense he almost collapsed on top of her. He caught himself on a forearm at the last minute. He slid his other arm around her body, his hand slipping between her legs.

He leaned over her, watching her lips part as she realized what he was doing. She gasped and twitched as he stroked her too-sensitive clit.

"Please," she sighed.

He couldn't tell if she was asking for more or less. But then her eyes blinked open, and she met his gaze.

"I need to catch my breath. I—" She groaned as he pressed his fingers harder against her.

Her pussy clenched around him, sending an aftershock of pleasure through his whole body. The bond in his chest was pleasantly warm, soothed by being connected to her in every way.

She squirmed, trying to escape his touch, but Teddy didn't relent. He kept stroking her.

He nipped at her earlobe. "I like you like this, *Minyha*. Dripping down your thighs. So wet and needy. So afraid you have more to give me." She gasped and her pussy twitched again. "One more. Let me feel one more."

Her eyes pleaded with him, but she pressed into his fingers. She looked gorgeous—her hair wild, eyes hooded, cheeks flushed. He wanted to see her like this every day.

The thought startled him, but he didn't have time to react. Stella's hand came over his, trying to direct his pressure on her clit. He ripped her hand away and pinned it behind her back.

Teddy clicked his tongue. "What did I say, Stella? I'm in charge here. You take what I give you."

She shuddered, cursing into the pillow as he rubbed her harder and faster. Then she froze and her whole body spasmed, a guttural moan spilling from her lips as she surrendered to one more orgasm. It rolled through her in waves. Her thighs trembled violently, and when he slid his other hand up to pinch her nipple, her whole body seized, gripping his cock so hard it was just on the edge of painful.

As she came down from the high, she shoved his hand away from her sensitive clit. "No more," she rasped.

She blinked her eyes open and smiled at him. Teddy liked the glazed, satisfied look on her face too much.

He pulled back and instantly missed the warmth of her soft skin. These stolen moments in the treehouse were a fantasy. He could not keep this. She was in love with someone else, for the love of the gods.

How quickly he'd forgotten she didn't really belong to him. It just felt like she did.

Stella had plans that didn't include him. He'd wanted to be there for her in the worst moment of her life, and he'd been the one sucked into the escapist fantasy. She was the one who would go home to someone else.

He was angry at himself for forgetting. He'd lost control and gotten sucked into the vortex of Stella, likely for the same reason he'd avoided her. She was joyful and imaginative and gentle with him, and he was falling for her.

This cosmic joke by the goddess of love could easily become a cosmic curse if he wasn't careful. Stella didn't want him. She was in this tournament to fight for someone else.

"We should head out soon," Teddy said.

Stella laughed and flopped onto her back. "You just fucked me senseless, Your Grace. I think you're going to have to wait a few minutes for my legs to work again."

She stayed sprawled on the bed as Teddy rose to get dressed. He considered bathing, but the thought of reliving the previous night's trauma was unappealing. He wiped the sweat from his skin with a damp cloth, watching Stella out of the corner of his eye.

Her expression had morphed from pleasant satisfaction to serious contemplation. She rose from the bed, her energy shifting to match his as she rifled through her bag for something to wear.

The fantasy was over. It was time to get back to the fight.

30

TEDDY

The cave mouth stretched before Teddy, dark and wide, like the mouth of a great beast waiting to swallow him whole.

He was finally going to retrieve his piece of the memory challenge. All he had to do was walk in and watch whatever horrible memory was waiting for him.

"I think you should wait until I'm finished so I can go with you," he said.

Stella shook her head. "We're losing daylight. We don't know how long the memory will be, or how long it will take you to pull yourself out of it. We already lost too much time in the river and the recovery and this morning." She blushed and looked away.

Funny that she felt suddenly shy when she'd been so wild and uninhibited earlier. But everything was different in the light of day, staring down the second challenge. Their momentary escape was over, and now it was time to face their futures.

She looked down at her feet, her hands subconsciously running over her vest to check that her blades were still there.

"I hate that you'll be alone, but I know you can do it," Teddy said.

Stella smiled, but her eyes were full of apprehension.

Teddy knew that look—knew the way she was picking up a

memory over and over, like pressing on a bruise to see if it still hurt. He'd tried to deliver her from the worst of it, but it was written in the tension in her body—the crease between her brows as they silently walked through the forest, the way her hands came to her short swords every time a creature scampered through the underbrush.

He didn't like that she was going to continue on alone to her cave, or that she was about to watch what was probably a very difficult memory when she was still traumatized.

Teddy took her face in her hands, and she startled, her wide eyes meeting his. "I will see you by nightfall and we will both be safely out of our memories and ready to hike back to the crossroads and ride home tomorrow."

She smiled weakly.

Teddy wanted to kiss her, but that seemed a comfort reserved for more intense moments. They were just getting each other through this tournament. It was just an impulse of this bond. Nothing more.

"Be safe. Don't let the magic hold you too long," she said. "Memory is tricky when you don't wield it regularly. Be careful of going in too deep. I don't know how the challenge works, but there could be trapdoors to other memories. Try not to wander."

He forced a smirk. "It's just a memory. How bad could it be?"

Stella's lips formed a tight line. "Don't take too long, Your Grace. I don't want to have to come back and save you...again."

He rolled his eyes at the jab. "I'll see you in a couple of hours."

She turned and disappeared into the trees. Teddy waited for the sound of her footsteps to retreat before he faced the cave again.

A strong pulse of magic seemed to beat from somewhere inside. He knew from the stories how it worked for the witches of the Gauntlet. All magic required an exchange. He just needed to step into the dark, cut his hand, and spill his blood onto the medicinal plants inside. Then the memory would come into his mind.

At least, that was how it was supposed to work.

He snapped his fingers, sending a surge of fire magic into his palm. He walked forward into the cave.

As he moved away from the entrance, the darkness became

greedier, eating up his torchlight until he could only see as far as his next step. That was how he would find what he needed. One faithful step at a time.

Finally, when he'd wandered far enough that he worried his descent would never end, the toe of his boot nudged a dense bunch of greenery. He tried to flare his torch brighter, but the dark just closed in tighter.

Teddy sighed. He placed the memory stone on his open flaming palm, drew his dagger, and sliced the blade across his skin just below the stone. Making a fist around the memory stone, the flame snuffed out, and he allowed his blood to drip onto the greenery below.

Witch's blood held magic that would help sustain the medicinal plants that were foraged by healers in the two kingdoms. It seemed gruesome, but it was part of the complex magical ecosystem that kept the realm balanced.

He stood there for a few moments, wondering how he would know that it was enough.

Teddy blinked and suddenly the cave was blindingly bright.

It took a moment for his eyes to adjust. He knew this room. It was the first-floor sitting room in Castle Savero, which led to the main dining room.

Teddy's heart pounded. He glanced around the space and his gaze fell on a familiar face—his father's cousin, traitor to the kingdom, who had briefly usurped the throne twenty-five years ago: Vincent Savero.

This was the night of the invasion and Teddy was inside Xander's mind, but this was like no memory he had experienced before. He could sense the wild spinning of his father's thoughts.

This wasn't right. Memory magic had all the senses—a fully embodied experience—as well as emotions, but it didn't have thoughts.

Except now it did.

Teddy squeezed his eyes closed as if that would wrench him from this nightmarish magic, but when he blinked his eyes open, he knew there was no choice but to play it through. He surrendered to the storm.

Cecilia stopped moving immediately and dropped her blade.

"Smart girl," Vincent said.

Xander turned wildly, summoning his storm magic. It was hard to use this deep in the castle. He could blow out the windows in the room, but trying to funnel a storm through a small opening was not very effective. He wanted to stand and fight, but doing so now would get his closest friends killed. It would probably get him killed as well.

"No shame in admitting when you're outmatched, cousin."

Xander felt crushed under impotent fury, but he dropped his blade and held his hands up. Guards charged him and Cece, snapping Unsummoner bracelets on their wrists.

He narrowed his eyes at Vincent, trying to remember the young cousin he'd grown up with. He looked nothing like his old self. The years had carved away any kindness and left him with sharp features and the dark eyes for which he was known. Xander was sure they hadn't always looked like that. He would have noticed.

The moment Xander's magic severed, he wanted to slump in defeat. He forced himself to hold his head high.

"Those are spelled," Vincent said. "You won't be able to get them off without magic. Ancient magic. You may have sneaked those witches away, but not before they did me a few favors. Not your basic everyday Unsummoner bracelet. You're quick, taking so many of my men out before they could subdue you. Honestly, you all nearly foiled my well-laid plans when you had the wedding so soon. I almost couldn't get my men here in time."

Vincent grinned as he looked at the three of them. "I thought a couple of fake princesses would add enough chaos to the mix, but I must admit, you weathered it much better than I expected. There were so many moving pieces and I nearly missed my timing." He brushed his hands down his fine tunic. "I see the gears turning. You're wondering about the eyes. Unfortunately, Cato's power is not what it once was. It wore off sooner than expected this time, since the lovely Lady Reznik temporarily stole his memory of how to use it. So she noticed when I was mesmerizing her with my charm at brunch."

Both Xander and Rainer bristled at that, but Cece laughed.

Oh, gods. Please, Cece, don't be yourself right now. Don't be brave. Be sweet and timid. Just this once, *Xander silently begged.*

"That's funny?" Vincent asked, a slight grin on his face.

"Yes. It's just that all of you Saveros think you're so different, but you equally overestimate your ability to charm women."

Vincent tipped his head back and laughed. "You are certainly spirited. I'll give you that. I love a feisty woman." He walked toward her, and Cece paled. "I understand you're still available," Vincent taunted, looking from Rainer to Cece.

"I'm engaged," Cece said.

"Until the deal is sealed, I consider you still available. It's McKay's fault for not securing you when he had the chance." Vincent reached out a hand and stroked her cheek.

To Cece's credit, she didn't shrink away.

Beside Xander, Rainer thrashed against the guards. Xander met his eye and shook his head as if to say, "Don't give him the satisfaction."

Vincent looked at Rainer as he let his fingers trail down Cece's neck, over her exposed shoulder, and then along the neckline of her dress, letting his finger skim right under the edge of the lace. Cece's heart raced loud enough for Xander to hear from where he stood, but she didn't move.

"So soft," Vincent whispered.

Rainer stilled, his brow creased with helpless worry as he watched.

Cece met Xander's eyes over Vincent's shoulder and gave the slightest shake of her head.

"I'll make this simple. Why is it that the trickster hasn't been able to get into any of your heads? Or the king of Olney's?"

Xander shook his head. "I don't know."

"If you're a good king, that's a lie. But if you're a good friend and lover, it isn't. As I understand, you spent quite a bit of time protecting Guardian McKay for your dear Cece. Is that true?"

Xander wasn't sure how to answer. He felt like he was struggling in an undertow, and every wrong answer was going to sweep him into deeper water. He'd been strategically outmaneuvered for months. He wouldn't suddenly be able to come out on top, but he was the king. He had to do something.

Just holding Vincent's attention might be enough. The longer they distracted Vincent and his men, the more time the staff had to escape. He crossed his fingers that they were smart enough to flee and had somewhere to go. Hopefully, Evan was intercepting people. He prayed their friends made it to safety.

Vincent nodded, and two guards dragged Rainer forward. They stripped him of his fine tunic and undershirt so that he stood shirtless before they bent him over the mahogany table. They bound his wrists to either side, immobilizing him.

Cece faltered, taking a step toward him. His gaze was locked on hers, and he shook his head. Tears welled in her eyes, but she smiled half-heartedly as he sent something through their connection. "I love you," he mouthed.

Cece gritted her teeth and dug her nails into her palms to keep herself from crying. The frustration on her face mirrored Xander's own. He hated feeling helpless.

Vincent pulled off his fancy tunic and rolled up the sleeves of his undershirt, revealing scarred forearms. "Here's what's going to happen. You can tell me why the trickster can't get into your heads." He picked up a switch. "For every minute it takes you to tell me, I'm going to give Rainer a lash. If you tell me now, he won't get any. Look at that perfect skin, Lady Reznik. You've done such a good job keeping him in one piece all these years. Are you willing to throw that all away now? As I understand, lashings are very hard to heal, even for talented healers, because of the way the skin splits. They almost always leave scars."

Reality set in. They'd faced cruelty before, but never such sharp violence. Cato's psychological warfare had been brutal but always with a goal in mind, and he hadn't relished physical pain in conjunction with it. His violence was a means to an end. Vincent seemed to bask in their fear, his eyes lit with excitement at the prospect of inflicting pain.

"We'll start in one minute. If you tell me before, then I won't whip him at all."

Cece glanced helplessly from Rainer to Xander. Rainer met Xander's *gaze and gave the slightest shake of his head. He wanted the king to know he could take it.*

Beside Xander, Cece was standing tall, but he could tell by the look in her eye and the way her heart pounded that she was crumbling.

"Let Lady Reznik go. She doesn't know anything. She only recently recovered from her ordeal," Xander said.

Rainer looked relieved by the plea. Xander didn't understand why he was doing it. Cece wouldn't leave, but he just wanted her out of the center of Vincent's attention. She did not deserve to be the object of any more cruelty.

Vincent just laughed. He smiled at Cece as he brought the switch down on Rainer's back. The sound reverberated through the room like a crack of thunder.

Rainer gritted his teeth against the pain, immediately meeting Cece's gaze. She closed her eyes and tears streamed down her face. Rainer's face went calm and serene with her. Xander was struck by the juxtaposition of the horror of the violence combined with their beautiful way of silently communicating.

Xander didn't know how much Cece could take. She already looked like she was about to crack.

"Lady Reznik, perhaps I'm asking the wrong people. Perhaps you know. Why can't the trickster get into your friends' minds?" Vincent said.

"I don't know," Cece gritted out.

Vincent slammed the cane down again. Xander and Cece flinched.

The same game went on for far too long as Vincent taunted and tortured them. The more frustrated he got with their defiance, the more brutally and faster he hit Rainer. No matter how many times they said they didn't know, he didn't believe them.

Vincent whipped Rainer three times in quick succession and Cece yanked herself free of the guard who'd been holding her back, running to Rainer. He squeezed her hand, and she kissed his knuckles. Her cheeks were flushed and damp with sweat.

Xander couldn't imagine the agony of both watching and feeling the pain of the person she loved most. If it had been her on the table, Xander would have cracked instantly. But all three of them had managed to keep this secret this long, and none of them were going to break now.

Rainer's back was a sliced-up, bloody mess. The pain must have been staggering. The air smelled like copper. The table, the floor, and Vincent's clothes were speckled with blood and sweat.

Cece met Xander's eyes. He saw her waver. Her hand was poised over her heart as tears poured down her cheeks. It wasn't Vincent's torture that had her sobbing. It was that Rainer was hurting but still sending reassurance through their bond. Xander knew what it was to protect Cece at his own expense. He'd done it for months while Cato tortured him. He saw it now in the way she cried harder a moment after the strikes, her palm pressed to her heart. Xander had never respected Rainer more.

"I can do this all night—until he's fucking dead. One of you is going to crack," Vincent snarled, preparing to strike again.

Cece curled over Rainer's body protectively, and Vincent drew up at the last second.

"No," she snapped. "We don't know. I made Cato forget how to use his magic. Maybe it has to do with that, but none of us know why he can't do it."

Vincent laughed. "You are very tricky, Lady Reznik. The problem is that I'm a liar, and I know a liar when I see one. This is the last piece of information I need to fulfill my deal with the trickster. I'll have it now, and I'll enter this era with myself as a king with no debts left to pay."

"He is barely conscious," Cece said.

"Are you offering to take his place?" Vincent challenged.

Rainer looked up at her sharply, but Cece said nothing.

"I am," Xander said.

Vincent blew out a breath. "Oh, cousin, come on! We've seen this little drama play out before. Plus, I need you able to move around freely and charm these people. You are part of my succession plan. I need the goodwill you've harnessed with the common folk and aristocracy. I also need you to smooth things over with your new in-laws, so we'll eventually need your new wife as well. You're lucky, you know. You have a longer-term purpose than your two friends. Unfortunately for them, they were caught with you. Once I have what I need, and I've closed off my deal with Cato, they have no purpose. I do hate waste," Vincent threatened.

He turned back to Cece. The feral look on his face made Xander's stomach plummet.

"Very well. If none of you want to talk, perhaps I haven't tried the right strategy yet," he said.

Vincent grabbed Cece, pulling her back flush to his front. He held her securely around the waist. He didn't need to say anything for Xander to recognize the look in his eye.

"There are much worse things than death," Cato had told Xander years before.

Once again, Cato was right.

Ever since Cato had reappeared like a living nightmare the day before, dread had prickled Xander's skin. The hairs on the back of his neck stood on end, reminding him that a reckoning was coming. Now that Vincent held Cece against his body, Xander knew what it was.

Two guards untied Rainer from the table and dragged him to a chair. He winced as his back hit the wood, slumping over, unconscious. He quickly regained consciousness as they tied his wrists to the chair—as if he needed restraints. The man looked half-dead.

"If the two of you won't talk, there's only one of you left to hurt," Vincent said. "Now, while I assume she's the one pulling the strings in all of this, I know that the two of you must also know why it is that Cato can't influence Marcos."

Xander looked warily at Cece, but she looked resigned.

Somehow, that was no comfort. Xander knew she could take the pain, but he wasn't sure he could.

"No takers? Good! I was getting bored with this. I have something else in mind for the lovely Lady Reznik."

Vincent put a hand around her throat, caressing her bodice with the other.

Xander's stomach dropped. He went rigid. The guards tightened their grip on his arms. Rainer rolled in and out of consciousness beside him, in too much pain to connect the dots. If Cato was the brilliant psychological strategist, Vincent was the ruthless, brutal tyrant. He had Cato's flair for manipulation and, thanks to his time undercover in their court, a deep understanding of the dynamics that played out between the three of them.

Cece was doing a good job of hiding her fear, but her heartbeat raced, and if Xander could hear it from ten feet away, Vincent could most certainly feel it at the pulse point in her neck.

He didn't seem satisfied with their reaction. His hand tightened on her throat.

"In fact, I think I'll do it right here. Let you both watch. How many men can say they've fucked a goddess?" Vincent taunted. "And I'll have proof. Maybe I'll let my men each take a turn after me."

Vincent's guards grinned at each other and chuckled as if he'd told a hilarious joke. Every story Xander had been told about the trail of violence Vincent left in villages along Argaria's borders rushed into his head at once.

"Maybe if she's as good as you all seem to think, I'll keep her," Vincent chuckled. "Would you enjoy that, goddess—having my men and your men watch me take the spoils of this war?"

She refused to cower. "The only thing I will enjoy is watching you bleed out from my blade."

Vincent stepped back and backhanded her.

Xander tried to stand, but two guards forced him into a chair.

Cece quickly stood up straight and lifted her chin in defiance as Vincent admired the blotchy red mark rising on her cheek. He brushed his fingers tenderly over it.

Xander was desperate for a way out. He looked at the dagger on the hip of the guard to his left. He could probably get it and take the man down, but Cece would be on her own and there were six other guards in the room. Two beside Rainer, two beside Vincent. There were probably men outside the sitting room doors as well.

No matter how badly Xander wanted to help her, if he acted rashly now, they'd all suffer for it. He'd get one chance, and he'd have to make it count. "Stop this. You should keep her for yourself—as a queen," Xander said. "She's a goddess. No one would cross you. If you shame her in front of your guards, she can never be that."

Vincent laughed. "She was never going to be my queen, cousin. I saw the game you three played in your library. She doesn't fuck like a queen. She fucks like a whore, and that's what she'll be to me. She will be treated to every deviant, twisted thing I can't do to a wife. What a lucky girl you are,

Lady Reznik. I have so many creative ideas for you. So many dark, destructive things for you to try."

Cece paled, her panicked gaze shifting from Rainer to Xander.

"You smell so sweet." Vincent's nose grazed up the column of her neck, and she shuddered as his tongue darted out to lick up the same line.

Rainer mumbled something between breathless grunts of pain.

"Trying to give me pointers, McKay?" Vincent chuckled. "I think I know what she likes after that day in the library."

Her knees buckled, but Vincent held her firm. He sank his teeth into the place where her neck and shoulder met, and she flinched. The guards holding Xander in his seat tightened their grip on him. All he could do was watch as Cece tried to squirm from the pain.

"The only way out is through," Vincent whispered. "My patience is wearing thin. If you tell me now, I won't hurt you, Cecilia."

A hysterical giggle bubbled from her lips.

Vincent went rigid. "Why the fuck is she laughing?"

"Because you already hurt her. She feels what Rainer feels," Xander said.

Vincent was quiet, considering this. Then, with deadly precision, he cut through the strap of her gown and the front folded down to her waist, revealing her lacy mauve bustier.

Vincent clicked his tongue. "Would you look at that? It's like she was expecting me."

Several guards laughed.

Cece tried to squirm away, but Vincent pressed his blade to her throat again. "Move again, and I'll have my men break the bones in your fiancé's fingers one by one. Hold still."

His hand brushed over the lace.

Xander watched as Cece's eyes glazed, like she was trying to send herself somewhere far away. She tipped her head back and stared at the ceiling.

"Please stop," she whispered.

"I'll stop when you tell me what I want to know," Vincent said, his gaze meeting Xander's once again.

There was no winning now. Xander knew enough about interrogations to know the pain would not end if she or Xander told Vincent what he wanted to know. Interrogations ended in death or escape, and Xander had no escape route for them. If Cece gave up what she knew, she'd no longer be valuable.

"I don't know," she whispered. "None of us do. Only Marcos knows for sure. We compartmentalized knowledge for this very reason. I would have told you when you were brutalizing Rainer if I knew."

Vincent clicked his tongue. "Perhaps you all truly don't know. Only one way to know for sure." He stood straighter. "Enough games, Xander. Be a king for once in your pathetic life. Be a leader and make the right choice. Tell me now, or I'm going to take her to the other room and find out what all the fuss is about. I'll fuck the information right out of her, and if that doesn't work, I'll let my men take turns until the truth comes out. There won't be anything left of her."

Rainer shook his head violently. He mumbled her name, but he was barely conscious.

Two kingdoms balanced on the edge of a knife.

Xander clenched his jaw so tightly he worried his teeth might shatter.

It was Cece or his kingdom. He could give Vincent the answer he craved and maybe that would be enough to protect Cece. Or he could keep his mouth shut and let this nightmare play out.

Xander hated being king. It was a thankless job that he could never do right because it was impossible to know what was right for so many people when he was just one man.

But he loved his home, and he knew that Vincent would destroy it.

Cece met his gaze, a faint, resigned smile on her lips, like she knew before he did what he would do. But he did not want this. He did not want to have to choose between seeing a person he loved hurt and the safety of his kingdom. There was no real greater good.

There was only the man he was now who had learned that being king was about surrendering selfish desires for the safety of his people. It felt wrong to choose anyone other than Cece, but he forced himself to stay still.

It should have felt like a triumph. Like he was finally evolving from Storm Prince to Storm King, but the victory felt hollow.

Cece nodded at Xander. It was barely perceptible. "Don't," she said, her *voice low enough that only he would hear. "Don't take this on. You're doing the right thing."*

"Very well," Vincent huffed. "Get her ready for me, Grant."

He shoved Cece into the arms of his guard, who dragged her kicking and screaming into the connecting dining room.

"Last chance to save her," Vincent said, his dark eyes roaming from Xander to Rainer.

Rainer surged in his chair and it tipped to its side, landing him in a heap on the floor.

Vincent laughed and sauntered into the dining room, leaving the door open a crack—so they could hear, Xander realized.

A new terror gripped him as a scuffle echoed from the adjoining room. It all went briefly silent. And then the screaming started.

Teddy wanted to run toward the doorway—to do something, anything. His own emotions were tangled up in the memory. It was no ordinary memory magic. It was tossed with thoughts and emotions. He felt his father's panic and grief, his bone-deep fear and love for Cecilia.

It's just a memory. Not real. Teddy called to mind the cave. The dank smell, the oppressive darkness, the cool air.

He closed his eyes, and when he blinked them open, he was standing back in the cave.

The memory stone was still warm in his hand and glowing subtly.

It was worse than he'd ever imagined. Teddy's father had drilled the lesson into him: *You must always be king first.* But Teddy had always thought that was driven by some projected desire to keep the throne. He had not fully believed until seeing that memory that his father did not want the seat, and yet he'd allowed the woman he loved so deeply to be hurt so he could keep it. Xander had kept the secret and sacrificed his love.

Teddy thought his father had never had to choose—that he'd sulked over choosing a wife after losing the love of his life—but he did not know how his father had chosen to be king at her peril. How Cecilia had looked at him with pride and fear when he did it. Teddy hadn't known the way that look broke his father more than anything else had.

He'd expected to see the night that Isla left, but he knew all at once why Endros had chosen this memory. The god of war was trying to rattle Teddy off the throne. He'd seen Teddy in that interrogation and had him pegged immediately. The god knew fear and how to amplify it. Endros knew how to mark an opponent's weakness the way all great warriors did.

Teddy's chest seized, fear and grief pouring in, the bond growing taut. The horror hit him, knocking the air from his lungs.

He took off running toward the cave mouth in blind darkness. The need to get to Stella as soon as possible pressed in on him from all sides as he stumbled from the mouth of the cave into dusky light. He tore through the forest in the direction of her cave, his memory stone still burning in his bloody palm.

He'd thought their trip couldn't get worse than Stella making her first kills. But if Teddy had seen this memory, Stella was probably seeing the same one from a different, more horrifying point of view: her mother's.

31

STELLA

Stella stared into the mouth of the cave, feeling a mixture of dread and excitement. Her mother had stood before seventy-seven magical caves like this and walked into every one to retrieve a memory. This magic was in her blood, and it called to her, a curling sensation in her stomach urging her forward.

Still, she was apprehensive because this was not the same as the Gauntlet. That magic had been created by the witches of Olney to preserve balance. This magic was part of a contest that Endros was using as revenge against those who had bested him.

Stella glanced at the darkening sky and drew in a bracing breath. Then, she stepped into the cave. She snapped fire to her fingers effortlessly, letting it rise into a large flare as she walked deeper into the velvet darkness.

The cave stretched on longer than expected, until finally she came upon a large, wild patch of greenery. She knelt before it, brought the memory stone into her right hand, and drew one of the blades from her vest in the same hand. She let her flame flicker out on her left palm and drew the knife across her skin in the darkness.

The cut stung, and she hissed as she placed the memory stone in her bloody palm and squeezed a fist around it, letting the blood dribble into the plants. By feel, she carefully tucked the blade back into her vest. The minutes ticked by; the longer she waited, the more afraid she was that she'd done something wrong. Her knees were going numb against the dirt floor.

Finally, something illuminated in front of her. The first flicker of soft light burned into the flare of a fireplace. Stella squinted into the sudden brightness.

She was no longer in the dank cave. Now she was in a fire-lit room that smelled of smoke and something metallic.

Blood.

She glanced around the room as her eyes adjusted. Stella recognized the woodwork around the fireplace because she'd once asked her father if he could replicate it in their home. It was the only time he'd ever denied one of her requests outright, so it stuck with her. It was in a dining room in Castle Savero, where she'd had lunches on their winter holidays.

She turned and came face to face with her father, looking so young and beaten nearly to death. His shirt was torn and blood-soaked. His hair was plastered to his forehead with sweat and his brow was furrowed in pain.

Something was very wrong—Stella wasn't watching the memory through her mother's eyes with just the sensory experience and emotions. Her mother's thoughts raced through her head as well. Usually there was a slight detachment to shared memories, even with all their senses, but this was so visceral that Stella felt the raw fear in her mother's body as if it was her own.

The embodied memory was disorienting because Stella was so much shorter, seeing the world from a whole new angle in her mother's eyes.

Strong arms dragged Cecilia away from Rainer, who was bloody and half-conscious, and King Xander, who was being held in his chair by two guards.

She glanced over her shoulder at her captor.

Stella didn't know his face, though something about it was vaguely familiar—the dark hair and olive skin reminded her of King

Xander, but this man had a cruel glint in his eyes that made him look nothing like the king.

Adrenaline coursed through her blood, making her tremble as the memory took over.

Tears streamed down her face as she was forced to bend over a table.

No, no, no, this wasn't right. This couldn't be real. Stella would have known if this had happened. But the terror in her body was real—the memory was clearly her mother's. Stella squeezed her eyes closed, but it was useless. The vision remained.

"Don't cry, love." Vincent ground his hardness against her. "I have a feeling you'll enjoy it."

"Fuck you." She jerked her head back, connecting with his cheek, and he stumbled, cursing.

"Hold her still. You're going to pay for that, Cecilia," he said as the guards held her more firmly against the table. Their hands were like iron bands on her arms.

Vincent brought the butt of his blade down on her left hand. A bone snapped, and she yelped involuntarily.

"That's right. Let me hear those sweet little screams. Let your men enjoy your agony."

She bit her lip as he brought the butt of his blade down again, refusing to give him the satisfaction.

"Yes, please defy me. It will make it so much more satisfying when I break you," he whispered before shattering another bone. "Scream," he commanded. She kept her mouth shut. "Scream, or I'll give you a reason to really scream."

Fear sliced Cecilia in half. Rainer tugged hard on the other side of their connection, but everything in her was ice-cold fear. She'd hoped he would be unconscious, but there he was trying to fight his way back to her, if only through their bond.

Vincent dropped to his knees, and she felt a blade slice into her left inner thigh. She screamed in surprise and pain.

She bucked wildly, and his hand slapped her ass hard again.

"Stop it, Cecilia." Vincent's angry whisper cut through her. "Stop moving! I'm not doing what you think. I'm marking your inner thigh with

my initials so that every man who ever gets between these legs will know I was here. So that you'll never forget. Now scream your fucking head off, or I really will fuck you."

She couldn't understand what was happening. Confusion clouded her mind until she felt another slice of the blade, and she screamed.

"More," he threatened.

She screamed louder. She begged him to stop.

Stella was breathless. Terrified. Split between embodied memory and distant horror.

Rainer's love surged through their bond, mixing with his fear and her pain.

You're not alone, it seemed to say. That broke her. She sobbed because she didn't want to be alone, but she didn't want him to feel her fear and pain either.

It was so cruel. Vincent wanted Rainer and Xander to think he was hurting her, and he was, but not in the way any of them had expected. Her relief was short-lived when she realized that in not doing it now, he could keep the threat of it fresh for whatever lay ahead.

Time slowed, marked by the fiery slash of his blade on her thigh and the hysterical sobs that ripped out of her. She waited for the fear to leave her, but she couldn't stop shaking.

By the time Vincent was done with his carving and yanked her shredded skirt back into place, Cecilia's throat was ragged from screaming, but he hadn't done what she was afraid he would.

She told herself that she'd been through worse, but it was cold comfort. She felt dazed and unable to concentrate. The first glimmer of her goddess power flickered to life in her chest, but she couldn't focus her mind. The pain was too bright and her fear too biting. Her skin flashed hot, then cold.

Cecilia screamed.

Stella screamed, too, in embodied agony. In grief that was new to her but old to her mother. In terror that was so cold and left her breathless.

The light of the room faded into blackness, and Stella was vaguely aware of her body. Gasping sobs rattled through her as her senses returned. Her hip was numb against the cave floor, but she curled into a ball anyway and continued to sob.

Stella wanted to run. She wanted to escape the memory—rip it out like an invasive plant that had rooted down deep and was taking over. She wanted to bail out of the Games—to stop the horrible mess she'd set into motion.

She'd wanted her parents' story so badly, but she'd not once considered there were such horrifying parts she didn't know. The omission felt partly of betrayal, partly of love. It was no comfort to know her mother was whole and hale now.

Stella remembered moments when she was young—when Cecilia had crawled into Rainer's lap, crying, and he sat heart-to-heart with her, trying to help her breathe. She'd watched her mother sitting alone on the swing in the backyard, her father watching from the window.

"I want Mama," Stella had cried.

"Mama needs some time, Stell-bell. Let me tell you a story instead."

She'd listened to his story and pretended to fall asleep, but she'd jump up as soon as he left the room and watch him go to her mother and whisper soothing words while Cecilia cried.

Stella remembered it so well because she'd spent so long trying to figure out which of her dolls would make her mother feel better that she'd fallen asleep in the process.

But she could not go to sleep now and wake up safe. She could not unknow what she now knew, and that was exactly what Endros had wanted. To punish her parents by making them relive this. To subject her to the same pain because there was no worse way to hurt a parent than to hurt their child.

Much as her mother made her crazy, Stella never doubted that she was deeply loved. She'd seen it in Cecilia's teary eyes when she'd sent Stella off on this trip. Cecilia had known what she was sending her daughter into; she was already grieving it, but unable to speak a word of it.

Stella rolled onto her back and squeezed the warm memory stone in her blood-slicked palm. Her body was sore, as if she'd lived through that pain, the memory in her bones and muscles as much as her mind.

Endros wanted her to learn what it took to challenge powerful men. He wanted her to learn to be afraid.

Stella lay in the dirt, shattered between past and present, between her own memories that were sliding into context with the puzzle pieces she'd just received from her mother's past.

She wanted to stand. To run from the horrible place where her life had just split between fantasy and reality. The perfect story, the history that had formed Stella, that had been so foundational in her life, was only half of a history. Her whole world was ruptured.

There were the stories her parents told and the ones that lived silently inside them.

Most were shared freely. Her father's voice echoing through the hallway, joyful, teasing. *"Let me tell you about the time your mother—"*

But the story written in a mess of fine white scars on his back was the one he never told. She still remembered the shadow that drew over his face when she asked about them once when they were swimming in the sea. The memory sprang to mind with ease now.

"Papa, what happened to your back?"

He'd frowned, his eyes going hard. "That's a grown-up story, Stell-bell. I'll tell you when you're older."

He'd been out of sorts the rest of the morning until they walked back to the house and he'd disappeared into the backyard with her mother. Stella had watched them through the window—her father, her hero, his broad shoulders sagging as he curled into her mother. Cecilia holding him with the same tenderness with which she held her children when they had a scraped knee.

Stella wanted to ask so many times, but the moment never seemed right, and the question always froze on her tongue. She was more afraid of the stories they didn't share freely than the expectation to live up to the ones they did.

Now she felt breathless, like just seeing that memory had broken something in her.

A new undeniable revelation rose in her mind after seeing the conviction in her father's words, after seeing him fight to get to her mother, after seeing her mother's love in trying to keep him from feeling her pain.

Suddenly, it was so clear. Stella had thrown herself into the Gauntlet Games, said she would walk across the fire to be with Arden. But that was not how Arden felt for her.

He didn't fight for her even in the small ways. He'd taken the first detour on the course to their happily ever after, and she wanted to blame him. She wanted to say he was a selfish, vapid prince who only cared about himself.

But she knew the truth. Deep down, Arden did not love her the way she wanted to be loved—he might not even be capable of that kind of love. She'd let herself be blinded by his charm because she liked how it felt to be in his orbit, even if she was only occasionally at the center of it. And she had always known that. But surrendering that fantasy would have meant facing a reality in which she had no prospects and no idea if she'd ever meet someone who made her feel that way.

Stella had settled for less because she was afraid of having noth-ing. Wasn't *something* better than nothing?

Now that she'd seen the real thing, it ripped open the aching wound at the center of her. Stella wasn't special. She was just another silly girl living in a fairy tale in her head. There was no one coming to save her.

She sat on the dusty cave floor so long that her legs began to go numb, the cold creeping into her bones. Finally, she pushed to her feet and snapped fire to her fingertips. She had to scale back down the ridge before it was fully dark.

Footsteps pounded from somewhere behind her. Stella spun, drawing her short swords. She did not feel prepared for a fight, but her fire magic had been simmering beneath the surface the whole time she was in the memory and now she was made of rage and grief.

A small fire illuminated the cave, drawing closer by the second. The source of it rounded the corner and Stella was ready to pounce until she realized it was Teddy. All the fight leeched out of her as she sheathed her blades.

He looked haunted, his eyes wide but relieved, and his tunic torn.

"I saw the night Vincent invaded. I saw—" Teddy's voice cracked, and he swallowed hard. "I saw the hardest choice my father ever had to make and felt the way he loathed himself for making it."

They stood there suspended, uncertain of how to move forward in a world where they knew too many of their parents' secrets. How were they supposed to hold this history they had no right to—these private hurts that their parents had tried to shield them from?

Stella couldn't count how many times she'd told her mother how lucky she was to have found Rainer and how Cecilia would never understand what it was like to struggle to find someone to love.

"I didn't know that happened. I—" Stella sucked in a breath. The grief was still alive. "I felt what my mom felt. I was there. I felt every broken bone. I felt the dagger cutting into her thigh—saw the sadistic way that the monster smiled at his handiwork when it was over. I felt—"

Her voice broke, and a sob ripped up her throat. She'd felt their bond—the way her father had tried to force his way through, the way her mother had tried to prevent him from feeling something so awful. Something she had done a magnificent job of sheltering Stella from.

Teddy took a step toward her, and she flinched. If he was too gentle now, she would fall apart completely. She'd never get up off the cave floor.

Maybe it was the bond, but Teddy seemed to understand. He didn't touch her like he thought she was fragile. He touched her like he knew she was strong.

He cupped Stella's face firmly in his hands. "You did what you had to do and now you know you are stronger than that nightmare."

"How did they survive this?" Stella said between sobs.

Teddy rubbed her back. "I don't know. But they did, and you did too."

She drew back and met his gaze. "What did you see?"

Something like grief passed over his eyes. "I saw the choice my father had to make. I saw the night the kingdom fell to my uncle. He was so haunted. I heard your mother screaming." A muscle ticked in Teddy's jaw. "I think he's doing this to punish them. I think Endros is finding a way to punish everyone who was involved in his downfall. Your mother is an obvious one, but the best way to get revenge on any mother is to go after their child."

Stella felt sick just thinking about her foolishness. Her mother, pregnant for the first time in twenty-three years, trying to keep calm and collected while watching Stella fight for her life in a tournament. She'd been so reckless and selfish, throwing herself into this fight. So angry at Arden for not loving her more. So shaken by losing her status as the only biological child. It was idiotic to be jealous of a baby who hadn't even been born yet. A baby *she* already loved. She hadn't stopped to consider that Endros could be the gamemaker, because it had never happened before.

Teddy ran a hand through his hair. "I keep thinking about how he even seemed to be trying to humiliate Cato with this part of the challenge. Making him the map-keeper. The way he had the ancient witches who created the Gauntlet involved in this, creating this bastardization of the original Gauntlet designed just to hurt the competitors. Not to mention the magical cost to them."

"Because of the memory stones?" Stella asked.

Teddy nodded. "Think about it. It takes a tremendous amount of magic to make memory stones. My father said it permanently robs the creator of some of their magic. Those witches had to make a stone for each of us. I'd say it's an appropriate punishment to rob the women who sabotaged Endros's plans by also robbing them of some of their power."

Teddy's theory made sense. Stella had been stunned to see a pile of memory stones. They were so rare and precious that she'd only seen one in her entire life—the one Cecilia had made for Rainer.

"And now with these memories, it feels clear he's trying to haul all our parents' most painful moments back to life. They had to relive them to put the memories into the stones."

"And then we had to suffer along with them," Stella finished. It was diabolical. "It's like this whole tournament is reminding everyone how terrifying he is."

"That's what I'm worried about. Even if he's not working with the Sons of Endros, he's still benefiting from their work, and from having a platform," Teddy said.

Stella shuddered thinking about it. Centuries ago, the gods had lived among people, in mortal bodies, but greed and infighting and fearful humans forced most of them from the realm. The ensuing war that their parents had eventually brought to an end was a ripple effect of the end of the rule of gods in Olney and Argaria.

When the gods died, they ascended to the Otherworld and, while they could still visit and influence the mortal realm, their power was much more limited and they couldn't stay corporeal for extended periods of time.

Endros's power in the realm came from belief in him. His sudden presence as the gamemaker of the Gauntlet Games was a reminder to fear him, and the way he'd conducted the interrogation the other day, staying in corporeal form the entire time, was a flex of his strength. As far as Stella knew, no god had ever been born a second time into the realm of the living. But if Endros wanted to test if it was possible, he'd chosen a strategic time to do it.

"I know this is probably the last place you want to be, but I think we should rest here for the night," Teddy said. "We're only a few miles from the Muddled Mind and if we wake at first light, we'll be home by nightfall tomorrow." He studied her for a moment. "Is there something else bothering you?"

Stella couldn't meet his eyes, but she shook her head. She was still trying to come to terms with the fact that her romance with Arden had been a fantasy she'd conjured out of loneliness. She wasn't ready to admit to Teddy that he'd been right all along.

32

TEDDY

Stella and Teddy rode back into Olney just before sunset on the sixth day of the memory challenge. They went directly to the arena, where a small crowd was gathered to await the nightly showing of memories.

Teddy had expected that the priestesses would need to summon Endros, but the god was seated in his place of honor, waiting for them when they rode into the arena.

Out of the corner of his eye, Teddy watched Stella. She was looking at her parents in the royal booth. Cecilia was pale and very poorly hiding her relief.

Teddy couldn't bear to look at his father. He'd been so focused on putting one foot in front of the other, in completing this task so he could move on to the next one, that he'd hardly had a moment to process the memory he'd been given.

Xander had raised him with the knowledge that being king meant making impossible choices for the sake of the kingdom. Teddy had always thought he was speaking about the personal relationships his role had cost him. Now, Teddy knew that it was so much more.

It was looking into the eyes of the person most dear to you and saying that you couldn't save them. Back then it had been Cecilia, but only months ago the king had done the same with Isla, and Teddy had been cruel about it.

He'd never felt so young, foolish, and uncertain if he had the strength to do the same. His entire life, he'd sacrificed his personal happiness to be the symbol his kingdom had needed. But it was one thing to surrender his own well-being and another to sacrifice someone he loved.

Teddy didn't know how the king had done it, or how he seemed so publicly at peace with it now.

Stella glanced at the booth again, and the reality hit Teddy like a gut punch. She wasn't just looking for her parents. She was looking for Arden, and Arden wasn't there. Only King Marcos sat stoically in the booth, his wary gaze fixed on the gamemaker's dais.

Endros stood and clapped his hands slowly as Teddy and Stella dismounted their horses. "Excellent work. We weren't sure we would be seeing you two after reports from your fellow competitors had you wounded and lost in river rapids," Endros said.

Teddy had been looking for Rett and his friends since they'd arrived at the arena, but they had probably already completed their task and could no longer attack competitors per the rules of the tournament.

Endros held out his hand. "I'll take those memories now."

Stella went rigid beside Teddy. The blank expression she'd worn while riding in had morphed into narrow-eyed anger. Her rage seared through their connection.

"Steady," he whispered.

Stella's gaze snapped to him, and Teddy could practically read her mind. Endros had just made their parents relive their worst memories *and* share them with their children. Now he wanted the pleasure of enjoying them personally and sharing them with the entire audience.

She looked from the stands to the large white tarp at the far end of the arena. Raven Whitewind and the other witches who had created the Gauntlet stood beneath it. There must have been some magical mechanism for a witch to project the visual for the onlookers.

Stella looked ready to burn the tarp down.

Teddy loved her conviction, but he was afraid it was that stubbornness that would keep her from completing the challenge.

Endros smiled at her hesitation. "For my collection and for the good of our people, I find it's good to occasionally reflect on the mistakes of other important figures in the kingdom so that I can learn not to make the same ones myself."

Teddy turned to face Stella head-on. She looked so angry and so beautiful. "I'm choosing to believe my father wouldn't have given this over if he didn't think this was a possibility."

"I can't believe this," she said in a hushed whisper. "He wants to keep them like little trophies. He has no right to their pain. He has caused them enough heartache already."

"I know, but we don't have a choice."

"Don't we?"

Teddy cocked his head to the side. "*Minyha*, you know we don't. You know the price if you don't complete the task to the best of your ability. We made the same magic binding agreement to the Gauntlet Games. It's one thing if you're too wounded to complete the Games, but you're standing here with the task completed. If you don't forfeit the memory stone, you'll forfeit your life instead."

Stella looked away. Gods, she was stubborn. Perhaps Teddy would be too if he had seen what she'd seen. He had only the implication, but she had lived it and felt her mother's pain. He didn't blame her for not wanting that to be entertainment for a heartless god and a bunch of ghoulish onlookers.

"If you won't do it for you, will you do it for your mother?" Teddy asked. "She looks like she's about to climb out of the box and jump down here."

Stella huffed a laugh. "I bet she's planning all the ways she would kill him again."

Teddy smiled sadly. "She'll have to get in line."

Without another word, Stella walked up to the raised dais where

Endros was waiting and plopped the stone into his hand. Teddy followed suit.

"Very well. Stella McKay and Theodore Savero, you have completed the memory challenge. Congratulations and enjoy some much-earned rest," Endros said.

A smattering of applause broke out in the crowd.

"And do be careful with those Sons of Endros causing havoc. I want to see both of you in the final challenge in two days' time," Endros said.

Stella nodded curtly and returned to Shark. Teddy followed and mounted Poker. They rode together to the stables, gathering their bags and leaving the horses with the stable hands.

Teddy paused outside of the stables. Stella looked weary but still lovely in the last dregs of daylight. He searched for what to say after all they'd endured on their short quest.

She'd saved him, and he'd saved her back. He'd seen her elated, grief-stricken, angry, sexy, and vulnerable. Nothing felt weighty enough to capture that.

Stella smiled and kissed him on the cheek. "It doesn't have to mean anything, Teddy. You were just trying to hold me together when I needed it, and I'm grateful for that. I'll be fine."

It was like a door slamming closed in his face. The subtext was loud. *I don't need you.*

She didn't, and Teddy liked that she didn't—but he hated it just as much.

When they were close, the bond felt like a powerful connection, but now it seemed the barest of threads stitching them to each other. He'd been a comfort for her in a dark moment, and that was all. It wasn't like Teddy to be so sentimental about it.

The sex was incredible—he'd never felt so connected to someone else—but it went far beyond that. He didn't know how to be casual when he knew her so much better.

Now they were home, though, and the escapism was no longer necessary. She would go running back to Arden, who was entirely unworthy of her, because that was what she'd fought for.

Teddy would go back to trying to win the Gauntlet Games, but he had no clue what favor he'd even ask for. He'd started off fighting for the freedom to marry who he wished, but he wasn't sure what he wanted anymore.

For now, he just needed to face his father and apologize.

"I should walk you back." He sounded so pathetically eager to spend just five more minutes with her.

Fortunately, Stella didn't seem to mind. She just fell into step beside him.

He wished he had anything clever to say, but all their passion had been spoiled by reality. Maybe Stella was right. They had just helped each other through a difficult time and now they could go back to the way things were before.

Except Teddy was fighting a whole new set of impulses. He could barely keep himself from leaning into her as they walked, from shoving her up against the garden gate to kiss her senseless one more time.

Stella paused just inside the McKay Estate garden and Teddy hovered awkwardly beside her.

She glanced at the house. Her father was waiting at the back door.

"Thank you for walking me home," she said. "Thank you for— everything."

Teddy wasn't sure how to say goodbye. He leaned in to hug her, then felt awkward doing that in front of her father, so it ended up being a sideways half-hug.

"Be safe," she said. Then she ran to the back door and threw herself into her father's arms.

Teddy turned and walked back to the castle, unable to shake the feeling that he was walking in the wrong direction.

THE NIGHT WAS JUST BEGINNING AND ALREADY IT FELT TOO LONG.

Teddy had bathed, stretched, and assembled his weapons for the final challenge, even though he still had days to prepare.

When he felt ready to climb the walls of the foreign castle, he finally left his room and walked down to the guest sitting room.

He wandered inside and helped himself to some whiskey as he stared out into the dark queen's garden. Somewhere in the castle, Arden was doing something more important than waiting for Stella to arrive. And Stella would probably be up all night waiting for him to show. Did he have any idea what he had? Truly, Teddy could not imagine being so oblivious. What a fucking luxury.

He felt a strange aching loneliness that had nothing to do with the bond in his chest and everything to do with the fact that there wasn't an infuriating wild woman beside him.

The sitting room door creaked open and the telltale static of his father's magic crackled through the air. Teddy didn't turn. He took a sip of his drink and waited. A moment later, Xander sat down in the chair opposite Teddy.

"Rough night?" Xander asked.

Teddy nodded. "Restless."

"Ah. I've never been a very good sleeper myself. Worse since Isla left."

Teddy had been careless when talking to his father about Isla before. Guilt lodged in his throat. "I'm sorry I doubted your decision to ask her to resign. I should have realized that's not a decision you would have made lightly."

His father studied him with practiced silence. Finally, he set his glass on the table beside him and began to spin it slowly. "None of my decisions are ever made lightly. It's been many years since I was carefree. Not since the night of that memory."

Teddy stared down at his boots. "I'm sorry you had to make a decision like that, even if you knew it didn't matter. I felt—" Teddy took a deep breath and finally met his father's gaze. "I felt how much it cost you to let her down. I've never seen a memory like that before, but I could hear your thoughts. I could feel everything you felt, and I understood for the first time how much you loved her."

Xander blew out a slow breath. "I know you have resented the pressure your mother and I have put on you. You've managed the weight of that responsibility admirably. You are the one who has to live with your decisions, so you must find a way to be at peace with them. King is a role you inherit, but what no one tells you when you're growing up is that the moment you earn the title will be one of the worst of your life. Kings may ascend in calm, but they are forged in chaos. I've tried my level best to ensure that isn't the case for you, and the thing that keeps me awake at night is that I might fail, anyway."

The king took a long swig of his whiskey. "That is still one of the worst moments of my life. I pray it remains that way and that neither you nor your siblings know that or worse."

Teddy bristled. "The moment Isla left wasn't worse?"

His father shook his head. "There are things you see on the outside of a relationship and things you see on the inside. Don't pretend to know how I feel or that you can understand anything other than the fact that I made a hard decision for our kingdom at great personal sacrifice."

"And how did that turn out?" Teddy countered. He didn't mean to be so curt. He was supposed to be apologizing, but he couldn't stand being patronized.

Xander ran a hand through his hair. "I suppose we'll find out soon at the rate this violence is escalating." He watched his son over the rim of his glass as he took a sip. "Are you up this late because you're worried about tomorrow?"

Teddy shrugged and rubbed a hand over the back of his neck. "In part."

He thought of facing Stella in the arena. What if she got hurt? What if they were pitted against each other? What if he'd won the right to choose his future partner but had to remain connected to her forever? Would he feel her fall in love with someone else from a kingdom away?

"Oh, I know *that* face." Xander barked out a laugh and shook his head. "I saw it in the mirror myself twenty-five years ago, when I met her mother. I know the 'oh fuck' face of realizing you are in love with the person you're very much not supposed to be in love with." His father studied him in his narrow-eyed, assessing way. His mouth softened into a smirk. "Does Stella know?"

Teddy's mouth went dry. Could he really call this love? This incessant desire to go see her, to stand close to her just so he could feel the glow she gave off... It was so hard to tell what was the bond and what was his heart alone.

Stella was beautiful, clever, and fun. There was no denying that. But did he love her?

"Not sure *I* know," Teddy said after a long silence.

His father laughed. "You know. Gods, it seems like you've inherited my timing." He grinned widely.

Teddy rubbed a hand over the back of his neck. He remembered the way his mind had flashed to her when he was thrashing in the tub, trying to fight off the assassin.

His father studied him. "Not like you to be so lacking in composure or focus."

"Not like me to fall in love with the most infuriating woman in the two kingdoms."

Xander laughed. "Yes, well. It will keep you on your toes. I'm glad you found someone who is a better fit than Grace."

Teddy stared at him. "You knew Grace was unhappy?"

His father shook his head. "No, I can't take credit. It was your Uncle Evan. He sees all—knows all. You know how he is."

Teddy slumped into his seat as the mortification settled in. "He could have just told me."

"You needed to hear it from Grace. She can be a little more reserved about her feelings—more like Evan than Sylvie in that regard, at least." Xander leaned over and clapped a hand on Teddy's shoulder. "Look, it's good to have something or someone to fight for, but you must know that Endros will test you with it in the final challenge. I hope you're ready for that."

"I'm certain I'm not. Stella saved me out there. I had a cord around my neck and all I could think was how to protect her. What an idiotic thought—" Teddy choked on the knot in his throat. He'd let one admission slip, and now it was as if every secret he'd ever kept was trying to claw its way out at once.

He'd been so worried about the tournament, but what if Stella was the thing he couldn't survive?

His father offered a knowing smile. "She gives you hope. That's a valuable thing at a time like this. Probably the most valuable thing. Dying is easy, Ted. It's the living that's hard."

Teddy looked at his father and thought of the horrible memory that he'd needed to give back to Endros. "I'm sorry you had to relive that night."

Xander swallowed and pursed his lips. "I'm sorry you had to see it."

Teddy looked down, rolling the golden liquid around in the glass. "I shouldn't have assumed that you make choices like that lightly."

"He would have hurt Cece no matter what I did. The choice I made was to let her know I was willing to sacrifice her. She wanted me to—"

"I know. You don't have to explain—"

His father held up a hand. "I do." He cleared his throat. "Until that point, I was still sure there was a way I could get out of this role. I didn't want the responsibility and gods know that I never had the temperament for it. Still don't. But I've learned. But you are the best of your mother, thank the gods. And the best of Isla. And I like to think that you're even the best of me, though I put that in third place because that's absolutely where it belongs."

Teddy smiled.

"You have your mother's temperance and she is not so well mastered as you think," Xander said with an affectionate smile. "Jess struggles with it still. She always has, but she learned, as you have, how to control it so that she could rule and make a difference. I like to think you have my sense of fortitude, to keep pushing no matter how others doubt you. But you have Isla's sense of strategy and patience. She never knew when to quit on a lost cause—" He cleared his throat again. "Well, I suppose that's not the case anymore."

Teddy winced. "That's not true."

His father grinned and winked. "No, it's not."

A knock on the door startled them. Xander rose to answer it.

Teddy crossed his arms, trying to compose himself. "Any advice? From one heir to another?"

His father paused with his hand on the doorknob and smiled sadly over his shoulder. "Don't lose."

He pulled the door open and Alexandra stormed in, her golden eyes narrowed on Teddy. She was wearing her leather armor, and her long hair was sweaty, strands that had slipped out of her braid stuck to the back of her neck as if she'd been training.

"Alexandra, to what do we owe the pleasure at this late hour?" their father asked.

She crossed the room and poured herself a glass of whiskey. "I need to speak to Teddy." She sat down in the chair their father had vacated and glared at Teddy.

Xander arched a brow. "I'll leave you to it, then." He paused in the doorway. "Alexandra?"

"Yes, Papa?" she asked sweetly, not bothering to meet his eye.

"Be kind to your brother. He's had a rough day and the next few will be worse," Xander said. He closed the door and left his children alone.

"Hard challenge, brother? Finally meet your match?" Alexandra taunted.

"In more ways than one. This time two nights ago, I had an assassin's garrote around my neck."

She froze with her glass halfway to her lips. "How?"

"Caught me while I was bathing," Teddy said.

Alexandra was quiet for a long moment as she sipped her whiskey. "I've always said you were a little too vain."

He ran a hand through his hair. "Well, it hasn't gotten me yet." He shifted in his chair. "How did the competition look when they got back?"

Alexandra blew out a weary sigh as if it was a huge imposition, but she relented immediately. "Jeneva and Katerina looked a little weary, but no worse for the wear. Fionn Silver had some bumps and bruises—friend of yours, isn't he?"

Teddy glared at her. "Hardly."

Alexandra smiled. "Well, he had a pretty good wound on his side and his fancy armor was shredded." She paused. "Dixon looked fine, but Christophe was half-fried. I could tell that was your handiwork from the lightning burn and the fact that he had a tremor in his hands. Drew had burns all over his left arm. I assume that was Stella. And the Roach had a limp from a wound in his leg that hadn't fully healed."

Teddy nodded.

"You should have seen our parents when that group wandered in." Alexandra whistled. "I thought Cece was going to climb out of the booth and throttle them. Would have liked to see it, honestly. The waiting was awful for everyone."

Teddy swallowed his guilt. He counted off the competitors in his head. "So Tristas Dahlien and Remington Patrico died out there. Do they know how?"

Alexandra sighed. "Rett and his cronies were bragging about taking them out. But—"

Teddy leaned in. "But?"

"But Cato's network said that both men were found behind the stables at the Muddled Mind. They said they had been poisoned."

Teddy leaned back in his chair. "You think it was Jeneva and Katerina."

She nodded, giving him a moment to absorb the information. She took another long sip. "Now, if you're satisfied with my report, I just want to know one thing." She set her glass down on the table and leaned toward him. "Why did you have Stella make me forget I was going to enter the tournament?"

Teddy froze with his glass halfway to his mouth. He'd almost forgotten that her remembering was a possibility, but now her anger made sense.

"Because I couldn't worry about you *and* her."

Alexandra looked ready to lunge at him. "You wouldn't have needed to worry about me."

"Of course I would have."

She glared at him as he continued.

"It's not a marker of your skill. You'd be an easy way to get to me and I am an easy way to get to Stella." Teddy ran a hand through his hair. "I could not abide that kind of chain reaction in the middle of the dumbest decision I've made in my life. If it makes you feel any better, even if I win the third challenge, it will be the most miserable win of my life."

Alexandra rolled her eyes. "Why?"

"Because even the heir can't have it all, Alex."

His sister appraised him warily, and when she seemed to assess that he was indeed as pathetic as he seemed, she slumped back in her chair.

"I wanted the chance to prove myself, and you robbed me of it. I can't believe you would do that when you know how hard I've been trying." Her voice was tight in a way that unnerved him. As far as he knew, Alexandra hadn't cried since she was a child. "I don't see why Jalen should get to lead the Argarian military when I have trained under Isla almost as long."

Teddy sighed. *This again.* "You know why."

"Because I'm a woman?"

"Because you are young and impulsive and lack the experience or composure to lead," Teddy said. "I don't say that to hurt you. I say it because I love you dearly and it's my job as your brother to tell you things that are hard to hear privately, so I never have to publicly. You know I respect you as a fighter and a leader, but you are untested and young and the men don't trust you."

Alexandra looked away, the white-knuckle grip on her glass the only sign of her displeasure.

"Also, you fuck around too much and too obviously. I know that the men do as well, but the standards are not the same." He held up his hand before she could protest. "I'm not saying it's right, but it's true. If you want to be a leader, you have to first prove you can master yourself, Alex."

She slammed her glass down on the table beside her. "And how am I supposed to learn to do that when you're coddling me?" She shook her head. "I need to get the fuck away from this whole family. You all do this. Mother with her dresses. Juliana with her invitations to tea that are actually just set-ups with available lords. Jalen and his military missions that are just pointless tasks to keep me out of his hair. I'm tired of being smothered. I'm a grown woman and if you won't all treat me like it, I will find a way to make you."

"Don't do anything rash, Alex."

She arched a brow. "Like what?"

Teddy truly could not imagine, but he knew the look in her eyes. It was the same one she wore every time she was working on some devious and terrible plan. She would pay him back or find a way to redeem herself.

When she was little, it was easy to manage those impulses, but now that she was grown, he couldn't contain her. Especially with Isla gone.

Alexandra got to her feet and walked across the sitting room with purpose, pausing at the door to glare at him one more time. "By the way, Nathan could probably use some consoling if and when you stop feeling so sorry for yourself. Rumor has it that Rosie McKay very publicly shot him down while you were gone," she said.

"You're a fucking menace, Alex."

A smirk passed over her lips. "I know." She ducked out of the room.

Teddy wasn't stupid enough to believe this was the end of her anger. Alexandra had a temper, but she was a strategist at heart and understood how to choose the ideal moment for maximum drama.

He had his own feelings to contend with and a tournament to win —he couldn't also prepare for whatever chaos Alexandra was about to unleash.

33

STELLA

Stella hadn't been able to face her mother when she first got home. She needed time to process everything. She had dinner with her father, who watched silently, constantly trying to feed her more, and then she'd bathed and locked herself in her room. She'd wanted to reassure her parents that she was fine, but so much had happened and she needed the night to untangle all the complicated things she was feeling.

She'd slept heavily, waking at nearly midday. She'd bathed again, and it wasn't until she found herself scrubbing the skin of her hands raw that she realized she couldn't even reassure *herself* that she was fine.

Stella stared at her bright red skin for several long moments, listening to the steady drip of water from her body. She rose from the bath suddenly, sending water sloshing over the sides of the tub.

She dried herself in a hurry, slipped into a simple cotton dress, and patted the water from her hair with a towel.

Finally, she felt ready to face her mother with honesty. Stella crept down the hall and tapped on her parents' bedroom door.

"Come in," her mother called.

Stella cracked the door open and stepped inside.

Late afternoon light poured in through the large windows, the curtains stirring with a breeze that held the salty tinge of sea air. One of Rosie's dangling dried flower sculptures hung from the ceiling over the bed. Vases of Rainer's carved star flowers and roses were squeezed into every crevice of the overflowing bookcases on the far side of the room. His oldest and most rudimentary carvings were combined with the new, intricately detailed ones in a small glass jar on Cecilia's nightstand.

Stella didn't know how to start. She felt suddenly, keenly aware of how her secrets had formed a rift between them. There was a time when she'd told her mother everything. Stella had no idea why she stopped. Some part of her had always been afraid of her mother's knowing assessment, or maybe she'd subconsciously known that her romance with Arden wouldn't hold up against her mother's scrutiny, the same way it hadn't with Kate.

She couldn't remember the last time she'd laid in bed beside her mother and whispered stories in the dark. She'd wanted to be part of her own fantasy so badly that she had shoved Cecilia away.

"You know, I picked this room because it doesn't get morning sun and I could easily sleep as late as I wanted. But now, being pregnant again and taking afternoon naps, I remember how much I love the light this time of day," Cecilia said as she pushed herself up. She patted the bed beside her. "Come here, Little Star."

Stella crossed the room and lay down beside her mother. Cecilia wrapped one of Stella's damp curls around her finger and waited in the quiet, patient way she always did when she knew Stella needed a moment to untangle her feelings.

Stella traced her fingers over the flower pattern on her dress as the sadness in her chest began to unravel. "I thought that Arden was the hero in my story."

"And now what do you think?" her mother asked, gently stroking her hair.

"Now I think I'm the hero." Stella burst into body-wracking sobs.

She was shocked by the grief. She hadn't expected that being her own hero would be so stunningly lonely.

Her mother hugged her like she understood. She was maybe the only person who could.

A lump formed in Stella's throat, and she pulled back to meet her mother's bright blue eyes. "I didn't know you went through that, Mama—that someone hurt you like that. Endros had no right to your pain."

The grief and fear were still fresh in Stella's chest. The ragged agony of her father trying to get to her mother, desperately fighting across their bond so she wouldn't feel alone in the worst moment of her life. Her mother's harrowing grief that he would feel what she did and suffer alongside her.

It was one thing to hear the pretty version of a story, but what they had been through was so brutal and ugly.

Stella had never been under the impression that what her parents went through was easy, but she hadn't realized how much she'd bought into the folklore when the lived reality was right in front of her.

How many times had Stella seen quiet moments where they'd both seemed haunted by something only the two of them could see?

Cecilia offered a watery smile and brushed the tears from her cheek. "The fairy tale is the story everyone else tells. The truth is messier, full of heartache and frayed edges. We didn't tell you not because we didn't trust you to be able to handle it, but because we tried to make a world where you wouldn't be exposed to the horrors we've endured—" Her mother took a shuddering breath. "You saw the worst parts of it, but the real magic is in the healing. It's in loving someone in their weakest, most vulnerable moments the same way you do in their triumphs."

Stella squeezed her hand. "It's okay, Mama. You don't have to explain—"

"I do. You saw the worst of it, but you didn't see what good care your father took of me when I was healing, how he kept me safe and let me lead the way, how he built folklore into our relationship that guided both of us out of our darkest moments. Fairy tales are just stories, Stella. And sometimes stories save us. They have that power.

But they are never the *whole* story. There's an entire ever-after that is all about healing. Love is finding someone you can heal with. Someone who will sit with you in your darkest moments and love you when you can't bear to love yourself."

"Is that what Papa is to you?"

Her mother's face softened. "You saw firsthand through those memories. Your father has always been a focal point for me. He has anchored me through every storm. Is that what Arden is to you?"

It was all too much. Stella was overloaded with information. Her need for love was a deep, yawning cavern that Arden had not even tried to fill.

"Papa fought so hard for you," Stella whispered. "Arden couldn't even defend his choosing me to his own parents." It hurt so much to say it and face the ugly truth. "He doesn't love me how I need to be loved, and I only loved what we could have been. I tried to keep something alive alone, and I felt so resentful and furious at him for not wanting me enough when I only ever loved his potential. I don't know why I couldn't see it."

As a child, Stella thought her parents were gilded by their love, blessed with the matching golden scars they bore over their hearts. Now she could see how those marks were probably as much a reminder of their pain as they were a reminder of how much they loved each other.

A real man would have greeted Stella when she returned from the worst day of her life. A partner would have been beside her in the mess the way her parents were for each other.

She thought about the mix of terror, grief, and love her father had sent through the bond in her mother's memory. Stella wanted someone to feel that way about her. Desperate and wondrous and terrified.

Her father used to say that fear and love were a pair. As a child, she'd never understood it, but now she did. To love someone for real was to show them where you could be hurt and trust them to be careful with you.

"It's all right, Stella. I've got you," her mother said, petting her hair softly. The movement was so soothing that Stella didn't even care if it made her hair frizz.

"Sometimes it's no one's fault," Cecilia whispered. "Some people can't love you the way you need to be loved, and it's no one's fault. It just is. I'm sorry you're hurting, because I know how badly you wanted this."

Stella had imagined an entire relationship for herself. She'd invented an intimacy made of empty promises. She'd summoned that from the longing in her heart, all because she was too desperate to see the truth. Stella wanted to feel *wanted*.

She hated that Arden didn't love the way she loved. She could have begged, but the kind of love she'd been desperate for since the first time she knew love existed wasn't the kind that someone pleaded for. It was the kind given freely, helplessly, unflinchingly. And though some wisdom in her bones had felt that truth the first time she'd held Arden's hand, it felt newer now—harsher. Like she'd helped sharpen and aim the blade, but was still surprised it struck true.

That was the trap of a charming man like Arden, someone who pretended to be good while actually being quite selfish. It wasn't what he gave her so much as the possibility of more that he constantly dangled. Stella felt so stupid for not seeing it before, but it wasn't until—

No, she would not think of Teddy. Not now. She would break.

Her mother stroked her cheek and spoke again. "I can't tell you what love is because it's something different to all of us. To me, it has been the way your father cared for me so steadily, and how he learned to adapt to the ways I needed to be loved. He learned to stop fixing and sit beside me and support me when I needed to do the fixing. He learned how to choose his own path instead of letting someone else aim his sword for him. It's all about finding the person who can love you when you're at your most tender."

Stella squeezed her eyes closed. There was only one face those words conjured.

She wanted to banish Teddy from her every thought. She could not even face him in her own head. When she thought about him, she thought about everything else. She thought about the fact that he had only touched her that way because she needed the distraction.

No matter what complicated thing she felt for Teddy, he did not feel it back. He was just a good man who felt responsible for the blood on her hands because he was the reason she'd had to get her hands dirty in the first place.

"That's not all that's bothering you," her mother whispered into her hair.

Stella hesitated. She knew the admission wouldn't make her mother love her any less, but she didn't want to burden Cecilia with anything else.

"I killed someone. I—" Stella's throat tightened. "I killed three people."

"Oh, my Little Star." Her mother pulled Stella into her arms and held her tight as she sobbed. "I'm so sorry. We hoped you would have it better than the two of us, but you did what you had to do."

Stella gulped in a breath. "I know it sounds so silly. I knew it was a possibility going into this contest, but I just didn't think it would happen like this. It was so fast, and I just reacted. And it was—" She gasped out a sob. "It was so *easy*."

Her mother kissed the top of her head and squeezed her harder. "I know. It's okay."

It had been so long since Stella had been held that way. How had she forgotten her mother's gentleness? How had she forgotten the person she always wanted most when she was sad or hurt? How had she forgotten how soothing it was just to be hugged and enveloped in the summer scent of her mother?

Stella cried harder. Of course Cecilia knew what it was to have blood on her hands and to be shocked by her own ability for violence.

Stella pulled back and met her mother's watery gaze. "How many people did you kill while pursuing the Gauntlet?"

"Eighty-nine. I was eighteen the first time I killed a man." Cecilia sighed. "Don't look so surprised. I never forgot. That number is just the men I killed with my own hands. It doesn't include the battalion I killed accidentally with my magic or anyone in the battles after that. It never got easier. It just became more of a reflex to protect myself." She swallowed hard. "I did what I had to in order to survive and my grief now doesn't come from being disappointed in you or your choices. I just hate that you have to fight when I wanted you to know only peace. All of you." Her hand slid to her stomach.

Stella imagined Leo and Rosie in the tournament. She'd do anything to keep them from feeling this way.

"I think about your grandfather a lot as I watch you in the games," Cecilia said. "I was so much like you at your age. I see now how the choices your Grandpa Leo made for me were out of love and protectiveness and not control. As I watch you compete, I have a whole new appreciation for the terror he must have felt watching me go off to try to finish the Gauntlet. Being a parent is always wanting better for your kids, while knowing that you can't save them from making their own mistakes."

"But I don't want to make mistakes."

Cecilia smiled softly. "You sound just like your father."

Stella sobbed a startled laugh.

Cecilia took her hand. "We are forged by our mistakes. I wouldn't wish you perfection because you'd be bored. I knew from the first moment you set your father's sleeve on fire at ten months old that you would be a *force*, and here you are, choosing yourself. It's a hard, lonely lesson, but it will serve you well. Sometimes it comes down to you or someone else, and I'm happy that you love yourself enough to fight."

Tears welled in Stella's eyes. She'd always felt so messy and out of control, a bright spark in the shadow of her mother's grace. But Cecilia's pride made her feel seen in a way she hadn't realized she needed.

Stella didn't know how to say that she hadn't killed for herself. When it was her life on the line, she couldn't do it. It was seeing Teddy in danger that had made her capable of such violence. That was what really frightened her.

How easily she'd lost herself in Arden and how quickly she could do the same thing again.

But it was not the same. Teddy was not weak, and he had fought for her. He had killed to protect her and he'd done it without a second thought.

"Is that all that's bothering you?" Her mother's voice startled her from her thoughts.

Stella couldn't possibly begin to unpack how she felt about Teddy. She'd been certain she had him pegged, but now she was so confused.

Maybe she'd have the words eventually, but she needed a deflection. She glanced at her mother's stomach, just the hint of a curve to it under her cotton dress. "How are you feeling?"

Cecilia smiled, and Stella understood in that moment what people meant when they said pregnant women glowed. Her mother looked lit from within by joy. "I'm still getting sick a lot—like I did with you—but your father's excitement is contagious. He's working on a new crib and it's been good for him to have something to focus his anxiety on with you in the tournament. I'm happy to have him fussing over his projects instead of over me or you."

Stella laughed. "I'm happy about the baby, but also a little jealous, which sounds so ridiculous. I'm a grown woman."

Cecilia smiled and pulled her close so Stella's head was tucked against her chest. "I know you're worried about this new baby, but you will always be my first baby, Stella. You were so dearly wished for. You taught me how to be a mother and Leo and Rosie have benefited from having you as a big sister. This new baby will, too. I'm so proud of the beautiful, passionate young woman you've become."

"But everyone else has found their place. Leo is a fighter, and he helps Papa with his woodwork. Rosie has her art and flowers," Stella said.

"And you will find yours, too. It's okay if it takes longer."

Stella thought of the look of intense concentration and pleasure on Rosie's face as she knotted flowers onto threads, weaving artful, intricate, hanging floral sculptures as if she could see a thing in the world no one else did.

Stella had none of that. No ability to see invisible patterns or create. She only knew how to destroy. Friendships, opportunities, relationships, and, now, people.

"Leo has always been good at making people feel welcome and Rosie has always been good at making things beautiful. I only seem to know how to burn things down," Stella said.

Cecilia kissed her temple. "It's like your father with his wooden flowers. I could never make something beautiful like that. But the world needs both the creators and the revolutionaries. I only knew how to break things, but that's important when things are stale. Your Aunt Sylvie, King Xander, even your father—they are the ones who know how to make something beautiful. But the world needs change-makers too. They need people who burn and burn and inspire other people to burn too. I think you underestimate your-self. You know how to make people great. Do you know what I see?"

Stella shook her head.

Her mother smiled. "I see your confidence in Leo. You have always pushed him harder than your father or I could. You broke him out of his shell. His first few years with us, he was so afraid of every-thing. The more of a wild child you were, the more he saw that the world could be a safe place. When he fell, you were the one who picked him up, and he got braver every day. That was your doing. You showed him how to grow out of his fear and look at what a wonder-ful, confident young man he's become."

A lump formed in Stella's throat. She'd always been so close to Leo. After her initial disturbance at his arrival, she came to agree with her parents that he belonged with them. He just fit in. But they were so close in age that she'd never stopped to see how she had helped shape him.

Her mother stroked her cheek. "And I see your softness in Rosie."

"That's *your* softness," Stella said. Her voice wobbled.

Cecilia shook her head. "No, Little Star. Rosie has her mother's creativity, your father's steadiness, and my warmth. But she has your strength of heart and vulnerability. I see you in all the beautiful things about your siblings, just like I sometimes see myself or your father. But you have always had a way of seeing their beauty and reflecting it back to them in a way they can take."

"Papa says I get that from you."

"Perhaps. But you have always been so fiercely your own, and that is the thing I am most proud of," Cecilia said. "That is what I fought for—for you and every other woman in the two kingdoms to be themselves and make their own choices."

Again, Stella couldn't remember why she'd pushed her mother away. Sometimes it felt easier to be loved so intensely from a distance, especially when she wasn't certain she'd done anything to deserve it.

"Why is this all so hard?"

Cecilia smiled softly. "Oh, my Little Star, you're just growing up."

"Don't be nice about it. It makes it worse," Stella sobbed.

Cecilia laughed and kissed her forehead. "It's my job to love you no matter what. Best job I've ever had." She shifted and the top of her dress gapped, revealing the golden scar over her heart. Stella stared at it for a long moment.

"Don't romanticize this scar like everyone else, Stella," her mother whispered. "You have always loved it, even when you were a baby. But I would spare you from ever having to make that choice—from looking into the eyes of the person you love most and knowing that it's you or them. I don't want you to love like that. I want someone to love *you* like that. I want you to be safe because you're my baby."

"What if I fail?" The question slipped out.

Gods, Stella didn't even know what she was fighting for anymore. She'd thought she was so unique, but she was just another woman giving too much of herself up for a man who didn't appreciate it. It was such a disappointing end to this story she'd expected to be grand.

"What if you fail?"

Stella pulled back and met her mother's gaze. "I thought you would reassure me."

Cecilia sighed. "What I mean is: What are you making failure mean about you?"

Stella frowned.

"You're my baby. I cannot even fathom that kind of failure,

because it terrifies me and I have only survived thus far by putting my complete faith in you. I'm white-knuckling every challenge, hoping that if you can't win, you'll at least be safe."

Stella sat up. "I don't want to upset you. The baby—"

"I'm fine, and so is the baby. You worry about you, Stella."

"How?"

Her mother laughed loudly and suddenly. "I don't know. I've been missing your grandfather. I'd love to know how he handled me running into danger like this. Now I know how terrified he must have been, but he never showed it. I'd love to know his secret. I wish I could tell you that I'm not afraid, that I have every confidence. But being a mother is redefining fear daily, and when I see you hurt, it makes me want to rip the world apart."

Stella rested her head on the pillow next to her mother. "Can I stay here tonight?"

"Of course."

Stella snuggled into Cecilia's arms and breathed in the lemon-lavender scent that had been so comforting to her since childhood. Sometimes a girl just needed her mother.

34

STELLA

The following afternoon, Stella sprawled on her bed, making a list of all the herbs she wanted to have in hand for the final magic challenge.

A light knock on her bedroom door startled her. She looked up to find her father leaning against the doorframe.

"Arden Teripin is in the sunroom again," her father said. "Is this going to be a regular thing?"

Stella didn't move. She should have been prepared for Arden to show up, but when he wasn't there to greet her at the end of the memory challenge, it had solidified where she stood with him.

When she'd heard someone at the front door, a part of her had hoped it was Teddy. He had no reason to come looking for her, but after her conversation with her mother, she couldn't get him off her mind.

"Stella?" Rainer frowned, a deep crease forming in his brow. "I can send him away."

"No, it's not that. He's just not who I was expecting." She met her father's gaze. "I'm sorry I took your spot last night."

He smiled, and the crease in his brow softened. "That's okay. You needed your mom. I'm happy you talked to her. She's been missing

406

you and I think you've been missing her too, even if you're too stubborn to say so."

"I didn't mean to kick you out of your bed, though."

"It was fine. I just slept in Aunt Clara's old room. That room has the best morning sun, anyway."

Her parents were so opposite, and yet somehow so well-suited to each other. Her mother's grumpiness in the mornings and her father's energy. Her father's neatness and her mother's mess. Her mother's emotional nature and her father's steadiness.

For so long, she'd admired the way they fit together like puzzle pieces. Now she understood how lovely it could be to have someone to balance her out.

"What's on your mind, Little Star?" Her father cocked his head to the side. "Who were you expecting?"

Her mouth went dry. "No one." Stella swallowed hard and looked toward the bedroom doorway. "I don't know what to say to Arden."

Her father's eyebrows shot up. "I'm happy to ask him to leave—"

Stella laughed. "No. I mean—" She meant she'd already made peace with him in her head and telling him felt redundant. "I mean that I don't think Arden is who I want to tell all my stories to."

"You were hoping it was Teddy," Rainer said.

Stella's cheeks heated, and she nodded. She sat up, smoothing her dress over her legs. "How did you get so good at loving Mama?"

Rainer walked to the bed and sat down beside her. "Practice. It took a long time for me to learn how to hold your mother tight enough that she could grow, but not so tight that I smothered her. To give her room to wander, but to make certain she knew I'd never truly let her go. It took years to even understand where her soul ends and mine begins. It took a lot of practice to figure out that balance, but it's possible." Her father paused. "Is he the one you want to tell all your stories to?"

When she didn't say anything, her father squeezed her hand. "You've had all this time to be just you—to grow into yourself," he continued. "So now you're challenged with trying to figure out where the edges of Teddy's heart are and to try to learn that territory together. That's the joy and the terror—to learn that softness—to learn how badly you can hurt someone else even without meaning to. And Stell-bell—" He smiled and the crease in his brow disappeared. "It's okay for no man to ever be good enough."

Stella laughed. "Papa."

He wrapped an arm around her shoulders and kissed the top of her head. "I have to say it, okay? I'm trying not to be that father who thinks no one is good enough for his baby, but just know this." He pulled back so he could look her in the eye as he spoke. "I'll never think a man is good enough for you unless *you* do, Little Star."

Stella swallowed hard. "I know."

"Well then. I'll leave you to it." Rainer kissed her cheek and left her to gather her courage.

Stella rose from the edge of the bed, checked her hair in the mirror, and smoothed her dress. Normally she would have changed into a more elegant gown, or made sure her hair was styled more neatly for Arden, but she was done trying to convince him she belonged in his world. The fact that she'd ever felt that way to begin with should have been a sign that Arden didn't make her feel at home. She couldn't be bothered to pretend anymore.

She descended the stairs slowly with a sense of grief creeping over her, like she had already watched her dream die and was now going to speak next to its funeral pyre.

Arden stood when she walked into the sunroom. The afternoon light made the embroidery on his tunic look too bright, almost garish, and out of place in the cozy room. He thrust a bouquet of pink roses toward her.

"Thank you," she said, setting them on a side table and urging him to sit down beside her on the couch.

Arden studied her like he was trying to figure out what was differ-ent. Could he see the newfound weight she'd taken on?

It was irrational to think that people would be able to read it on her. Teddy had witnessed it, and it also seemed like he could read it on her face in moments when she went quiet.

But Arden had never killed someone, and he was oblivious to that feeling.

"You didn't stop to see me and let me know you were okay," Arden said, finally breaking the silence.

"That's because I'm not okay." Stella hadn't realized until she said it aloud that it was true. She'd recovered from the initial shock of killing three men, but now she had a new revelation to contend with.

She felt awkward, like everyone could see her heart on display. Like she'd underestimated the very thing that she thought would deliver her the romance she wanted so badly.

Arden clearly had no idea what to say to that.

"You weren't waiting for me when I returned. I almost drowned in a river. I almost bled out. I would have if it wasn't for Teddy. I—"

I killed someone for you.

She almost said the words, but they weren't completely true. She had entered the contest for Arden, but she'd killed those men for Teddy—one of those things she'd never do again, and the other she'd do without hesitation.

It wasn't worth explaining to Arden. She'd already given him too much of her time.

Arden cast his gaze down toward the floor, chastened by her words.

"I went through all of that while you were here courting Grace, safely tucked away behind your castle walls. I was gone and in danger and you didn't even bother to change your social schedule—"

"But I—"

Stella stood and held up a hand to stop him. "I can only blame myself. I can see now how you have always shown me exactly who you are. I was the one who hung on to every crumb you gave me because I was so hungry to be loved by the man I thought you were— by the man you could someday be. But you aren't that man now. I deserve better than a bouquet of flowers a day late and I deserve better than to waste my time listening to you make one more excuse as to why you couldn't be there for me."

"I'm sorry I wasn't there when you needed me." Arden looked so sincere, and perhaps he truly was, but it didn't really matter.

"I've never needed you," Stella said. "You never made yourself available enough for me to need you. You came here to clear your conscience, and you should consider it clean now, but I have another challenge to prepare for, so I hope you'll see yourself out."

He stared at her in mute shock, his gaze burning into her as if trying to recognize her as the same woman he'd wanted to court at the start of the tournament. He wouldn't find that girl.

Mercifully, Arden didn't argue. He stood and bowed to her.

"I'm sorry for your troubles," he said. "I simply wanted to tell you that I spoke with Grace and we decided to go our separate ways and let the bond dissipate."

He waited for her to react, but Stella truly didn't care what he did. When Arden realized there was no anger or joy to cling to, he turned and left Stella standing in a triangle of sunlight.

Stella waited to feel regret, but she only felt relieved. She walked into the kitchen and found her mother sitting at the kitchen table, a vase of daisies prominently displayed in front of her.

"What are those?" Stella asked.

"Teddy left them for you. He stopped by when you were with Arden. I wasn't thinking when I said who you were with."

A bouquet of pale pink roses sat next to the daisies. Stella nodded at it. "And those?"

Cecilia touched the flowers tenderly. "Those were for me. He saw that memory of Xander's and I think it made him see me in a new light."

Stella felt the heaviness of her mother's gaze. "What did he say?"

"He said, *'Your daughter is very brave, and she saved my life and I can see now where she gets it from.'* He brought you the daisies as good luck for tomorrow."

Stella pressed a hand to her heart. She couldn't compose herself under her mother's assessment, not that there was a point to trying. Part of her mother's gift was to read emotions. Perhaps she could make sense of the chaos that Stella felt.

"You don't have to know right now, Little Star. You're very young. You have time to decide who you want to be and who you want to be with. You have always been in a rush. I know you want what I have, but remember, that was almost twenty years in the making. Your father and I had our hardships, and we took the long way home to each other. It would be okay to give yourself the gift of time, but you have to figure out what you want."

Cecilia nodded toward the garden. "He only left a short time ago, and he seemed like he needed somewhere to think. I gave him the cottage key. I did a lot of thinking there myself back in the day. You could probably find him there."

Stella turned to go and stopped immediately, her hands going to her hair. It was so silly. Teddy had seen her half-drowned and half-dead, splattered in blood, and naked, and she was worried she didn't look good enough to face him in the light of day.

She smoothed her dress and turned back to her mother. "Do I look okay?"

Cecilia's lips twisted into a soft smile. "You look beautiful."

Stella blew out a breath and took off through the back door of the house, into the garden and down the path back toward the cliffside cottage.

The cottage, which had originally been a one-room art studio for her grandmother, had become her mother's apartment growing up, and then a place where her parents had started their life together. Stella had lived there with them until she was three, when Rosie's mother had needed a place to stay.

Cecilia had been heartbroken to move back to the family estate where she'd grown up, but still kept the cottage. In recent years, it had been transformed back into an art studio by Rosie's floral sculptures and tapestries, though Stella liked to spend afternoons there watching her sister work.

Stella hesitated, her hand poised to knock on the salt-stained blue paint of the cottage door. The walk was short, but her heart pounded like she'd just run a great distance. It was strange to knock when it was her family's property and Teddy was the visitor. Instead, she pulled the door open and stepped inside. The key was still in the inside lock. Stella turned it, listening to it click into place. Whatever was about to happen between them required no interruptions.

Teddy sat on the window seat, staring out the full wall of glass at the sea down below. A gentle breeze blew in through the open windows, ruffling his dark hair. He turned and smiled at Stella, and her heart beat harder in her chest, the bond unfurling in instant relief at the sight of him.

Stella allowed herself a moment to stare. He was dressed in a finely pressed tunic fitted perfectly to his broad chest, his hair immaculately styled, and his face clean-shaven. She preferred how he'd looked in the forest—messy and half-feral. Now he was back to playing the part he always had and the fine clothes just looked like a costume for a part he had never wanted to play.

"I didn't want to disturb you, but I thought you might want company," she said.

What did she even want to say to him? What could be said? Tomorrow was the final challenge—the magic challenge. She'd assumed they'd be allied with each other, but Endros might not give them a choice. She might have to hurt Teddy.

"Thank you for the daisies."

Teddy looked away. "I figured you should get at least one bouquet of your favorites today." He gestured to Rosie's floral mural. "Had I known you had all of these, I would have realized a few more daisies were pointless."

Stella beamed with pride. "I wish I could take credit, but it's all Rosie. I mostly just sit where you are and distract her while she's trying to work."

He studied the mural for a few moments and then pointed to the strings of flowers hanging from the rafters—Rosie's newest installation that she referred to as a dangling sculpture. "I've never seen anything like this. I should hire her to make something for my mother's birthday."

"I'm sure she'd be happy to."

"This whole place feels like it's right out of one of your fairy tales," he whispered.

Stella kicked off her silk slippers and crossed the room, the old floorboards creaking under her bare feet. She swiped a dried daisy crown off of the bookshelf, walked to Teddy, and placed it on his head.

"There you are. The only thing I've made in this room and the only crown you wish to wear."

Teddy smiled up at her. This close, she found it impossible to contain her emotions. All the fear and grief were scratching at her chest, begging to be let free.

She took a shuddering breath. "I ended things with Arden for good. I thought you should know."

Teddy's eyes went wide, and he stilled. "Why?"

Stella licked her lips, her mouth suddenly dry. "I realized when I saw my parents' memories. I wanted so badly to have what they had and that wasn't something I could have with Arden. He can't love me the way I need to be loved, and I finally found the courage to admit that. Thanks to you."

Stella used to marvel at her parents. It seemed so simple for them. They sustained each other and never seemed to grow tired of it. She feared she'd never find that satisfaction. Now she feared she'd found it and it was so much worse to know it existed with the same certainty that she knew she could not keep it—that she could not keep Teddy.

She was painfully in love with him, and he was in love with Grace.

His throat bobbed, and he nodded. "I'd be lying if I said I wasn't happy to hear that, though I'm sorry you didn't get what you hoped for. You deserve the love you want."

"So do you," she countered.

He rubbed the back of his neck and brought his hand to rest over his heart. "I spoke with Grace earlier today. I apologized for not listening to her when she was trying to be honest with me. You were right that I shouldn't have to change, but she was right that I didn't love her as much as I loved the way she made me feel. That wasn't fair of me."

They stared at each other, the moment taut with everything they couldn't say.

Stella's heart pounded. He didn't want Grace anymore.

Then, the reality hit her. She remembered at once the reason Teddy had entered the competition. He wanted to choose his partner. If he didn't, he'd have to relent to a political marriage. To be with him would mean going back to Argaria with him but also being forced to perform alongside him at court. It would mean watching him suffer daily as he tried to fit himself into an impossible mold of perfection.

"It's a shame it didn't work out." Teddy smirked up at her, tapping the flowers on his head. "You would look beautiful in a crown."

"I didn't want to be queen anyway," Stella said.

Teddy held her gaze and licked his lips. "You don't want to be queen, or you don't want to be *his* queen?"

The question felt like too much and also like an inevitability.

They'd been headed here from the moment the goddess linked them together, or perhaps the moment he'd been so tender with her when she was too raw for anything but human touch.

But how could Stella leave her life in Olney for Teddy when she was still getting to know him? When she was just getting to know herself? When she was going to have a new baby sister or brother and Rosie and Leo needed her still? When her whole life was here?

Because even if she could give up some parts of that, she knew deep down Teddy couldn't love her enough to make up the difference. She would compromise many things. This was her home, and it was already a stretch when she'd thought of being queen of Olney. To move so far away to a foreign court and be away from everyone she loved while having the unimaginable burden of being queen... She couldn't do it. Love was supposed to feel like freedom. This felt like a trap, even if she'd be in the same cage as someone she loved. Even if she could look at him every day and know he saw her.

"I don't want to be queen," she said, her voice barely a rasp. "But maybe—"

Here she was again, looking down another ending and still unwilling to let go. Teddy's disappointment hit her in the chest, knocking the wind from her lungs.

His eyes were as soft as his touch on her side. "What future could we have? You don't want to be queen."

"And you don't want to be king."

He huffed a laugh, but all she felt was his grief mingling with hers. "Unfortunately, you're the only one who can opt out."

Stella tapped her chest. "Too bad we're already stuck with each other."

Teddy smiled sadly. "Can't regret the one reckless choice in a lifetime of careful ones."

"Speak for yourself. I'm not about to start being careful now," she said.

Teddy laughed—a real laugh that sent a curl of pleasure through her.

Stella had been so close to what she wanted, but timing was everything.

"It's for the best," she rasped. "I'm not your peace. I can't love you the way you deserve to be loved. When I win tomorrow, I'm not going to ask for Arden's hand. I'm going to ask for the bond to be broken so we can both be free of this." Her voice broke, and she swallowed the lump in her throat.

It hurt to even admit it out loud, but it hurt more to see the understanding on his face. It would have been better if he were angry. She knew how to meet his fury, but had no idea how to meet this quiet compassion.

The adversity she faced hadn't been a set-up for a grand fairy-tale romance. It was the set-up for Stella to finally figure out what she wanted and walk away when she couldn't get it. Maybe that's what her mother had meant—that the greater love story was about loving herself. It was a good lesson, but it didn't make it hurt less.

"How can this be it?" She hadn't meant to say it, but it slipped out anyway.

Teddy's face softened, and he pulled her into a kiss. It was soft, the barest brush of his lips, like a whispered goodbye on his way to grander things.

She pushed him back against the glass, straddling his lap and kissing him harder. He groaned, one hand coming up to cup her cheek and the other pressing her body against his so hard it hurt.

"Don't let me down easy," he whispered between kisses.

Stella pulled on the back of his tunic until he relented, breaking their kiss to grab the collar, yank it off, and toss it to the floor. He unbuttoned the front of her dress, nipping down her chest and pressing kisses to each mark he left behind.

He moved slowly, languidly, when she wanted him to go fast, or at least faster than the wave of grief that was crashing down on her. Teddy groaned into her neck as she rolled her hips against him. He brushed his nose along her jaw, and finally kissed her again.

"Please," she murmured against his mouth.

Could he feel the agony in that one word? Did he know that she meant *my heart is in your hands* and *please don't ruin me*? Or maybe she really wanted a reckoning and that plea was *Please ruin me. Please wreck me this once so I'll know it before I meet my end. Please destroy me so I can die knowing I've risked my heart at least once—that I've had the real thing this once.*

Funny that she thought she'd loved before. This felt like being tossed unprepared over some cliff edge and only realizing when she felt the stomach-plunging terror of free fall that there was nothing she could do but surrender.

There was no saving herself from this. It was just another thing she would need to survive. It was so messy, like a sparring match where they were both bloodied, but neither of them was willing to surrender. She could see it in Teddy's eyes; the silent confession, the game of chicken they were playing. *I'll pulverize your heart as you pulverize mine. I'm already devastated. May as well devastate you too.*

Stella had felt bottomless for so long. No amount of love could fill her up. She wanted to be cherished, exalted, and convinced of her worthiness. But no matter how much her parents doted on her or how Arden showed her affection, she still felt restless, certain there was something she was missing.

Until now.

Teddy hiked up her dress as she fumbled with the button on his waistband.

"Slow down, Stella," he teased, popping the button open and freeing himself from his pants.

But Stella didn't want to go slow. Her chest was tight, eyes burning. If she didn't replace this hurt with something more intense, she would dissolve into a crying mess and that was not how she wanted to make peace with letting him go.

She shoved the top of her dress down, pushed her undergarments to the side, and sank down on him, watching his expression morph from surprise to agonized pleasure.

"*Fuck*," he groaned.

She held his gaze as she started to move—slowly at first, then quickly gaining momentum. He hugged her close, pressing her chest against his, keeping her from moving too fast. He gripped her hips, forcing her to ride him the way he wanted, making certain she knew that if this was their last time, he wasn't going to let her rush him.

Joy and lust soared through their bond. Teddy looked at her with awe and she'd never felt more beautiful or more broken.

He kissed her slowly, his lips trailing up her cheeks to kiss away tears. Gods, she was crying again. He tucked his face into her neck, murmuring soft praise that sounded something like a promise to make it better.

His hands gripped her hips, moving her faster, angling her for more friction. Stella held on tight, fingernails scoring his shoulders as the pleasure wound tighter and tighter inside her. Her toes cramped, but she refused to let go. Once it was over, she wouldn't be able to do it again. Why had she ever wanted it to end when it felt so good?

Teddy met her movements with an intuitive rhythm that sent her gasping over the edge whether she wanted to or not. Then he moaned against her chest and shuddered, and they were left panting in the almost-dark cottage.

The connection in her chest buzzed pleasantly. If she didn't win tomorrow, it would always be there. Perhaps over time Stella would become accustomed to the ache. The bond pulled taut across the miles between them. The random swells of his anxiety with no idea what was happening to him.

Maybe with him far away, this fever between them would cool and they could see each other once a year and not feel cleaved in half when they had to go their separate ways again.

Stella was furious at Goddess Desiree for messing with their lives like this. She had no regard for the pain she caused for the sake of making a point.

"What does *Minyha* mean?" Stella whispered.

Teddy looked almost pained as he leaned his head back against the window and closed his eyes. "It's hard to translate. It's such an old word."

"Then why use it?"

"Because it describes you perfectly."

His lips tipped into a smirk and Stella knew he'd never tell her.

It was probably for the best. The sooner she forgot that nickname, the sooner she'd forget everything else and be able to move on with her life.

35

STELLA

Stella stared at the table of refreshments in the royal family tent. The small white linen tent was set up just behind the competitors' tent and Stella needed the private space to mentally prepare herself.

Bees buzzed around the plate of fresh pink melon, and berries overflowed from bowls, spilling onto the white tablecloth in an array of reds, blues, and purples. The fresh-baked lemon cakes smelled sweet and citrusy, but her stomach was too twisted in knots of anxiety to enjoy any of it with the final challenge looming over her.

She'd left Teddy asleep in the cottage just before dawn. He'd looked so peaceful and she couldn't bear to wake him, so she'd left like a thief in the faint dawn light and proceeded to spend the entire day chest-clenched, trying not to cry. Mercifully, her family was giving her space.

Stella reached for a lemonade, but the glass was slick with condensation and her hands were trembling so much that it immediately slipped from her grip. A delicate hand snapped up and caught it before it could shatter on the ground.

Stella looked up and met Juliana Savero's hazel eyes.

"Easy," the princess said, smiling warmly.

"Doesn't bode well for the challenge," Jalen said as he stepped up beside Juliana.

The Savero twins' movements were an eerie echo, like they always understood where the other would be next.

"Jay, don't say that," Juliana chided. She smiled sheepishly at Stella. "Sorry, he's such a man sometimes. I don't know why he even bothers to speak when he has nothing intelligent to say."

Jalen threw an arm around Juliana's shoulder.

Stella sipped her lemonade. "It's fine. I'm just a little jumpy."

Jalen looked around the tent. "Where's your competition?"

Stella shrugged. "I don't know. He'll probably show up any minute to tell me how I should be outfitting myself differently, and that I shouldn't be having lemonade, and calling me *Minyha*."

Juliana froze with her glass halfway to her mouth. "He called you *Minyha*?" She locked eyes with Jalen.

The prince burst out laughing.

Stella glared at the twins. "Yes. Do you know what it means?"

Juliana pursed her lips. "Well, yes. It's just—" She looked away. "It's just not really a nice nickname."

Stella huffed a laugh. "Just tell me."

"It means *pain in my ass*," Jalen said with a grin.

Juliana rolled her eyes and sipped her lemonade. "It does not. It means '*one's greatest trial or test.*'"

It was Stella's turn to laugh. The tension that had been coiled tight in her chest all day finally unraveled. She sounded half-hysterical.

She'd made *Minyha* out to be some romantic nickname in her head when Teddy was just referring to how she tested him. The laughter shook through her, but when it died, she was left with the empty ache of wishing it had meant something more.

"I suppose that's an appropriate nickname," she said.

"You're both wrong."

Juliana cursed as they all turned to find Alexandra standing at the tent entrance. She cut an imposing figure, tall and statuesque in her leather armor and gilded by sunlight.

Alexandra sauntered into the tent, snatched a lemon cake off the table, and took a bite. "I expect that kind of idiocy from Jay. He's been coasting on looks for years. But you're usually better at languages, Jules, though I suppose you focus more on the contemporaries than the old languages. In modern Novumi it means one's greatest trial or test, but I don't think that's what Teddy means. He's using the Old Novumi translation."

Juliana put her hands on her hips. "Well, what does it mean if you're such a scholar, Alex?"

Stella had been alone with the two princesses of Argaria so infrequently, but those few occasions had left her feeling like she was navigating some strange emotional weather. Sibling dynamics were often complicated, and she supposed being royal only made things more complex, but Juliana and Alexandra had always felt like they vacillated between being best friends one moment and adversaries the next. No one else could say something bad about Juliana, but Alexandra had free rein and vice versa.

Alexandra turned her intense golden eyes on Stella. "There are no direct translations from the old language." She smiled sadly. "It's a sacred word of claiming. The closest translation would be '*my heart*' or simply '*mine.*'"

Stella didn't realize she'd stopped breathing until her chest started to burn. *A sacred word of claiming. My heart.* Her magic involuntarily drew up the memories of the moments he'd used the nickname. *Mine.* They were all linked together in her mind by a little golden thread.

The first time, Teddy had said it in that taunting tone, full of playful exasperation. Surely he meant "my trial" that time.

But later—when he'd said it in the cabin, when he made her come so hard she'd cried. When he'd looked at her with that wild, possessive intensity that she found so intoxicating. When he knew she couldn't give him the answer he wanted, and still he'd looked at her with so much tenderness.

He'd meant "*Mine*" when he whispered it against her pounding pulse.

Gods. She hadn't realized she'd said it aloud until Alexandra laughed.

"I'll say. If there ever was a time to pray, it's when Teddy is mooning over you." She made an exaggerated gagging motion.

Stella's eyes pricked with tears. This was a distraction she did not need. Why not at least tell her what the nickname meant? How could he keep something so monumental private?

She froze, realizing it was because she'd rejected him. He'd called her Stella after she told him she didn't want him. He'd made the change when she let him know that she was not in fact going to be his.

Her eyes burned, her chest wound so tight she could scarcely breathe.

Alexandra smiled thoughtfully. "Which do you think our dear brother meant, Jules?"

Juliana stared wide-eyed at Stella. "Oh my gods. He's in love with you."

Stella shook her head, trying to swallow the lump lodged in her throat. "I don't think it's that deep. It's just this bond. It's very compelling."

But the words were more wish than truth. And Stella was more raw wound than warrior. She could not have this now when she needed to be clear-headed and strong. When she needed to be the fighter she'd been when she'd saved Teddy's life.

Stella needed to be someone who could survive. Someone like her parents.

The revelation changed nothing. It couldn't. When Stella stepped into the arena, she would need to do whatever it took to win. She needed the bond gone. Surely that was a blessing the gods would grant her. She couldn't bear to face the torment of knowing Teddy so intimately when she could not have him.

A throat cleared from the tent doorway.

Fionn Silver stepped inside and sauntered over to Stella. "Hey, princess." Juliana and Alexandra both looked at him for a long moment before realizing he meant Stella. "I need to call in that favor."

Stella crossed her arms. "If it's something about throwing this challenge, it's not going to happen."

He held his hands up in surrender. "Nothing so serious. Besides, there's no fun in surrender when you can be an outright victor. I promise it won't take long. We'll be back in the arena in no time."

Alexandra stepped forward, her fingers brushing the blade tucked into the back of her armor. She looked to Stella for approval.

"I appreciate the solidarity, but I'll be fine, Your Graces." Stella curtseyed and turned to leave, but not before she saw Fionn wink at Alexandra and the princess answer with an obscene gesture.

THE DOCK AIR WAS ROTTEN WITH LOW TIDE, BUT THE PIER WAS QUIET and free of its usual hustle and bustle. The percussive sound of boats gently bouncing against the dock bumpers in the rough waves matched the urgent rhythm of Stella's pounding heart.

Stella leaned against the fence, looking out at the sea. "You need me to do *what*?"

"I need you to wipe the harbormaster's memory."

"Of everything?"

Fionn laughed. "No, princess. Just a little bit. I'd appreciate if you could make it look like he just hit his head and forgot."

Stella stared at Fionn. That wasn't exactly a big ask. What she'd done on Alexandra was intricate and meticulous. It took a lot of magical finesse to remove a memory without making it obvious that something was missing. But to bluntly remove a chunk of time was relatively easy—for Stella, at least.

She tried to puzzle out his angle. If he didn't have magic, he wouldn't have realized the simplicity of the task. Maybe he hoped to wear her out before the magic challenge. As far as she could tell, Fionn did not have magic, and if he did, it had to be meager for Stella to have no sense of it at all after being so close to him.

Witches could always sense magic on each other. Stella could sense it every time Teddy was close, and not just because of the bond buzzing in her chest. His storm magic sent a soft crackle through the air. All of the Savero siblings were like that.

Fionn looked at her expectantly.

"Why?"

He cocked his head and smiled flirtatiously. "That wasn't part of our agreement. Information is power. I just need this small favor."

"What if he forgets something vital?" Stella asked.

"You seem like a smart girl. I don't think I should have to tell you that's kind of the point," Fionn said.

Stella tried to read anything else about this request in his eyes, but Fionn's face was a mask of calm indifference.

Maybe he'd slept with the man's wife and simply wanted the dalliance forgotten so he could come and go from the Olney ports without being sabotaged at every dock. The harbormaster did have considerable power in Olney City. He was in charge of the comings and goings of every visiting vessel, and while he did have the help of a team of tide witches and several deputies, he was ultimately the keeper of everything related to sea travel. It was an important role because having one man who knew everyone who came and went in Olney meant a wealth of information, all of which funneled back to the network of spies run by her Uncle Evan and Aunt Sylvie.

As if on cue, the dock bells rang out, signaling the end of the day. That meant only a half-hour to get back to the arena to check in for the third challenge.

"Time's wasting, princess. We have somewhere to be mighty soon, and I have to think this work will take some doing."

"What do you need me to erase? How much?"

"Just the last day, and I also need the corresponding incoming and outgoing ledger page for the last day as well," Fionn said, polishing his fingernails on his tunic.

The move was too forced to be casual, but Stella didn't have time to puzzle this out and she couldn't go back on the bargain she'd made even if she wanted to. If she did, word would spread and no one would bargain for anything with anyone in her family. While that didn't sound so bad now, she couldn't imagine a situation where Rosie or Leo needed help and couldn't get it because of something stupid she'd done. This was her mess, and she'd need to deal with the fallout. It would be easy enough to tell her parents when she saw them. She'd hold the stolen memories in her own mind until she had a chance to comb through them for anything suspicious.

"I'll do it," she said.

"Good lass. I knew you would. I know the honorable type when I see them, and I had you pegged on sight. Makes sense. They say your father was the honorable sort, too."

Stella didn't like that he brought up her father. It wasn't a threat—everyone knew who her father was—but there was something about a mercenary referring to him directly that made her feel oddly protective.

"Don't speak of my family."

Fionn bowed his head. "I meant nothing by it, princess. Merely paying compliments."

Stella frowned. Mercenaries were not known to compliment someone for being honorable. The only honor they respected was timely payment. But she had no choice.

The salt crust gritted on the hinges and a bell above her head jingled as she yanked open the door of the harbormaster's office and walked inside.

"We're closed," a gruff voice called out from somewhere behind the tall wooden counter.

A large metal spike on the countertop was crammed full of port entry passes. When Stella leaned over the counter, she glimpsed an older man with gray hair bent over a ledger. He was muttering quietly to himself about something not adding up.

"Excuse me, sir," she called.

The old man's head snapped up at the sound of her voice. When he saw her face, he jumped to his feet. "Good evening, Lady McKay. How can I help you?"

Sometimes it was nice to be a familiar face. It instilled trust, even when she didn't deserve it. Stella put on her best damsel-in-distress voice.

"I'm so sorry to bother you. I was actually wondering if you had a record of the ship that arrived from Novum, the one that was carrying Fionn Silver. As you know, my father likes to be very prepared and, given that I'm competing in the Gauntlet Games, he is trying to figure out how long each competitor has been here to prep."

It was a terrible lie, but Stella had always understood the weight her parents' names carried in Olney. She rarely threw them around, but when she did, people were eager to oblige her.

The harbormaster stood from his desk, grabbed the book, and walked to the counter. The wood groaned when he hefted the heavy tome onto it.

He turned back a few pages. "I remember myself. It was two weeks ago, but this book keeps me honest. Let's see here—" He broke off as he scanned the page.

Memory magic could typically only be used with physical contact. But Stella's magic was a remnant of her mother's, unique in that it could work from a distance instead of just by touch.

She pressed gently against the harbormaster's mind. The man didn't even flinch. He went right on scanning the page. Stella closed her eyes and searched his mind. Time was difficult to track in another person's memory, so she needed to try to have him call up something that would serve as a marker.

"I know a bunch of storytellers arrived from Novum yesterday. They're here to record the story of the end of the festival," Stella prompted.

Memory magic was an exercise in what to keep and how to organize it. When Stella was little and first learning to wield the magic that was her birthright, her mother had taught her to think of her mind as a giant library full of books. Eventually, the shelves would be full if she tried to save everything. Even magic had its limits. She'd learned to vent the unimportant memories before bed each night, imagining that she was pulling boring books from the shelf and tossing them out of her mind library.

The more important memories stayed tucked away in the back of the library for safekeeping, unless she wanted to pull them out and watch them for the sheer enjoyment of it. The front of her mind held memories that she needed to refer to more frequently—spells, appointments, and healing herbs.

And in a secret room off the side, she kept other people's memories—moments her mother had shared with her from before she was born, and Rosie's favorite memories of their childhood. That was where she would store the harbormaster's memories.

Stella closed her eyes and pressed her magic into him. As he called up the memory of the previous day, the golden threads of his mind connected to that memory flared brighter.

She could see both the vision of the memory and the spiraling tangle of golden threads related to it in her mind's eye. When someone was actively thinking of a person or memory, their mind naturally connected it with other related memories. That magic could be used to help heal the minds of those who suffered from memory loss. In this case, those same connections would allow her to uproot all the memories that she needed to extract.

She twisted the golden threads into a braid, and then gently tugged. They broke away with ease. Crowded brains were easier to manipulate in this way since they were eager to let go and make space. She tucked them into the secret room in her own mind for safekeeping until she had time to look through them and figure out what Fionn was trying to hide.

Before she finished, she removed the memory of her visit.

When she blinked her eyes open, the man was staring at her and rubbing his temples.

"I'm so sorry for this," she said.

He frowned as she slammed his head into the desk. He crumpled to the floor. Stella checked his pulse before carefully removing the page that Fionn had requested from the ledger.

Stella scanned it quickly, committing it to memory before ducking outside.

Fionn's face lit up when he saw her. "No problems?"

"No problems, but we need to get back," she said, shoving the page into his hand as she brushed by him. She walked down the dock and up the trail to town with a sick roiling in her stomach.

A little memory was no great loss, but she'd assumed when Fionn offered to trade that he'd wanted help to recover a relative's memory. This task left her feeling like she'd unwittingly become an accomplice to some unknown crime.

Stella shook off the anxiety and forced herself to focus on one challenge at a time. The Gauntlet Games' final challenge was upon them, so the mystery would have to wait.

36

TEDDY

The blindfold was just loose enough that Teddy could make out his boots when he looked down. Gravel crunched beneath his feet as two guards escorted him into starting position for the final challenge. The night was hot and oppressively humid—like every summer night in Olney—and the low light made it hard to tell what sort of environment he was in. Beneath his leather armor, his shirt was already damp with sweat.

The noise of the crowd was muted in a way that suggested he might be in a pit again. He shuddered as the sense memory of the first challenge came back to him in a rush—the cold water on his skin and the panic that tore through him when he'd realized his armor was stuck.

A soft, calming sensation swelled in his chest.

Stella must have sensed his panic and was trying to calm him down. He took a deep breath and tried to narrow the funnel of their connection so she wouldn't feel so much from him. He didn't want to distract her from what was sure to be the most violent challenge yet.

He stumbled over a rock but was steadied by the guard on his right.

"Godsforsaken blindfold," he grumbled.

Just like the first challenge, this one had started with him being blindfolded and dragged helplessly through a series of twists and turns. Teddy had no idea where he was, but without sight, his other senses were sharper. He could smell the overpowering sandalwood scent of the hunter on his right and the hint of onion on the breath of the guard to his left.

"Stay here. You'll hear the rules read off in a few moments, once the other competitors are in place," the hunter on his left said.

The two of them retreated, leaving Teddy alone with his swirling thoughts.

"I'm not your peace. I can't love you the way you deserve to be loved. When I win tomorrow, I'm not going to ask for Arden's hand. I'm going to ask for the bond to be broken so we can both be free of this."

Stella was so calm when she spoke those devastating words—like she'd already grieved the loss and was whispering the message to his ghost. It was the most rational she'd ever been, and Teddy was so angry at her for being steady when he felt so out of control. Stella wanted him, but not enough.

He couldn't even blame her. He didn't want this life. It would have been cruel to cage her alongside him—but gods, if he didn't wish he was selfish enough to do so.

Olney was Stella's home. He saw the way she cared for her siblings, the way Leo and Rosie looked up to her, the way her parents poured their love into her and how that had made her such a brave and kind woman.

Teddy had never known someone like that—had never let himself be known. She had studied him in the practiced way a warrior studied an adversary. But she hadn't wounded him on the field of battle. She'd unearthed the most tender part of his heart and made sure to hurt him there—in the way only a lover could.

And now it was over. He didn't know what to say about it or how to move forward. Instead, he kept turning the memory over and over, waiting for it to hurt less.

He needed to think of something—*anything* else. Patting his pockets, he took inventory of the herbs he'd stocked up on in case he needed a spell. The magic challenge, like each of the others, had varied historically. Some gods tried to level the playing field between those who summoned and those who couldn't. Those were the years when the final challenge was most entertaining and violent. Endros seemed the type who was out for blood and Teddy doubted he would give Teddy and Stella an edge.

The number of competitors had dwindled from sixteen to nine, and the final challenge typically produced the most desperation and bloodshed. He had no doubt that this event would follow that pattern, and that made him even more worried for Stella. She'd been able to hurt someone else to protect him, but not to protect herself.

Teddy had become so accustomed to the constant swirling pulse from the bond in his chest; thinking about losing it left him bereft. Would Stella really wish it away if she won? Would he?

He imagined the bond like a thread connecting the two of them and gave a gentle tug on it the way Rainer had taught him. A moment later, Stella's responding tug echoed back to him. She was somewhere straight in front of him. Just sensing her there at the other end of the connection was a relief.

Footsteps approached from behind Teddy.

"Your Grace, my name is Tani. I'm one of the tournament priestesses. We need your assistance for this final challenge. I cannot tell you why, but I need you to channel your storm magic into this bracelet." She took his hand and placed a cold metal cuff on his palm.

That was unexpected. Teddy's magical advantage over half the competition would be depleted. However, being granted magic and understanding how to wield it were entirely different things.

That settled the churning in his gut.

He called up his storm magic and, instead of using it to generate a storm in the sky, he sent it directly into the enchanted metal.

The priestess took the cuff he'd filled and replaced it with an empty one. It wasn't difficult work. Teddy had been channeling storms since he was ten years old. It was like calling a soft melody that played on the wind and feeding it into the enchanted bracelet.

He repeated the same steps twice more, blindly trading the filled magical bands for empty ones each time.

"Are all the other witches having to create so many?" he asked.

The priestess shifted, and Teddy heard the cuffs click together. "We need to get each of you witches to make the same amount so that each non-magic-wielding competitor will have the element of surprise. This way they could end up with any of the cuffs and you won't know by process of elimination which they have."

Dixon's primary affinity was fire magic. Stella's was also fire, but they could ask her for memory. According to what Stella had told him at the beginning of the tournament, Katerina Shank was a water witch. The only affinity Teddy wouldn't need to worry about was earth magic.

Tani placed one last cuff in his hand, but it was already pulsing with magic.

"I don't need this. I have my own magic."

The priestess closed his hand around the cuff. "You do. Your magic will be limited to what fits in this cuff, just like all the other competitors. You may encounter obstacles that play to any affinity."

Teddy didn't like the sound of that. Not only would he have to be mindful of his fellow combatants, but he needed to use his magic wisely, and at any moment he could be hit with power he was unable to deflect.

"Endros thanks you for your contribution to his historic tournament." The priestess's tone was full of reverence. "A bell will ring, preceding an announcement in a few moments, and once you hear your task, a second bell will ring, signaling the start of the challenge. Only then may you remove your blindfold."

Teddy frowned and listened to her footsteps retreat.

He peeked out the bottom of his blindfold. Dim torchlight illuminated the bottom of an ivy-covered wall to his right. Teddy walked over to it and pressed his hand against it. There was hard stone behind the ivy. He could tell by the way his footsteps echoed that the space wasn't entirely open. There was another wall or door somewhere a few feet in front of him.

Teddy strained to hear anything. He could barely make out the crowd noise from the other side of the wall, or perhaps above it. It was hard to tell.

A loud bell clanged and shattered the night air. Applause rose from all sides, somewhere up above Teddy's head. He could tell by the way the noise ricocheted that the surrounding structure was more intricate than a wide-open arena. The week-long second challenge had offered the time they needed to construct a new nightmare.

"Greetings, competitors, and congratulations on making it to the final challenge." Endros's voice sent a chill through Teddy's blood. It seemed to be coming from everywhere at once. "This magical challenge will push you to your limits and test your ability to use a limited amount of magic wisely. Bear in mind that strategy is required to win."

Teddy shifted from foot to foot, trying to shake the nervousness from his limbs.

"Your final task is simple," Endros said. "When the next bell sounds, you may remove your blindfolds. You all stand in a maze, equidistant from the center. Whoever gets to the center of the maze first will be declared the winner. You will encounter magical obstacles of any of the elements, but you will only have access to the limited amount of magic in the cuff you've been provided. If you burn through it all and need it later, you'll be out of luck. And as a reminder, you may fight each other during an active competition. Best of luck and may the most worthy competitor win."

A hush fell over the crowd and Teddy's heart pounded, sweat rising on his lower back.

The bell sounded and Teddy sprang into motion. He slid the blindfold off as he started to jog. A few feet in front of him, the maze wall turned, and Teddy followed it. He wanted to sprint, but he needed to be on the lookout for magical traps.

The crowd roared from their perch along the outer walls of the maze. Teddy tried to ignore the audience and keep moving forward.

The corridor ahead of him split into multiple routes. He paused and started down the right pathway. It curved farther to the right, then the left. He made the next turn left and ran into a dead end.

Teddy cursed and retraced his steps, taking the left pathway instead. He made a mental map of where he'd gone so far to keep track of his progress.

The first sounds of steel on steel rang out from somewhere deeper in the maze, but his bond with Stella was steady, just a humming baseline of anxious urgency.

He rounded a corner, and a stone beneath his foot pressed down with a loud click. Calling on his magic was a reflex. He pulled it up just in time to catch a bolt of lightning that shot out of the side wall and deflect it into the wall a few feet behind him. The stone shattered and shards sprayed in all directions.

His arms stopped most of the shrapnel, but when he touched his stinging temple, his hand came away bloody.

Lucky break that it was a storm trap. He stood there for a moment, panting and staring at the scorched, crumbling stone the bolt had left behind.

When he turned, he continued through the maze more cautiously. Every corridor looked like the last and every second spent doing anything but all-out sprinting to the center of the maze felt like risking not only *his* life and future, but Stella's.

Footsteps rapidly approaching from his left gave Teddy pause. He crouched low and waited. The second the assailant came around the corner, Teddy drove his shoulder into their gut. It was like slamming into a wall. Their opposing momentum knocked them both back a step.

Christophe Wallthrew was a beast—six feet of broad muscle with a chip on his shoulder, known for using his fists over any other weapon. Teddy ducked the first punch from one of Christophe's meaty fists, but the second caught him in his ribs. The blow knocked the wind out of Teddy. He gasped in an aching breath just in time for Christophe to pound into his back with a two-fisted blow.

Teddy fell to his hands and knees, rolling to the side to narrowly avoid a knee to the face. He leaped to his feet, ignoring the searing ache in his side and the snap of his spine cracking back into place as he came to standing.

As long as he tried to fight Christophe this way, he would lose. Teddy called magic from his cuff and shot a bolt of lightning into his opponent's chest.

Christophe flew backward into the wall. His body shook and twitched violently until Teddy dropped the magic.

A blur of movement to his right caught his eye as Katerina Shank darted by.

"Shit!" Teddy turned to give chase when a body barreled into him and sent him sprawling.

The pain of his knees hitting the gravel stunned him. He stayed on the ground, assessing his battered body. He looked up in time to see Jeneva Lampry, the huntmaster's daughter, disappear down the corridor after Katerina.

It took every bit of Teddy's willpower to launch himself back to his feet. Instead of giving chase, he took the path they hadn't, praying it would be a shorter journey to the center.

He ran as fast as he could. Keeping a mental inventory of the twists and turns in the narrow corridors was becoming more difficult with the distraction of his labored breathing, his probably broken ribs, and the fact that every turn looked the same. The ivy cloaked any identifying features on the walls, and more than once, he wondered if he was just being led in circles.

As he jogged down a long straightaway, the crowd noise escalated. He was getting close. He could feel it. That, or he'd been made delusional by pain.

He rounded a corner at the same time Dixon darted out of the corridor across from him. The crowd roared and Teddy couldn't tell if it was in reaction to the two of them clashing or something else in the maze.

"You're so close!" It was Alexandra's voice that cut through all the noise and the rush of blood in Teddy's ears.

The sound filled Teddy with a raw, animal desperation.

Dixon's face whipped toward the crowd. He'd heard it too. Before

Dixon could take a step forward, Teddy tackled him to the ground and punched him in the face. Dixon's head snapped back, and Teddy doubled down. He threaded his hand into Dixon's dark hair and slammed his head into the ground again.

Teddy didn't wait to see if it had been enough to kill Dixon. He was so close to the finish.

He pushed to his feet and breathlessly stumbled onward.

37

STELLA

Stella sprinted down the narrow corridor of the ivy maze, gulping in humid air.

The magical cuff they'd given her could limit her summoning, but it had just occurred to her that she knew a spell that could help her avoid any magical booby traps.

The maze itself was a marvel. She had no idea how they'd managed to create the massive stone walls and keep it under wraps, but she probably shouldn't have been surprised by anything about the tournament after fighting an Octobear in the first challenge.

She could tell by the pulse of her bond that she was gradually wandering closer to Teddy, but she tried not to let that distract her.

Rosie had insisted she put some dried lavender in her vest in case she needed to do a spell. Stella was relieved for that now, since she had foolishly assumed she'd have full access to her elemental summoning magic. She paused before a split in the maze and pulled out a few sprigs of lavender. Slowing her pace, she gripped the lavender buds in her palm and pulled up the spell in her mind.

Stella squeezed the lavender and whispered the incantation. "Grant me vision to light my way, so from this path, I won't stray. Keep me calm throughout this fight, and bring that which is hidden into sight."

A tingling power rushed from the lavender in her hand, through her body and up to her eyes. Stella blinked and opened her palm. The lavender had turned to dust, but it had done the job.

The spell cast the torchlit path in front of her in a pale purple haze. According to the memory she'd pulled the spell from, that haze should cling to anything magical in her path. With her clear sight, Stella continued at a faster clip. She took the left path at the next split and had to quickly double back when she reached a dead end a few turns later.

As she turned down the opposite hall, she stopped short. The lavender haze gathered around the wall in front of her. It all seemed to be tied to a faint line across the ground that looked almost like a magical trip wire at the end of the straightaway. If she could jump it, she could duck around the bend in the corridor just beyond it for cover.

Stella steeled herself with a breath and took a running leap. As she landed, footsteps pounded from the hallway she was about to step into.

She rounded the wall and narrowly ducked a flying punch from Rett. Stella used his momentum, bending lower to wrap an arm around his knee. She yanked his leg up.

He slammed down onto the ground back-first and Stella vaulted over him to continue down the long straightaway.

Rett grabbed her ankle. Her knees crashed to the ground, and she cursed.

The second that she was stunned by the pain, Rett struck. He grabbed the collar of her armor and hauled her down. They rolled several times until she came up on top of his chest.

She punched Rett hard in the face. His nose snapped beneath her fist with a loud crack, and blood poured down his chin.

"Two for two, Roach," she taunted.

He roared in frustration and tossed her off of him. Her impulse was to run, but if she didn't stand and fight, he'd catch her too quickly. She grabbed two blades from her vest just in time for him to charge at her with two daggers of his own.

She slashed across his leather armguards, her blades glancing off the magical metal cuff on his wrist. It was as if the sound reminded both of them that he had magic now.

"You stupid bitch. Why do you refuse to die?" the Roach snapped.

"Could ask you the same." She kicked him in the stomach and grinned at the satisfying sound of air rushing out of his lungs.

The bond flashed with a bright flare of pain. Teddy. It was there and gone quickly. Panic drenched her in ice.

Rett's cuff lit up and Stella braced herself, sheathing her left blade so she could clamp her hand around his wrist. If he wanted to use magic, she'd make sure he felt it, too. If he was summoning, he couldn't be hurt by the power itself, but it wouldn't protect him from the explosive blowback of releasing too much at once. It was a common mistake even for witches who'd had years of learning how to channel their elemental affinities.

Stella had seen Rett fight enough to know he was a "more is better" kind of fighter.

The moment she felt magic rise like a pressure drop popping her ears, she summoned her fire magic.

A huge fireball exploded between them, blowing them apart. Stella slammed into the ivy-covered wall behind her so hard that she felt her ribs crack.

The crowd cheered loudly, but she couldn't tell if it was for her or someone else. It was disorienting being down below them.

She fell to her knees and glanced up at Rett. He lay in a heap, half-propped against the wall. His chest rose and fell slowly. Still alive. She could have closed the distance between them and killed him, but she needed to get to the center of the maze and now every breath was agony.

The crowd roared again as Stella continued toward what she hoped was the center of the maze. She had to be close.

A hand shot out from around the corner and gripped the neck of her leathers.

Suddenly, she was flying.

Stella brought her left arm up in time to break some of the impact, but her temple cracked against the stone wall and her vision went temporarily dark.

She forced her heavy eyelids open and rolled out of the way of a vicious kick.

Drew. She'd been literally thrown out of the way by Drew the Crew and now the massive brute was bearing down on her.

She should have known. He, Christophe, and Dixon always followed where Rett went. She was impressed with their uncanny ability to find each other in the maze.

She scrambled away from another kick. Drew bent, hauled her up to her feet, and slammed her back into the wall. Fiery agony burned through her broken ribs.

Stella gasped for air.

Drew's scarred hands closed around her throat, choking off the air she desperately needed. Her whole body was alive with agony.

"You scarred me for life, you stupid bitch," he said, squeezing his rough hands tighter.

She pushed against his eyes, but he didn't relent. She scratched her fingernails down his face. He cursed, but still held on.

Stella's vision went dark. Her broken ribs ached with the frenzied need for air.

She slammed her hand against Drew's mouth and he bit down on it. Stella forced herself to hold it there through the pain. She funneled her magic through her cuff and shot a fireball directly into his open mouth.

Drew's eyes went wide, and he stumbled back, choking on a soundless scream. Stella rubbed her throat and drew in deep, gasping breaths as her vision sharpened again.

She immediately looked away, listening to the horrifying sound of Drew trying to breathe through his fire-ravaged throat. It was a gruesome way to kill someone, but she was dazed and panicked, and it was the only idea she'd had in the moment.

She'd been stopped too many times already. It seemed the maze was designed to lead the competitors toward each other. But every second that slipped by brought her one second closer to being stuck with this bond and never being able to escape Teddy.

Stella ran blindly through the next few turns. The crowd shouted and clapped and she was certain she had to be close to the center. She rounded another corner and noticed the charred remnants of a fire trap that had already been sprung.

She turned left at the next split in the ivy walls and crashed directly into Fionn.

"Fuck," she grunted.

He immediately threw up his hands and went on the offensive, hitting her with a complicated combination of footwork and brutal punches. She'd learned this particular Novumi fighting style from Isla and Queen Jessamin, but it had been a long time since she'd practiced and her movements were slow. The lack of practice, the broken ribs, and the head injury made her feel off-kilter. Her movements were sharp, the fighting pattern trained into her body so that she struck on instinct, but she was only fast enough to deflect his moves, not to counter them.

His fist connected with her eye, and she ignored the blistering pain to hit him in the chin.

"You really need to work on your form. Left side is the weak side, princess," Fionn said, sliding a dagger along her side to prove the point.

Stella was pissed, pained, and tired of being hit. As he took a step toward her, she grabbed a blade from her vest and jammed it into his groin. He stumbled back and she kicked the hilt so it dug in deeper. He wouldn't be able to remove it until he could get medical attention.

"*Your* weakness is between your legs. Just like every other man," she said, elbowing past him.

Fionn grunted something that sounded like a laugh. "You're not wrong." He grinned and turned to limp in the opposite direction. Stella couldn't tell if he was disoriented or just messing with her.

"You're going the wrong way," she said.

He glanced at her over his shoulder and winked in that handsome, roguish way of his. "I know exactly what I'm doing. Good luck, princess. Sorry about the shiner."

She only took a second to watch him go before sprinting down the straightaway and turning left, then right, then left again. The crowd noise crescendoed as she moved and she had the distinct feeling they were cheering specifically because she was close.

Two paths stretched before her. She took one step toward the left option, and the crowd quieted. She paused and backtracked to the right, and the crowd went wild.

Stella put herself at the crowd's mercy and followed the curve around to the right. The corridor widened into a straightaway and she could finally see a larger open space up ahead with white marble floors. It had to be the center.

Her heart leapt into her throat as she dashed toward the opening at the same time a figure cloaked in shadow hurtled from the doorway directly across from her.

As she crossed the threshold into the center of the maze, her joy morphed into shock and then relief because she was standing face-to-face with Teddy, and they had entered the room at the exact same moment.

38

TEDDY

As Teddy stepped into the center room, a loud grinding sound cut through the air, a stone door closing behind him. The door behind Stella did the same, as did the doors on the other two walls of the room.

They were finally safe. All their adversaries were barred on the other side of the heavy stone. This victory was theirs alone.

For a moment, Teddy could only stare at Stella, scanning her for injury. The roar of the cheering crowd and the bell signaling the end of the challenge muted out, and his entire focus narrowed to her.

The hair at her left temple was matted with blood. The first hint of swelling had set in around one of her eyes and bright purple bruising circled the pale skin of her neck. Blood stained the left side of her waist beneath a cut in her leather breastplate. It had turned the brown leather a deep red, but it was a horizontal slice and not a puncture, so it had probably already healed.

He blew out a shaky breath of relief. Stella's shoulders relaxed at the same time and he realized she must have been doing the same assessment of him.

Teddy hesitated. He wanted to drag her body to his and kiss her, but he wouldn't ruin her reputation with so many spectators watching.

Stella took the choice out of his hands. She took a running leap into his arms and hugged him tightly.

Teddy tucked his face into her neck and breathed in her wild-flower scent. "I'm so glad you're safe," he whispered.

"You're hurt. I felt it."

He rubbed her back and squeezed her a little tighter. "Just a couple of broken ribs, I think."

"Me too," she mumbled into his neck.

There were so many things Teddy wanted to ask her.

A slow clap broke the silence.

At the top of the maze wall, Endros stood in front of a throne-like chair on the gamemaker's dais, beside the royal booth. "Excellent work, both of you. I'm very impressed with your strategy and viciousness."

The crowd cheered in approval. Teddy could feel the weight of his father's gaze, but he didn't want to take his eyes off Endros until he had his favor in hand.

The god lifted his hands and the noise of the crowd died again.

"It pains me to say this, but unfortunately, there can be only one champion and only one favor."

The crowd voiced their dissent immediately and loudly, but the moment Endros lifted a hand, they quieted again.

"I didn't make the rules, but I must enforce them. There can be only one. That is what was written into the rules of the Games."

Teddy set Stella back on her feet and took a step forward. "Stella can have it. She beat me by just a second."

It was a quick lie. They'd run in from opposite sides at the same time, but Teddy couldn't bear to look Stella in the eye while he took something from her.

Endros clicked his tongue. "Gallant of you, Your Grace. But you did indeed enter at the same time and the Gauntlet Games rules must be honored. It's how we keep the peace."

The crowd voiced their displeasure with a chorus of outraged shouts.

The god pressed a hand to his chest in the perfect imitation of sincerity. "Would that I could change it, but as you all know, this contest is bound by godly bargain, and I am as much a prisoner of the rules as the contestants. I didn't write the covenant of these Games. I only signed it."

The crowd settled.

"I have no choice but to use the tiebreaker," Endros continued, turning to face the kings. "King Xander, did I not give you a sealed envelope at the beginning of the Games and ask you to hold on to it, but not open it?"

Xander stood and walked to the front of the box. Reaching a hand inside his vest, he removed a letter with a red wax seal and held it up.

Endros grinned menacingly. "Would you mind reading it?"

Xander broke the wax seal, read it, and frowned. He glanced to Stella and Teddy and then to Cecilia and Rainer, who sat beside Queen Jessamin in the royal booth.

Teddy tried not to fidget, but beside him Stella picked at dry blood crusted on her hands.

"Ready the challenge," Endros said, waving a hand at the priestess beside him. He turned to the king. "Are you going to read the tiebreaker aloud to our contestants and the crowd?"

Xander stood tall. "'The final challenge is simple. Few moments in the history between our two kingdoms are as memorable and ingrained in the hearts and minds of our people as the great exchange. It's the swipe of a dagger between two mortals that eventually sent Cato from this realm.'"

Stella froze. "Teddy, does he mean—"

A door opened beneath the dais. A priestess in crimson robes strode into the center of the maze and paused in front of Teddy and Stella. She held an ornate golden box in her hands. She set the box on the ground and reached for Teddy's hand.

"Your cuff, please. They don't want you restricted for the final challenge," the priestess said.

Dread clenched in Teddy's chest. He didn't want the full force of his magic if he would need to use it on Stella.

The priestess whispered something, and the band slipped free of his wrist. Stella held out her hand, and the priestess removed hers as well, then tucked the glowing bands into a pocket in her robes and stooped to pick up the gold box again.

Teddy studied her face for any hint of the chaos she was about to unleash on them. The priestess just smiled serenely and opened the box.

Teddy braced himself as if it might explode, but the box only held a dagger with ornate silver leaves on the hilt.

Stella stepped up beside him, her jaw slack. "That's my mother's Godkiller dagger."

Teddy had seen it only in a memory his father had once shown him so that he'd recognize the signature magical feeling that a Godkiller weapon gave off in case he ever came across one. He'd been led to believe that those few weapons that were powerful enough to kill a living god had all been lost to time, but clearly that was not the case.

The blade seemed to hum and pulse in the same way all powerful magical objects did.

Xander cleared his throat and continued. "'In the case of a tie, this dagger will be placed on the centermost stone in the centermost room of the maze. The competitors will stand with their backs to opposite walls, equidistant from the blade. When the bell rings to start the match, the first person to plunge the blade into their challenger's heart will win the Games.'"

The world was suddenly airless.

The crowd went deathly silent.

Teddy couldn't help it. He looked up at the royal box.

His father's characteristically calm expression was gone, and in its place was one of horror. Cecilia was on her feet next to his chair, the first hints of a gathering storm roiling in the sky above her.

"I object!" she shouted. "He conceded. It's over. I will not stand by while you take your vengeance and pretend it's part of the Games."

Endros clicked his tongue. "Surely you won't ask for special treatment for your daughter, Little Goddess. Not when she has the advantage of your blood." The god smirked. "Shame that she also has your heart to cancel that out."

Cecilia looked ready to launch herself into the arena. Rainer's arm around her waist seemed to be the only thing stopping her.

"Careful, Cecilia. We are all bound to the covenant of these Games," Endros warned.

Stella looked at her parents, her face pained. The recognition crashed over Teddy. Endros was recreating a scene from Rainer and Cecilia's history and projecting it onto the next generation. They had already survived the horror of reliving their parents' worst memories, but that still wasn't enough.

Endros wasn't just out for blood. He was trying to shred their souls.

Teddy searched his mind for any other solution, but they'd talked about it back in the McKay Estate sitting room on the day he and Stella had done the tournament binding. As long as the peace held, so would the binding magic of the Games. There was no way out.

The priestess took Stella's arm and ushered her away from Teddy to the far side of the room.

Teddy walked to the opposite wall, trying desperately to find a loophole in the challenge. Could there be another definition for a heart? Could he plunge it into his own?

No. The rules said he must plunge it into his challenger's heart.

As Teddy finally turned and pressed his back against the wall, the futility of it all settled into his bones.

He couldn't do it. He could not kill Stella. Not when he loved her. Not when he knew how badly she deserved to be loved. Not when she hadn't had the chance to find someone worthy of her.

But she wouldn't do it either. Stella had killed for him. Teddy had been the dividing line between her conscience and action. She wouldn't be able to turn the blade on him now. They'd be stuck in a stalemate.

"One last thing," Endros said. "If you don't attempt this last piece of the final challenge, you'll begin to feel that burning in your blood again until you show an effort. And in three minutes, those doors will open and any competitors still standing will have a chance to steal the blade and beat you to it. Good luck."

Teddy's heart pounded, dread flooding his bloodstream as the god lifted the bell and began to ring it.

The high-pitched sound was loud and clear because the crowd wasn't cheering. They were watching in mute horror, their nervous glances bouncing from the arena to each other to the god who had orchestrated this.

Teddy didn't run toward the dagger. Neither did Stella. They slowly walked toward each other until they stood just an arm's length apart.

Stella swiped the dagger up, but Teddy's relief was short-lived, because instead of plunging it into his chest, she handed it to him hilt-first.

Her eyes shone, face awash with agony. "You know I could never."

Teddy shook his head. "Absolutely not."

"If we don't do it, someone else will run in here in a minute and do it for us. I'd rather it be you," she whispered.

She was so calm. Teddy was furious at her for being so rational now when she was so unreasonable the rest of the time.

It was like they'd switched roles. He could not master himself.

His chest was tight with panic, the same breathless vise-like fear descending on him as it had in the tent before he'd entered himself into the contest.

Stella pressed her hand to his heart. "Breathe with me."

He couldn't. It was like his body had forgotten how.

Teddy knew how to kill. He'd practiced enough that it was easy now—reflexive. But he didn't know how to kill someone he loved.

"You won't be able to come back," he whispered.

Stella touched his cheek. "You aren't replaceable."

"Neither are you. I have three siblings that could rule."

"But can both our kingdoms survive the upheaval?" she rasped. "We could stand here all night and debate it. We could kill anyone who comes in to face us until it's just the two of us again. But that will just leave us with more blood on our hands as we face down the same exact decision." She unbuckled her breastplate. It fell to the marble floor with a hollow thud. Stella unbuttoned the top three buttons on her shirt and pressed the tip of the dagger's blade to the flushed skin over her heart.

Just last night, he'd brushed his lips to that spot, murmuring how much he loved her in Old Novumi.

Teddy looked around wildly for any other option. He wanted to scream—to charge at Endros and fist-fight the god. But it was pointless. There was no escaping this decision.

"If you don't do it, the magic of the competition might kill both of us," she whispered, her voice barely audible over the murmuring of the crowd. "If we slay all our foes, and it is you and me again, we will be forced to finish this until the binding magic decides the game is over."

Teddy glanced up at the faces of the spectators. Some looked angrily at Endros; others looked sympathetically toward Teddy's plight. If there was one thing the people of the two kingdoms respected, it was the fairy-tale story Endros was trying to recreate in an eerie next-generation echo. They didn't like it.

It wasn't fair. Teddy and Stella had played the game. They passed every challenge. If anything, they should have both received a favor.

But Teddy wasn't a child, and he'd learned long ago that life was not fair. He'd followed every rule, and he'd been impeccable his whole life—until a few weeks ago, when he went to the Temple of Desiree. He couldn't even call it a mistake anymore because the more he'd gotten to know Stella, the more he'd let go of their history as adversaries, and the more the bond seemed like the hands of fate moving them around a board.

Why had all of that happened if only to end in tragedy weeks later?

Stella looked at him with such conviction, squeezing her hand around his on the hilt of the blade, her eyes glassy. "Teddy, we have minutes before someone else gets here and wins instead. I don't know how much time has passed. Our competition won't hesitate. Just do it."

He shook his head. "I can't."

A broken sob rattled out of Stella, tears streaming down her cheeks. "You should have told me what *Minyha* meant," she rasped.

"How could I when you didn't want me?" Teddy asked. The question was wrenched up from beneath his heart—from the very place where the bond connected him to Stella.

"I do want you. I just don't want to lose myself to have you."

"How is *this* not losing yourself?" Teddy snapped. He was so angry at her for putting him in this position.

"Because it's my choice," she sobbed. "I used to think I wanted exactly what my parents have."

"And now?" He could hardly breathe around the fear.

She looked up at the booth where their families looked on. "And now I'm afraid I do. Now I wish I didn't care about you because I'm not strong enough to kill you, and I'm terrified that we have the same weakness."

Stella flinched at the same time Teddy started to feel a low-grade warmth spreading through his blood.

It was already starting. They had hesitated too long.

Teddy shook his head. *No.* He could not do this. The burning came in a wave, and he gasped, squeezing his hand tighter around the dagger hilt.

"Come on, Stella. You fight me on everything else. Fight me now."

She blinked away tears. "I've already fought you and lost. I have no fight left. Not for you, *Minyha.*"

The term of endearment took the wind out of him. He rested his forehead against her shoulder, trying to compose himself.

"I cannot destroy my heart. I will protect what is mine," she murmured into his hair.

"You have to," Teddy rasped. The burning was becoming unbearable, the pain so bright he could barely keep his grip on the blade.

"Do you understand what I'm saying? I am my mother's daughter. I'll repeat history because that is what it takes to save the man I love."

Stella winced. "My blood burns. It's the magic of the contest because I'm not trying to kill you like I'm supposed to. One of us has to do this, and it needs to be you."

"Why?" It was more a question to the fates and gods than one he expected an answer to.

She smiled weakly. "Because I love you too much to hurt you more than I did yesterday. Because you are kind and smart and you will be an amazing king."

The dagger pressed against her skin, just enough to draw blood. Teddy looked her in the eyes, his hand trembling and slicked with sweat.

Stella gripped his hand tighter on the hilt, but Teddy couldn't do it.

She groaned in agony from the burning and bent toward him, the blade sinking into her chest. The burning in Teddy's blood lessened ever so slightly, but he yanked the dagger back in horror.

A loud explosion split the night and sent them both stumbling.

The dagger fell from Teddy's hand and clattered to the ground. Stella snatched it up and slipped it awkwardly into an empty slot on her vest.

He turned toward the sound. "What the—"

"Is it a magic trap in the maze or—"

Another explosion rent the air—much closer this time. Teddy dragged Stella to the ground, covering her body with his as shards of wood and ash rained down on them.

After a few moments, Teddy rolled off of Stella and looked around, but the explosions hadn't come from inside the maze.

Smoke snaked up from somewhere behind the bleachers and royal booths. An entire section of the crowd was missing.

The stands where the spectators had been watching were in total chaos.

"Mama!" Stella's shout was breathless.

Screaming and pained groans broke out in the crowd. Bloodied spectators rose from the remnants of the bleachers and frantically made their way toward the stairs.

A loud grinding sound filled the air as the doors to the center of the maze slid open.

Roaring voices rose in a chorus through the night. "For the old ways!"

Stella's wide green eyes met Teddy's. "It's the Sons of Endros."

Teddy glanced up at the gamemaker's booth just in time to see flames rise around Endros. He smirked as he faded into them.

Teddy felt the burning in his blood lift.

"I guess that concludes the Gauntlet Games," Stella said. "My blood stopped burning."

Teddy felt suddenly guilty for wishing for a solution to the tiebreaker—this wasn't at all what he had in mind. The tiebreaker was personally devastating, but a full rebellion would bring massive loss of life for the people of Olney and Argaria. If whatever was happening outside of the arena was bad enough that it broke the covenant of the Gauntlet Games, things were about to get so much worse.

He glanced at the royal booths. The left side of the makeshift wood platform had splintered, and the railing dangled at an odd angle. Terror shot through him. There was no sign of his parents or siblings, or Stella's family.

Stella took off running toward the carnage, but before she could get to them, Jeneva and Katerina sprinted into the center of the maze.

Jeneva immediately lifted her blade, preparing for a fight. "What's happening?"

"Sons of Endros attack," Stella said, lifting her hands in surrender.

Katerina looked back and forth between them. "Who won the Games?"

"Teddy did," Stella said without meeting his eye. "Or else the rebellion broke the covenant of the Games and we have much bigger problems to solve. Now, are you satisfied? Can I pass to find my family?"

"Can we leave?" Katerina asked.

Teddy's blood was no longer burning. "Stands to reason that an active rebellion attack on the Games would effectively end the peace."

Stella nodded. "The burning is gone. I don't know what else would stop it."

Jeneva turned her fierce gaze on the smoking remnants of the royal booth. "How do we find the quickest way out?"

Teddy turned in a slow circle. There were four entrances off the center of the maze. "Does anyone remember the exact route they took to get in here?"

Jeneva frowned at him like the question was insulting, which it probably was for the Olney huntmaster's daughter. All hunters were trained to have an impeccable sense of direction. "Of course." Her gaze wandered toward one of the maze openings. "Which competitors are still standing?"

"Dixon is alive but unconscious," Teddy said.

"Fionn and the Roach," Stella said.

Katerina wrinkled her nose in disgust. "Drew was, but if he didn't realize that my blades were poisoned, then he probably won't be for long."

"He's dead," Stella said flatly.

Their bond was as steady as her affect, but Teddy still searched her face for any sign of apprehension. He found none.

"I need to get to my father. He'll be a target in this," Jeneva said.

"So will you," Stella said, nodding to Jeneva's fiery red hair.

Jeneva tapped her short swords together. "They'll have to catch me first." She nodded toward the opening from which she'd come. "I'm going to find my father. I'm guessing he'll be on the castle walls."

"You shouldn't go alone," Stella said.

"She won't," Katerina said, stepping up beside her warrior friend. She smiled sheepishly at Stella. "Sorry we tried to kill you at the Muddled Mind. It wasn't personal. I just really needed that favor and you were in the wrong place at the wrong time."

Stella shrugged. "I don't blame you."

Teddy felt far less inclined to forgive than Stella was, but when she turned and gave him an irritated look, he sighed and said, "Yes, we understand. Just be careful who you trust. Security was tight around this event especially."

Jeneva frowned. "It was supposed to be, but two unscheduled ships landed at the pier right before the start of the challenge. My father was called away from saying goodbye to me because of it. The harbormaster was beside himself, afraid they were under attack, but it seems he just misplaced a page from his ledger. My father had to pull some of the security detail to investigate what was happening at the pier."

Stella paled and something like dread hit Teddy through their connection.

"What is it?" Teddy asked.

Stella's gaze darted around the room. "Before the event, Fionn called in his favor. He brought me to the pier and asked me to erase the last twenty-four hours from the harbor log and to remove the page of arriving and departing ships from the ledger and give it to him."

Jeneva stared at her. "You think it's a diversion?"

Stella shook her head. "If it is, it's a good one. It draws guards away from the event but—"

Another loud explosion erupted into the night. The four of them braced against the ground-rattling aftershocks. Smoke poured into the sky, the night turned momentarily orange by a fireball.

"The docks," Katerina rasped. "My father's shop is near there."

"Wait!" Stella said. "About Fionn—when I ran into him in the maze, he was headed the wrong way. He wasn't going toward the center room. He was running away from it."

Teddy had never trusted that fucker, and not just because he flirted so freely with Stella. There was something oily about him. He was too perfect, too smooth, just too much to be believed. He didn't like the way Fionn latched on to Stella and, in context now, the attack on the street where Stella had nearly been killed felt like a test— either of her skill or Teddy's attachment to her.

"Which way was he going when you saw him?" Teddy asked.

Stella looked up at the castle and Teddy's blood went cold. "That way. I'm sorry. I should have known. I'm not stupid enough to actually trust a mercenary, but mercenaries tend to not care for revolutions."

"Unless he's not really a mercenary," Katerina said.

"Regardless, we have to get moving," Teddy said. "Jeneva, head toward the docks to find your father. Light the barracks torches along the way if they're not already lit. We need to get this whole place on high alert. Stella and I will go to the castle to try to find our families and get the spectators to shelter." He paused. "And be careful with the other competitors. Rett and his friends have never been proven to be actively involved with the rebels, but that doesn't mean they're not."

Jeneva and Katerina nodded, then ran off back the way they'd come from.

Stella was already halfway to the door when Teddy caught up with her.

"I'm sure everyone is fine." He was trying to be reassuring, but he only sounded doubtful.

Stella led him back along the path she'd taken through the maze —past Drew's crumpled body and ivy splattered with blood, twisting and turning through the narrow maze until they heard the sound of footsteps coming from around a corner.

Adrenaline coursed through Teddy's blood. He would fight his way out of this maze if he had to. He was going to protect Stella and get them both back to their families.

A lump formed in his throat when he thought of the remnants of the royal booth, but he shoved the thought from his mind. He needed a clear head and he would not default to despair in a moment like this. Not when Stella needed him.

She was frozen beside him. Her hands rested on the hilts of the short swords at her hips. They both stood waiting, muscles coiled for action.

A familiar whistle sounded above them. Teddy's gaze snapped up. Alexandra smirked down at him from her perch atop the maze wall beside them. The fear in his chest unknotted as she held a finger to her lips, gestured to the corner he was approaching, and held up three fingers.

Stella shifted beside him, drawing her short swords as quietly as possible.

Together they advanced, pausing at the corner to look at Alexandra. She held up three fingers, silently counting down. Teddy stepped around the corner with Stella on his heels at the same time Alexandra jumped down onto the back of one of the men.

Alexandra drew a dagger across the throat of the man in front of her as Teddy took on the man to the right. He easily deflected a swipe from the rebel, plunging his sword through the embroidered Sons of Endros sigil at the center of his leather breastplate.

Steel met steel beside Teddy as Stella took on the third attacker. She spun away and Teddy took over, shoving the man against the wall and cutting his throat with a dagger.

Before the rebel's body hit the ground, Teddy had swept Alexandra into a hug.

She patted his back. "I know I'm your favorite and all, but we have to go. Our father sent me to get you both and we need to get beyond the castle walls now."

"He has a plan?" Teddy asked.

Alexandra nodded. "He said to find you and Stella and that Stella would know the way through the queen's garden." She looked at Stella. "Apparently both royal families are aware that you had a way to sneak in to see Arden."

Stella blushed. "What about my family?"

Alexandra nodded. "They're safe for now, but we have to move."

Stella's shoulders relaxed, and she started forward, leading the way back through the maze. They didn't encounter any other bodies along the way, but when they finally broke free from the arena, they could see the full carnage of the attack. Several of the bleachers lay in crumpled piles of wood; no bodies, but there were distinct blood spatters on the wood.

Alexandra urged him forward. "We don't have time to investigate now. We have to fight to see another day," she said.

A faint flicker in Teddy's peripheral drew his attention. He turned to watch a flaming arrow arc through the night, striking a shadowed figure to their left.

A scream rent the air as the arrow's flame caught the shirt of the figure. He turned to run, seemingly to escape the range of the archer, but the wind fanned the flames so his whole shirt caught and he fell to his knees and howled in pain.

Teddy finally recognized him. It was Dixon.

Stella gasped. Reaching out her magic, she yanked the flames away from his shirt and caught them in her palm, realizing as soon as she did it that she'd drawn attention to them.

They watched in mute horror as an arrow hit Dixon's throat. He let out a horrible gasping sound that they could somehow hear even over the chaos.

But it wasn't just one archer watching the field—it was a whole host of them. A horde of flaming arrows rained down on them. Stella had left her breastplate in the maze, leaving her unguarded. Teddy searched helplessly for any cover.

Stella threw her hands up and her magic surged into the arrows, burning them to ash that rained down on Teddy and Alexandra like remnants of a bonfire.

"Move," Alexandra said, grabbing both of their collars and dragging them forward.

They sprinted across the field to the cover of the castle wall. They needed to get inside before they were mistaken for rebels.

Stella led them along the outer courtyard wall until finally the dense shrubbery that surrounded the queen's garden came into view. She walked up to the hedges and sent out a surge of magic. The bushes bent apart, leaving a gap just wide enough for the three of them to squeeze through.

Once they were inside, Stella let the tall hedges fall back into place.

"What I'm about to show you is a secret you must immediately forget," she whispered.

"You sure you wouldn't rather just steal the memory from us when you're done?" Alexandra taunted.

"That was one time and only because your brother begged me," Stella said.

Teddy and Alexandra followed her down a path bracketed by roses. She moved soundlessly, falling back into her training as if she'd been as involved in combat as Teddy and Alexandra.

As they crossed into a water garden, Stella stopped suddenly, her hand clamping over her mouth.

At the far end of the pond, a large group of fifty rebels stood in formation. A tall man stood in front of them, speaking animatedly.

Fionn Silver.

He paced back and forth down the line, a subtle limp in his step. Although they couldn't make out what he was saying through the sound of running water in the pond, it was clear that he was a leader. His men listened with rapt attention.

"We can find another way around," Alexandra whispered.

Stella shook her head. "You don't understand. They're standing on top of the way in. I'm trying to figure out if they know that or not. If they do, we have a much bigger problem."

Teddy waited, peering over Stella's shoulder, holding his breath. To his horror, the men parted, and Fionn bent down and tipped up the grate in the ground below them, ushering his rebels into the secret passageway to the castle.

Stella gasped. There were too many rebels for the three of them to take on. There had to be at least fifty men, outfitted in high-end leather armor and beautiful weapons, not to mention the strong pulse of magic emanating from the group. At least some of them were witches. It would have been stupid to attack without knowing which ones had magic and what their strongest affinities were.

One of the rebels lifted his arm and Teddy spotted a glowing cuff on his wrist.

"It's our magic they're planning to use. That's why the priestesses had us make so many. It wasn't for the Games. It was for the rebellion," Stella whispered.

Teddy swallowed down his fury. Much as he wanted to charge across the garden and rip those cuffs off of the men, he needed to be strategic. Even Alexandra, always eager for a fight, was holding completely still so as to not attract attention.

"Our father is expecting us to come through that passageway," Alexandra whispered, peering at the men through the hedges. "What elements do those cuffs hold?"

"I gave fire and I'm assuming that Dixon would have given fire also—"

"Did we not just watch him panic over fire on his shirt?" she interrupted.

"Yes, but I hit his head pretty hard. If he just woke up, he was probably disoriented, and he still had the cuff restricting his magic..." Teddy let his voice trail off, trying to get the image of Dixon out of his head.

Alexandra shifted, her gaze still fixed on the men who were now beginning to descend into the tunnel. "Once they're all in, we need to follow them. We can pick them off one by one if we can do it quietly."

The wait for the men to descend into the passageway was excruciating, and then they waited a full minute after the grate slipped back into place with a metallic clang before they darted across the garden. They rounded the large pool full of lily pads and lotus flowers.

A scrape of boots on gravel behind them drew Teddy up short. He spun and came face to face with two men in rebel regalia. Both had bows drawn and aimed at Stella and Alexandra.

39

STELLA

Stella's heart was in her throat as she stared down the arrow pointed at her chest. For the second time in a night, she worried she'd met her end.

The men were too close for her to use magic to counter. The second they felt the flames, they'd loose an arrow, and it would be the same if they felt her nudge at their minds.

"Your Graces," one of the men said, a wicked smile passing over his face. "What a welcome surprise. I hope you'll forgive us for not welcoming you sooner, but we needed you to step out of the shadows so we had a better shot."

Alexandra's hand lifted to her vest, but Teddy grabbed her wrist.

"You won't be faster than an arrow," he whispered. "Be strategic."

"You should listen to your brother, princess," one of the rebels said. "You might train like a man, but women do not have the capacity to strategize."

Stella could practically hear Alexandra's teeth grinding, but the princess relaxed her hands to her sides.

"Now, if Your Graces would be so kind as to let us escort you. We're happy to take you in right through the front doors since we already have the castle," the other rebel said. "You can drop your weapons here."

Stella and Alexandra tossed their short swords to the ground. Teddy stepped forward to do the same but paused as a hooded figure darted out of the garden from the left, moving with familiar grace. A second figure moved behind the first like a shadow.

The rebels did not even have time to turn before they were on the ground, one bleeding from his throat, the other with a dagger in his heart.

Stella gasped as one of their saviors shoved down their hood. It was Juliana Savero. The skirt of her red dress was shredded, but her hair was still somehow perfectly styled.

"Honestly, Jay, must I do everything myself?" Juliana said as she bent to pull her dagger from the rebel's body.

Jalen grinned as he shoved his hood back. "You had it in hand and it's good for you to get those perfectly manicured hands dirty from time to time."

"You two are supposed to be inside," Alexandra said.

"We were tired of waiting. You're so slow," Juliana said.

Stella grabbed her short swords and sheathed them at her hips, stepping back to allow the siblings their reunion. The Saveros had always been a unit she had orbited, and here she was again, watching them hug while she stood awkwardly off to the side.

Teddy noticed her watching and dragged her in, and to Stella's surprise, Jalen, Alexandra, and Juliana hugged her just as tightly.

"Thanks for not killing our brother when he was being a moron," Jalen said.

Teddy sighed. "I was not being a moron, I was thinking of—"

"Your *Minyha*," Jalen taunted. "Yes, we know. Spare us the sentimental declaration of love. We have to get inside." He pulled back and patted Stella on the shoulder. "Now show us this passage."

Stella rushed over to the grate and heaved it open, laying it on the ground as gently as she did when she'd been sneaking in to meet Arden.

They funneled down into the dark corridor quietly and Stella snapped her finger, sparking a flame to light their way. She smiled at the quiet bickering of the siblings as she started to walk down the narrow tunnel.

The journey was short, but it felt like it took an eternity to get to the end of the passage.

"Where does this come out?" Alexandra asked.

"The kitchens," Stella said. She walked up the steps, paused outside the wooden door, and listened for movement on the other side.

She'd done this so many times before, but her heart was beating so loudly in her ears that she could barely hear anything else. When she was certain it was clear, she pulled the door toward her and ducked under the shelf into the pantry. Teddy was close behind her as she paused again with her ear against the door to the kitchen.

His hand came to her waist, and the bond in her chest pulsed with warmth.

After a few moments of silence, Stella cracked the door open.

Instantly, the knob was yanked from her hand and someone dragged her from the pantry. Stella was shoved, stumbling, into the center of the kitchen by one of the rebel fighters.

Teddy grabbed the man's shoulder, but stopped when he saw that a second rebel had a blade to Stella's throat. There were at least twenty men in the room and they had every exit but the window covered. With her eyes, Stella pleaded with Teddy not to fight.

Teddy held up his hands in surrender.

"Wise move, Your Grace," the rebel taunted. "You should tell your siblings to do the same."

Teddy rolled his eyes as his bickering siblings filed out of the pantry.

If a look could raze a building, Olney Castle would have crumbled under the glare Alexandra leveled at the rebels. Jalen and Juliana looked around the room, taking inventory of the opposition.

Stella just needed a diversion to squirm away from this man.

"Weapons down, Saveros," someone called from just outside the room.

Stella knew the voice. Fionn Silver.

The mercenary stepped into the kitchen doorway, dagger in hand. "Don't worry, I'll be sure to let everyone know how it was Stella McKay who laid the groundwork for my rebellion," Fionn said. "Lovely of you to prop open the kingdom doors for me. A regular old McKay family welcome."

She noted with a frisson of pleasure that he was walking with a limp as he closed the distance between them.

"Don't look so smug, princess. Everyone gets a lucky shot in every once in a while," Fionn said.

"Should have aimed more to the left," she grumbled.

"If you had, you would have disappointed many women in the two kingdoms."

Alexandra made a gagging noise.

Fionn's gaze snapped to her. "There she is. The Savero I thought I'd be facing off with in the tournament. Fed you the idea and everything. What happened?"

Stella happened. It was frightening how long he'd been working on this plan.

Alexandra didn't take the bait, though Stella could see that she was furious.

"Lucky for you, I was unwillingly diverted," Alexandra said.

Fionn grinned wickedly. "Should we have a showdown now? A little entertainment for my men. I know you're the type to want to prove a woman's worth. I can't think of a better place for you to do it than in a kitchen."

Rage flared in Alexandra's eyes and energy crackled through the air. She stepped toward Fionn.

A loud battle cry sounded in the hallway and Nathan Aiger came running into the room, slicing through the two men closest to the door with brutal efficiency.

Stella took the distraction to wrench the blade away from her neck and smash her head back into her captor's face.

The whole room erupted into chaos, the Saveros and Nathan each taking on several rebels. It wasn't until Nathan stepped aside that Stella realized someone had charged in on his heels, and that someone was her brother.

Leo sprinted toward her, running his blade through the chest of the man who'd been holding her. Then, he dashed past her into the fray.

Stella stepped up beside Nathan and helped him hold off a new group of rebels who were trying to get into the room to help. She glanced over her shoulder at the fighting. Teddy, Jalen, and Juliana were fighting on one side of the room. On the other, Alexandra was engaged with Fionn, the two of them exchanging vicious blows with matching looks of murderous delight on their faces.

Nathan settled back-to-back with Stella.

"So, Stella," he said between fending off sword swipes. "I have been trying to get to know Rosie and I would love your blessing to—"

"Nathan Aiger, I swear to the gods, do not even think about going near my sister," Stella said, sending a fireball at a man charging toward her. He stopped and dropped to the ground and Nathan spun to drive his sword through the back of the man's neck.

"Come on, Stella. I'm serious this time. I just want to get to know her. Take a minute to think about it." He looked so sincere. He turned to fight off another guard, then pivoted and looked at her expectantly.

"This is hardly the time," Stella said. "Did you ask Leo about it?"

Nathan's handsome face paled. "No. I'm going most terrifying to least terrifying sibling."

Stella laughed. "That would be more believable if you weren't so pale. Also, I'm a little offended."

"You're loud-scary. Leo is quiet-scary. He's a harder read and your thoughts are written all over your face, *Minyha*," Nathan said.

Stella huffed a laugh and threw a dagger at the guard charging at them. It sank into his shoulder and he twisted just in time for Nathan to cut him down.

"Have you asked Rosie if she wants to be courted?" Stella asked. "I'm giving you a hard time, but it's her permission you really need."

"I asked before and she said she had to think about it." Nathan fumbled a step, looking sincerely afraid. "What if she says no?"

Stella shrugged. "Then I guess you're out of luck."

Another group of rebels rushed in from the hall before he could say another word. Nathan cut off as many as he could, but one rushed past him toward Stella. She brought her blade up to stop his blow, but the cuff on his wrist lit up and he unleashed a fireball. Calling up her magic was so second nature that Stella caught it right away, but not before it dropped her to the floor. The searing pain of her sore ribs hitting the stone knocked the air out of her lungs. The fireball fizzled out.

The man was on her in an instant, straddling her waist, his hands fastened around her neck. Stella clawed at his fingers, kicking her legs to try to knock him off, but he wouldn't budge.

Something struck the man in the head and his eyes rolled back. His hands went slack, and he fell to the side.

Rosie stood over him, a large cast-iron frying pan in her hands.

"Don't touch my sister," she said, dropping the pan on the man's unconscious body.

Stella jumped to her feet and pulled her sister into a hug. "You shouldn't be in here."

Rosie held up a short sword in protest, but as Stella sat up, she realized the fighting had largely come to an end.

Their group looked tired and marked by minor wounds, but everyone was still standing.

"Looks like the McKays really did give them a warm welcome," Leo said with a smirk. "Too bad Fionn isn't here to see it."

Stella looked wildly around the kitchen. "Where did he go?"

Alexandra rushed toward the back door with a hand pressed to her bloody side. "It's my fault. He got the upper hand, and he ran out the back door when I was wounded. I'll catch him."

Teddy grabbed her wrist and pulled her to a stop. "We should clear this floor and find our parents. If they really did take the castle, we have bigger problems."

Alexandra looked like she wanted to argue, but she cast one glance out the kitchen door and then nodded in resigned frustration, still clutching her side.

Teddy led the way, and they all ran into the hallway, clearing rooms one by one. When they came to the east wing, they found a group of rebels engaged with a solo fighter.

The hooded figure moved swiftly through the remaining rebels, bodies dropping in their wake. The figure's movements were familiar —the smooth, efficient pattern of a Novumi fighting style.

Teddy watched as the figure rose from a crouch. "Is that—"

"Isla," Alexandra finished.

She yanked her scarf down and smiled at them. "You didn't really think I'd leave you both without a word. That I would leave your father. What do you take me for?"

Both Teddy and Alexandra looked overjoyed at the sight of King Xander's consort.

Isla looked somehow elegant in her bloodstained scarf and leather armor, her curved blades still at the ready for any adversary. Her black hair was braided back in an intricate design. She bore a strong resemblance to Queen Jessamin since the two were cousins. They shared the same regal posture, high cheekbones, and assessing gaze, but Isla's skin was a lighter shade of brown and she had a smattering of freckles over her nose and cheeks that gave her a more youthful appearance. She also tended to wear armor more than evening wear, much like Alexandra.

"You're back," Alexandra said thickly.

Isla's smile was beautiful and a bit frightening. "And I'm not alone. What have I always said?"

Alexandra's face lit up. "A battalion of women is better than an army of men."

Isla smirked. "And this is no army. These men lack true commitment to their cause."

"This was your plan," Teddy said.

His relief hit Stella in the chest.

Isla nodded. "We needed to do something drastic to get all the rebels out at once. The strategy we had been using for years of trying to pick them off one by one as new syndicates popped up was simply not working anymore."

"You knew they wouldn't be able to resist the hope of a real rebellion," Teddy said.

"Especially with me out of the way," Isla said. "Their attack is already frayed. Half their men abandoned the fight when they met our opposition, escaping on a fishing vessel."

Alexandra pointed down the hallway. "We have to get to Father—"

Isla looked offended. "You think I would leave your father unguarded?"

"I think he'd probably be annoyed to be guarded by anyone other than Mother," Alexandra said.

"Well, Nicholette has a long history of trailing your father. She's excited to remind him how rusty he is."

Stella knew the name from her parents' stories. Nicholette was one of the four princess guards who had protected Queen Jessamin when she first went to Argaria, and she'd since remained in service to the queen—and, apparently, Isla.

"You think he really doesn't know?" Alexandra asked.

Isla shook her head and smirked. "No. But I like seeing the two of them argue about who is protecting who. I've missed it."

Teddy stared down the hall. "How did you do it?" he asked.

"I have been preparing for months," Isla said. "We knew the tournament would draw them out, we just weren't sure how. Your Uncle Evan had several informants who kept us abreast of the plan and the players. Their leadership structure is nebulous and ever-shifting, we think by design. It makes it hard for them to stay organized, but it's also made it almost impossible for us to stop them. The only way we could ensure we hurt the Sons as a whole is to draw as many of them out at once. We figured that my being fired and the tournament on the heels of that decision would be too great of an opportunity for them to ignore."

Stella was both awed and terrified of Isla. "How did you know it would work? What if the spectators got hurt?"

"They surprised us at the docks, so we had to adapt our plan."

The guilt over Fionn's favor finally caught up to Stella. People were hurt because she'd been so stubbornly against working with Teddy for the first challenge.

"What do you mean they surprised you?" Stella asked.

Isla ran a hand down her vest, checking that all of her blades were secure. "We were ready for them to attack the tournament, but when the huntmaster and one of his battalions were called away to attend to two ships that arrived late in the day, it left us with less hunters watching the arena. That's how they planted the bombs."

Stella's mouth was so dry, she could hardly speak. "What happened at the docks?"

Isla's eyes narrowed at Stella. "The harbormaster misplaced some pages from the ledger and had no recollection of three ships arriving yesterday that had just been sitting there. When two others arrived and parked next to them and rebels started streaming from all five ships, it took us by surprise."

Alexandra stepped forward. "How did you handle it?"

Isla smiled affectionately. "Ever the strategist, Alexandra. How would you have handled it?"

"I would have helped the huntmaster hold the docks, secure the ships, and then fight back toward the castle and arena," Alexandra said.

Stella frowned. That strategy would secure their escape route, but at what cost?

"And that's basically what we did. I sent half of my battalion to the docks and the rest of us fought to secure the arena and get the crowd to safety on the upper level of the castle."

"It's my fault people were hurt," Stella said.

Isla shook her head. "This is war, Stella. Let go of whatever guilt you're carrying. You didn't start this fight. A few hunters lost their lives and many spectators were wounded, but your mother and the rest of the witches in the crowd were able to heal all of those injuries and the more gravely injured were brought to the healing suite for Lyra to work on."

Teddy placed a hand on Stella's lower back in comfort.

Isla's brows shot up. "We have much to talk about, it seems." She glanced out the windows. "We let them have enough to believe they were in control—the castle, the tournament. We let them have the docks until they divided their forces and sent more men up to the arena. Then, we immediately took it back. With this type of group, we had to play to their egos. A man lets his guard down when he thinks he's already won. What you see out in the courtyard is the very end of their so-called revolution."

"Did you catch Fionn Silver?" Stella asked.

Isla's face contorted with confusion. "The mercenary from the tournament?"

"He was leading them," Teddy said.

Isla shook her head, looking confused. "If he's their actual leader, that's news to us. I didn't realize he was involved. We chased the remaining rebels to the pier, but a group of them escaped on some well-hidden boat on an older, less-used dock. But it was only one boat's worth, and if whatever is left of this revolution exists on that boat, Queen Karina will take care of them the moment that they land in Novum."

"Assuming they're going to Novum," Teddy said quietly.

It made Stella uneasy. Fionn had seemed important and she would have felt more settled if he'd been captured with everyone else.

"Don't look so nervous. We have been planning this for months and we knew it was our greatest chance to find all of them at once. We are taking this very seriously and we estimate we have captured or killed ninety percent of their known network," Isla said. "Rest assured that we will find them wherever they land. My battalion is clearing the area around the castle now. It's finally over. For good this time." She looked at Stella. "You should go see your parents in the sitting room down the hall. Your mother has run out of people to heal and she's making everyone crazy."

Stella didn't wait for her siblings. She turned and sprinted down the hall to the sitting room. She had believed it when Isla said her parents were safe, but it wasn't until Stella laid eyes on them herself that she really trusted it.

Her father's shirt was torn and bloody, but he smiled when he saw her. Her mother's dress was smudged with soot and her eyes were rimmed in red, but she ran to Stella.

"Mama." Stella hugged her mother and, finally, all the feelings that she'd shoved down for the past few hours hit her at once and she started to sob.

"You're safe, Little Star. I've got you," Cecilia whispered. "You did so well. Everything is okay now."

"How are you all okay? I saw the royal booth," Stella rasped.

"It looked worse than it was," her father said, hugging both of them.

Cecilia huffed an exasperated sigh. "Your father means that he threw all of us down and covered us and took the brunt of the wood shards."

Rainer kissed her cheek. "And I'd do it again."

"Once a guardian, always a guardian," her mother grumbled.

Stella's relief brought on a wave of exhaustion. "I know there is probably a lot to do, but I need to sleep."

Her mother smiled. "Of course, but it looks like someone is waiting to talk to you before we head home." She nodded to Teddy, who was standing in the sitting room doorway.

Stella wiped away her tears and smoothed her shirt. "I'll just be a few minutes."

Cecilia smiled. "Take your time."

Her parents crossed the room and fell into an animated conversation with King Xander and Isla. Teddy caught her eye and nodded toward the hallway.

Stella hesitated a moment before following him out of the room.

In the dim torchlight of the hall, he looked exhausted but handsome. There was a bruise on his temple and blood on the neck of his shirt, but she didn't care. She still wanted to shove him back against the wall and kiss him.

The only thing stopping her was the look on his face when they'd said goodbye to each other in the seaside cottage.

The final challenge didn't change anything. She'd been willing to die for the greater good, but she wasn't ready to live for him when doing so would mean making him the center of her world. She'd barely had a chance to become her own person and she couldn't give that up and disappear into the role of queen. Many women would have seen that as a boon, but she knew the perils of royalty firsthand.

Teddy reached up and brushed his thumb against her neck. "Are you well?"

She must have looked a mess—dried blood crusted on her temple and neck, her clothes charred and filthy, and her hair hanging in a ratty braid down her back. But the way Teddy looked at her made her feel beautiful.

"As well as can be expected," she said. "And you?"

"As well as can be expected."

She smiled. "I'm glad you won."

Teddy shook his head and sighed. "I didn't win."

"Fighting again. It feels just like old times." The joke fell flat, but if Stella tried to be serious she would break down all over again. "You deserve the win and you deserve the choice. A good queen will make all the difference in your life, but it will also be what's best for the two kingdoms."

Frustration surged through their connection. "Fuck the two kingdoms. What do you want?"

She tapped her chest. "I can live with this just like I have through this whole tournament, and you can too. What I could not live with is knowing you're in a miserable political marriage with no one looking out for you."

Teddy glanced back toward the sitting room and blew out a slow breath. "I know you're probably eager to go home and rest, but I just wanted to ask you one last question."

The bond swam with a nervous energy.

"Has your answer changed?"

Stella stilled, meeting his golden eyes. "What answer?"

He hesitated. "Do you really not want to be anyone's queen? Even mine?"

Mine. Minyha. My heart. My greatest trial. The word was so accurate and so painful.

She loved Teddy, but, much as she'd wanted a fairy tale—and this would have been a neatly tied-up happily-ever-after—it was too soon to commit in that way, especially when committing meant leaving her family and her life behind. She'd learned the hard way not to simply slot herself into some man's life. While she knew that Teddy didn't just want a warm body—that he truly wanted *her*—there was no doubt that every choice he would have to make would put his kingdom before her. That was the role of a good king, and she'd learned enough to know that she couldn't be a woman whose needs fit after everything else a king had to attend to.

Stella swallowed the lump in her throat. "Yes, I'm sure. I'm not cut out to be queen."

He nodded and stepped away from her.

"I hope you find someone perfect for you," she said softly.

She smiled at Teddy as he walked away, and it only hurt a little to wish him well. She meant it when she told him she was happy he won. She just didn't know how to live with knowing what she had lost.

40

STELLA

Stella paced the Olney Castle sitting room, wringing her clammy hands.

The past two days had been a whirlwind that put the Gauntlet Games closing ceremony on hold. The rebels who had been captured were being held for questioning, but Isla and Evan were confident that they'd rooted out all but about thirty of the rebels. While it wouldn't instantly solve the unrest in the two kingdoms, the mood in Olney City was already calmer.

The full-out rebellion had angered people who were sympathetic to the Sons of Endros' cause because of the hunter lives lost, wounded spectators, and property damage it had caused to local businesses. Stella was relieved to see the people of Olney coming together to help each other rebuild.

Now that the most urgent matters had been dealt with, it was almost time to officially close the Games. Stella was uncertain how they would handle the favor since the tiebreaker hadn't fully been decided. In a few short moments, Stella and the remaining competitors would find out how the gods would proceed.

Stella's stomach tumbled at the thought. She suddenly wished she hadn't sent her mother and Rosie away after they'd helped her get ready. Now she had nothing to distract her from her racing thoughts. It was taking every bit of her self-control not to accidentally send every confusing emotion directly through the bond to Teddy.

She crossed the sitting room to the table where refreshments had been set up, poured herself a whiskey, and knocked it back in one gulp. Immediately, she refilled the glass and drank down another. She was refilling the glass for a third time when a shadow fell over her.

"Slow down, sailor. You don't handle your liquor well enough to keep that pace."

Stella glanced up as Kate walked into the room. She froze mid-pour and turned to face her friend, blindly setting the bottle of whiskey back on the tray.

Kate looked beautiful in a sage-green silk dress that floated behind her as she walked. Her dark hair was twisted into an updo on top of her head, and her mouth was set in a determined frown.

Stella took a wary step toward her. "Kate, I'm—"

"Now *that* is quite a dress. You really should wear red more often." Kate crossed the room and gestured for Stella to spin.

She appeased her friend, doing one slow turn. The bright red scalloped layers of silk ruffled as she spun.

Kate whistled low. "I saw the final challenge, so I'm guessing this isn't for Arden."

Stella shook her head. "I picked this one for me—so I'd feel confident, but now I'm afraid it will just draw attention to me when I can't keep it together out there."

Kate's frown morphed into understanding. "Well, if even some small part of you picked this to impress someone else, I think it's safe to say they will regret walking away from you."

Tears pricked at Stella's eyes. "He didn't. I walked away from him."

"What? Why?" Kate stared at her in shocked disbelief.

"Because when I finally stopped thinking about what 'we' wanted, I had a chance to think about what *I* want, and I don't want to be queen."

"But you love him."

The lump in Stella's throat was so large that she feared she would choke. "But I love him. He's ridiculous and uptight, but I love him."

"So you're drinking to—"

"Numb out the fact that I'm going to be attached to him for life."

Kate's eyes went comically wide. "We don't know that. The gods might grant no favors—and are you so sure Teddy won't ask for it to be broken if he is granted a favor?"

Stella took a sip of whiskey and shook her head. She looked out the sitting room window at the roses in the queen's garden. Daylight was fading into the golden light of late afternoon, which made the garden look even more whimsical than usual.

"No. He's going to ask for a blessing for him to choose his own wife instead of having a politically advantageous one chosen for him."

"So, you?"

Stella shook her head. "I already told you I don't want to be queen."

"He's gorgeous and in love with you, and from how loose your hips looked in that challenge yesterday, he knows what he's doing in bed—"

Stella scoffed. "You can't possibly have read that from watching that challenge. It was chaos."

Kate arched a brow. "So he is good? I knew it! No one is that hot and repressed without being wild in the bedroom."

Stella's cheeks burned as her friend eyed her.

"Well?" Kate prodded.

Stella looked away. "Yes, he knows what he's doing."

"I knew it!" Kate screeched.

Stella clapped a hand over her friend's mouth. "Keep your voice down, pervert."

"Say more and I will."

"He really knows what he's doing. I couldn't walk for a full ten minutes afterward and if you breathe a word of that to anyone, I will set your brother up with Colleen Ruby."

Kate froze. "You wouldn't dare."

"Wouldn't I?"

"You wouldn't curse me with the chattiest sister-in-law in all of Olney."

Stella clasped Kate's hand. "Try me."

Kate stared her down for a full minute before she blew out an exasperated sigh. "Fine. You are no fun at all. I can't believe you tumbled that broody prince, and you won't even share the details. Honestly, it's selfish."

Stella was so relieved to have their old dynamic back. She dragged Kate into a hug. "I should have listened to you about Arden. I know you were right, but I wasn't ready to see it and I needed to get there on my own."

"I think our friendship will go so much smoother if you just recognize that I am right about everything." Kate drew away and frowned. "Are you well? That tournament was scary—you were really hurt. Did it scar?"

Stella nodded stiffly. "I'm getting better every day. Are we okay, though?"

"That depends." Kate glanced toward the doorway. "Is your father out there in the throne room waiting? Do you think there's room in the family section?"

"Kate, don't even start—"

"What's he wearing? He looks so good in green—"

Stella swatted at her friend, and Kate ran from the room, cackling.

Her visit had the desired effect. Stella was bolstered by her teasing and felt as ready as she'd ever be to watch Teddy bargain with the gods for the right to fall in love with someone else.

THE WORST THING ABOUT THE LOCATION FOR THE FINAL EVENT OF THE Gauntlet Games was that the walk from the rear entrance of the Olney Castle throne room to Stella's place of honor in front of the dais was way too long. As soon as she stepped into the room, the weight of the collective gazes of half of the court pressed into her. The crowd parted as she walked toward the large dais.

She wasn't sure what she was expecting when she walked out into the throne room, but it wasn't to find Grimon, the god of death, in the godly seat of honor. He leaned back and casually ran a hand through his black hair, his lips tipping into a lopsided smile when he saw Stella. He nodded to her and his pale blue eyes momentarily flashed with power.

His brother, Samson, the god of lust, stood on Grimon's left, running his hands down his iridescent golden vest and grinning widely at Stella. His dark, curly hair was fastened in a bun at the nape of his neck and Aurelia, the goddess of the harvest, hung on his arm and whispered in his ear.

The rest of the gods milled about behind them. Stella spotted Adira, Desiree, and Sayla huddled together with her Uncle Devlin, all of them recognizable as the children of Clastor by their bright blue eyes. On the other side of the dais, Cato leaned against the wall, his witch friend Skylar beside him. She winked when she caught Stella staring.

The royal families were seated on opposite sides of the raised dais.

Stella reflexively looked at Arden, but he was either fascinated by the marble floors or ignoring her presence.

Taking her place at the end of the line of surviving competitors, she saw Teddy all the way at the other end of the line beside Katerina Shank.

It was remarkable how the field had dwindled. With Christophe and Drew's deaths in the final challenge, Dixon's death in the battle afterward, and Fionn in the wind, only five competitors remained— Stella, Teddy, Katerina, Jeneva, and Rett. Unfortunately, it seemed the Roach truly did live up to his name.

Rett sneered at Stella when he caught her eye and she quickly snapped her attention back to the front of the room.

"Nice of you to join us, Lady McKay," Grimon chided.

The bells began to toll, signaling the end of the day, and Stella gestured to them as if to prove she was right on time.

The god of death waited for the ringing to stop before he spoke again. "I've taken over as ceremony master as we are holding Endros for an inquisition in the Otherworld. This was a very unusual year for the Gauntlet Games. The rebellion broke the covenant of the Games and allowed you all to be freed from your binding pact, even though the final tiebreaker was still underway."

Stella's mouth was so dry. Her heart hammered in her chest as her mind called up the memory of how it felt to stand there with her hand around Teddy's, trying to help him guide the dagger into her heart. The panic hit her the same way it had in the moment.

A soft, buzzing calm feeling filled her chest.

She wanted to sob. The awful, beautiful bond that she hadn't wanted in the first place—that had become so dear to her and much too personal—was something she was going to have to learn to live with forever. Whenever she was sad, she'd feel Teddy sending comfort, and whenever he was worried, she'd have to stop herself from sending him peace. It suddenly felt impossible.

Her eyes burned and her lower lip began to tremble. Stella drew in a deep breath, trying to compose herself and focus on what Grimon was saying.

"The rules of the Games state that if the tournament is interrupted by an act of nature or any unforeseen emergency, the winner will be whoever was leading at the time of the interruption," Grimon continued. "Now, there would be more room for interpretation of who was winning, but Teddy had a dagger pressed to Stella's chest and he drew first blood."

A twinge struck Stella through the bond, as if Teddy was trying to disagree.

"I've conferred with the rest of the gods and we have deemed Theodore Davide Savero the winner of this year's Gauntlet Games."

Thunderous applause broke out in the crowd and Stella forced herself to clap along with them.

Grimon held up his hands, and the applause died. "Step forward and make your request."

Teddy took three steps forward. "I've given this a lot of thought. Having spent my entire life as heir to the Argarian throne, my focus has been only on what's best for everyone else. My entire existence was about thinking of the kingdom first, as I was taught by my father. It's logical to think that it would be easier to be loyal to your people when you don't have to be loyal to yourself first. Although that's a decision that was made for me out of love—I can see now how it's limited my ability to truly understand what it is to have something to lose personally. This tournament and surrounding events have given me a glimpse of the heavy responsibility that comes with the crown as well as what it feels like to have something to lose."

Stella steeled herself. He was framing his request so eloquently, but she wished he would just spit it out.

"So many things come together to make a great king," Teddy continued, ignoring the whispers in the crowd. "My parents have been fortunate to have a wonderful collaborative relationship that grew out of a political marriage. But my father had the chance to choose his wife. I wanted that same honor—"

Gasps rose from the crowd and Stella couldn't breathe.

Teddy waited for the murmuring to lull before continuing, "But I've realized that the wisdom with which my father made that choice was gained through having a chance to fully become his own person in his time away from court. He had a chance to know himself outside of his role in succession. He had a chance to lose something personally—to understand how to fight for something out of love instead of just responsibility. I love my kingdom and my people, but I've spent my life as a symbol for them instead of a person. I feel I'd be doing Argaria a great disservice if I tried to rule without first having the chance to be a real person."

The murmurs in the crowd had turned into full-fledged conversations.

Queen Jessamin whispered in one of Xander's ears as Isla leaned over to whisper in the other. Stella felt their assessment. She felt *everyone's* assessment.

Grimon raised his hands. "Quiet, please. We need to hear his request." He nodded to Teddy. "Your Grace?"

Teddy cleared his throat and stood tall. "I would like the blessing of the gods to abdicate the throne to one of my very qualified siblings. They are all brilliant and capable leaders who have had the benefit of becoming their own people, without the pressure of being heir their whole lives, and it's for that reason that I think they will make great leaders. A good leader must know their own mind. I'd like the time to learn to understand mine."

Stella stared at Teddy's back, breathlessly trying to comprehend his words. Her brain felt muddled and slow. He hadn't asked for the freedom to choose his own wife. He'd asked them to let him be free in all things.

Shocked, boisterous chatter broke out around her, and Stella couldn't even hear her own thoughts over the noise.

Katerina elbowed her. "He's choosing you."

Stella shook her head. "No, he's choosing *him*," she said thickly. Because it was true. He hadn't asked for her. He'd asked for freedom.

Grimon stood from his chair and the room instantly fell silent. Stella had always been close with the god who'd insisted on being called Uncle Grim, even though he wasn't actually an uncle by blood. But the god of death frightened the people of Olney, always quick to fall in line when he spoke.

"We have heard your request. Would any among us object to granting it?" Grimon asked.

The entire room seemed to collectively hold their breath as the gods remained silent. Not one of them spoke.

"Well, then. Consider your abdication blessed. Theodore Davide Savero, you are a prince and a prince you'll remain. That concludes this Gauntlet Games."

Teddy's relief hit Stella in the chest at the same time his shoulders relaxed. Then he promptly turned, cut through the gaping crowd, and left the silent throne room.

Stella wanted to chase him down, but the moment she turned to follow him, the crowd broke up into animated smaller groups to gossip. She ducked around a few, but the more she darted around, the more attention she drew to herself and the more whispers followed her. She turned and collided with a solid body. A firm hand clamped down on her upper arm and she stumbled.

Rett Roachelle towered over her, his rat-like face pinched in a scowl. "You must have a golden twat to get that uptight prick to abdicate."

"Get your hands off of me. The tournament is over and the only thing preventing me from breaking your nose again is—oh wait, nothing," Stella snapped.

Rett leaned closer to whisper in her ear. "You and I have unfinished business. I—"

Stella looked over his shoulder to see what had stopped him so abruptly. Jeneva was standing behind him with a blade to his throat. She glanced around at the crowd, but no one seemed to notice their scuffle.

"It's poisoned," Jeneva said softly. "You'll be dead before your body hits the ground, and we will be long gone. Understand?"

Rett nodded carefully.

"Good. Now apologize to the lady," Katerina said, stepping up next to her friend.

Rett's jaw ticked. "I'm sorry."

Stella bit back a smirk. "Thank you for teaching this monster some manners," she said.

Jeneva offered her a mock salute. "Happy to." She leaned close to Rett, and he flinched, nearly cutting himself on the poisoned blade. "Now, my father would like to interrogate you, but I've seen enough of your antics for one lifetime. Leave Olney in the next hour. If you don't, you'll be arrested and questioned about your connection to the Sons of Endros and their rebellion. If you ever return, you can expect the same." She glanced at Stella. "Any parting gifts for the man?"

Stella kneed Rett in the balls and he doubled over, then she kicked the knee she'd hurt in the tournament, and he fell to the ground. "Have a great trip home and enjoy your limp, Roach. I hope it's permanent."

She spun and ran into the crowd, pushing out of the throne room and into the castle hallway, darting up the stairs to the guest wing. She found Teddy's room with little trouble, but he wasn't inside. Instead, she found Alexandra sitting in the chair by his window.

"He's not here," she said.

"Do you know where he is?"

Alexandra shook her head. "What did you do to him?"

Stella swallowed hard. "I loved him."

She didn't wait to see what Alexandra said. She ducked out the doorway and down the hall to continue her quest.

41

STELLA

Stella paused at the top of the cliff trail, staring down at the beach far below. Teddy paced the line where the ocean met the sand. His summons had arrived just moments after she'd returned to the McKay Estate. She'd been delighted to escape her family's scrutiny after the pandemonium in the throne room until she got to the beach trailhead and realized that escaping their knowing looks meant facing Teddy when she had no idea what to say.

The salted breeze whipped the loose curls around her face into her eyes, and she batted them away.

"You shouldn't make him wait," Rosie said. "I'll leave the cottage key in the door in case you need to hide out—or need some privacy."

Rosie had come with her for support, but Stella suddenly felt the irrational urge to cling to her little sister. Maybe it was because the last few weeks had been so monumentally tumultuous. Still, Stella had a feeling that whatever she was walking toward now was somehow bigger and more life-altering.

"I don't think I've ever seen you look so scared, Stell-bell," Rosie whispered, squeezing her hand.

"What do you think he's going to say?"

"I think he's going to propose."

Stella stopped breathing. "What?"

Rosie giggled. "Gods, you should see your face."

Stella held up her hands. "It's not that I—" She blew out a slow breath to compose herself. "He kind of already did—poorly. It's just very fast."

"The man gave up the Argarian throne to be with you. That sounds pretty serious to me."

"We don't know that's why he did it," Stella snapped.

Rosie grinned and wrapped an arm around Stella's shoulders. "You didn't see the way he was looking at you because you were too busy being frozen in shock. He looked at you like you were his salvation."

"Well, I was—several times."

"Stella, gods!" Rosie shook her head. "You are truly exasperating. You've always given him a hard time, but Teddy is a good man. You shouldn't be so afraid to believe in him. You two clearly have something. You must be the only two *not* to notice that you always have."

Stella was afraid to be disappointed again—afraid she'd invented another fairy tale from the ashes of her wildest dreams. Teddy wasn't charming in the way Arden was, but they'd been through something truly traumatic together, and couldn't that make myth of what was simply survival?

She didn't want to be another person who wanted too much from him—not when he'd just had the courage to break that pattern in his life. It wasn't fair, and she wouldn't walk down the trail until she was certain of what she would do.

She turned to face Rosie. "Do I look okay?"

Rosie nodded emphatically. "On the slim chance that he's going to end things instead of profess his love, it would be really hard to do so with you looking that good." She smoothed Stella's hair and pulled her into a hug. "What does Mama always say?"

Stella groaned into her sister's hair. "To be brave with my hand and brave with my heart."

Rosie pulled back and smiled at her. "Go get him, Stella."

With that, her sister turned and walked back toward the cottage.

Stella listened to her footsteps fading away. When she could no longer find any reasonable excuse to delay, she kicked off her silk slippers and walked down the sandy path slowly. She welcomed the sting of the rocks and cool sand against her feet and breathed in the salty sea air.

Normally, being on the beach made her feel calm. But that was because she was normally on her way to a morning swim, not a seaside...whatever this was.

She paused at the bottom of the trail and the bond in her chest pulsed to life at the same time Teddy turned and spotted her. Something like relief broke over his face as Stella walked toward him. She had no idea what to say, so she fell back into their old familiar pattern.

"You summoned, *Your Grace*? I must admit, I thought the royal commands would cease when you ceded the throne."

Teddy shrugged. "Glad you didn't ignore it."

Stella was suddenly so nervous. She couldn't begin to find the words to say to him. It had been an hour since his shocking request was granted by the gods and her heart still hadn't ceased its racing. Perhaps it never would.

"What did your father say? Was there yelling? Honestly, I can't imagine King Xander yelling."

Teddy laughed. "He doesn't ever yell. I think he knows the silent disappointment is worse. He said it took me long enough. I guess he'd been waiting for me to make a hard decision. That's why he left me that memory, apparently. He saw me floundering, and he wanted to remind me that the hard decisions didn't end once you become king. They just get harder. He said that they fought to take out the Sons now so that I could have the choices he always wanted me to have. My mother reminded me that I'm not in the same position that he was in because I have three other siblings who could do the job."

"Teddy, I'm so happy for you. I don't know what to say—"

"Don't panic." He smiled sheepishly and pressed his fingers to his chest. "I can feel how nervous you are. I didn't do it for you—or, rather, I didn't *only* do it for you. I did it for me, because I needed time to get to know you. Gods! I need time to get to know *me*, Stella. My entire existence has been about keeping other people happy. I'd like to finally learn what makes me happy and you were the first thing that came to mind."

"I make you happy?" Stella asked skeptically.

He sighed. "And crazy and honest and curious and brave, Stella. You make me brave."

Tears pressed against the backs of her eyes. "That's not true. You made *me* brave."

Teddy took her hand and placed it over his heart. "I mean in here." He lifted her hand and pressed a kiss to her palm. "You gave me the courage to be honest with myself—to listen to my foolish heart."

Stella couldn't quite process everything he was saying—everything that had happened in the past hour. Her heart was racing and her nerves were completely shot from the ups and downs of the day. Much as she had wanted to deny Desiree and say that she was just messing with them, Stella had seen the wisdom of her aunt's vision. More than that, it was suddenly so obvious how they just fit together.

"It was this dress, wasn't it?" Stella asked.

Teddy bit back a laugh. "It's a spectacular gown, but no. It wasn't the dress, though I like seeing you in it almost as much as I'd like to see you out of it."

"The swords, then?" she teased. "Double-wielding blades usually catches some attention."

He blew out a breath. "It was the swords and the wearing my shirt and nothing else—and the rain."

Stella burst out laughing. "I knew it. That recipe always works."

Teddy ran a hand through his hair and smiled. "It was more than that, although the sheer amount of nudity certainly didn't hurt with helping me see you in a new light."

Stella pretended to flip her hair. "A wise man once called my ass legendary."

"Maybe if you do him the honor of allowing him to court you, he'll write a drinking song in its honor," Teddy said.

"*Your Grace*, have you been hiding musical talents?"

"Absolutely not, but I'm nothing if not determined. I'm sure I could whip something up with the right motivation."

Stella's chest clenched. This playful side of him was so new and disarming and she was thrilled at the prospect of seeing him this relaxed all the time now that the pressure of perfection was gone.

He tilted her chin up so she would meet his eye. His smile was teasing. "I'm going to need your help, Stella. I have so little practice being imperfect, but you're *so good* at it."

She slapped his arm. "Shut up and kiss me, you perfect liar."

Teddy kissed her and all the nervous energy from the day bled from her muscles until there was nothing but the urgent press of his lips, his hands in her hair, and his firm body against hers. The bond in her chest pulsed, and she wanted to draw him in, to have him closer. She wanted him to lay her down on the sand and make her forget the stress of the past two days.

When he finally pulled away, Stella was breathless. The orange glow of the sun, low on the horizon, was almost blinding.

"I thought we could finally go on a date that doesn't involve people trying to murder us."

"Sounds boring." She glanced down the empty beach. "Why here? Why not bring me flowers or ask me on a proper courting date?"

He grinned and began tugging his shirt up and over his head, tossing it into the sand with the same nonchalance with which he'd tossed away his crown earlier. "Well, I was hoping you'd be willing to give me my first swim lesson—you know, so that I don't almost drown on our next adventure."

Stella smirked and gestured down at her dress. "And ruin this exquisite gown?"

Teddy licked his lips. "Oh no, *Minyha*. Take that dress off. If I'm going to get in the sea and flail around embarrassing myself, I'm going to need a little motivation—for courage."

Stella cocked her head and smirked. "For courage?"

He unbuttoned his pants, letting them hang dangerously low on his hips. Stella drank in the sight of him. Teddy glowed, his brown skin gilded by the setting sun. His smile was more relaxed than she'd ever seen it and that combined with the lines of his defined abdomen disappearing in a point just below the waistband left her breathless.

"For courage and maybe for a reward when I'm finished," Teddy said with a wink.

"So certain you'll earn one?"

He shook his head and let his pants fall, stepping out of them so he stood naked before her. "Certain you'll make me."

A laugh bubbled up from Stella's chest, the sensation rising as if it came directly from the bond.

This was it—the fairy tale she'd been searching for. It didn't end with a walk down the aisle in a fancy temple; it started with a walk across the beach to the man she could truly be herself with.

Stella unbuttoned her dress, let it slip into the sand, and followed her handsome, naked prince into the sea.

SONG OF THE DARK WOOD

The first in a series of interconnected standalone gothic fairytale romances

Never stray from the main trail. Never meet the eyes of the dead or the monsters that lurk in shadows. Never bleed in the Dark Wood. And above all ... keep the Wolf happy.

For centuries, the people of remote Ballybrine have kept the peace with their gods by sacrificing a Red Maiden to ferry souls from the Mother's realm of the living, through the Dark Wood, to the Wolf's realm of the dead. Soon it will be Rowan's turn.

Ripped from her family as a young girl, Rowan Cleary has been forced into a cloistered life learning to please the wolf and wield her spirit-enchanting voice. Though none of the previous maidens have survived their five-year term, Rowan is determined to beat the odds and protect the women who have become family to her.

When a deathly blight breaks out in the Dark Wood, and the acting maiden is murdered, Rowan vows to strike a new bargain with the god of death to ensure her survival. The Wolf has always been someone to fear—even more so now that the townspeople blame him for the blight—but he's far from the vengeful death god she expects.

To unravel the mystery, Rowan must seduce the Wolf. Soon, the attraction between them grows into a relentless magical force, threatening to shatter the delicate balance between realms and unleash a darkness eager to swallow their world.

Book One in the Fable Song Series is Out Now!
https://www.amazon.com/dp/B0D1M81771

or scan the code to order:

ACKNOWLEDGMENTS

First and foremost, I'd like to thank Adderall. I no longer have to imagine what it's like to have an attention span. What a concept. I could not have done it without you.

Now onto the more normal stuff.

My brain was not quite ready to let go of this world when I finished The Godless Kingdom, but it still took about two and half years for legacy to fully come together. Once I got into it, my characters ran away with the story, as they often do. Stella and Teddy are so dear to me, not just because of who they are, but also because of what they show about the legacy of the original series. Hopefully their story won't be the last. Time will tell.

To Tanya - Thank you for listening to me cry on the phone the day I finished drafting The Godless Kingdom and for saying "Maybe it's not over yet." You gave me the nudge to write this one and it's grown into a story I love so much.

To Liz - My personal broody prince, thanks for being my muse for Teddy, for meeting me at my most dramatic with a bone dry sense of humor, and for talking me through this romance arc. FOR SCIENCE!

To my indie writer friends - Helen, Nicole, Courtney, Callie, Jenessa, Victoria, and all the other indies who have shared their wisdom and expertise with me. Thanks for helping me build something from nothing but my tired brain.

To Megan - You've always been the best mirror I could ask for. Thank you for seeing me, for your brilliant business mind, and for being so genuinely invested in these stories and me.

To Erin - Thank you for being so kind and thorough in your feedback. Your sharp eyes keep this revision train sane(ish).

To Tabs - Thanks for keeping it real. Your kind, honest feedback is always valued here.

To Charlotte - Thank you for this gorgeous cover, for letting me say "brighter" 20 times, and for giving me a next generation map to go with my next generation story. You are the food bowl to my Moo Deng.

To Nicole (Rainer's Bad Girl) -Thanks for making the family tree with minimal questions asked. Rainer would love it.

To my beta readers - Anastasia, Fil, Jenessa, Jenny, Lauren, and Tayla. Thank you for bringing both knowledge of the OG series and fresh eyes to this book so that I could make it into a truly tense tournament and feet-kicking romance.

To my sensitivity readers - Thank you for lending me your experiences and helping me craft the delicate parts of this story with care.

To my business witches - As always, thank you for your support in this an every other thing I do. I'm tremendously grateful for your wisdom and magic these last five years.

To my family and friends - Thank you for supporting my stories. Let's all agree to pretend chapters 25, 28, and 29 didn't happen.

To my Little Doves - You are a *force* and I'm so grateful for all of your creativity, humor, and support. This book and Kate, are my love letters to all of you.

To my readers - Thank you for coming back to Olney with me or for visiting for the first time. I'm so grateful you're here. I hold your kind words and encouragement in my heart with every book I write.

ABOUT THE AUTHOR

A LEGACY OF STARS is Sheila Masterson's sixth novel. When she's not writing fantasy romance novels, you can find Sheila practicing yoga, or curled up reading tarot or a book. She lives outside of Philadelphia with a small army of underwater houseplants that survive out of spite. Keep up with her online at sheilamasterson.com.

instagram.com/sheilareadsandwrites